Books by Julie Midnight

<u>Monstrous Hearts</u>

Wolf's Wife

Wolf's Bane

Wolf's Kin

<u>The Werewolves of Crescent City</u>

Secrets in the Moon

SECRETS IN THE MOON

The Werewolves of Crescent City
Book One

Julie Midnight

ISBN: 978-1-7367836-3-4

Any references to historical events, real people, or real places are used fictitiously. Names, characters, and places are products of the author's imagination.

Front cover image by Julie Midnight
Book design by Daniel Young

First Printing Edition 2021

Hellcat Press LLC
www.hellcatpressllc.com

TABLE OF CONTENTS

Cora Marshall had dressed with great care in anticipation of the detective's arrival. She wasn't sure what a murderer looked like, but with every newspaper in the city implying she might be one, even her outfits fueled debate about her guilt. Hopefully, a black suit where the skirt reached her knees was proper enough attire for a girl who had lost her father. She certainly wasn't about to wear anything dowdier.

Her fingers played with the diamonds in her necklace while she paced throughout the study. The maid had already been told to show in Detective Hayes as soon as he arrived, so now there was nothing to do except wait or worry. Cora detested both options.

Determined not to fidget, she picked up the nearest newspaper and read its headline. PACK VIOLENCE SHATTERS CITY.

The details left her wincing. More severed heads had been found in the streets. The werewolf kings were always at war with each other over expanding their territories, but lately the fighting had spiraled close to human areas.

Well, that was the price to pay when living with monsters, wasn't it? Glittering days hid bloody nights. If Crescent City was a lush rose admired by all, then werewolf packs were the sharp thorns hidden behind its leaves.

Still, as Cora read through more of the article, part of her wondered if she'd made a mistake in seeking out Detective Hayes. He had an outstanding reputation for solving crimes, and surely a werewolf living among humans held some restraint, yet a beast was still a beast no matter how fine of a suit he wore.

Then she huffed at herself and folded the newspaper to hide its grim words. What good would it do to worry? She had no one else to turn to, and time was running out. Besides, if this wolf tried to make a nice meal out of her, he'd quickly learn she was one bunny that bit back.

Just as she returned the paper to her father's desk, the doorbell chimed. Her heart jumped into her throat while she hurried for the nearest window. She had never been reserved in her life but would now give her best attempt at it. She checked her reflection in the glass panes to make sure she looked perfect and then stared out at the sprawling gardens below.

The maid's diffident words drew near. "You'll find the lady right through here, sir."

"Thanks a lot."

A deep voice, clear and confident. Brimming with a snap to the syllables that marked an inner-city dweller from high society and its arch manners. Anticipation shivered through Cora, but she pretended to be absorbed in a ridge of pink hyacinths, even when footsteps sounded against the polished wood of the study's floor.

"Miss Cora Marshall? I'm Detective Samuel Hayes."

Finally, she let herself look over. Her careful expression thawed into a smile, and all rehearsed words flew out of her mind. "Oh! You're nothing like what I expected."

What had she expected? After weeks of interrogations from the police, a vague figure had formed in her mind, merging with the portrayals of private detectives found in plays: someone older, perhaps even her father's age. Flabby from chasing down criminals with his intellect instead of his feet. A wrinkled mess of a suit, fingers stained with nicotine from countless cigarettes, and a suspicious air that required a lot of coin to smooth into diligence.

She couldn't have been more wrong.

For one thing, this Samuel Hayes looked to be in the prime of his life, without a strand of grey in his dark, neatly combed hair. His well-tailored suit emphasized a lean, powerful body, and his tie was in a perfect knot against his collar. Yet his eyes were what truly captivated her—deep gold like a wolf's and just as wild.

Frankly, he was the most handsome creature she'd ever met, human or otherwise. Cora's smile grew. Well. She wouldn't have to feel nervous at all. A big, bold, good-looking fella was something she was *very* used to dealing with.

In response to her surprise, the detective raised his eyebrows. The corner of his mouth twitched with humor. "Expecting something hairy and panting?"

"Of course not. I know a little about werewolves. Anyone living in the city has to. Please, sit down." She gestured at the pair of leather chairs placed in front of the desk.

The maid had already set out a tray of light refreshments, and as they settled in, Cora added, "Coffee?"

"Sure."

She poured some for them both while covertly watching him from beneath her lashes. He took in his surroundings with sharp glances here and there, his expression serious once more. When she handed him the cup, he knew how to hold the saucer but drank all the coffee in one go—someone who understood manners without curbing his appetite. He really was a smoldering fella, and she was glad of it. She'd had enough of stuffy old men frowning at her.

"Thank you for driving out here for a mere consultation," she said, keeping her voice brisk while she took her own cup in hand. "I realize my letter was a little obscure about why I need your services."

"More than that. Your letter was so vague that I would've thrown it out if I hadn't recognized your name." His tone kept the words an assessment rather than a rebuke, but he leaned forward as if already hunting for an explanation.

"I worried about someone from the newspapers intercepting it. I may sound paranoid, but my situation really is that bad. Last week, a journalist crawled through a window and rifled through my writing desk. Thank God there wasn't anything besides a note to my dressmaker. Even that was juicy enough for them. 'Heiress worries about diamond-stitched frock while father remains missing and presumed dead.'"

Cora eyed her reflection in her coffee before adding, "I think I'm starting to get frown lines. It's all so vexing."

Detective Hayes cocked his head to the side. He looked amused again. "I did my research, Miss Marshall. If there's one thing I know, it's that you're the most beautiful girl in the city and no one can say otherwise."

Her brilliant smile returned. "You're very kind."

"I also found out you're no stranger to scandal. In fact, you get a real thrill out of it."

"Oh, well..."

When she offered no other reaction, he needled for one. "I can rattle off examples if you think I'm bluffing."

She took in his steady gaze, realizing it was her first glimpse of how he would bite at whatever puzzled him until its secrets spilled out. Her laugh was sudden, delighted, and entirely unfeigned. "All right. Show me how busy you've been."

He blinked, seeming surprised. "You had a fling with the railroad baron H.B. Stevens after meeting him on a cruise along the Copper Coast."

"Oh, yes. It was my seventeenth birthday as well as the first time I sailed on the ocean. I liked him very much. He made me laugh until I was dizzy."

"Mrs. Stevens didn't find anything funny about it."

"Of course not. She was too busy taking private tours of the ship that always ended in her bedroom. I saw her with a different crew member every day." Then Cora sipped at her coffee. "That's one thing. What else did you find out?"

Hayes scoffed and leaned back in his seat. His eyes held a peculiar glint, as though he respected her boldness in the face of such details. "You once spent a year modeling for the biggest artists in the city, which meant your nude portraits were hung in galleries for all to see. Some are still there as permanent exhibitions."

"Did you go to look at any? Which was your favorite? I very much like Rigg's interpretation of me in his *Evening Star Comes to Life*. I look very tall in it. As you can see, I'm not tall at all."

"You don't care, do you?" murmured Hayes. "Not even a hint of blushing. You like getting in trouble, Miss Marshall."

"I grow bored very easily. It's fun to ruffle the feathers of those who just ache to be upset." Her smile faded as she remembered where it had all led to.

"But now you're so nervous about the newspapers that you won't write a full letter."

"Well..." She paused under the guise of finishing her coffee. "It's much different to be accused of my father's murder. That's not fun at all."

"No, it's more than that. You quit your antics about a year ago. Disappeared from all the gossip rags because your behavior became as modest as a nun's. What happened, Miss Marshall? What made you afraid of the scandals you once thrived on?" Those striking eyes absorbed every movement while he waited for an answer.

When Cora only hesitated, he added, "You have to trust me if we're going to get anywhere. I can't hunt down the truth if you don't give me all the facts. Even the nastier ones."

"Everyone has secrets. Can't I keep some of mine?"

"Sure. I just won't take you on as a client."

She drew in a deep breath. Really, she wasn't good at this type of negotiation. She had been perfectly happy as a thoughtless socialite sparkling with the rest of the city. "I would like to be honest. It would be such a relief."

"What's stopping you?"

"People would only grow further convinced of my guilt."

"Try me."

In silence, she set aside her cup for a cigarette. Hayes leaned forward to close the space between them, extending his lighter in a

silent offer. She accepted it, their faces inches apart as her cigarette flared into life against the heat of the flame. With the slightest shift on her part, they could be kissing. With the slightest shift on his, teeth could sink into her throat.

Then his gaze met hers, patient yet inscrutable. She found herself wondering why he had left his pack to live among humans. They were kindred spirits in a way, two creatures fighting against the currents of society. Was that connection, tenuous as spider silk, something she could trust?

"Everyone thinks I hate my father," she said, without looking away. "That it's my motive for killing him. But everyone's wrong. You see, I can't hate my father. He took that away from me."

After a final puff on her cigarette, she left it in the tray and rose from her seat. She would have to reveal the wretched thing for him to truly understand.

As Hayes stood with her, she added, "You're right about my sudden good behavior. Even the newspapers point it out. Their most common theory is that he threatened to disinherit me, which scared me into becoming a good girl until I decided murder was easier. They're wrong about that, too."

She turned around and let her head fall forward. The rest of her body remained stiff and uncertain. No one else had seen what he was about to—no one except her father. "It's somewhere on my scalp. Go on, take a good look even if it means mussing my hair."

When he drew close, her stomach knotted itself in a ghostly reaction to a procedure she couldn't quite recall. His fingers brushed up the nape of her neck, and she drew in a quick breath to keep still. But his hand was gentle and smelled like tobacco, sensations miles

away from the cold touch and antiseptic stench lingering on the edge of her memories.

Her hair was cut short in the back, following the latest fashions, and it didn't take long for him to pause at a tender spot on her scalp. When his thumb brushed over the area again, she knew he'd found it. A binding sigil, placed so discreetly as to be invisible.

When Hayes spoke, a growl slipped into his voice. "That's been illegal for decades."

"My father still found an enchanter who could do it. This is Crescent City, you know. Money wins over everything else."

"Did he have memories stripped away, too?"

"Yes." Now she faced him, refusing to feel ashamed of her next words. "You're very good with your research, Detective, but my most sordid scandal remains a secret. I tried to elope with someone. I loved him. I know I did, even if I can't feel it anymore. He was a servant who worked on the estate and was therefore very unsuitable. When my father found out, he kept it from happening. Somehow, he even kept it out of the public eye. But it was still the final straw for him and after that..."

A vague wave at her head was enough to draw a nod from the detective. Then the sigil throbbed with the same dull pain as pressing on a bruise, warning her that any further discussion about its presence would lead to outright agony. She moved for the window to give herself time to recover. "I don't remember his name, his face, or how quickly I fell in love. And I don't know what happened to him. He's a mere shadow in my mind."

While staring out at those wretched hyacinths, she wondered what her last words had been to him, this mysterious man who

survived as an ache in her heart. Her eyes burned. The sigil hummed against her skin. She ignored both feelings and looked over at Hayes.

He stood a polite distance away, hands in his pockets while he watched her. Silent. Remote. She had heard wolves scorned any signs of weakness; to be vulnerable was to be prey. And yet she found no contempt in his expression. No mockery. She couldn't tell what he thought at all.

She raised her chin, daring him to dismiss her. "Telling the truth would mean sticking my head through the noose with my own words. Surely, I wanted my father dead. Surely, having all of his money and none of his control is worth the risk of being caught and hanged."

"But you didn't do it."

"No." Now she moved closer, desperate for him to understand. "And I don't know what happened. But I *must* clear my name. He took away my future once already. I don't want his disappearance to do the same."

For a few agonizing moments, Hayes studied her as if seeing clear through to her heart. Then he took the final step needed to erase the distance between them and smiled, a hot, crooked one hinting at the feral nature behind his perfect tie and polished shoes. "In that case, we better track down your father and find out what happened."

CHAPTER TWO

"You have a wonderful car." Cora beamed as they flew down a road that took them away from the city, every twist and turn handled with aplomb by Detective Hayes. It was a convertible model, and he had put the fabric top down to let the crisp air whip at their hair and clothes. After three weeks of hiding from reporters in a house stuffy with worry and wilting bouquets, hurtling through the elements felt utterly refreshing.

As she looked out at the scrubby grass and untamed blackberry hedges flanking the road—the first signs of entering wild land, no man's land—she remarked, "I've never ridden in a KB Victoria before. The engine runs as smoothly as butter."

And in her very short acquaintance with Detective Hayes, she'd never seen him as relaxed as while behind the wheel. His mouth had eased into a slight smile, and the gold of his eyes glinted with boyish excitement. She had no doubt that, on his own, he would lose himself in the thrill of speed, in an unseen chase that left behind all troubles.

Her comment now brought some wryness to his grin. "Big fan of cars, Miss Marshall?"

She leaned her head back against the seat as the first aspen trees appeared, slender as matchsticks and just as neatly lined up. "Since I agreed to tell the truth, I'll admit I worried about the car more than my father when he disappeared. Well, the car and Tierney, although I didn't know him very well."

"Dominic Tierney. Your father's driver."

Cora nodded, unsurprised that the detective already knew about him. Poor Tierney had been under severe scrutiny in the papers for the first few days. "He's been with us for three years. Father hired him after buying the car—it was a Bugatti Royale, you see. Monstrously big, and my father didn't want to muscle around such a beast."

"Did you ever take it out by yourself?"

"All the time. It was a stately old thing but handled the road beautifully for its size."

Admiration slid into Hayes' voice. "Elegant, too. Whalebone knobs, walnut steering wheel, and a shiny blue-and-grey paint job. Anyone who has one is driving art."

Cora turned from a view of ducks bobbing in a pond to stare at him. How did he know such details? The papers had only printed photos of the charred wreck found by police. Then the answer came to her, and she found herself smiling. "Well, Detective, you might be the first good decision I've ever made. You looked into the entire case before meeting me this morning, didn't you? Even to the point of reading through classified police files."

"I wanted to know what I was getting myself into."

He had a way of saying things with that voice of his. It was how Cora had always imagined a werewolf's would sound—deep and smooth, with just enough of a growl to turn innocent syllables into something suggestive. Listening to it was like the afterburn of whisky on the throat.

If he was the first thrilling man she'd met, she would have been too flustered to do more than run a hand over her hair like a schoolgirl. But he wasn't, and anyway she wanted to know what the police had learned. "Do you still have them? The case files? I'm curious how close they are to arresting and charging me."

Her question brought a certain gravity into the air, and after a moment he said, "Close enough that I want to work fast on this, Miss Marshall. It's another fifteen minutes to the site, so let's hear your version of what happened the day your father disappeared."

"I don't know much. I really don't."

"It's all right. Just tell me everything you remember, no matter how small or silly."

Cora looked out her window, taking in the green countryside. The clusters of flowers, the little wooden fences, and the distant cottages with their chickens and chimney smoke all looked so innocent. So tranquil.

Then she looked at what waited ahead: a glowering ridge of birch that marked the beginning of Corpsewood, the forest that butted up against the east side of the city. The forest where her father's car had been found.

"Three weeks ago exactly, Father told me over breakfast that he was going into New Obsidian on business and would be back home the next morning. He often did that—stay overnight if he knew he'd

be working late in another city. No one likes driving through the forest after dark.”

“Did he give any details on what he’d be doing or who he’d see?”

“No, but that was normal as well. Father had no intention of grooming me to take his place at the banking firm. He always made that very clear. I know it sounds like another motive for killing him, but I completely agreed with the decision. Not one peep of protest from these lips.”

Hayes raised an eyebrow. “Too much responsibility?”

She gave him a shining smile. “Exactly. I would run his financial empire into the ground within a year.”

“I bet you could do a good job if you tried. You have the smarts for it.”

That drew a laugh out of her. “The only other time I’ve been called smart was when a man thought he needed flattery to get a dance with me. What’s your reason, Detective?”

He shrugged. “It’s just what I’ve observed. The cops think the same. A pretty face with no brain behind it couldn’t scheme up a murder like your father’s.”

“A murder that I didn’t commit.”

He acknowledged the words with a nod and then said, “What happened after he told you about going into New Obsidian?”

“Not another word passed between us. He finished his toast and coffee and then left. It was all completely normal.” It was frankly embarrassing how little she knew.

“Did the driver check over the car before they took off?”

“Oh yes, Tierney always did that since Bugs can be so temperamental. But it looked and sounded fine when they pulled out of the driveway. And that’s all I know firsthand. Everything else

is what I read about later on, and I can hardly believe newspapers to be accurate about anything when they always lie about me." Then she shot him a significant glance, hoping he would let her in on details from the police files.

He did. "The car was found on the road through Corpsewood, about three miles in. The terrain there is hilly, and parts of the road are cut through the earth, leaving high sides of exposed rock. Somehow, that huge car had been flung halfway up a ridge of limestone and caught on fire. The flames set the surrounding trees and brush alight. By the time it was all put out, the crime scene was a muddy, compromised mess."

It sounded ghastly, and for a moment Cora remained quiet. "Why didn't they find any remains in the car? They never told me they didn't, but if they had, I would have been pulled down to the station to identify my father. And if there wasn't anything recognizable, then one of the police enchanters would have scried the bodies to confirm who they were."

That drew a wry grin from Hayes. "See? Brains. The fire was so damn hot that everything burned down to ash and metal. There was no way to recover any remains."

"Or maybe the bodies weren't in there."

"The cops don't like to think about complicated scenarios when there's a simpler explanation to grab at. A car as large as a Royale could have only been tossed like that by a bomb planted inside it. Nothing else would be powerful enough."

Cora stared straight ahead, feeling like her blood might boil. "And no one else has as good a motive as I do."

She kept calm for a heartbeat before her next breath exploded out in a huff. "What a bunch of faff."

"You ran around with Ephram Harper for a while," said Hayes, voice neutral.

"That was before I found out he was a maniac mailing dynamite to people."

"He prefers being called an anarchist."

"I don't care what he prefers. He could have blown *me* up. If he's so against the rich and spoiled, I should have been his biggest enemy. He always had clammy hands whenever we touched. I should have thought about that more carefully." Then Cora shuddered, wishing she had taken along one of her stoles for the sheer comfort of soft fur against skin. "Anyway, he didn't teach me how to make bombs and I didn't plant one in my father's car. I *didn't*."

"Relax, Miss Marshall. I wouldn't take you on as a client if I thought you were guilty." Then his voice softened a little. "Sick of talking, or can you stand a little more?"

"Please, let's continue. I know you'll have to work quickly to save my neck."

"What do *you* think happened to your father?"

He was the first soul who had asked after her own thoughts on the matter, and for once, the words struggled to come out. "I don't know. Father was a rich and powerful man, but there are dozens of businessmen like him in the city and they're walking around very much alive. It's not the kind of life that gets you killed, is it?"

The detective made a nonchalant noise. "Unless he crossed the wrong person during a business deal."

"It's possible, but that never stays secret for long. The biggest men of the city spy on each other so carefully that each one knows what the rest ate for breakfast by the time they're all in their offices for the day."

"No enemies that you know of?"

She shook her head.

"What about bad habits?"

"I'm the only one in the family with those, Detective. I really can't imagine who'd want to kill Father... besides me, anyway. No wonder the police are licking their chops. This must be the easiest murder case they've ever had."

Then her voice faded to nothing, for the line of silver birch that marked the edge of Corpsewood now loomed ahead. They were weedy, spindly things, still bare so early into spring, but their stark trunks somehow seemed more of a warning than the shaggy spruce trees that filled the gaps. Despite herself, she shivered. "Why did you want to come out here if you've already read up on everything?"

Unlike her, Hayes seemed even more at ease when the first leaves cast shadows upon them. As the road roughened beneath the car, he said, "I like to see things with my own eyes. Maybe the cops missed something. Maybe they misinterpreted what they found."

"And why bring me with you?" She was dying to know the answer to that.

He considered her words, hands still relaxed against the wheel and expression still faintly amused. "I could tell you wanted to come along. You should've picked better shoes, though."

Cora glanced down at her high heels. They were a pretty maroon with bands of gold leather for the straps. "These pop perfectly with the color of my dress."

"We'll be ankle-deep in ash slurries."

"Which is why I'll go barefoot once we reach the site." She felt pleased at how his gaze flickered down her exposed calves and ankles. She thought she had very nice legs and saw no reason to hide them.

"I seem like a silly fool, and I am, but I always know how to keep my clothes unharmed. Only men are allowed to ruin them."

At that, his focus snapped back to her face, and he looked like he wasn't sure he'd heard right.

"I hope you don't mind me being a terrible flirt, Detective. It's been over a year since I could say exactly what I thought, and now I'm determined to speak every little thing that pops into mind, no matter how unladylike or scandalous."

"Don't worry about it, Miss Marshall. It takes a lot to make my ears burn."

"I'll try my best," she said, sunnily, and smiled as her words drew another look. Oh yes, it was fun to tweak a wolf's tail.

Corpsewood was a gloomy place, the tall firs so close together that their branches choked out the sunlight. The road had turned into little more than a gouge of asphalt running between rises of earth and rock and root. It was also very quiet compared to the city, with only the roar of the car intruding an unearthly stillness.

Cora found herself peering through the windshield, anxious to see the first signs of scorched earth that would mark where her father's car had been found. To their left, two blackened trees rose within view.

Her reaction was nothing more than a sharp intake of breath, but Hayes still answered her unspoken question. "That's it."

Then he fell silent while steering the car off the road to park.

"Is it dangerous at all?" said Cora, already unstrapping her shoes.

Her freed toes wriggled before he replied. "No, but stick close. It's easy to slip."

He was right; although the trees and foliage had been burned into brittle sticks of charcoal, the soil proved as treacherous as sand when

they began a cautious climb up the side. Every step soon became a fight.

"This is awful," she said to Hayes, who navigated the scorched skeletons of the brush without pause. He only stuck his hand out to her in reply, helping her over a ridge of tree roots protruding from the earth.

It was easy to see the great chunks carved out from where the car had rolled upward. The fire had left even uglier wounds, and they stopped at the area where the flames had burned the hottest.

"The scorch marks on the limestone go up high," murmured Hayes, intent on the scene. "The car burned for a while."

Cora nodded, pretending that she saw something equally insightful in a stretch of earth that looked like ashes in a fireplace. Yet she didn't, and perched on a blackened rock to stay out of his way while he prowled. "What are you hoping to find?"

"Anything interesting." His voice had grown absent, but his eyes remained razor sharp.

"You're very vague."

"Ask me something specific and I won't be."

There *was* a question on the tip of her tongue. Now seemed as good a time as any to ask it. "What made you leave your pack and live among humans?"

There was no change in his expression. "I wondered when that'd be coming."

"I suppose it's one you hear quite often." When he nodded, she added, "And I also suppose you'll give me whatever your usual answer is."

"That would mean ignoring what you said, and I doubt you'll take that quietly." Then he looked over at her. In the dappled light of

the forest, his eyes had gone dark and inscrutable. "How much do you know about city wolves like me?"

"Not a thing."

"Then there's no snappy answer to your question."

"I'd be just as satisfied with a long one."

"You're not paying me to gab, Miss Marshall." The words could have been harsh but only sounded wry as he made his way back to where she waited. He eyed her as if he couldn't make head or tail of anything she did. "Packs have strict hierarchies. Stepping outside of the lines drawn around you is a sure way to get killed for committing treason against the alpha-king. You're looking at a rare example of someone who did that and survived."

"Why did you do it?"

"You mean 'what.'"

"No. Why? Lots of people break laws. It's the reason that tells you everything."

He drew in a deep breath and then let it out, as if deciding against the first answer that had come to him. "I didn't agree with what I was told to do."

Cora took in the wry twist to his mouth and the sudden hardness in his eyes, and sensed he'd told her more than most humans knew. That what he *hadn't* said still made him furious. She supposed she should have felt unnerved by this first crack in his composure, but she didn't. Not one bit. "Does... does it have anything to do with how wolf packs are attacking humans more than ever?"

He relaxed again, which told her the answer even before he said, "No. That's happening because they're on edge. Very defensive about the borders of their territories."

"Against humans?"

"Against everything. It's all shaping up to become a city-wide pack war." The words sounded much too calm for what they revealed.

Cora was aghast. "All of them fighting each other?"

At this point, Hayes seemed grimly curious about how far her questions would go. "Let's just say there'll be a lot more bodies on the streets before the survivors can return to their gold thrones and bleed."

She scrambled to make sense of it all. More than half of the city shared borders with wolves. It would be torn apart as surely as a deer caught between teeth. Then she remembered the detective's casual inquiries about her father. "There are humans involved in this, aren't there? Do you think my father was one?"

"Just for driving through Corpsewood? No. It's no man's land. But if he loaned an alpha-king some funds for war supplies..."

"I doubt it. He considered you all worse than beasts. But then again, he knew the city's underbelly well enough to find someone to bind me, so what do I really know?" Despite herself, her fingers brushed at the back of her head. The sigil throbbed in response, reverberating throughout her skull. She had become very good at not wincing, but somehow Hayes still noticed.

"Never stops hurting?"

She looked up to find him intent on her. He still stood casually, hands in his pockets and hat tilted at a devil-may-care angle, but his voice had fallen quiet, even sympathetic.

"Never," she admitted. "I always feel it."

Then her hand dropped to her side, and she found herself asking, "Will you be in particular danger if it comes to a city-wide war? Will they make you pay for what you did?"

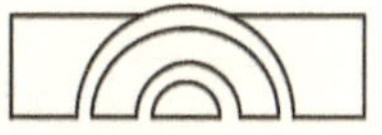

At that, he gave her a lopsided grin. "I'm not part of a pack anymore, Miss Marshall. Right now, that's the safest thing for a wolf. And believe me, nothing's dragging me back into one."

Then he moved away, adjusting his hat against the glare of the sun as he looked down to the road. "I'm not as convinced as the cops that a bomb was what blew up your father's car."

It was an obvious change in conversation, but the tactic worked. Hope speared through her so hard that her next words came out breathless. "Just from what's here?"

"The gas tank of a Royale is as massive as the rest of it. Holds over fifty gallons. That's enough to start a fire this size. And the road is clean. Not one scorch mark from burning shrapnel. I think the car went up in flames from rolling up the hill. All that metal crushing together like a tin can... As soon as the tank got damaged, it exploded."

Cora grinned. "Oh, that's *wonderful*. Everyone said you were the best, and I believed them, but seeing you in action is something else."

Hayes didn't smile back. "That doesn't explain how the car was flung up the side. If we want to hamstring the case against you, we need a better answer than 'I don't know.'"

When he held out a hand, she took it, glad for the help down. "What do you suggest?"

"A visit to the police station."

She immediately pulled free. "Oh, no. If I see any of those faces ever again, I'll slap them."

"They have the car stored in their evidence room. I want to see it, and it'll be easier with you beside me to vouch that I'm acting in your interests." Then he extended his hand again.

"What if I give you a note to show them instead?"

She half-expected him to laugh, but he merely stepped closer, pushing up his hat enough for the sunlight to catch his eyes and brighten them back into their normal gold. "You're frightened."

"No. Yes. I don't know. Yesterday, I read an article in the newspaper about the different ways I could die when they hang me. If my neck doesn't break, then I'll choke to death, and it'll last even longer if the arteries and veins aren't compressed by the rope enough. How am I supposed to face the police with *that* in the back of my mind?"

Cora realized how fast and shallow her breath had become, and how her jaw ached with repressed tears. "What if I start crying in front of them? I'd never forgive myself for showing how scared I am. It's what everyone has hoped to see for weeks."

Then Hayes' hand caught her own, stilling their trembling with a gentle squeeze. As she looked up at him, staring into those wild eyes, he murmured, "You're not on your own anymore, and I wouldn't take you along unless I knew I could bring you back out. Trust me, Miss Marshall, I won't leave you to a cell and I won't make you take any guff. All you have to do is stand there and look smug while I pester them until the veins in their neck pop."

It coaxed a laugh out of her, imagining the two police inspectors assigned to her case—one with the beefiness of a bull and the other small and insistent like a terrier—turning red in the face. "I suppose I can manage that."

As they began the climb down, she added, "But I insist on going back home first. This outfit won't do at all. I always make sure to look my best while being accused of something."

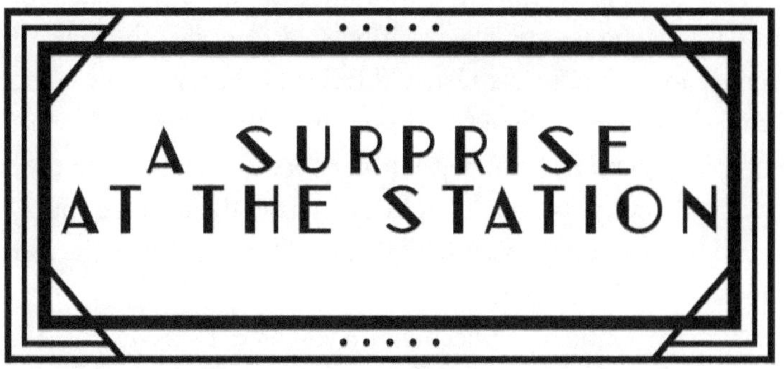

CHAPTER THREE

In what seemed like much too short of a time later, Cora found herself approaching the Crescent City Police Department with Detective Hayes by her side. A massive building, its towering, square pillars ushered visitors up many stone steps to the main entrance. Suspects and criminals were dumped off at the back entry to be processed and put into interrogation rooms or holding cells. Cora fervently hoped she'd never see that side of the station.

As if sensing her growing tension, Hayes brushed her elbow before reaching for the door handle. In the brief moment before the slab of reinforced glass swung open, she drew in a breath and tried to find some courage. She surely flirted with disaster, putting so much trust into a wolf she hardly knew, but the shadow of a noose already adorned her neck like a twisted necklace. What did she have to lose?

And so she stepped inside with confidence, not missing nor minding how Hayes' hand hovered at her nearest elbow, guiding her through the swirls of people inside.

In contrast to the building's outer appearance, its interior was old-fashioned, with yellowed light shining upon worn benches for visitors and wooden cubicles partitioned by glass near the back of the room. It looked more like a bank, this part of the station, except for the massive oak desk placed mere steps from the entrance. A police officer sat behind it, scribbling at paperwork while waiting to check in each and every visitor and direct them from there. Hayes simply steered her past, offering a grin that flashed his teeth when the cop glanced up and then glared.

"Just what kind of connections do you have, Detective?" she murmured, as they took the hallway to private offices.

"I don't. I want to get straight to the point, that's all."

The hubbub behind them faded as they passed by doors with frosted windows and brass plates bearing names. Cora found it increasingly hard to bite back questions while glancing around at the dull paint and cobwebbed corners. This was nothing like the corridor that led to interview rooms, which was marred with shoe scuffs and brightly lit to discourage shadows. This felt much more like the quiet of a slumbering snakepit.

She found herself drifting closer to Hayes while their shoes sounded against the floor, surely alerting anyone and everyone working there of their presence. In response, he smiled at her. "Easy. I always hold onto my promises. You'll leave this place as freely as you walked in."

Just then, they reached the end of the hallway. When he knocked on the last door there, she read the nameplate and felt her heart thump faster. In the few private moments they had left, she hissed, "The police captain himself?"

"Highest man in the station," he replied. "Only the police commissioner has more power, and I always avoid dealing with politicians or administrators if I can help it. Dempsey started out patrolling the streets and has the scars to prove it. It gives him a different view from most who make it to the top."

Then the door opened, and Cora quickly rearranged her expression into a pleasant smile while facing Captain Dempsey, the man who wanted her neck in a noose.

He wore a scowl over the interruption, and it deepened as his gaze jumped between them. "Don't tell me you picked up the Isaac Marshall case, Hayes. It's just about wrapped up and tied with a bow."

Hayes gave him a wolfish grin. "Always a pleasure when our paths cross, Al."

The police captain didn't look inclined to agree, but stepped back and waved them inside.

Cora studied the office with unabashed curiosity, finding grimy windows that let in just enough light to reveal a desk overflowing with paperwork and makeshift ashtrays. A haze of smoke filled the room, but she thought she could make out maps of the city tacked to the walls.

When the police captain pulled back one of the chairs facing his desk and gave her a sardonic bow, she sat with an ease that she didn't feel, primly crossing her ankles. As Hayes settled beside her, he winked.

Dempsey noticed. "I should ban you from the damned building. Every time you skulk in here, you blow a case of ours to pieces."

"I also catch the real killer."

Dempsey pointed at Cora. "She had the motive, she had the means, and she had the opportunity."

"And *she* is sitting right here," said Cora, keeping her posture demure. "I know most people say I don't have much of a brain, but I can certainly keep up with a conversation."

"You have enough smarts to hire him, anyway." Then Dempsey sat behind his desk with a sigh. He was a handsome man, with a hard look to his eyes and the type of strong jaw that showed the darkness of stubble no matter how close of a shave it had. Grey streaked his hair, but he still looked fit and strong and steady, like a hound that had years of experience to hone its excitement while tracking game.

He lit a cigarette before glancing between them again, voice slowing a drawl. "DeLuca and Fuller are on the case. What did you tell this hairy bastard that you didn't mention to my men? He only accepts clients if he thinks they're really innocent."

"No bodies found," said Hayes, voice affable. "No witnesses, either. Your fellas built their case on the likely explanation, but I always dig for the real one."

The police captain scoffed. "The bomb detonated in a lonely stretch of the forest and the resulting fire was so hot that everything burned to ash. But sure, let's hear the theory on how Isaac Marshall escaped something that sent a 7,000-lb car hurtling up a hill."

"I'll have one after I look at the vehicle itself. I know it's being stored here as evidence."

Cora kept her gaze on the police captain, curious about his reaction to such brashness. She half-expected him to go red in the face, or bluster insults about a wolf demanding anything from a human.

Instead, he took another drag from his cigarette. "There's nothing that says you have any right to see it."

"No. But it's always helpful to keep on my good side, isn't it? Especially for those situations where it's wolf pack vs. city and no one from the police force can act without disturbing the delicate treaties and inter-territory laws that keep us all from killing each other."

A slow, hot grin appeared on Dempsey's face, and Cora felt herself stiffen in her seat. It wasn't a nice smile at all, but one that said, *Well, if you're going down that road...*

"You want to talk about helpfulness? Then take on the mess with the Saxby Pack."

For the length of a heartbeat, Hayes fell very still. "No, and you already knew that would be the answer. You know my one hard rule. I don't—"

"Ever take on cases for us if they involve your old pack. Yeah, well, plenty of times we find ourselves committing to things we hate."

"Don't do this, Al," said Hayes, voice dropping low. Not quite a growl, but close enough. "Pushing me to take them on as a client will only cause a bigger mess for everyone."

The police captain glanced over at Cora. "Might want to encourage him along, lady. We're close to charging you, and every second he and I spend arguing is one more that you lose."

"I didn't hire him to tell him what to do," said Cora, glancing over at Hayes and hoping he could read what she felt from her expression. *Don't let these bastards bully you around.*

But Hayes didn't look back, instead focused on Dempsey as the man leaned back in his chair. There was a savage amusement in the police captain's eyes as he said, "We both know how this has to shake

out. One of us just isn't ready to admit it. You can't pretend to be free from slipping off whatever leash your old pack had you on. Just like I'm not free to throw their diplomat out on their ass whenever she comes in here. No one can do what they really want unless they're willing to live alone in the woods. I don't feel like picking ticks off me for the rest of my days. Do you?"

There was a short silence after that. Cora knew that if he'd said all that patronizing claptrap to her, she would have responded by choking him with his own tie. There was nothing she hated worse than a lecture.

But Hayes looked unfazed, neither angry nor abashed as he said, "I'm not a rookie on his first beat, and this has nothing to do with fear or pride. I'm telling you no because it's a terrible idea."

"I wouldn't prod you unless it was serious. It's a weird one, Sam. I've seen a lot, but never any like this." Then the police captain sighed, all traces of humor fading from his face. "At least hear me out. If you do that, I'll let you look at the car without another word."

When Hayes' eyes narrowed, the police captain jerked his head at Cora and added, "And I'll get her out of the room if you don't want anyone else listening in."

She stopped a nervous glance at Hayes just as he shook his head. "No. She's fine."

When Dempsey shrugged, Cora sensed herself becoming invisible. Normally that would annoy her, but at the moment she was only curious to hear more about the dark details behind something as mysterious as a wolf pack in trouble.

After another hit on his half-burned cigarette, the police captain began. "A week ago, two human lovers were necking over by Beake

River, right near the bridge that separates no man's land from city territory. It was around midnight. Everything was quiet. And then—and this is where the witness descriptions get shaky—*something* chased them and tore that bridge to shreds doing so. Everyone ended up in the water, pulled downstream until the two lovers managed to crawl up the river bank. Problem is, they ended up in pack territory with the creature still after them."

"Who survived?" Hayes sounded grim.

"The lovers escaped back to city territory. A goddamn miracle, considering how the pack was also on their heels. Whatever chased them was killed, but not quickly enough to keep it in pack land. It stumbled over the border and died slumping against the fence of a junkyard."

"Wilson's Wrecks," murmured Hayes, as if to himself.

The police captain nodded and then leaned forward on his desk. His gaze had hardened into something deadly serious. "Sam, a few of my boys made it to the scene in time for its final breaths. I trust them when they say it didn't look anything like a wolf. Too big. Too deformed. But when it died, it transformed into a human body right in front of them."

Cora felt her mouth drop open. Only wolves could change into humans and back, and it was an act of their nature, something as instinctive as a pair of jaws snapping shut. If the body had changed *after* death... well, that suggested strange magic at work. Perhaps some mad enchanter performing forbidden experiments. The burn of the sigil buried beneath her hair suddenly sharpened into blistering pain, and she had to fight hard to keep her hand from darting to the back of her neck.

As she struggled to keep her breathing steady, Hayes rubbed at his face. "How many from the pack were killed by this thing?"

"The Saxby diplomat won't say, but one of the lovers swore to seeing two wolves ripped in half. Barehanded."

There was a long moment of silence before Hayes spoke again, hand still working at his eyes. "They want the body."

It wasn't a question, but Dempsey nodded, anyway. "They're not getting it. Anything that ends up with a pack is as good as dead to the human world, and even you aren't slick enough to deny it."

When Hayes said nothing, the police captain added, "They're desperate, Sam. Getting pushy. You know the city can't let even one pack muscle around the law. Show an ounce of weakness in that department and they'll all lunge in for blood."

"Who's the diplomat?"

"Rowan Saxby."

Hayes grimaced.

The reaction brought a glitter of humor back into the police captain's eyes. "So you know her."

Before Hayes could confirm the obvious, shouting echoed through the hallway, shattering the conversation like a rock thrown through a window. Cora jerked in her seat, turning toward the sound on instinct. Both Hayes and Dempsey rose from their chairs, already reaching for their side holsters. Then one voice rose louder than the rest, and Hayes dropped his hand, expression changing.

The police captain laughed. "Speak of the devil. I'd recognize that nasal yawping anytime. I don't suppose you're willing to try talking her down first?"

"I'd only stir her up more," said Hayes, his head cocked toward the door. The glass pane shivered whenever the shouts reached a

certain pitch. It sounded like two or three other people were also arguing, either with her or against her.

As Cora rose from her seat, too fascinated to be unnerved, Dempsey brushed past them with a sigh. "This is the third time in a week. Sometimes I'm sure that all you mutts are better off dead."

Before Hayes could stop her, Cora followed the police captain. She'd never had an ounce of self-preservation, and it wasn't about to guide her actions now. When Hayes hissed her name, she only walked faster, heels clicking down the hallway as the yelling strengthened, and was soon close enough to make out distinct words.

"Let me simplify this for your thick skull. There is a body in your morgue that killed four pack members. It committed crimes on pack land. We need this body sent back to us so that we can examine it."

"Ma'am, it died on city property and therefore is under the care, duty, and law of the city. Any requests or claims for it require the proper paperwork."

"We've given it."

"It takes up to six weeks to process paperwork for initial approval or rejection, as I've said five times already."

In the entrance room, the single officer behind his desk still scowled, but had also risen from his seat and braced his hands against the polished wood surface as if to turn his body into a shield against the diplomat and her three guards glaring at him. The rest of the room was cleared out, visitors ushered elsewhere, and several of the officers that had been behind their glass windows were now gathered around him in a bristling wall, stone-faced as they waited for the she-wolf to escalate from bark to bite.

Cora hesitated at the mouth of the hallway, giving Hayes the chance to catch her arm. Despite the excitement of the scene, she glanced up at him, expecting a rebuke. Instead, he only pulled her back a few steps, just enough to put his body between hers and the argument—just enough to protect her.

"It's about to get that bad?" she whispered, pushing her mouth close to his ear to make sure she'd be heard above the cacophony.

"Just be ready if it does." He remained focused on Dempsey as the police captain stepped into the fray.

"What's going on, Ogden?"

"Ms. Rowan Saxby of the Saxby Pack is here, sir." The officer kept any note of irritation from his voice, but his neatly combed hair had fallen into his face as if he'd swiped a hand through it more than once. "She wants to see the body."

"Can't do that and you know it," said Dempsey, facing her square.

"Captain, the legal paperwork necessary to extricate the body back to pack land may take up to a year to be approved, signed, and sealed. It'll be nothing more than bone by that point. We need to know what's going on *now*." The diplomat's expression remained tight with rage while her voice gained a chill that might have passed for politeness. She was all angles in her pinstriped suit, with dark hair slicked back into sharp, nearly geometric waves close to her skull, but any sense of sleek efficiency was ruined by bloodshot eyes and a muscle jumping in her jaw.

"If we skip over everything and hand over the body, it'll start a damn riot. We can't show favoritism no matter how urgent the case is."

"If it's done quietly..."

"Yeah, well, you already made sure it won't. Your voice carries across the entire station. There's probably already a gaggle of journalists fighting over the phone booth across the street to get the details into their newspapers."

When the diplomat hissed in a breath as if to say more, Dempsey sighed. "We'll pass on anything we learn in our investigation over to your royal inspector. Like always."

"That's not good enough. Secondhand information from human sources is hardly suitable for my king."

When Dempsey only shrugged, her voice turned hot. "At least give us information on the humans connected with the body. There were two that were chased by the killer. Several members of our pack saw them flee into human boundaries. They're witnesses and our inspectors wish to interview them."

"Lady, I wouldn't give you the name of my worst enemy. I know what wolves have been doing to humans. My boys have been cleaning up the messes on the streets for almost a year."

"Cross-fire casualties aren't the same as investigating witnesses."

Dempsey laughed. "Is that what you're calling it?"

"Do you think this is funny?"

The police captain's voice finally hardened. "I think you've got a lot of arrogance to come in here and act like your king rules over us. As far as I'm concerned, he's an animal itching at fleas no matter how many jewels shine in his crown."

The diplomat's eyes constricted to pinpoints. "How dare you?"

In the hallway, Cora felt her breath catch from the sight of sudden fangs. Hayes pushed back the side of his jacket enough to hover a hand by his holster.

The police captain didn't even blink. "I killed Rusties in the Tin War. Snarling like a junkyard dog won't scare me."

They drifted closer to each other like snakes, unblinking while both the pack guards and the officers twitched with tension, waiting for the first strike.

Then Hayes stepped out from the hallway, approaching them empty-handed. His voice cracked through the air. "Rowan."

Cora watched the diplomat recoil at the sound of his voice. "You."

"You know this isn't the way to go," he said, as easy and calm as Cora had ever seen him despite being under the scrutiny of everyone in the room.

"Pet," she hissed, taking another step back. The guards rippled around her, various expressions of confusion and disgust crossing their faces. "Don't speak to me. You're nothing more than a tool for these humans."

Then she stalked off, heels rapping against the floor as the guards slunk after her. One, a red-haired man with a scar on his chin, glanced back at Hayes with troubled eyes, but none of them stopped.

When the door slammed shut behind them, Dempsey pulled out a fresh cigarette and lit it before giving his officer a light slap on the shoulder. "You did good, Ogden. If the bitch files a complaint, it'll come to nothing. The rest of you get back to work, too. If she follows her usual pattern, she won't return for a few days."

As the officers dispersed, the police captain glanced over at Hayes. The grin was back on his face. "One day, I'll want to know what you did to get booted out. Every wolf who sees you acts like they'd rather run into a leper."

"I left it. That's good enough for most. I want to see the car, Captain."

Something had come over Hayes, a sort of change that Cora couldn't quite describe. It wasn't the snarling bluster of the wolves who had just left, but he had still stood there sharp and tense and ready to move onto blood if any more words were used to prod at him.

Dempsey saw it, too, and only nodded. "Sure. You know where it is."

They took a different hallway this time, one that led to a stairway down. Cora cast sidelong glances at Hayes while their footsteps scraped against the rough concrete, trying to gauge his mood. He looked as cool and pleasant as ever while nodding to the officer who met them at the bottom, and his hand remained light at her elbow when they passed warehouse-like shelves storing evidence boxes. But once they were led to the room full of cars and left alone, his expression hardened into remote concentration. He obviously didn't want to talk.

Cora tried watching quietly, but she had never been blessed with patience and soon grew bored. And it was so *silent* down there. She never knew what to do with herself when she wasn't talking or listening to someone else.

She studied the pathetic remains of her father's car, unsure how the mangled lump of metal could help her case. Then she found herself saying, "It's such a shame."

Hayes nodded. "I heard it was a real looker."

"No, I mean... That everyone is so beastly to you."

Now he glanced over. "I sometimes come away from cases with bruises or broken bones. A few insults are nothing, Miss Marshall."

"I suppose that's one way to look at it," said Cora, still doubtful, but she took the hint and turned her attention to the remains of the Royale again. "Do you see anything that could prove it wasn't a bomb?"

As he circled around to what she guessed was the left side of the car, he said, "Hard to tell. The fire distorted a lot. Except for..." Then his hand reached out as if to touch it. Just before his fingers brushed the twisted metal, they flexed and drew away again.

"What is it?"

"I'm not sure." He sounded absent, and she nearly huffed in indignation at his mysteriousness.

Then his head snapped toward the door, and his eyes darkened to amber, which she had begun to recognize as a sign he was on edge. It took a heartbeat for her to hear footsteps approaching, and another to look over, too. It sounded like a man's shoes, and she expected to see Captain Dempsey or one of his men.

It wasn't him. It was one of the guards who had hovered around the Saxby diplomat—the fella who had looked torn up over the diplomat's insults toward Hayes. In the harsh overhead light, his uniform was all dark leather and shiny brass buttons, and his red hair gleamed like a burnished penny.

The other wolf hesitated while glancing at her, but his posture remained rigid as he refocused on Hayes. "Sir."

"You're not supposed to call me that anymore, Brom," said Hayes, suddenly sounding very tired. "Were you sent here?"

The guard's silence was answer enough, but when Hayes shook his head, he said, "I know the risks I'm taking and I'm here, anyway. Please... help us."

Hayes hesitated. It was the first time Cora had seen him do so. Then he jerked his chin at the door. "Let's go outside."

His glance was enough to reassure her that they wouldn't go far, and she politely turned away, pretending she was still interested in the car. It worked well enough that she was able to sneak over to the slightly ajar door and listen without being caught.

"We need your help no matter what that jumped-up diplomat says. The king wants it solved, and that means all the higher ups want it solved *bad*. We've lost seven from the guard, sir."

"All from the creature?" said Hayes, his voice turning sharp.

"No." Now a trace of bitterness entered the guard's voice. "Four from the creature. The other three... failed in various ways to help the investigation. Their pelts are on the royal inspector's wall. He needed to show the king he was doing something to save *his* skin."

Hayes swore. "Is the diplomat still near the building?"

"Probably throwing up in a nearby alley. Her head's coming off if she comes back with nothing."

Before Cora could hear Hayes' reply, Captain Dempsey's voice sent her jumping back from the door. "You look like you feel sorry for her."

He stood a few feet away, cigarette still in hand. Somehow, he had slipped in through another door unnoticed.

"Captain," said Cora, heart ramming against her ribs. "You gave me a terrible fright."

He continued as if she hadn't even spoken. "He'll hate himself for it, but he also knew it'd come to this sooner or later."

"What do you mean?"

The police captain laughed. "What story did he give you? Something that puts his situation in a happy light, I'm guessing. He

was exiled from his pack, Miss Marshall. Most wolves give up and die from that. He's managed to make himself a cushy career, at least."

"It's that hard for them?"

"Their pack is their identity and Hayes was close to the very top. The royal inspector. That's a higher position than mine, but now he has to sit there and listen while I dick him around. And when he goes to other wolves, he has to sit there and listen while they insult him for being a dog performing for humans."

Cora raised her chin. "And then he makes all of you look like fools by solving cases that stump everyone else."

Dempsey smiled. "No one can pull it off every time. Though if you *are* innocent, I hope he proves it. I don't like seeing innocent people swing."

"You make it sound like you have nothing to do with it either way."

For a moment, the police captain didn't respond. He walked around the car, now letting the soles of his shoes sound loudly against the tile floor. "Everyone's nervous with how pushy the wolves are getting, Miss Marshall. So many bodies are being found, and some of them are human. So many bodies, but not one of the murderers. It makes the regular Joe and Jane types who fill up this city nervous. They start demanding that something needs to be done, and that if it can't get done, they start demanding for heads themselves. It's making all the politicians and administrators sweat, because they're the first to be targeted by the rage of the common fella. There needs to be something given to people to show that we can all still do our jobs. That justice can still be carried out, quick and smooth and righteous. Do you get me?"

"I think so," said Cora, trying to keep her voice steady. "Charging and convicting me for my father's murder will do just that, won't it?"

Dempsey nodded, but didn't look gleeful or even satisfied. Instead, he suddenly seemed very weary, as if there was a great weight on his shoulders and it had just turned into something crushing. "If it helps any, I sent for the best hangman around. He's the chief executioner of New Obsidian. He knows how to tie the knot and place it so that your neck will snap as soon as you drop."

She took a moment to calm herself by pretending to readjust her grip on her clutch, wondering how much trouble she would get into for calling the police captain a jackass to his face. "No, Captain. That's not helpful at all."

He shrugged. "Just telling you how things are, lady."

Hayes' voice cut between them. "It won't get that far."

He stepped back into the room, alone once more, and added, "I'm taking the case, but I'll only tell you everything if you give me unlimited access to all information and resources at your department's fingertips."

"Done. It's not like we can keep you out, anyway. How the hell did you squirm into the case files for Isaac Marshall? Those were with Fuller and DeLuca at all times."

"We all have our secrets, Captain. I'll see the body after finishing up here."

He waited until Dempsey left before turning to her. For the first time since seeing the pack diplomat, something in his face softened. "Are you all right? I didn't mean to leave you alone with him."

"I'm fine. He didn't make me cry at all," she said, flashing him a smile. "What about you?"

"Don't worry about me." He glanced away before adding, "I need to visit the morgue."

"And I suppose I'll have to stay here and wait for you out of respect for client confidentiality?"

"I haven't signed anything yet. It's more that the morgue isn't exactly a pleasant place."

She studied him, not liking the new, grim set to his mouth, and then tucked her arm into his. "It's true that I've never seen a dead body before, but I can't imagine it's any worse than feeling my skin crawl whenever reporters take pictures of me."

The morgue proved to be bright and sterile, much more so than any other room they had visited in this furtive, subterranean level of the police station. It was cold of course, and smelled like disinfectant, but she had frankly gotten worse scares while volunteering for charity work at the local hospital, even once they entered the autopsy area and met the medical examiner, Dr. Morris, who looked like a corpse himself with his pallid face and wizened body.

He frowned at her. "I don't like her being here. Women always faint, cry, or go into hysterics. Take her outside, Hayes."

Cora managed to keep a smile in place as Hayes said, "You've been hanging around the dead too much, Morris. It's shrunk your social niceties to nothing. She's staying."

With a grumble, the medical examiner waved at them to follow him. Sheets covered bodies but left faces exposed, and Cora found herself looking at each one. It really wasn't as bad as she'd feared. They looked dead all right but bore no grotesque wounds or even an expression of pain.

"Here we are." The man's spectacles flashed as he reached the rows of metal lockers and pulled on the handle of one. When it slid

out silently, the body fully covered by its sheet, he added, "The John Doe who came to us last week. I'm not surprised you're here to see him, Hayes. He started a murder spree in pack land and ended up dead in city territory. Very messy."

"Once they get him, it'll be swept beneath the rug like plenty of other things," murmured Hayes, stepping closer as the man folded back the sheet.

The words were flatly spoken, even colorless, but Cora found her watching him instead of the medical examiner's reveal. There was still something in the detective's eyes—bitterness? Anger? Whatever it was, it hardened his gaze into a piercing amber attention. Then he leaned over to better study the body, and the brim of his hat hid his face from view.

With nothing left to distract her, Cora reluctantly glanced over at the dead man, hoping it wouldn't be too horrifying. Then the walls around her tipped and tilted. At her strangled gasp, Hayes' focus snapped over to her.

"Ms. Marshall?"

She was too busy sinking to the floor to answer. He caught her before her head cracked against the cold tile, and her spinning senses grew further confused by the press of a body against hers and by the strong arm wrapped around her waist to keep her upright.

"I told you," said the medical examiner, dryly. "Let's hope she recovers without falling into a fit of crying."

If he were a few steps closer, Cora would have tried to beat him with her purse. As it was, she couldn't even keep her voice steady. "I'm all right. It was just a shock."

Hayes' free hand brushed her cheek, guiding her to look up at him despite the lingering unsteadiness of the ground. Lines of

concern furrowed his brow, but when he spoke, the words were soothing. "You're all right. It's a dead body. That's tough to swallow for anyone who hasn't hung around them much."

"No, it's not that. It's... I *know* him." Then she sucked in a shaky breath, unable to keep from looking over at the body. "That's Tierney. My father's driver."

CHAPTER FOUR

Captain Dempsey rubbed his eyes while slouching over his desk, shoulders twitching reflexively each time Cora's crying took on a particularly loud pitch. Without looking up, he said, "And you're sure it's him?"

"I'm positive." Cora mopped at her tear-stained cheeks with the handkerchief that had been given to her. The sodden fabric muffled the rest of her words. "As soon as I saw his face, I knew it. Even through all the b-blood and filth and those awful *bite* marks..."

Then her expression crumpled into another sob.

The police captain had interviewed enough upset women to recognize one on the verge of hysteria, and said nothing else while pulling a cigarette out of his pocket. As he lit it, his attention flickered to the third figure in the room.

Detective Hayes hovered behind Cora's chair, his attention unwavering. The brim of his hat cast his eyes in shadow, but the grim set to his mouth and his utter silence revealed his tension. One hand rested against her upper arm as if to steady her, squeezing gently whenever her breath hitched. At the sound of the police captain's disgusted sigh, he glared over.

Dempsey remained unabashed. "Don't give me that look. She can get plenty of cuddles from you. I need answers."

Cora blotted her eyes and said in a thick voice, "How many more times do you need to hear it? That was Tierney."

"Miss Marshall, the body is almost hamburger. I want to be sure we're upending two cases based on irrefutable facts. It's going to take hours to get Dominic Tierney's dental records and make a comparison, and in the meantime I'm not about to make any hasty —"

"Is there a tattoo of an eagle on his back? A big one with the wings on each shoulder?"

In the short silence that followed, she lowered the handkerchief from her raw face and looked at the police captain, too miserable to even enjoy his expression. "It's in red and black ink and there's writing beneath the talons. The words say—"

"You convinced me." His voice had also changed, now deathly serious. "There's no way you could've seen the back of the body from where you were standing."

Then the man grabbed at a pile of coffee-stained papers on his desk and pulled one free. The scratch of pen strokes sounded overloud in the office as he quickly scrawled a few lines, and Cora found herself shifting uneasily. Hayes watched him feed the note into the glass pneumatic tubing system but remained silent as the paper shot out of sight.

When the police captain only resumed puffing at his cigarette, thumb rubbing at one eyebrow as if he was lost in thought, Cora fidgeted with the handkerchief in an effort to keep quiet. It didn't

work. "What's going to happen now? Will your men have to interview me again?"

The question drew a hard smile to Dempsey's face, and his eyes seemed to clear again. "Feel free to celebrate, Miss Marshall. We've got nothing more to do with you. The fact that you identified the thing that killed members of the Saxby Pack, a case that was officially handed over to Hayes while you were busy having hysterics in the morgue, means the Isaac Marshall case is now connected to it. You and your father are now entirely Hayes' responsibility."

"You mean, you're..."

"Throwing you to the wolves."

"That is a horrible attempt at humor, Captain."

"It's not supposed to be funny. It's just the bald truth."

She drew in a breath to ask how he could be so cold about things, but Hayes spoke up first. "How are your boys handling the loss of a big case? Will they fight against giving me their files and any collected evidence?"

"I'll send everything over before they find out it's more than a rumor." Then a sardonic gleam appeared in the police captain's eyes. "I won't lie to you, Sam. There'll be bad blood over this. A lot of people inside the station and out of it will think she's escaping justice."

Cora nearly choked. "You can't still believe I had something to do with this."

"Why not? You hire a wolf to prove your innocence and then your father's murder turns out to be related to a case involved with his old pack. Now it's out of our hands and there's no one on our side who can make sure Isaac Marshall's killer is found. It's a damn lucky coincidence, especially for someone close to being charged and

tried. DeLuca had just picked out the suit he would've worn while formally arresting you. Said he wanted to look good in the papers."

Despite everything, Cora felt a laugh bubble up. "Captain, your men—who all dress *terribly*, by the way—have interviewed me three times. You all very well know I'm not bright enough to scheme up an intricate conspiracy like that."

Hayes had started prowling around the office, hands in his pockets while listening to them. Now he stopped by one of the maps tacked to the wall, studying it as he said, "She's not safe, Captain. In fact, she's in more danger now than before. It's never a good thing to be connected to somebody who's killed wolves."

Dempsey shrugged. "I didn't say the gossip would be right. Just that it'll exist. Giving you control of a case where pack members died and the killer was found on human land is one thing. But people are going to be mad at finding out a wolf is in charge of solving what happened to one of the city's elite. They're going to be mad and they're going to be scared."

"Then it's a good thing I don't worry about being popular." Hayes made a final circuit around the room before stopping behind Cora again. She twisted enough to look up at him as he added, "Shoot the files over to my office and have the car put *in* my storage unit. Don't think I forgot about the cute joke your boys pulled the last time I took on a case involving a vehicle. That $500 parking ticket was tough to swallow."

The police captain shrugged. "I'll make sure the transition is smooth. After that, no promises."

When Hayes glanced at her, Cora knew it was time to leave. A wave of dizziness ran through her as she rose, still clutching the handkerchief. "I take it this means we'll never meet again, Captain."

"I hope not, Miss Marshall. Despite everything, I wouldn't enjoy seeing you behind bars or on a slab."

Somewhere behind her, Hayes growled, but she only nodded, refusing to be shaken. "I certainly won't miss your way with words. Goodbye."

"Good luck." The man's voice was drained of its usual sting, and as he watched them go, the expression on his face seemed more appropriate for someone staring at two corpses.

It left her unusually silent as Hayes guided her through the hallways and into the public area of the station. The sharp glances and outright glares from officers and citizens alike made her all too aware of how puffy her eyes felt from crying, and it was suddenly hard not to stare down at her shoes. A strange dread gripped her as they approached the massive door that led outside, the thick glass distorting the view into vague, unrecognizable blurs. What if everything remained bewildering once they were outside? What if nothing ever felt normal again?

Then Hayes' voice brushed her ear, low and sure and rock-solid. "Easy. We're almost out of here."

She drew in a shuddering breath as he reached for the handle. "I feel like I'm in a nightmare."

The flash of camera bulbs certainly convinced her she was awake, and so did the hubbub of voices as reporters rushed around them, jostling each other for the best positions and shouting questions.

"Miss Marshall! Is it true your father's driver was found?"

"Did you have a hand in his death?"

"Did you hire wolves to kill your father?"

"Oh, my God," she moaned, trying to duck her head before her swollen eyes and reddened nose could be seen.

Hayes snarled, a guttural sound that shook anyone who heard it bone-deep. Still covering her face, she sensed more than saw him lunge past. Then one of the reporters yelped, and all voices fell silent as the crack of a bulb against concrete rang out. The bodies around her pulled back in a wave, leaving one man choking in Hayes' grip while staring at his broken camera.

As soon as Hayes dropped him and grabbed at the next man, they all scattered like rats. Cora watched, dumbfounded, as they ran in different directions, leaving her and Hayes alone on the steps.

He caught her arm, eyes still feral. "Come on. They won't follow us."

"Won't you get in trouble for that?" Despite her words, she was smiling, and twisted back for one last glance at the sad remains of the camera.

"It's my job to get in trouble. A little more won't hurt."

They both fell silent as they reached his car, and it was only once they were on the road, the police station safely out of sight, that Cora finally relaxed enough to sigh.

Hayes didn't look away from the traffic, but his head angled toward hers. "Do you want me to take you home?"

"No. I don't want to go back just yet. I'll only sit there in an empty room and think about what I saw."

"Then let's get you somewhere quiet."

He took her to a small cafe in a section of the city that was clean but drab, away from the frivolous boutiques that drew in shoppers and the business blocks that belonged to harried bankers, doctors, and lawyers. In the distance, factories whistled shift starts and belched smoke from their blackened stacks, and the cars that passed by looked like people on their way to someplace more important.

Right at that moment, Cora appreciated the sensation of being invisible.

Inside, no one flinched at the sight of Hayes' gold eyes, and the waitress sounded bored as she led them to a table. Cora rubbed at her temple while Hayes ordered coffee for them both, too worn out to maintain any composure. When they were alone, she nervously played with the fringe at the edge of the tablecloth, admitting, "That was an awful experience. I'm glad it's over."

"Are you feeling any steadier?" His voice sounded even, but concern gleamed in his eyes as he watched her.

"Yes, I'm feeling much better. It's just... the poor man."

The words didn't seem to reassure him, and he kept searching her face. "You knew him a lot better than you let on."

It wasn't a question, and she drew in a shaky breath. "I didn't, actually."

There was a soft growl from him. "Miss Marshall, putting aside the fact that you knew about a tattoo that couldn't be seen with his clothes on, you'd be the first socialite I've met to cry over a servant who was nothing more than a familiar face."

"Detective, I swear to you, I don't know what's going on. The moment I saw him there on the table, my head started spinning and it still hasn't stopped. Yes, Tierney was good-looking and charming, and yes, he proved irresistible whenever I saw him stripped down to his braces and covered in engine grease, but I wouldn't call mere sex the same as actually knowing a person. Would you?"

His eyes narrowed slightly as he studied her, their gold heavy and intent, but then the set of his shoulders relaxed, and he looked away to run a hand over his hair. "I need your trust, especially now."

At that, she leaned forward, desperate for him to believe her. She needed at least one person on her side, and the idea that he might see her as a liar hurt more than expected. "You have it. I don't know anything about what he may or may not have been involved in. Our fling started the day he was hired and ended a month later, and during that time his first name was the only private detail I teased out. After that, he was simply Tierney, staid driver for my father. I really didn't think I was hiding anything by failing to mention a brief affair that happened years ago."

"Why did it end so quickly?"

"He wanted the job more than me." Then she felt her cheeks sting.

Hayes nodded, some of the tension leaving his body, but whatever he might have said in response was lost as the waitress approached with their coffee. Cora thanked her with a subdued smile. Hayes just pushed the cream and sugar to her side of the table.

"I suppose the police reports went into detail about what I had for breakfast the morning Father disappeared." Despite the sour words, her expression brightened as the rich, heady smell reached her, and when the waitress returned with a plate of chocolate-dipped cookies, she immediately grabbed one.

Hayes stuck to the coffee. "Just a lucky guess. I don't think you take anything plain, Miss Marshall."

Her smile warmed as she glanced at him, almost forgetting how raw her face felt from all the crying. "You're being very kind, trying to cheer me up instead of dumping me off at home."

"Seeing your first dead body is rough." Then he nodded at her hands, which had absently braided the fringe. "Especially when you keep thinking about it."

She managed a hiccup of a laugh while smoothing it back into place. "I've done this since I was a girl. Braided anything possible whenever I was caught up in unhappy thoughts. Luckily, I don't think very often. They say ignorance is bliss and I believe it."

When she looked up again, she found his gaze had slipped up to her face. Something about the way he sat there, intent on her even with his body angled toward the entrance and one hand within easy reach of his holster, drove the last of her shivers away, and she sipped at her coffee with steady fingers.

As she bit into the cookie, he suddenly said, "You know, most socialites I've met in this line of work didn't cry over the hired help even when they *did* know them."

"Oh, I can think of one. Lady Cagni. Her husband is from across the sea, a count of something or another. Anyway, his valet died from the flu and she was *so* upset because she had just finished matching the servants."

"What?"

"She wanted them all to have red hair and blue eyes. And they did... until the valet died. It's a rare combination, she said. It takes her months to find replacements. I thought she was going to hyperventilate while explaining it all to me."

Hayes raised an eyebrow. "I'm not talking about someone who thinks it's the same as a knife missing from a set of silverware. You hide it well, Miss Marshall, but you really feel things."

"I guess that's true. Even though it should be impossible, I still miss..." Then her voice faded, and she felt a frown crease her forehead as she struggled to remember the name. Sometimes it seemed at the tip of her tongue, as if the sigil hadn't been able to fully erase it. But the sensation didn't harden into anything she could

hold onto, and she gave up with a huff of breath. "I still miss the man I planned to elope with, even though I can't remember his name or how he looked. And before you ask, I'm sure it wasn't Tierney."

Hayes nodded. "Your father would've fired him after finding out."

"That and he was only a fun fling. This was something different. I know it, somehow, even if I can't explain why."

Something changed in the wild eyes that watched her. The natural harshness of a hunter's gaze seemed to soften for just a moment. "You would have been happy with him."

"Yes." She felt the truth of it ring in her heart. "It's funny, Detective, but drinking myself silly throughout the night and waking up in strange beds in the morning became as dull as sitting at home like a spinster with her knitting. Oh, it was fun at first, make no mistake, and Father's face would turn such an *amazing* color whenever the latest scandal would hit the papers. But I started feeling empty, like nothing really mattered."

"And then?"

"I don't know. All the memories of meeting him are now gone. But I know it was very serious, and that I was, too. They wouldn't have taken so much of my mind away otherwise, would they?" Then she drank some more coffee, suddenly feeling awkward. "Why are you curious about all this? Surely, it has nothing to do with my father's disappearance."

He hesitated, as if choosing his words carefully, but in the next moment his expression changed. Then his head snapped toward the doorway. His eyes brightened into a feral hue that she was beginning to recognize. "We've got company. No, don't turn around. I'm about to tell you who it is. It's the diplomat from the Saxby Pack."

She worked hard to keep her voice hushed. "So they *do* want to work with you."

"We'll see. Avoid meeting her eyes or showing your teeth when you smile. Wolves who don't live among humans take those as signs of aggression." He dropped his hand from his coffee to his side holster, and she knew then that the diplomat was approaching their table.

The back of her neck prickled as the she-wolf stopped within polite speaking distance, ignoring her entirely. "Detective Hayes."

The hours that had passed since her outburst at the police station hadn't improved her disposition any. Her face was still tight with anger, and her words still glacial.

Hayes kept his own voice pleasant while stirring his coffee. "What is it, Rowan?"

The diplomat's mouth twitched as if she fought not to snarl. "Alpha-king Saxby has agreed to put his *faith* in you to solve the mystery of what this creature was and who set it upon us. But the news of it being the driver of your client's father has left him wary. He wishes to see her and ascertain for himself that she isn't involved in a conspiracy with you."

Cora bit back a stunned laugh. Perhaps wolves weren't so different from humans after all... at least not when it came to ridiculous suspicions. "Ascertain how? That could mean anything from a truth spell to old-fashioned torture."

The diplomat curled her lip at the question, but when Hayes straightened in his seat, eyes flashing in warning, she reluctantly answered. "We're not about to risk human wrath. We want a simple interview. No human can erase the scent of guilt from their skin."

The day was already too strange to feel anything as normal as fear, and Cora answered without a hint of trembling. "Detective Hayes knows much more about these matters than I do. I just follow his advice."

There was a terse nod from the diplomat before they both glanced at him. He was still stirring his coffee, gaze traveling around the neighboring tables almost absently, but when he spoke, his voice was clear and hard. "We're not stepping onto Saxby territory. If we agree to this, we'll meet you on no man's land or with a pack willing to play neutral host. Even then, we'll only walk in once I've got a Mange locked in place."

The name was completely unfamiliar to Cora, but the diplomat obviously recognized it. Recognized it and didn't like it, for her mouth tightened again. "Is that necessary? We've never been the ones to break an oath."

At that, Hayes met her gaze for the first time, and his eyes were so hot and feral that the she-wolf actually stepped back. "Don't pull that moral act on me. I knew the wolf who last held your role in the pack. He never had a disloyal moment in his life and yet I saw his bloody pelt nailed to the traitor's wall. Tell the alpha-king that *if* we meet him, it'll be under the security of a Mange. Now get out of here."

The diplomat stiffened but said nothing else. A nod to them both and then she turned and left, heels crisp against the floor. A few people at other tables watched her go with mild curiosity before returning to their drinks or conversations.

Cora watched Hayes drain his coffee in one go. Except for a muscle twitching in his jaw, he already appeared calm again. "Well. You're really something when you bring out your dominant side."

His eyes darkened to their usual gold. "You don't have to see them even if they agree to everything. It's your decision."

"I meant what I told her. I *do* trust you, Hayes."

Her answer turned his glance into a full stare, one completely unlike what the diplomat had received. Cora found herself quickly adding, "But I have to ask: what *is* a Mange?"

"It's a long explanation, but if you really want to know, I'll tell you."

"Oh. No, that's all right." She picked up the remaining half of her cookie and dipped it into her coffee while adding, "Whenever people try to explain something complicated, I never understand them. As you can imagine, my tutors all hated me. One even called me a pea-brain and expected me to cry over it, but I just laughed at her. I've always known what I was, even as a child."

To her surprise, he offered a wry smile. "I like a challenge and I promise I won't call you a pea-brain."

Then he reached for the salt and pepper shakers discreetly set to the side and placed them in the center of the table. "Let's say these are two packs with a lot of bad blood between them: the Salt Pack and the Pepper Pack. One day, the Salts send their diplomat over, claiming they want to negotiate a peace treaty on their land. The Peppers are just as tired of fighting but aren't about to trust their enemy. In reality, both packs would then start fighting over *who* holds the negotiations until too many wolves die to keep it up, but for the sake of this conversation, we'll say the Pepper alpha-king immediately agrees to travel into Salt territory to discuss the treaty. The catch is, he'll do it only after a professional hostage is set up on *his* land."

Cora watched him set the cream pitcher by the pepper shaker.

"Meet a member of the Mange Pack," he said, looking up at her again. "The Mange Pack lives on the outskirts of the city. They don't have control over good land, they never whelp any tactical geniuses to get them on the map, and they never want to form alliances with other packs. But there are a *lot* of them and they all fight like berserkers. Snuff out one and you'll have the whole damn pack after your throat, no matter who you are or where you are. Absolute killers."

"What makes them good hostages?"

"They're mercenary instead of egotistical. They love hiring themselves out as bargaining chips among other packs because they get paid a lot and they also get to kill a lot if it all goes wrong."

Cora studied the arrangement before her. It was utterly silly, comparing merciless wolf packs to tableware, but it also made more sense in her mind than droning textbooks or bitter tutors. "So, the Mange wolf stays among the Peppers as the Pepper alpha-king steps into Salt territory. And if the Salts did anything to him, then I suppose as a hostage the Mange wolf would be killed in response."

"Exactly. And then the rest of the Manges would go after the Salts in vengeance for breaking their promise of peace talks and triggering the death of the Mange being held hostage."

"And that's truly enough to keep the Salts from trying anything horrible?"

"Let's put it this way. Two years ago, the Farrogut Pack tried using a similar setup as a trap. The Manges overwhelmed them, skinned the bodies to drive home the point, and carried off anything valuable. The pack that later took over the territory had to rebuild certain rooms because the bloodstains were too deep to be scrubbed out."

Cora took the pitcher to add more cream to her coffee. "That does sound very definite. So, if you hire a Mange, we won't be in any danger at all."

"It's a better than average chance of surviving, anyway." Despite the grim words, he winked at her. "You sound like you understood all of that."

She smiled over her cup. "I suppose I did."

Silence fell between them, relaxed and unhurried. She watched his hands as he replaced the salt and pepper shakers to their original positions. Despite the grisly nature of their conversation, his fingers remained precise. Nothing about this—not the revelation about Tierney, not the diplomat from his old pack, and not the dire warnings from the police captain—had shaken him. She'd never met anyone so steady.

Frankly, she'd never met anyone like him at all. It was easy to recognize that bubbly feeling filling her full despite her scratchy eyes and lingering headache; it was that cherry-sweet warmth that came with a man making her feel good, whether it was a simple compliment or a sticky-skinned night. But she was surprised to feel so... comfortable around him. Yes, that was it. Comfortable, as if he would never sell his memories of her to a newspaper, or grow angry after too many drinks and try to strangle her, or throw her out of his house in the morning before she could find her shoes.

She'd heard him snarl like a beast and talk about murder as casually as most people discussed the weather, and yet it was suddenly clear to her that, even under far better circumstances, she'd put her life in his hands in a heartbeat.

The waitress approached, then, the smell of nicotine heavy on her clothes. "Anything else?"

Cora demurred with a polite smile, but it was as if the woman's presence pulled the rest of the world back into existence, and when Hayes set out enough coins to cover the coffee and leave a decent tip, she glanced around at the other patrons hunched over in their seats, eating or arguing or reading. Everything had shifted in a way she couldn't pinpoint, and now the coziness of the cafe seemed remote and dim.

Then Hayes stood and offered a hand. "The sun's going down. Let's get you home."

She nodded, realizing there was no way to postpone the inevitable.

The drive home was quiet, and Cora felt a throb of misery at the sight of the house lit and waiting for her arrival. The servants would be tired, the rooms would breathe the lingering presence of her father, and the sigil would be its own form of his ghost, burning at her scalp as she tried to sleep. Suddenly, she didn't want to go in. Suddenly, she wanted to run off screaming in the night.

Instead, she tried a smile as they pulled into the long driveway and got out. "What do private detectives do at night?"

"I'm betting nothing as glamorous as a socialite." In the darkness, his presence was solid and reassuring, encouraging her forward even when she glanced over at the car garage, unlit and empty.

The maid opened the door without any change in her expression, even when Cora turned to Hayes and asked with a trace of desperation, "Will I just be trapped here again?"

He smiled a little. "Miss Marshall, I'm going home to a mountain of paperwork. You're not about to miss anything interesting."

"I know, but... what am I supposed to do tomorrow? And the day after that? Wait until you either hear back from the diplomat or catch a break in my father's case?"

"What did you used to do to keep busy?"

"Whatever Father told me to." She didn't need to raise her hand to the back of her head to explain why; a flicker in his eyes showed he understood.

In a different tone of voice, he asked, "What about before that?"

"Whatever he told me *not* to do."

At that, Hayes sighed and stepped inside with her. Surrounded by the gilded wood and plush carpet of the hallway, he appeared wilder than ever. "It's killing you, isn't it?"

Hope rushed through her, leaving her breathless. "I want to find out what happened. I don't want to read whatever letters you send me, or listen to you after it's over. I'm in this mess up to my neck, and I can't just sit here like a little bird in its cage and wait for the cloth to be removed. *Please.*"

There was a beat of silence before he nodded. "Tomorrow, I'm planning to interview the two lovers who saw Tierney while he was a monster. If you want to tag along—"

"Yes!"

"But there's a condition."

"I don't care." Suddenly, it didn't matter that she'd be sleeping in an empty house, or that none of her old friends returned her calls, or that the morning newspapers would have screaming headlines about her. Now she had something to *do*.

As if sensing her distraction, Hayes stepped closer. "I still want you to hear it. If I keep involving you in some of this investigation, then in return you'll never strike out on your own. I don't want you

looking for evidence, talking to witnesses or people who might know something, or otherwise going into something dangerous by yourself."

"Agreed," said Cora, immediately. She could feel herself beaming.

Hayes didn't look nearly as happy. "I'm dead serious. The revelation about Tierney threw everything about your father's case up in the air. Whoever was responsible for that has a nasty streak, uses magic no one recognizes, and doesn't want to be caught. You could walk right into a trap if they're clever enough. So no sleuthing on your own, all right?"

When Cora nodded, sobered by the words, he searched her face, his eyes dark and intent. "I know you've been going through hell, but I'll help you out of it. You won't be trapped anymore."

She nodded again, heart pounding against her ribs from his closeness as much as his words. And when they said their goodbyes, she barely heard him mention that he'd return around noon, instead caught by an insistent whisper in her mind even after the door closed between them.

You've felt something like this before, haven't you? Not with him but another. The sigil couldn't burn everything away. But is this an echo of that, or something new?

CHAPTER FIVE

Cora studied herself in the mirror, trying to gauge whether grey was too drab without the flash of jewelry. It was, and she quickly stripped down to the lace of her lingerie, tossing the dress onto a pile of others on the floor. Her outfit needed to be *perfect.*

After so many interviews with the police, she knew how uncomfortable it felt to be questioned by grim figures. She certainly didn't want to appear dour. But she also wished to be taken seriously, not dismissed as a frivolous socialite who only knew how to smoke, seduce, or scandalize. And most importantly, she needed to make Detective Hayes' jaw drop the moment he saw her.

A skirt tried on and tossed off. A shirt dismissed as too fussy. She was just reaching for a seafoam green dress that would look striking with her hair when Maisie appeared in the doorway. The maid's voice remained as crisp as her uniform as she said, "Excuse me, miss. Miss Violet Granbury is here to see you."

"What? But why on earth would she...?"

The answer came in the form of Violet herself as she pushed the maid aside, still wearing her kid gloves and sable coat. "Because, darling, I saw the papers and just had to rush over and congratulate my dearest friend on getting away with murder."

As Cora blinked, still shocked, the other girl swept her into a hug and kissed the air by her cheeks. Just as quickly, Violet spun away and sank into the nearest chair with a sigh, the movement parting her coat enough to reveal how she wore only a silk negligee beneath it. She really had come running over. Cora didn't know whether to shriek or laugh at her oldest friend for disappearing along with all the others and returning only once the clouds of suspicion had cleared.

And to sit there and act as if she hadn't avoided Cora's letters, hadn't sat in a different box at the theatre to keep from speaking to her, hadn't told reporters that Cora Marshall was nothing more to her than a fellow party girl sharing the same social circles. "Vi, I ought to slap you silly for all the things you said about me to those vile journalists."

Violet only smiled and lit a cigarette. "None of us can afford to keep grudges, ducky. Now really, how did you manage it? I want all the details, especially the sordid ones."

It was hard to find a response that didn't involve pulling the other girl's hair out, and Cora gave herself time by trying on the dress. It looked fantastic, giving her a soft, carefree appearance, but her reflection's expression remained troubled. "There's nothing to say. I didn't get away with it because I didn't do anything in the first place. I'm innocent."

"Innocent? Is there such a thing these days?" As she spoke, Violet removed her sunglasses, revealing her face in full.

She was completely unlike Cora in looks, her hair a deep auburn that made her unusual violet eyes all the more striking. Her mouth was sharp and thin, perfect for the sardonic smile she always wore, and her long body had the starved elegance of a greyhound. Yet worrying signs were visible as well. Her ashen skin and smeared makeup suggested she hadn't bothered glancing into a mirror, and her normally sleek bob looked like a rat's nest.

Despite the knot of anger in her chest, Cora found herself drifting over to clasp the other girl's hand. "Vi, are you all right? You look tired."

"Don't lie to avoid hurting my feelings. I have none. The only heart I have is this pretty little one right here." Violet pulled her hand away to catch the gold locket hanging from her neck, and continued to play with it as she added, "What I look like is roadkill, and I feel just as awful. There must have been something in the drinks last night."

"Where did you go?"

"Freddy's, as always. The boy can never stop partying. He also saw the papers, by the way, and told me how much he hopes to see you. He's throwing something else this afternoon—an event to watch him break world records in his new speedboat."

So, they really were all acknowledging her again. The fact ignited strange feelings in Cora's heart, far messier than mere indignation. A week ago, she would have killed for even a phone call from one of her friends. Now she was being welcomed back into their inner circle of gossip, parties, and sex, welcomed back into the *right* type of scandal, and yet when she pushed away that initial burst of anger... nothing replaced it.

Had she changed that much throughout this ordeal? She'd never minded hollow pleasures before, had never minded the fake smiles offered to her. Were they still enough?

At her silence, some of the archness left Violet's face. "Come off it, darling. No one turns down an invitation to Freddy's. Don't pout just because we worried about you bumping off your friends next."

Suddenly sure of what she wanted, Cora began searching through her shoes. "To be honest, it *was* all very vexing. But you're right, there's no use holding grudges. The plain fact of the matter is that I've already made plans today."

"To what, try on your entire wardrobe?"

Cora flashed a smile at her, unable to contain her excitement. "To investigate."

Then came the sound of a car pulling into the driveway.

Cora gasped. "He's here and I'm not even ready."

As she tore through her hat collection, Violet got up to peer out the window. "Oh, I see. This must be your private detective. My, my, he *is* a wolf."

"Isn't he fantastic? Just wait until you meet him." She picked a cloche with a brim that swooped low, wanting to emphasize her eyes. "He's very clever and perceptive, and nothing seems to shake him at all."

"Meet him?" The other girl's tone seethed with disdain. "Darling, you're speaking as if he's human. I know scandals are second nature to you, but it's a bit mystifying to hear you'd rather keep company with a wolf than spend time with us. Didn't you miss your friends at all?"

"Of course I did. But..." Unable to find the right words, Cora fussed with her hat instead.

Violet studied her, eyes widening. "Don't tell me you've gone silly over him."

"Well, and so what if I have?"

The other girl laughed, but it was a short, breathless one, as if the shock had driven the very air out of her lungs. "He won't take you seriously. No one takes any of us seriously. We're like stars, bright and hot and wonderful to look at... and then we burn out in one big flash. I mean, really, who would want to live with you or me? We know nothing, we do nothing, and we go through money so fast that if any of us live past thirty, we'll be worth nothing as well."

Cora blindly reached for some earrings, trying to ignore how the words stung at her heart like vicious little wasps. "Maybe I just want to pretend for a day or two that it's *not* like that."

"And then it won't hurt as much when he bills you for the extra hours?"

Cora flinched. Then she turned away, facing the mirror and trying to ignore how her reflection's mouth trembled. "What an awful thing to say."

"The truth always is."

In the heavy silence that followed, Violet joined her, dropping her chin on her shoulder just as they'd done since childhood. "Don't misunderstand me, darling. I'm not saying this out of spite. It's just... our kind of life is short enough. Why waste it chasing after something you can never have?"

A knock came at the door, the three raps that signified Maisie was about to open it. Cora wiped the tears from her cheeks just as the maid announced, "Detective Hayes is here to see you, miss."

"Thank you, Maisie. Tell him I'll be right down."

Hayes waited near the front door, still in his hat and coat and obviously impatient to be off and running. Despite his sleek clothes, he looked more feral than usual, eyes glinting with a hunter's excitement, but the closed expression on his face warmed as Cora and Violet descended the stairs. "Afternoon, Miss Marshall. Miss Granbury."

Violet brushed past as if he hadn't even spoken, instead giving Cora a parting glance over her shoulder. "I'll keep in touch, ducky. And remember, Freddy's invitation is an open one. In the meantime, have fun with your *pet* detective."

"Violet!" Cora's voice rose into an outraged gasp even as the door closed behind the other girl. "That's unspeakably rude!"

"Your friend seems a little miffed at me," said Hayes, the corner of his mouth quirking into a smile.

"I'm so sorry." Her cheeks stung with heat as she looked up at him. "We had a fight and I'm afraid she can turn very nasty when that happens. But still, she shouldn't have said that about you."

"I've been called a lot worse." Then he studied her face, long enough that she worried he might have noticed the redness in her eyes. Whatever he saw, he decided not to press on it. "Who's Freddy?"

"Oh, she meant Freddy Davenport. He invited me to one of his parties."

He let out a low whistle. "That's a big name to have among your friends. Sounds like you're popular again."

"Apparently, it's very different to get away with murder than it is to be accused of it." Then she patted her hat into the perfect tilt and brightened her voice. "Anyway, what do you think? Does this look right for investigating?"

To her gratification, he couldn't resist glancing her up and down. Although those gold eyes were still strange and thrilling to her, the look in them was *very* familiar, evaporating the hurt of Violet's words even before he said, "The boots are a nice touch."

She beamed. "Aren't they gorgeous? I fell in love with them at first glance even though they cost a fortune. The man at the shop said the pearls can only be harvested from a part of Mulgrew Bay that's in wolf pack territory."

"Not at this point." As they walked outside, he added, "The Upper Mulgrew Pack stopped existing, to put it gently, over five months ago."

"Wasn't that just awful? I was hoping to have some matching gloves made, too." The sight of Hayes' car chased away the last of the thoughts troubling her mind, and there was only sheer excitement in her voice as she said, "So. Who are these two lovers that we're about to interview?"

She soon found out. Jack Sutton worked as a patent illustrator for a law firm in the city. His sweetheart, Mary Barlowe, was a secretary there. Neither wished to be interviewed at the firm, and had reluctantly agreed to instead meet Hayes at Jack's home—a small apartment above a sandwich shop.

"Is there anything else I should know?" said Cora, as they walked up a metal staircase at the back of the building, which was the only way in from the outside. The air smelled like pickles and pastrami from the shop below.

"Just remember that people often lie. The trick is to figure out why." Then he knocked on the door.

As they waited, Cora studied their surroundings with interest, taking in the various alleys and apartment windows that could be

seen from their high position. A factory loomed like a giant in the near distance, belching steam and smoke as the ground shuddered from its machinations. Several squat buildings surrounded it, all of them as grim and plain as concrete blocks. It made the sudden low of a cow all the more startling, and Cora turned back to Hayes to see if he'd heard it, too.

He seemed to sense her unasked question. "There's a slaughterhouse nearby. I can smell it. Probably feeds supplies to that meat pie factory."

Then the door in front of them opened, revealing the suspicious face of a man about Cora's age. She couldn't say her first impression of him was favorable; he dressed neatly and had his hair combed back in the precise manner of a law firm employee, but there was a sullen look to his eyes and to his words, too, as he said, "What do you want?"

"Jack Sutton?" Hayes kept his voice friendly. "I'm Sam Hayes, the private detective you spoke with on the phone."

The man nodded and pulled at his collar, a nervous habit judging from the ink stains there. The act left his watch flashing at them as his gaze jumped to Cora. "Who's she?"

"His assistant," said Cora, keeping her voice prim while brandishing a small notebook. "He hates taking notes." Then she bit back a smile at the swift glance from Hayes.

After a beat of hesitation, Jack nodded and stepped aside to let them in. "Well, all right. Mary's already here."

The apartment and its furnishings were well-worn yet clean, without any sign of mold, infestations, or buckling walls that plagued many of the older buildings in the city. Instead, what caught Cora's interest was the sheer amount of loose leaf paper scattered

everywhere—finished artwork. There were ink portraits, field sketches, technical illustrations, and even a few watercolors. It was obvious that Jack Sutton truly loved to draw, and that he was good at it.

Mary Barlowe was near the kitchen, frantically pushing aside papers until she found a tray big enough to serve coffee and cookies. She was less dolled up than most secretaries Cora had met: her hair was left straight and pinned back from her pale face, and her skirt and sweater were practical instead of stylish. She also looked terrified whenever Hayes stepped into view, and shook so badly that Cora herself ended up carrying the tray over to the table to keep the coffee cups from chipping against each other.

As the percolator coughed and bubbled, Jack slouched forward in his seat, resting his elbows against the table while refusing to look at anyone. Mary moved about in the kitchen, trying to seem busy to avoid sitting with them. Cora took a cookie to give herself something to do and then glanced up at Hayes, who had remained standing. He gave her a smile that was both wry and reassuring.

When it became clear neither witness would volunteer anything, Hayes reached for a newspaper left on the table. "The papers are showing a lot of interest in what you saw that night."

Jack scoffed. "Yeah, only because it's now connected to that rich heiress who murdered her father. No one believed us at first."

"The reporters certainly did," said Cora, skimming through the article. The revelation about Tierney being the strange beast that puzzled both wolf and man was now public, and so was the fact that two human witnesses had seen him in his monstrous form. She hoped that in the coming days, the papers would be kinder to

Tierney than they had been with her. Even a dead man deserved better.

She glanced up and added, "At least your names weren't revealed."

Mary shook her head while coming over with the percolator. "We haven't talked to anyone from the newspapers. They must have gotten our story from the police somehow."

"Who didn't do anything, anyway," muttered Jack. "So why bother us for more information? This Tierney fella is dead and can't hurt anyone else."

Hayes offered them a slight smile, one that didn't show his teeth. "True enough, but we still don't know what happened to him or how he turned into that creature. Who's to say it won't happen again to someone else?"

Silence fell. Mary and Jack's faces paled. The hush lasted for several heartbeats before Mary nodded as if to herself, her expression firming as she came to some internal decision.

When she excused herself and left, Hayes refocused on Jack. "This thing he turned into, the thing that chased you that night... what did it look like?"

"It wasn't a normal wolf," said Jack, still sounding shaken. "It had the fur, and a few things about the head, maybe... but no. I never could have mistaken it for a wolf."

"It was far too big," said Mary, returning with an artist's portfolio tucked beneath her arm. "And when it moved, it looked nothing like any animal I've ever seen. Here. Show them, Jack."

When he hesitated at taking the leather case from her, she urged it on him. "Go on. Your drawings of it are perfect."

"It would be very helpful, Mr. Sutton," said Hayes, drinking from his cup of scalding coffee without so much as a flinch. "What we saw in the morgue now looks like a normal man."

Jack's mouth remained set in a sour line, but something in his eyes softened as he glanced at Mary while taking the portfolio from her. With a smile, she sat next to him, one hand settling on the bared skin of his forearm while he pulled out a sheaf of papers and thumbed through them.

Cora felt a twinge in her heart at the sight of such quiet, easy intimacy. It was the ghost of a grief that she couldn't fully feel. Once, she must have wanted her life to be something similar, luxury cast aside like a fur coat to bare her heart to love instead. Leaving her father's fortune behind—what did it matter? The weight of pearls couldn't possibly compare to the sweetness of a familiar kiss.

The twinge came again, stronger this time, and Cora abruptly looked away, afraid she might make a fool of herself with tears that had no reason to exist. Her gaze found Hayes, hoping to draw on his steadiness, expecting to find him absorbed in the drawings.

Instead, it was she who was under his scrutiny, and his gaze was so intent that she felt herself flush. What was it about the wolf-kind that suggested their eyes found more than flesh and blood? Surely an animal would only see the raw meat and hard bone of a body. Yet Cora sensed he had looked into her heart just then, and had seen the glimmers of that old pain. Had seen it and had understood it.

"Here," said Jack, and Cora gratefully looked at the papers spread out on the table.

On every sheet loomed a beast too grotesque to imagine. Jack had a neat, precise way with his pencil, rendering the creature in detail as fine as any scientific illustration. The drawing nearest to her focused

on the head of the creature. It had a misshapen muzzle, flatter and broader than a wolf's, and enormous, bristling teeth. Its eyes were small and so were the ears.

Hayes stepped closer to pick one up. Cora also looked at it, skin prickling as she realized this drawing was of the full creature.

"It really does look half-man, half-wolf," she murmured. The body was vaguely like a human's, at least in the shape of the chest and hips. Yet the hands were overly large and had pads like a dog's paw. And then there were those long, vicious claws...

"How did it run?" said Hayes.

"On all fours, but awkwardly. Lurching, like." Mary shuddered.

Jack rubbed at her shoulder before adding, "It didn't look any more at ease on hind legs." Then he pushed forth another piece of paper, one that showed detailed sketches of the creature as it stood.

Hayes looked at it for a second and then circled away from the table, giving Cora a meaningful glance. She understood what it meant—he was about to try something. "Your drawings are really nice, Mr. Sutton. Chilling to look at. How much are the newspapers paying for them?"

Jack stiffened in his seat. Mary gave an indignant gasp. "I already told you, we haven't talked to anyone else."

"You didn't. He did." Hayes' tone remained level.

Cora studied the man as he started to squirm. "Listen, I don't have to take this from some dog. I—"

"Insults won't work with me," said Hayes. His voice still sounded calm, but something in his eyes had changed. They looked sharp, feral, intent as if he were chasing a quarry and just saw it stumble. "There were details in this morning's papers that weren't in your police interviews."

Jack pulled at his collar, the fabric now damp with sweat. "They added that themselves. Juiced it up to sell more copies."

Then Hayes nodded at the other man's wrist. "Your watch isn't just new, it's a brand way out of your reach. You couldn't afford it with your salary."

Mary's voice rose. "The head of his firm gave it to him yesterday for doing such fine work on a big account."

Cora pointedly tapped a name in the newspaper article but kept her voice gentle. "Do you mean Mr. Leyendecker? The reporter mentioned he's Jack's employer. I've met him, Miss Barlowe, and he's a real penny-pincher. It's just not in his nature to give ostentatious gifts. Why, for her past birthday, his wife only received some stationary."

While Jack twitched, now freely perspiring, Hayes picked up one of the drawings. "These were carefully placed in a portfolio even though drawings and sketches are scattered throughout this apartment. You wouldn't need to take these to work for any reason, so why are they set aside, ready to be pulled out and shown to people?"

"All right!" Jack's shoulders slumped. "So what if I did?"

"What?" Mary stared at him. "Jack, how could you?"

"I don't see what's wrong with it," he muttered. "The amount they offered for the drawings is more than I'd make in two years working under that old bastard Leyendecker."

"You mean they already know these exist?" said Hayes, his voice sharpening.

"Yeah, but they tried underselling me, so I'm waiting for a better price. I thought it would be one of them when I answered the door earlier, not you."

Cora watched a muscle jump in Hayes' jaw as he started pacing. "Hayes, what is it?"

He sounded like he wanted to growl. "You let all this information slip, and now you've told reporters that even more is coming."

Jack's expression remained confused, but Cora suddenly shivered, catching on to what Hayes meant. "You believe that whoever's behind this will want to shut them up, don't you? Before anything else can be revealed to the public."

But Hayes didn't answer, instead stopping at the nearest window. When his shoulders bunched, Cora knew something was wrong. She was already rising from her seat when he lunged for her, his voice coming out as a snarl. "Get down!"

The windows exploded.

Cora found herself flattened to the floor, the weight of his body over hers as glass rained around them. Mary shrieked somewhere off to her right as footsteps pounded up the metal staircase. Jack wasn't making any noise at all. Blood spattered the floor near his chair.

"Hayes," she gasped.

"Stay low." The words vibrated against her ear as shots continued to puncture the walls. "The gunfire is coming from the street. Once I clear the back stairs, run."

Cora had never felt so frightened in her life while silence fell, leaving the squeak of the door abnormally loud as someone opened it from the outside. She caught the shape of a man just before Hayes took him out with one shot. Her heart hammered as he eased forward to check for more gunmen. The air was thick with the smell of fear and metal.

Then Mary's whimpering caught her attention. The other girl was hiding behind an overturned chair, her eyes as wide as a doe's.

Cora veered toward her, trying to ignore how glass pricked her knees through the thin fabric of her dress. "Mary. *Mary*. Are you all right?"

The girl didn't answer, merely twitched, but in the next moment Hayes murmured, "It's clear. Get the hell down those stairs and take the nearest alley out, because there was more than one shooter and they'll all be coming up here to make sure nothing's left alive."

"What about you?"

"The idiot survived being shot in the leg. I'll help him get out."

"But you don't know how many there are," hissed Cora. "You could be killed."

"No time to argue." His eyes flashed at her, wild and fearless. "Help the girl get out, too. Hurry!"

Cora bit back a retort and reached for Mary. "Take my hand. Come on, we've got a chance to go."

Mary still didn't say anything, but in the next moment her fingers blindly fumbled for Cora's.

Every second was precious, yet Cora couldn't keep herself from glancing at Hayes one final time even as she stumbled to her feet. "Don't you dare die."

He gave her a faint smile while reloading his gun. "Get going, Miss Marshall. I'll find you."

Mary was out the door first, silent except for her panting. Cora quickly followed, wincing as their heels rapped against the metal stairs. Just as they reached the final step down, a muffled gunshot rang out from somewhere inside the sandwich shop. Customers poured out, yelling and shoving and trampling anyone who slipped and fell.

"They're shooting up through the ceiling at Jack," said Mary, her voice sounding strangled. Then it rose into a shriek. "Oh God, I see one of them."

So did Cora, her gaze jumping to a big brute cutting through the crowd like a shark, his hat angled low to hide his face. When he saw them, his entire body stiffened like a hound scenting the fox it sought. Mary made a strangled noise and then took off down the nearest side street. Cora ran after her, voice dying on her lips as she realized calling the other girl's name would only alert more of the thugs.

The cobblestones beneath their feet were damp with stagnant water and littered with trash. When the air thickened with the smells of animal and manure, Cora realized where they were going. "Stop! There's nothing ahead but the slaughterhouse!"

Then a bullet hit the brick wall on their right, and Mary started screaming as they dodged sagging dumpsters and rotten crates. Her shrieking coaxed a few heads to poke out through upper story windows, but they quickly disappeared again at the sight of the gunman. Cora was gasping too hard to speak, praying her heels wouldn't slip on the slick ground, but Mary never once slowed down, not even when they reached the cattle lowing in their pens, eyes rolling white with confusion and uncertainty as Mary ducked between the wide bars to hide among them.

"Oh, no," muttered Cora, but a glance behind her revealed the hulking shape of the thug, panting from chasing them and already raising his gun. She quickly wormed her way into the pens as well, pushing past stamping hooves and shuddering hides. One cow shook its head, blunted horns lowering enough to catch her dress and tear it. Cora flinched but kept moving, hearing Mary shriek while waving

frantically at the men funneling cattle into the mouth of the slaughterhouse one at a time.

"Help us! For God's sake, help us!"

The two workers stared, as slack-jawed as the cows themselves. Then another shot rang out, and the cows surged, bowling into the men in sheer panic. Mary disappeared from view. Cora fought through the scrambling current of hooves and horns, expecting to be crushed at any moment, expecting to trip over the other girl's broken body.

Then she caught a glimpse of Mary's sweater, and darted through a gap between two shuddering cows to catch her hand again. Mary looked dazed but unbloodied as they ran into the mouth of the slaughterhouse, the stench already overwhelming.

They stumbled to a stop, their path cut off by a cow and the worker standing before it with the killing hammer. He stared at them in bafflement, lowering the massive iron head of his weapon.

"What..." he managed, and then a stray bullet caught him in the shoulder, sending him reeling back.

The other workers fled from their processing stations, sparing not a backwards glance.

"Cowards!" shrieked Mary, tears running down her cheeks, but Cora simply saved her breath, catching the other girl by the arm to drag her further inside.

They slipped and slid over the bleeding floor, heels scrabbling for purchase as skins hung on hooks swayed in front of them, raw and wet. Cora couldn't bite back a shriek as one slapped against her, coating her entire side in congealing clots, but the sound of heavy panting somewhere behind them drove her on.

Mary had fallen silent, just as bloodstreaked as they ran past carts of offal that steamed in the air. Then rows of butchered carcasses swung before them. Cora caught sight of a long knife and quickly grabbed it while they both hid among the forest of hanging meat.

Footsteps approached, slow yet steady. Cora heard Mary whimper, but she only tightened her grip on the knife and waited for the bastard to come close enough. Finally, a shoe appeared within sight, within *reach*, and Cora lashed out. The blade caught him with a satisfying *thwack*, slicing above his ankle just as she'd hoped. The man went down with a yell, dropping his gun to clutch at his leg.

She scrambled for it without dignity, feeling like her heart might burst as she rose to her feet, already aiming at his head.

The man hissed something under his breath, inching backwards. "Think you know how to use that?"

"I have a wonderful aim." Then she pointed the nozzle at his good leg. "Would you like me to prove it?"

He just panted for breath, keeping his head down as if still wishing to hide his face. Then Mary shrieked again, and Cora thought for sure she was dead.

But it was Hayes who appeared, hat missing and blood dappling his face. His eyes looked feral but his aim remained steady as he pointed his own gun at the thug. "Your pals aren't coming to help."

At that, the man sagged back with a grimace, finally giving a clear view of his face.

Cora gasped. "I know you! You're part of Roy Alemeister's crew."

"Don't know who that is," muttered the man, but he refused to meet her eyes.

"That's utter faff. Who told you to come after Jack Sutton and Mary Barlowe?"

When that question was met with silence, Hayes moved in close enough to step on the man's bad leg, driving his voice into a scream.

"Okay, I'll talk. I'll talk, you bastard." The man panted a few moments before adding, "But there's nothing to say. I was just following orders."

Cora huffed. "Well, you can still take a message back to Roy. Tell him these are Kitten's friends and that she's very displeased by all this."

"Kitten?" repeated the man, face going blank.

"He'll understand it." Then she looked at Hayes. "Unless you'd rather let the police have him?"

He raised his eyebrows. "Are you sure Alemeister will listen to you?"

"Oh, yes. Very sure."

As sirens sounded in the distance, Hayes jerked his head at the man. "Get out of here before I change my mind."

The thug staggered to his feet and limped off. As soon as he was gone, Hayes holstered his gun and stepped closer to her. "Are you all right?"

The question was low and urgent, and Cora suddenly realized how awful she must have looked. Her hat was gone, the color of her dress was unrecognizable, and her boots were covered in muck up to her calves. "I'm fine. What about..."

Then she reached out and touched one of the spots of blood on his cheek. He let her, the gold of his eyes darkening. "None of it is mine."

The words seemed to snap Mary out of her stillness, and she suddenly stepped toward Hayes, eyes glassy. "Jack. Is he…"

"He's all right. The bullet just winged him. I told him to wait outside."

They all left through the slaughterhouse's shipping door, weaving among the abandoned trucks and crates. Workers and curious spectators milled around, gawking at the broken windows of the slaughterhouse and trying to understand what had happened. Then one figure broke out from the rest—Jack.

"Mary!" He stumbled to a stop in front of her, a handkerchief wrapped around the calf of his left leg. "God, you're a mess."

"Well, thanks a lot for asking how I am," she snapped, eyes flashing. "I'm just fine except for being shot at by maniacs and nearly trampled by cattle."

"I didn't mean it like that. It's just… oh hell, Mary, I thought you were dead." Then he grabbed her and lunged in for a kiss, heedless of the blood smearing her clothes.

Cora turned away to give them some privacy, glancing up at Hayes as he remained beside her. "I think they really do love each other. Did you see the way he looked at her?"

"He's still an idiot." Then he shrugged out of his coat and offered it to her. His expression had gone very, very serious. "But maybe I'm not any better. I'm sorry, Miss Marshall, for putting you in danger."

Cora pulled on the coat with a sigh, sinking into its warmth. "Don't you dare apologize. This has been the most exciting day of my life. Besides, you weren't to know, were you?"

She had a feeling there was more he wanted to say. His eyes certainly looked that way, their wildness taking on a different sort of

intensity than the deadly glint she'd seen in them during the gunfight.

But whatever he felt, he kept it to himself and instead asked, "So, is there anyone in the city you don't know? How do you have friends in the Bruisers?"

"I wouldn't say we're friends, but I'm well-acquainted with their leader, Roy." Then she smiled. "Was that something else I should have told you right away?"

His voice turned wry. "Let's just say I'm all ears."

She wrapped the coat tighter around herself, starting to feel the chill of her sodden dress. "I'd rather have a long conversation after I'm cleaned up."

"All right. I'll come by tomorrow morning."

"No, I didn't mean *that*. Just come home with me right now and have a drink or something while I bathe. There are so many exciting things to talk about that I couldn't possibly wait until tomorrow."

He stared at her for a long moment. "Are you entirely aware of what just happened?"

"Of course. Someone tried to kill the witnesses, which must mean our investigation is making the guilty party *extremely* nervous." Then she beamed. "And now we have a lead into finding out who it is."

Cora sighed while pulling on a silk robe over her freshly scrubbed skin, already feeling miles better with the filth from the slaughterhouse washed away. The sunlight streaming through the windows warmed the vases of flowers in her room, tinging the air with refreshing scents of iris and tulip as she sat at her dressing table. Her reflection in the mirror grinned back at her, just as pleased the day had turned out so well.

She never could have imagined detective work to be so exciting, or so different from her usual sort of thrills. Laughter covering lies, bad behavior egged on to see who would sink into sin and who would become the queen of it, the reckless air of gambling... these were all sweet as sugar but melted away just as quickly. Sleuthing and the truth it unearthed felt so much more satisfying, so much more *real*, and she craved more.

Even the sting of losing a favorite outfit barely registered in her mind, and when one of the chambermaids arrived to take away her ruined clothes, she only said, "Oh, don't bother trying to save them. There's so much blood that they'd need cleaning spells."

"Would you like them sent out instead, miss?"

"No, that's all right. The papers would be all over it if I did, trying to take pictures and who knows what else. I'm sure there's already a pack of reporters outside." Then she approached the nearest window to peer through the lace curtains.

The front gardens were edged by a row of hats and faces hidden behind cameras, marking the property line as neatly as a fence. "I hope none are trying to sneak inside this time."

"Detective Hayes is speaking with them to make sure they aren't." It was Maisie who answered, passing by the other maid with a tray of coffee and shortbread in hand. "He also thought you might need something to steady yourself after this afternoon's events."

Cora felt her expression bloom into a smile. *You silly girl*, she thought to herself. *You* have *fallen for him, and hard.*

Just as she bit into a cookie, the bushes below the window rustled. Then there was a shout. Cora returned to it just as the line of cameras pulled back and broke up. Reporters ran in every direction as Hayes appeared in view, walking out from the house while dragging two men by their shirt collars. Cora leaned closer, nose nearly pressing against the glass as he shoved them into the street, ignoring their arguing.

One man soon slipped away, but the other remained, yelling at Hayes until his face looked purple against his starched white collar, growing even angrier when the detective remained so calm. Even as Cora hid her smile behind a hand, some part of her grew alert to the man's pompous tones. They were intensely familiar, as was the way

he straightened his tie with the sharp, angry movements of a cat that had just gotten its fur ruffled.

"Oh, dear," she murmured. "I think that's Mr. Forrester. Did I have an appointment with him today, Maisie?"

"No, Miss."

"That makes things even more interesting." Then Cora leaned through the window, uncaring of her disheveled state. "Hayes! Wait. My father knew him. Let him inside."

Even from that distance, Hayes' eyes flashed gold at her as he nodded, still impassive. When he stepped away from Mr. Forrester, the man grumbled a few last words and stalked toward the house, knuckles white against the handle of his briefcase.

"I'm sure he'll let himself in," said Cora, reaching for her coffee. Her gaze lingered on Hayes as he slowly followed the other man, scanning the grounds for anyone else who shouldn't have been there. "Maisie, when you have the chance, have Hayes come up here. He should know who this is."

"Here into your room, miss?" The maid was too used to Cora's behavior to pretend to be shocked by the request.

"Yes. We won't have much time before Mr. Forrester really starts shouting."

She remained by the window, sipping at her coffee until a brief knock came. When she turned around, Hayes offered her a lopsided smile, polite enough to wait in the doorway until she waved him inside. It was impossible not to notice how he looked slightly disheveled from chasing off reporters, collar and tie loosened and his hat missing. It was the roughest she'd ever seen him, and she liked it very much.

Yet he looked unmoved by her underdressed appearance, merely glancing over her room before focusing on her face and her face alone. She expected immediate questions about how she knew Mr. Forrester, but instead he said, "How are you?"

"Couldn't feel better."

When his gaze flickered down her robe and back up to her unstyled hair, still concerned, she understood the point of his question. "No, really, I'm feeling fine. You see, it always takes me ages to get ready. It started from wanting to annoy my governesses and then evolved into being fashionably late. Believe me, being this undressed has nothing to do with nearly being gored by cattle."

She'd kept the words light, but he only tensed up, eyes darkening.

Deciding it would be better to change the subject, she quickly added, "But it *is* very sweet of you to scatter those reporters. I'm not in the mood to be photographed without an inch of makeup. And I had no idea Mr. Forrester was coming."

Then she sat at her dressing table again, aware that the man in question would soon demand to see her.

As she started brushing out her hair, Hayes paced around the room, obviously on edge. "Who is he?"

"One of my father's earliest business partners. Technically, he's a lawyer, but also an old family friend. Well, as close to a friend as Father's ever had."

"When was the last time they met?"

The brush faltered in her hand. "Well, that's strange. Now that you mention it, I don't think I've seen him for nearly a year. Right around the time the sigil was put on me. Do you think there's a connection?"

His response was a tilt of the head that could have meant anything. "Did any new business associates or friends take his place?"

"Not that I noticed." Her fingers absently traveled up the back of her neck until they reached the familiar heat of the sigil. It pulsed against her touch like a second heartbeat, and she quickly pulled her hand away again, swallowing hard. "If he *did* have anything to do with it, I'll know. They stripped my memories away, but my body still remembers what happened. Being near my father leaves me absolutely nauseous now."

There was a pause before Hayes sat on the nearest piece of furniture, a pink velvet footstool that looked ridiculously dainty against his sleek power. It left them able to face each other, and when he spoke again, his voice sounded gentler. "Did you know this fella was coming today?"

"Not at all. He wasn't scheduled to. And I thought I signed all the papers needed to keep my father's estate running while he's missing, so I'm not sure why he's here."

"His attitude will tell us a lot."

The simple use of the word *us* brought a smile back to her face. "You're talking like we're a team now."

His eyes had been dark and musing, but now surprise flickered in them, as if he hadn't realized it himself. When he straightened up in his seat, already starting to amend what he'd said, she added, "I rather like being your assistant."

Her voice came out softer than she meant, and much more earnest. It left him silent. It thickened the air between them. Cora felt her heart start to hammer, felt a rush of sweet uncertainty that she hadn't felt since her first kiss at fifteen, when she'd thought she'd

found something that would make her feel alive and full instead of alone and ignored.

Just then, Mr. Forrester's voice rose from somewhere in the rooms below, obviously shouting at one of the maids over being told Cora wasn't yet ready.

She sighed, feeling the moment dissipate. "He's a very rude man when he knows he has the upper hand."

Hayes' eyes still looked very serious, but his smile was wry. "And you're sure it's him?"

"Positive. Why? Do you think I'm still in danger?"

"Maybe Roy Alemeister isn't too happy that we botched his job."

"I don't think he'd resort to murder." Then she reached for her makeup, hoping to apply the bare essentials before Mr. Forrester threw up too big a fuss to ignore.

"The humans call him their King of Crime. I'm pretty sure the fella resorts to everything."

"But I'm an old friend, and even better, an ex-lover. We were together for five months. If that didn't push him into killing me, then I don't see how anything else could. No, I'm much more concerned about Father's friend at the moment." She studied her hair critically, wondering if she had time to style it into waves.

Then Mr. Forrester's words rose into a roar.

Cora sighed, glancing down at the thin silk of her robe. "He's always been so impatient. Do you know what he was called in his earlier days? The Beast. If I don't go down now, he might come up and break the door in sheer rage."

"He'd try, maybe." Hayes sounded casual, but she didn't miss the flash of his teeth.

She smiled while rising from her seat. "Let's not wait and see."

Mr. Forrester was about her father's age, with his hair going to silver and his face craggy as a mountain, but he still looked robust and powerful in the body. It was as if his belligerence had preserved his strength, preventing the stooped shoulders and soft paunch that Cora associated with most of her father's friends.

He was also a man used to his imposing stature, to the point where he grew affronted when meeting anyone else taller. Hayes was one such example, and Mr. Forrester promptly ignored him as soon as they were all in the parlor together. The closest he came to acknowledging the detective's presence was to clear his throat and intone to Cora, "My dear, this is a discussion of a very private nature."

She didn't miss how quiet his manner had become, or how she felt nothing more than her usual mild distaste. It heightened her curiosity; he obviously wanted something from her. "Believe me, Detective Hayes is much better at keeping his mouth shut than I am. Let's get started."

The man sighed and minutely adjusted his tie. "Very well."

Within moments, he had paperwork spread out over the nearest table, frowning when a maid brought over a tray of coffee and sandwiches. Despite his lingering surliness, he took both. "There's not much to do. Merely sign a few papers to keep all the wheels running while your father's state remains unknown."

Cora thumbed through the pile before her, unable to pretend having any interest in it. "Didn't I already do this back when he first disappeared?"

"Those were in case you were shortly charged with his murder. As that nasty business has been settled, these are to make sure the transition is smooth when he can be legally declared dead."

"I suppose that makes sense." Cora peeked at him from beneath her lashes, taking in his stiff shoulders and open frown. He did look decidedly nervous, and she doubted it was from sharing a room with a wolf. For the first time, she considered actually reading through the contracts she was about to sign. "There's a lot here, isn't there? I hope everything's all right with my father's finances."

Mr. Forrester tried to grin. On him, it looked like a grimace. "These are precautionary measures, nothing else. All that's required is your signature on the dotted line."

"Maybe so, but a contract is a contract. I should really make sure I agree with what it says, shouldn't I?"

"Very wise," murmured Hayes from where he leaned against a recess in the wall a few yards away. "Any lawyer would approve of such caution."

The comment drew an aggravated glance from Mr. Forrester. "I don't see why you have him in here, Cora. Shouldn't he be out doing his job? You're certainly paying him well enough. I received the receipts yesterday."

Cora flushed, angry that he had needled her so precisely. She decided to return the favor and press at a question that had been turning in her mind for quite some time, ever since her father had disappeared.

"Mr. Forrester," she said, keeping her voice light and absent, keeping her gaze on the papers before her. "There's something I've been wondering about in regards to my father's finances."

"Yes?" he already sounded wary.

"Did he ever engage in anything illegal through them?"

"What an idea. I'm sure it's not yours."

"Oh, it's very much mine." She smiled sweetly at him even while the sigil burned a little hotter for a heartbeat. "You see, I know of at least one thing he's done that is very illegal. It made me interested to find out if you know of any others. After all, you're his oldest friend."

The man sputtered. "Miss Marshall, this is a ridiculous line of thinking, and I won't engage with it. Your father was a shrewd man. He would know better than to get into anything that might damage his reputation and his empire."

"What about potential ventures, then? Surely he would ask you for advice. Were there any that seemed unusual or risky?"

"There's absolutely nothing I can say." Even as he spoke, the man pulled out a handkerchief and mopped his face. "Why is it so hot in here?"

"I think it's pretty cold myself," said Hayes, circling around to Cora's side. When she glanced up, she found him intent on the lawyer.

"Was anyone speaking to you? As I was saying, I—" Then Mr. Forrester's body went stiff. He made a choking sound.

Cora gasped as his eyes rolled in the back of his head. Her breath came back out as a shriek when he slumped forward, scattering papers everywhere. Hayes said nothing but kept her from reaching out toward the man.

"Oh, my God. Is he dead?" She stared at the motionless Mr. Forrester, facedown in his cucumber sandwich.

"No. Something's happening. He smells like magic." Then Hayes grabbed her and pulled her out of the chair, dragging her back until a few feet separated them from the table. Mr. Forrester had started twitching.

For a few awful heartbeats, his muscles jerked and jumped like he was being electrocuted. Just as quickly, he fell still and drew in a wheezing breath. When the man slowly straightened up, unresponsive to her hesitant query, Cora had the strangest feeling of watching a puppet move on its strings, the movements stiff and unnatural.

Mayonnaise from the sandwich covered much of his face, and yet it looked... well, yes, like Mr. Forrester, but the expression was completely unlike him and yet completely familiar. Cora found herself drifting closer, caught up by it until Hayes' grip pulled her back. She didn't fight him, didn't even speak, because just then she understood what had happened, familiarity sharpening into recognition even as the man winked at her. "It's been awhile, Dollface."

"Roy?" she gasped.

"Who else?" He began wiping his face clean with a napkin. "Are you always this undressed around your pet detective?"

"Roy Alemeister, you cretin. And here I thought you'd stop doing this after we broke up. Couldn't you have just *met* with me instead of possessing an innocent bystander?"

"Who am I in?"

"My father's lawyer."

"Then he's not innocent." Mr. Forrester's—Roy's—gaze flickered to Hayes. "So. You're the one who killed three of my men."

"I guess that's introduction enough," said Hayes, voice easy, but his hand remained near his holster.

"Yes, let's talk about that," added Cora, fresh indignation rising. "I'm very concerned about the two lovebirds you tried to murder this morning."

"It's a job, Cora." Even his eyes looked the same despite being in a strange face, their sardonic gleam as alluring and infuriating as ever. "And anyway, who are they to you?"

"They're mildly involved with my father's disappearance. I can't see how they'd be a danger to anyone... except for whoever hired you."

Roy's expression immediately closed up. "Can't tell you anything. Sorry."

"Oh, so we're about to have our usual argument."

"You always seemed to enjoy it, Kitten. Especially the ending." Then he started rising to his feet, still looking at Cora.

Hayes stepped toward the table. "Sit down, Alemeister." His voice sounded pleasant, but his stare wasn't.

Cora watched Roy bring out the smile that always made people want to punch him. "Relax, wolf-man, or I'll make sure you don't interfere."

"Roy, don't you dare," hissed Cora, understanding the implication. Panic swelled within her as the two locked gazes, Hayes standing easy and calm, hands in his pockets, and Roy in the body of Mr. Forrester, bracing against the table as his muscles began to twitch.

Hayes remained still, watching as the twitching turned into shaking and then into Roy slumping back in his seat, panting as if he'd just run for miles. His smile had disappeared.

"Your tricks won't work on me. I'm not human." Then Hayes offered a grin of his own, one that showed all his teeth. "And it was four of your men. They're having trouble pulling the last body from the offal vat."

Even though it was on a different face, Cora still recognized the first crack in Roy's attitude. "Is all this really necessary? Let's at least be better as friends than we were as lovers. Can't you help at all?"

Roy was still sweating. "If I don't keep the job, the client will just go to someone else. Besides..." His voice resumed its wryness. "You already have help. It's panting right beside you."

"Don't be cruel to him just because you think he filled your place. I didn't see *you* reaching out to help when the rest of the city was calling for me to be charged, tried, and hanged. You never even returned my call, Pumpkin."

A strange look came over Roy's face: embarrassment. They both knew the things she'd done for him, and how much he owed her. "If you hadn't turned up your nose at my offer," he muttered, "You wouldn't be in this mess."

"Your offer?" Cora laughed. "Being a kept mistress would have felt the same as living with my father—stuck in a little cage until I was needed. Now perhaps some girls dream of such a stable situation, and I won't begrudge them that, but I don't see that as an offer so much as an insult. Although, I'm very sorry I dumped my drink on your head after you first asked me. Now let's not quarrel any further, Pookie. Just leave those poor kids alone."

"It's not that easy."

"Why?" said Hayes, watching him intently.

"Piss off, Furface." Roy shot him a look but didn't try to rise from the table again.

"Roy." Cora put an edge in her voice that he would recognize, the one that signaled she was fed up and needed him to be serious. "Please. They were in the wrong place at the wrong time, that's all. You of all people should know what that feels like."

There was a disgusted sigh. "The best I can do is delay the job."

"For how long?"

"A few weeks."

Cora bit her lip and then nodded. "Is there anything you can tell us about who ordered the hit? Anything at all? *Please*, Boo Bear."

"Will you stop calling me those things?" he grumbled, gaze not quite darting over to Hayes.

"I remember you used to enjoy all sorts of nicknames. Especially after we argued."

It was extremely gratifying to see the self-proclaimed King of Crime flush like a schoolboy. She sensed amusement radiating off Hayes, but he kept his expression neutral.

"All right. One thing and then I'm gone. The client isn't a fuzzball like your friend." Despite the insult, for a moment Roy looked almost affectionate. "Stay sharp, Kitten. I can't interfere again."

Then Mr. Forrester's eyes rolled back again. Hayes immediately approached the body.

Cora waited where she was, shivering slightly. In some ways, seeing Roy again had felt more exhausting than dodging bullets. "I really hate it when he does that. Sometimes they never wake up."

"When has he pulled this on you before?" Hayes sounded amazingly calm while easing the lawyer upright and checking his pulse. "He'll recover, by the way."

"We used to argue a lot. Whenever I'd storm away, he'd follow in different bodies until he got the last word in. We were a complete nightmare as a couple, and yet..." She shook her head, feeling her lips curl into a reluctant smile. "He always had this magnetism that was irresistible."

"Can't say I saw it. Are you sure he'll keep his word?"

"Oh, yes, he always does. He thinks it makes him different from the upper levels of society he claims to hate."

Just then, Mr. Forrester groaned. When his eyelids flickered open, Cora leaned closer. "Mr. Forrester? Are you feeling all right?"

"No. In fact, I can't remember the last time I felt this terrible. My head is throbbing like someone took a sledgehammer to it."

"That's just me," said Cora, smiling brightly. "Father always says I give him headaches, too."

Mr. Forrester managed a grimace. "What were we just talking about?"

"How Isaac Marshall's new business venture was a source of friction between you two," said Hayes, affably.

Even as Cora looked over in confusion, Mr. Forrester paled. "I don't know anything. As soon as he mentioned having an idea for a 'shadow' venture, I refused to listen to another word. We had a devil of an argument about it."

Cora recovered enough to say, "Nonsense. You and Father are as thick as thieves."

He looked at her with bloodshot eyes. "Miss Marshall, my entire career is to make sure things are legal and correct."

"Does that include the papers you brought me?"

"There may be some... discrepancies. Not on my part, but on your father's. The best thing to do is just sign where you're supposed to and keep everything running until we learn more."

"Why weren't you going to tell me this?"

"Cora Marshall, I've known you since you were a baby. You couldn't keep a secret if your life depended on it. It's what disappointed your father more than anything."

A wave of hurt rose up within her, but she pushed it back as the man rubbed at his forehead and added, "That's all I know. Truly. Whenever your father chose to step outside lines, I wouldn't follow. I *couldn't*. Now if you'll excuse me, I really must be going. I don't feel well at all."

Cora kept enough of her wits about her to see him to the door, but once the man had left and they were alone, she turned to Hayes. "Was that a shot in the dark, or do you know something I don't?"

He shrugged. "Educated guess. When an old business partner suddenly stops being involved, it usually means someone new was found."

"You really are clever, aren't you?" She smiled at him before smoothing out the wrinkles in her robe. "Well. I need to finish dressing. I'm itching to get ready and go."

When she hurried up the staircase, he stayed put, voice drifting after her. "Go where?"

"Wherever needed to find new clues." Back in the bedroom, she began pulling clothes from the closet.

In another moment, he appeared in the doorway. "After what happened this afternoon, I'm glad you're not crying in a corner, but there's real danger leaking into this case. You're not coming along on any other leads."

"What?" She turned to him, fingers clutching at fabric. "You can't. You mustn't. It's been too much fun."

"Fun?" he repeated, voice incredulous. "Miss Marshall, you almost died today."

"But I didn't. I can take care of myself, you know." Then she stepped behind the changing screen near her closet and shrugged off her robe. She needed to transform this silly mood of his in any way

possible, and with the nearby lamp on, she knew her silhouette would be visible.

As she hooked her bra into place, she added, "I proved that in the slaughterhouse, didn't I? And by holding my own against Roy. When's the last time someone embarrassed the King of Crime and lived to tell about it?"

"I don't want the risk hanging over my head. Especially when there's no good reason for it."

He sounded much steadier than she liked, and she made sure to give her hips an extra wriggle while shimmying into her panties and then her lace garter belt. "What are you talking about? I'm essential to the investigation."

"But not out in the field." His voice definitely sounded rougher, and not from exasperation.

She bent over to pull on her stockings. "What about when the pack diplomat returns with their offer? She made it very clear that they wish to speak with me."

"Frankly, Miss Marshall, I don't like that, either. I've been trying to work out a way around you stepping onto pack land at all."

"I can't just refuse." She straightened up again to attach the translucent silk to her garters. "And there's no way we can find out what happened on their side without meeting them, is there?"

"I'm not willing to concede that yet."

"You do seem very stubborn." Then she walked out from behind the screen under the pretense of reaching for her dress. When she glanced at him, she saw a muscle jump in his jaw, but he showed no other sign of being affected. His gaze even remained on her face, serious and uncompromising.

She felt herself deflate, wondering if all the insinuations made by others were really true. "Is it the money? Because I'll pay it all in advance if you'd like. You wouldn't lose a penny."

He stared, the gold of his eyes very warm and clear. "That's not what I meant."

Before she could ask what he *had* meant, the phone rang. In too much of a huff to wait for anything else, she answered it. "Yes?"

"Miss Cora Marshall?" The icy tone of Rowan Saxby remained clear even through the crackling of a bad connection.

"You're that diplomat, aren't you?" said Cora, more to signal Hayes over than to confirm the caller's identity. As he drew closer, she angled her face so they could both hear the she-wolf's next words. "What do you want?"

"I've spoken with Alpha-king Saxby. Our terms are ready and final."

"Let's hear it."

"We agree to meet on any pack land bordering ours. As I assume the traitor is still advising you, I won't bother listing the packs in question. Our only condition is that it must happen within the week. We've wasted enough time with the city's police force. We won't make the same mistake with you."

With Roy's warning still ringing in her ears, Cora couldn't say the time limit sounded like a bad thing. "How can I get back to you?"

"I'll call again in precisely one hour. If you haven't made a decision, it's all off."

"Which means?"

"A missed opportunity, nothing more."

Cora glanced at Hayes. He looked absolutely feral, but said nothing. "Well... what happens if you don't accept my first choice?"

"No negotiations on either side. We'll accept whoever you choose."

Hayes shifted suddenly, as if holding back a growl. Cora felt his tension heat her skin like electricity. "And this is just a simple interview with your investigators? Nothing more?"

"Of course. Do you think we would be stupid enough to hurt or kill you? One hour."

Then the diplomat hung up. Hayes broke away to pace around the room. Cora watched, her fingers tapping against the phone. "That sounds like good news, but it isn't, is it?"

He shook his head, eyes nearly yellow in the bright light streaming through the windows. "Anytime a pack offers you a choice instead of trying to take it away, it means you've already lost. No wolf gives up that easily. The Saxby Pack has figured out another way to get what they want."

"What *do* they want?"

At that he paused, shoulders bunching beneath his suit as if he struggled against changing into a form with teeth that could maul and savage. "Anything you know, and they won't care if you survive their questioning. We won't be safe with any pack that borders their territory, because that's exactly the choice they gave us. It means they've already made deals so that anyone you pick will double-cross us."

Cora had to admit it sounded chilling. "How are you so sure?"

"Because..." His voice dipped into a brief growl before he forced himself calm again. "Just take my word for it. Please."

"What about that professional hostage you told me about? The one from the pack that kills anyone who kills one of their own? Do they think we won't use that?"

"No, they know I'll never give them an inch of trust. They'll expect the Manges. Remember, it won't be the Saxbys feeling their teeth. It'll be the pack holding our meeting. And that pack will find itself stabbed in the back once the Saxbys kill us and trigger the Mange hostage into being killed as well."

There were a few moments of awful silence before she said in a soft voice, "But we have to do something. Two weeks isn't much time to figure out who's behind this all. We need every piece of information we can get. I'm still perfectly willing to walk into this."

The words drew out half a laugh and half a sigh. "You really aren't frightened, are you?"

She shook her head. "The only thing that terrifies me is being treated like a caged bird. Singing when I'm supposed to and keeping quiet otherwise. You've probably noticed a pattern by now—how the men in my life never want me to be anything beyond what they expect."

He nodded slightly, a hint of humor returning to those wild eyes. "Kitten."

"Exactly. I hate it. I'd much rather somebody gave me the chance to show I can do things."

"Is this where I come in?"

She smiled a little but realized she felt very serious. "I don't know. Is it?"

A breath of silence passed. He glanced away—an action she was beginning to recognize as his way to ease a tense atmosphere—and

then back at her. "Well, I'd never call you Kitten. You seem more like a Bunny."

It got her to laugh, and even as hope filled her, his expression turned thoughtful. "There's one thing we can try. It's not much safer. In fact, most would argue it's even more dangerous."

"Tell me."

"The Frosthound Pack." The way he pronounced it made it obvious that the very name should leave her reeling in shock. When she only shrugged, he added, "They're one of your choices, but the Saxby Pack would never expect you to pick them."

"Why not? If they've already made a deal, then..."

"Not with the Frosthound Pack. It's just that they're equally dangerous to us." Then he sighed. "To make a long story short, the Frosthounds are a very powerful pack, and because of the alpha-queen, very unpredictable as well. She believes in a death goddess that rules over fate, which means she sees any double-crossing that ends in death as an offense."

Cora nodded. "That sounds safe enough."

"I'm not finished. She believes the will of her goddess is more important than anything else. If she feels your fate should be tested by chance, then she'll do it. You won't be safe on their land just because you're human. It's risky as hell, but not the certain death that the other packs will offer."

Just as Cora opened her mouth to answer, he suddenly stepped closer, bringing his face within inches of hers. "Miss Marshall, I will do everything I can to keep you safe, but if you step onto pack land, you might not leave it."

The sweet rush of his body so close to hers went straight to her head, and for a moment, she couldn't speak. Perhaps his concern wasn't anything more than professional, but a girl could dream.

When she remained silent, he quietly said, "Are you sure you want to do this?"

"Yes." Then she smiled and meant it. "I think it's time people see that this bunny can bite."

The shopping trip had been very successful, and Cora was smiling even before she saw Detective Hayes waiting by his car in the driveway. She waved while parking. "Hayes! You're early."

He smiled slightly. "No, Miss Marshall, you're late. I said I'd be here at nine. It's nine-thirty."

"Oh. I have warned you that tardiness is a lifelong habit of mine." She got out just as he walked over to join her. "I had to get my hair done, of course, and there were a few items I needed for our meeting with the Saxby Pack today."

Then she pulled a hat from its box and brandished it for his inspection. It had a delicate veil that would fall over her eyes at an angle and was studded with real pearls. "I doubt I can convince them that I'm anything more than a frivolous heiress, so why not play that to the hilt and make them underestimate me instead?"

"And the rest of these?" said Hayes, eyeing how bags and paper-wrapped parcels filled every area of the car that wasn't the driver's seat. Multiple servants had appeared to take them inside.

"Detective, it's impossible to stop with just one thing."

His baffled expression suggested he didn't agree, but he only said, "Miss Marshall, I always admire your moxie, but we're going to be stretched for time and I need to brief you on what to expect. You'd better swap hats now so we can get going."

"Swap hats? Oh, no. I've got an entire outfit planned." She picked out two parcels in particular and began after the servants, who were trying to see over their armfuls.

"What's wrong with your current clothes?"

"Everything. I've thought about this very carefully and know just what to wear. It won't take me long to change. I promise."

He checked his watch but followed her with nothing more than a sigh.

It was strange to consider how they had reached an agreement about this meeting in much the same situation—her behind a screen while changing, and him pacing throughout the room. Now, though, she wasn't trying to tease him and could tell that he was in no mood for it, anyway. She had never seen him so tense.

She spoke while stripping down, tossing her clothes aside without care. Each piece of her new outfit waited within easy reach. "I'm listening, Hayes."

"So far, everything is playing out as expected. According to my sources, only the diplomat and the royal inspector from the Saxbys will be there. The alpha-king had second thoughts after hearing we chose the Frosthound Pack to host the meeting."

"Is that good news or bad news?" Then she unwrapped one of the parcels and studied what was in it. Her tailor was used to much odder requests from his various clients and hadn't even raised an eyebrow when she'd put in the order last week. He was a stiff,

humorless man but did wonderful work—she was able to fit the material around her thigh without any interference from her stockings and garter belt.

As she reached for the second parcel, Hayes said, "It's hard to tell. There won't be as many guards, but without their alpha-king to keep them cowering, the Saxbys will be more aggressive."

"You sound very sure of that."

"I've been in meetings like this. We'll all be on edge. Every wolf there will be under a spell to hide their scent. It's a common tactic during negotiations where no one wants to give anything away."

"Well, that doesn't affect me."

"No, but it makes us feel... blind. We judge a lot by what we can smell."

"That's very good to know." She meant every word, since it reassured her that the thaumaturgist she'd seen really had known his stuff when it came to slipping things past wolves.

Then her attention narrowed to the box in her hands, which was much heavier than one would expect for its size. Its contents gleamed back at her, just as striking as they had been in the shop.

These were the extras, and she thought it was better to keep them in her purse. Mr. Rye had given her very clear instructions and had sworn they would work beautifully. He hadn't been surprised by her initial request, either, and had in fact told her that such orders were on the rise with the recent pack-related violence throughout the city.

That fact drew a comment out of her even as she reached for her dress. "I must admit, I'm puzzled about why the Frosthounds are so feared when it seems as though *every* pack is very willing to kill."

There was a brief pause before he answered, and when he did, his voice sounded flat. "Packs are rigid about their roles, Miss Marshall.

They don't like it when someone flouts expectations, whether it's in their pack or out of it. It makes them nervous. The Frosthounds do just that."

"Yes, I remember what you said about their alpha-queen worshipping a death goddess."

"It's more than that. She used to be the royal duelist for the alpha-king. It's a rough position. Most court duelists don't survive beyond five years. It's also a *lower* position—you fight for members of the court, but that doesn't mean you're part of it. When the Frosthound alpha-king fell in love with her and wanted her as his queen, every wolf in the upper ranks of his pack was against it. Usually that's enough to stop a king's whim in its tracks. Not with Thane, though."

Cora couldn't help sighing. "That's so romantic."

"Not really. It meant he slaughtered most of his court to make it happen."

"Still. You'd be surprised at how many girls dream of having a fella who would do anything for her, and all because he really loves her."

Finished, she stepped out from behind the screen, pleased with what the nearby mirror showed. She had chosen an outfit of white and black, the sharp lines and colors softened by the luxurious stole over her shoulders and the sheen of pearls on her gloved wrists. She looked dramatic, elegant, and completely like someone who had trained herself to be helpless from having other people do everything for her. "Is that really all it takes to scare a wolf? Facing someone in love?"

Hayes still moved about the room with the restlessness of an animal in a cage. It wouldn't be right to say there were cracks in his

usual composure, but that affable glint in his eyes that could turn teasing or intent within a breath was now nowhere to be found. Instead, he looked very hard and guarded. "Wolves understand greed. Love, not so much."

There was an odd undertone to the words for all that he spoke evenly, enough so that Cora turned to look at him as he added, "All the other packs now consider Thane Frost to be crazy, and his queen equally so."

When she only nodded, more interested in tilting her hat to the perfect angle, he shook his head. "You're not frightened at all, are you?"

"I don't see the point of fretting. Besides, you've never scared me."

"I'm not like other wolves. I try to be nice."

She flashed a smile at him. "I doubt I'd be scared even if you were being very, very bad."

"Miss Marshall." His expression all but begged her to take things seriously.

She finally did, realizing there was likely more to his tension than merely trying to convince his client that she was in danger. "I'm sorry, Hayes. I don't mean to be this aggravating. Did your plan to hire someone from that one pack work out?"

"It's all set up. I have the Mange waiting with someone I trust. That doesn't guarantee things will go easy for us."

"I know. Really, I do. And I also know it will be much harder for you than for me, facing your former pack, but..." She grabbed her purse and took a final glance at her reflection while trying to find the right words. "We've done the best we've can to stay safe. As for what they might *say*, well, that's nothing worth thinking about. If they're

anything like their diplomat, then they're utter fools. They'd have to be, to believe they're better than you."

Then she realized the room had fallen silent. Hayes had stopped pacing and was now staring at her as if he still didn't know what the hell to make of her.

"Detective?" she said, puzzled more than anything. "Should we go?"

He remained terse throughout the drive, and she decided to keep quiet rather than distract him with chatter. It was easy to absorb her attention in their surroundings; she had never been this close to city limits. Yellow paint marked the borders shared between public streets and pack territory. Occasionally, barbed-wire fencing did as well.

Then the road itself became bordered with yellow, and Cora knew that meant they were now surrounded by wolves. Trees and shrubs and brick walls ran along the road, protecting whatever hid behind them from the most curious eyes. Occasionally, things opened up to reveal flashes of squat, industrial buildings or even the glimpse of houses far in the distance.

She wasn't sure how much time passed before Hayes said, "We're almost there."

Cora nodded, excitement bubbling up through her rib cage. "Any final advice?"

"Don't trust them."

Within a few breaths, he turned into a driveway almost hidden by the gnarled trees bordering it. They drove down a gravel path enclosed by tall hedges for nearly a mile before a huge iron gate appeared, already opened. Hayes hissed something beneath his breath at the sight of figures waiting there.

"Frosthounds?" she murmured, fixated on them despite the hedges falling away to reveal a massive white mansion and its grounds.

"No. Saxby fellas."

They were hard, ferocious-looking creatures, she had to admit. They dressed like normal men, wearing hats, suits, and nice shoes, but moved too smoothly, revealing their inhuman nature as they turned to watch the car. All five were broad, sturdy, and looked like they were used to being punched in the face. Perfect goons.

Hayes stopped the car just when it was close enough for her to make out the feral yellow of their eyes. "Not a damn Frosthound guard in sight," he said, his voice tight.

When the Saxby wolves approached, he glanced at her. "Stay in the car. If things get ugly, use it to get out of here."

"But, Hayes..." Heart in throat, she watched him get out and put himself between her and the approaching Saxbys. Her hands twitched against the folds of her dress as they stopped a few feet from him.

The goon in front had a neck thicker than his head, and his teeth flashed at Hayes as he said, "So, you came crawling in after all."

"Hello, Eddie. It's been a while since I've seen you out of that royal uniform." Hayes looked easy while facing him, but Cora didn't miss how he kept them all in his line of sight. "Why are you out here waiting for us?"

"Gotta check you over for weapons."

"Not happening. It's not your place to even request it."

None of the other wolves looked surprised as they slowly moved to circle him. Cora tried to keep calm as Eddie said, "That's rich, coming from a fella who makes a living serving humans."

Two of the other Saxbys mimicked the high-pitched barking of a lap dog while grinning.

Hayes glanced at them, but his tone didn't change. "The Saxby king has no authority here. We're equally powerless on Frosthound land."

At that, Eddie laughed. "Equally? You think you're *equal* to us?"

Cora gritted her teeth, finding it impossible to stay silent. She hated their contempt, but the vicious anticipation coming to life in their eyes was even worse. They were aching to attack.

She hid the anger in her voice while leaning through the rolled-down window of the car, offering one of those knowing smiles that men could never resist. "If you boys want to have fun, you should be talking to me."

All attention jumped to her. Hayes went stiff with fresh tension, but she kept her focus on the goons, who studied her as if they hadn't even realized she was there.

Then one of them said, "Think you can handle a real wolf, sweetheart?"

She remembered enough about wolves to keep her gaze away from their eyes, instead glancing over their bodies as if admiring their strength. Her fingers hitched the folds of her dress up over her knees. "I don't mind finding out."

That drew half-smiles, and even a step closer from one or two before Hayes snarled with enough violence to stop them in their tracks. "I'll break your goddamn necks if you move any closer to her."

Just then, a whistle rang out. Two wolves were coming out from the mansion. Cora felt her heart skip a beat until she realized they had to be Frosthound guards. Stark black uniforms emphasized the

guns and daggers waiting within easy reach. They moved efficiently, silently, well-used to working with each other. Most striking of all, though, were the masks they wore, shaped and colored like skulls. Only their eyes remained visible, flashing yellow while they approached.

The Saxby goons quickly moved away from Hayes, looking sullen and avoiding eye contact. Their well-tailored suits suddenly seemed ostentatious, even vulnerable compared to the Frosthound guards' severe appearance.

The taller guard spoke first, revealing a hard voice thick with sarcasm. "Well, now. Both your royal inspector and your diplomat said all the guards were inside with them. Who's been forgetful? You for leaving your posts, or them for leaving you outside?"

When none of the Saxbys responded beyond uneasy gazes that darted everywhere except at them, the second guard stepped closer, smaller in stature but with a wiriness that promised hidden strength. "Get inside before we decide to skin you."

Grim words, all the more so because of their neutral tone, but it was the guard's unmistakably female voice that left Cora leaning further out the window in surprise. If the Frosthounds noticed her movement, neither commented on it, instead watching the Saxbys slink back inside.

Then the male guard turned toward Hayes.

Cora wanted to smile at how he remained unflinching beneath the scrutiny, or how the growl hadn't quite left his voice as he said, "This is the first time I've visited a pack without seeing their guards everywhere."

"Alpha-king Frost wanted to see what the Saxbys would try."

When Hayes just growled again, the female guard added, "You knew coming to *us* for a neutral territory would be uncertain. All the king and queen promise is extending that same uncertainty toward the Saxby Pack. Drive over to the entrance. We'll meet you there and escort you the rest of the way."

Then they left, both barely making a sound against the gravel driveway. Cora watched until Hayes got back in the car.

"Miss Marshall." It was only her name, but the words seethed, warning her that his anger hadn't left with the other wolves. "What the hell were you thinking? I told you to leave."

Somehow, the fact that he was furious with her as well warmed her heart more than the sweetest compliment. It meant he really was taking what she said and did seriously. "I know, and I know you also told me not to speak to them, but something had to be done. They were about to bully you bloody."

"Look, I can handle myself."

"And I can handle a bunch of goons."

When he shook his head, mouth still grim, she added, "Hayes, I didn't come to you for protection. I came to you because I haven't got any brains. It's all this sleuthing that I need help with. When it comes to looking after myself, well... I was doing fine just now."

He made a sound halfway between a growl and an incredulous laugh. "You don't know these fellas like I do. They would've—" Then he broke off, obviously forcing himself calm. When he spoke again, the words sounded merely flat, but his eyes blazed gold as he looked at her. "Don't goad anyone else. They might not just laugh. All right?"

"All right," she said, her voice as demure as her hands while she smoothed her dress back over her knees.

Her sudden compliance drew a glance from him while they drove toward the waiting guards. "Why do I feel uneasier when you agree with me than when you argue?"

She just smiled, pleased at how well the folds of fabric hid the snub-nosed revolver strapped to her thigh.

CHAPTER EIGHT

Just as promised, the two Frosthounds waited by the mansion. Cora thought they seemed much more at ease than the Saxby goons had been, speaking quietly to each other while watching her and Hayes approach. The male guard had one hand resting on the hilt of his dagger, but his careless tone made it clear that he wasn't looking for a fight. "We're not checking for or taking away any weapons."

Hayes didn't look surprised. "Does that include ones containing silver?"

"It does," said the female guard. Like her partner, she didn't seem interested in intimidating them.

"Silver?" echoed Cora, using the distraction caused by the question to scan the mansion's entrance. The massive marble columns were carved with depictions of writhing skeletons. It was impossible to tell if they were in pain or ecstasy, whether they fought each other or were passionately entwined.

When her gaze returned to the guards, she realized they both studied her. It was the she-wolf who answered. "Aside from age, silver is the only thing that kills wolves. Again, you won't be safe inside. But at the very least, your chances will be absolutely fair."

Then she realized they weren't sure whether she understood *she'd* be in as much danger as Hayes. She gave them a broad smile, remembering to keep her mouth closed. "Detective Hayes was very clear about what it meant to come here."

The male guard simply jerked his head at them to follow and then led the way, but the female guard walked beside them, amusement obvious in her body language over how Hayes immediately angled himself between her and Cora. "Very gallant, Detective, but she's not even nervous."

Hayes ignored the comment, instead studying every corner of the room they were being led through as if an assailant might leap out at any moment. Everything was utterly white, from the ceiling to the walls to the floor. It was also very bare, with only a staircase spiraling up from the very center, twisting around a massive statue of a skeleton wrapped in a shroud. The top section of the steps circled its skull like a crown.

The effect was striking, and as they began up the stairs, Cora found herself saying, "Is this..."

"The Lady of the Dead," answered the male guard.

"A lot has changed since my last visit," said Hayes, his tone as neutral as his expression.

"I remember you. You were still a junior inspector then, investigating the potential alliance of mating a Saxby princess to our king. A polite formality between neighbors and nothing more. Really, a waste of time."

"I never said that."

"There was no need. The Saxbys never consider an alpha-king who built his name and lands over one who inherited it."

At that point, Cora was utterly confused by the conversation and glanced at Hayes. He seemed satisfied by the guard's knowledge, as if it had confirmed something for him.

Then the female guard spoke. "Instead, our king found love with a cultist and cluttered up his territory with shrines to the goddess that she worships and he ignores."

Cora blinked, surprised at how casually they spoke of their king and queen. She'd always heard that wolves cowered before their leaders. "I think that's sweet of him. Cults can be very trying."

"Experienced with them, are we?" said the male guard.

Cora took the question seriously. She always did when someone was being sarcastic with her. It was the easiest way to make them regret it. "More than most people expect. My uncle led one. It's not well-known, but it happened."

"Is that so?" The she-wolf's mask prevented any hint of her expression from showing, but she sounded genuinely interested compared to her partner.

The stairway they were on looked very long, so Cora kept babbling, realizing it would probably help if they thought she was a complete idiot. "Uncle Alfie used to be an archeologist, you see. He led all sorts of successful expeditions funded by my father. It was swell for them both. Uncle Alfie gained prestige and respect in all the scientific circles, and my father got his money back and more from selling the gold and artifacts Alfie found. Mostly private collectors, but sometimes to museums, too."

Hayes had glanced at her several times without giving any hint that she should shut up. If anything, he seemed to use the guards'

distraction to study the glimpses of what waited for them at the top of the stairs. It was the only incentive she needed to keep going. "Well, eventually, he found a strange idol during an expedition that changed everything. He thought it was a relic from an ancient cult and grew determined to resurrect it.

"My father didn't like that at all. Uncle Alfie had stopped making money for him and was now spending loads of it. He refused to fund any of Uncle Alfie's cult dealings, and the two had a very bitter fight. I heard some of it. You wouldn't think brothers could say such things to each other. They didn't speak again, and poor Uncle Alfie spent the final ten years of his life estranged from the family."

The male guard said nothing, perhaps having already learned his lesson, but the she-wolf still tried to be polite. "How sad."

"No, not really. They were always arguing. I remember Uncle Alfie smiled much more than my father, but the strange thing is, I wouldn't call him any friendlier. I think their natures were very similar, but their goals were very different."

"What happened to the cult after your uncle died?"

"Oh, I have no idea. We had no contact with him and weren't beneficiaries of his will. I don't even know what it was called. It was just another ascension cult. Those are a dime a dozen in the human parts of Crescent City. But I suppose it did all leave me with a very nonchalant view toward them in general. Once you see the figures behind the mystique, it all becomes very boring, doesn't it?" she said, finishing just as they reached the end of the stairs. A massive set of wooden doors waited in front of them.

"Maybe you just haven't met the right ones," said the male guard, and then laughed when Hayes glanced at him. "Relax, Detective.

We're not the ones to bristle at when it comes to protecting your client. The ones behind these doors are."

Then he and his partner pulled them open.

Murmurs flooded through, as did the echoes of shuffling footsteps and the rattle of weapons. Cora's anticipation quickly faded as she realized it was just another hallway, this one much shorter in length. Beautiful, though, with stained glass windows on either side that depicted bones entangled in the roots of rose bushes. An even more impressive pair of doors waited at the end, black as pitch and with what looked like genuine wolf skulls somehow embedded into the wood.

It wasn't exaggeration to call the sight ominous, but all of Cora's attention jumped to the figures waiting by the doors. Saxby wolves, twelve in all. Most either were or looked like the goons from outside. The diplomat, Rowan, was easily recognizable, but it was the two Saxbys in military-style uniforms who truly stood out. None of them looked happy.

Hayes stopped her from moving any closer and turned to the Frosthound guards. "What are you playing at? Why isn't the room ready?"

"The meeting before yours has gone late," said the she-wolf. "Everyone will have to wait in the hallway."

Hayes scoffed. "There's nowhere else it can be held? In a place this size?"

"Not for outsiders."

When Hayes just shook his head, the male guard added, "You're free to pull out of this and leave, if you'd rather."

Cora knew Hayes would be tempted, and quickly glanced at him. When their eyes met, she said, "I don't see how it's any different from being in the same room."

"There won't be a table between us, for one thing," he muttered, but then offered his arm to her. She took it, keeping her smile confident as they followed the guards.

Their escorts stuck close, and there *were* several other Frosthound guards near the Saxbys. Without a word between them, the Frosthounds moved together to form a living barrier while the Saxbys resituated themselves to stay away from her and Hayes. Even then, less than six feet separated them. When the Frosthounds melted back toward the doors, Cora wondered if the alpha-king and alpha-queen were already inside the room.

Hayes wasn't inclined to talk, and none of the Saxbys seemed to be, either. She found herself glancing out the nearest window and then realized they were so high up that there was nothing except sheer air surrounding them. Falling out of one would mean sure death. She was glad she'd never been afraid of heights.

It didn't take long for caution to soften into boredom, and she began peeking at the Saxbys beneath her lashes. Frankly, she didn't think they were very intimidating, not compared to the Frosthounds, anyway. The diplomat was as sour as ever, and the goons just looked like goons, which made the two dressed-up wolves stand out all the more.

The male wolf had the more intricate uniform. Gold braiding draped over his right shoulder, gleaming against the stiff, navy fabric, and he had a peaked cap tucked beneath his right arm. Cora disliked him immediately. He looked like a self-important fella, with an

imperious expression on his well-fed face and too much care put into that frankly ridiculous mustache.

The other uniformed Saxby was a she-wolf, taller than Cora by a head. Her blonde hair was pulled back into a braided bun, emphasizing the sharp beauty of her features. She looked like the dagger at her hip—no-nonsense compared to the male wolf she kept close to, and yet all the more striking for it.

There wasn't much chance for private conversation, but Cora still turned to Hayes, too curious about who they were to wait and find out. The question died on her lips at the sight of him staring at the Saxby she-wolf. She didn't look back but stood with a particular stiffness that suggested she was well-aware of his attention.

Cora glanced at him again and found his focus had jumped to one of the windows beyond—but not fast enough to keep her from seeing what flickered in his eyes.

"Oh..." she breathed, too softly for anyone else to notice, as if a human would be noticed at all in a room full of tense wolves. She recognized that look, for an echo of it reverberated throughout her heart whenever she remembered the ghost of a kiss, or caught sight of an almost-familiar silhouette in the distance.

A lost love.

Before she could say anything to him, the uniformed Saxby wolf turned to the Frosthound guards blocking the doors, frustration clear on his face. "This is ridiculous. I was told that everything would be set up."

The response could have come from any of the bone masks turning in his direction. "The alpha-king and alpha-queen will offer their apologies afterward."

"What good are apologies for wasted time?" he snarled.

Cora didn't miss how the Saxby she-wolf quickly whispered something in his ear, or how Hayes shifted his weight as if ready to fight.

Then the Saxby diplomat stepped forward, separating herself from the rest. Her voice sounded downright oily as she said, "We mean no disrespect, of course."

"You have a funny way of showing it," said one of the Frosthounds, and Cora recognized his voice as belonging to the male guard that had escorted her and Hayes.

"I apologize. It's simply that..." The rest of the diplomat's words faded to a murmur as she leaned closer, obviously hoping she could smooth her way into having a guard prompt the alpha-king and alpha-queen into seeing them sooner.

Cora used the distraction to turn her back on all the wolves and step closer to Hayes, fluffing her stole as if she were merely preening. Instead, she hissed up at him, "Why didn't you tell me?"

His reply was just as quiet, but he didn't look any less tense than the others. "Tell you what, Miss Marshall?"

"Hayes, I'm silly, but I'm not *that* silly. I'm talking about—"

Then the Saxby diplomat raised her voice. "Very well. The royal inspector is willing to conduct the interview here and now if you are, Miss Marshall."

Cora faced them with a bright smile but knew enough to let Hayes answer.

He shrugged, appearing indifferent except for the hardness of his eyes as he glanced at the uniformed wolf. "What's wrong with waiting?"

The simple act of him speaking, or perhaps speaking to a high-ranked pack member like the royal inspector, left several of the Saxby goons growling. The hallway suddenly felt much smaller.

The diplomat held up a hand in warning. "You're to speak only to me."

"I thought you didn't want to waste any more time. It'd be much faster talking to each other."

At that, the royal inspector responded, his voice as stiff as his posture. "If that's the case, why not let us directly question your client?"

The Saxby she-wolf leaned in to whisper something else to him. This time, he flashed his teeth at her and sent her flinching back.

Cora didn't miss how Hayes jerked in response, or how his next words deepened into a growl. "Because I wouldn't trust you with a dime."

"Favoring a human over one of us?"

Hayes smiled grimly. "You're missing the point by a mile."

Cora bit her lip hard enough to hurt, trying to keep quiet as they both stared at each other. The air thickened into something dangerous.

Then one of the Frosthounds spoke—the female guard. "If you start fighting, it's up to you two to finish it as well. You're both in the presence of the Lady of the Dead, and She doesn't care whether you believe in Her or not."

And neither do we.

Even Cora understood the implication. Any fight could be finished only with a death. The royal inspector lost some of the bloodlust in his eyes. Hayes didn't, and the Saxby diplomat quickly intervened. "Your king would really accept such risks to your court?"

"If it comes to that, and sometimes it does. Anyone who fights in here may fight to the death without being interrupted... or saved."

The Saxbys milled among each other uneasily, their eagerness suddenly snuffed, but Hayes still seemed ready to lunge. Cora knew she had to act. "If there's going to be all this fuss, then go right ahead and question me. I never mind being the center of attention."

She ignored Hayes' sharp glance, keeping her smile in place even when every other wolf shifted to look at her. When she was sure she had their attention, she breezily added, "What do you want to know?"

Hayes murmured her name, his voice still guttural, but the Saxby diplomat spoke over him, relief bright in her eyes. "Very well. Inspector?"

When the royal inspector turned to her, she acknowledged him with a nod, much too used to stuffy, important officials to feel cowed by his rigid manner. She briefly found herself wondering how Hayes had looked in such a uniform before the wolf said, "Crescent City officials have refused to give us any information about the creature who killed four members of our pack, or the man it turned into after dying, or the strange magic used to transform him in the first place."

Cora blinked, remembering how Captain Dempsey had told the Saxby diplomat that the police would pass along any information they learned. Even as she wondered which of them had lied, she said, "His name was Dominic Tierney. He was my father's driver."

"Who identified him?"

Cora glanced at Hayes, sensing his spike of tension. He answered for her. "Initially, Miss Marshall. Dental records confirmed it."

"We'll want to see them."

"Not up to me."

The royal inspector's face grew red. "Do you have any talent with magic?"

"No," said Cora, feeling that was a safe enough question to answer immediately. "Not at all."

"Have you ever hired a thaumaturgist?"

"No." It was the truth, but she couldn't help but notice how the sigil hidden beneath her hair suddenly burned hotter, as if it didn't like the mere idea.

When the royal inspector and the diplomat both looked disappointed, Cora suddenly realized they could smell the honesty in her answers—and didn't like it, either. "I really don't know anything. Why would you think otherwise?"

The royal inspector looked affronted at a human asking him anything. At his significant glance, the diplomat responded instead. "It seems obvious that transforming the driver with unknown magic was an attempted assassination against Isaac Marshall. We don't care about the affairs of humans, but this magic... our enchanters are baffled by it. It's unknown. Our ability to shift form is ours and ours alone."

"According to witnesses, it *does* resemble a wolf in some ways," said Hayes, watching the diplomat carefully.

"Bosh," said the royal inspector, his mustache bristling. "This thing shook off even silver."

"Then what killed it?"

"We don't know. That's why we need to find out what's going on. Whether there are more of them, and who *did* this." With those words, each and every Saxby stared at Cora.

She voiced their obvious implication. "And you believe that I know all these answers because I was the one who ordered the hit on my father."

"She's smarter than she looks," muttered the Saxby she-wolf to a nearby goon.

Cora gave her a sweet smile. "Oh, no. It's just that you're all being far less subtle than you think."

A laugh came from among the Frosthounds. The Saxby she-wolf glared at Cora, who looked right back. Beside her, Hayes had fallen very still as if forcing himself calm.

The royal inspector's face now appeared nearly purple. "We know your father was traveling to New Obsidian for business. Who was he going to see?"

"I don't know."

"Where's his body?"

"It hasn't been found."

"Yes, but where is it?" he growled. Cora couldn't help but stare at the vein that had appeared on his forehead. She couldn't remember the last time she had annoyed someone so quickly.

"No more games," said the diplomat, perhaps realizing he was ready to snap.

"I'm not playing any," said Cora. "I really don't know what happened. And anyway, why ask after my father so much? Surely you're more interested in Dominic Tierney."

"We're *interested* in what you're obviously hiding from us." The royal inspector's teeth flashed at her.

It was a threat that Hayes wasn't about to ignore, and he bared his own teeth. "That's rich, coming from you."

"Don't try to throw your weight around." The royal inspector seemed to have lost his earlier fear of starting a fight, the yellow of his eyes gone black. "You're lucky I haven't killed you on sight for your crimes."

Hayes laughed, but it was a brief, bitter sound. "You wouldn't even know how, since you always have others do your dirty work. And people ask how I can live with myself."

Snarls filled the air from the Saxby goons, and Cora felt her heart thump a little faster. Her fingers twitched at her dress. The revolver against her thigh felt hot enough to burn.

"Stop goading him," hissed the Saxby she-wolf, looking directly at Hayes for the first time. A muscle jumped in his jaw, but he didn't say anything back.

The royal inspector drew himself up. "I thought heeling to humans like a dog would've given you some humility, Sam. Instead, I see the same arrogance that nearly crippled our pack and killed our —"

Hayes punched him right in the face. The crack of fractured bone cut through the air. It was so sudden that Cora didn't even have time to gasp before the royal inspector reeled back. Then Hayes looked at her and growled, "Get out of here. Take the car and don't stop until you're in human territory."

"Hayes—" she managed, but the Saxby guards were already lunging at him with drawn daggers. The hallway exploded into chaos.

Cora squeezed herself into a recess, dimly aware of the Frosthounds watching in silence while Hayes disarmed one goon and threw him straight through a window. Glass shattered as the wolf fell to his death. Another sliced at him before meeting the same

fate. The rest snarled in frustration, the narrow hallway trapping them into waiting behind whoever was closest to Hayes.

Cora hesitated, unsure of who to go for since he was fighting just fine against the goons. The diplomat cowered in the corner, screaming something at the impassive Frosthounds. The she-wolf was prevented from reaching him like all the rest.

The royal inspector bled from the nose and still seemed dazed when Hayes grabbed him and hauled him upright, choking off his breath with a tight grip. He looked wild, mindless, like he wouldn't stop until the inspector was dead.

Then the Saxby she-wolf slipped through a space between two of the goons, dagger unsheathed.

"Hayes, watch out!" yelled Cora, pulling her revolver free even though she knew she couldn't get a clear shot in from her angle.

But he didn't react to his name, didn't react to anything until the she-wolf pressed her dagger against his throat. The silver edge gleamed wickedly. His eyes blazed at her, but not with the rage that had sent the first two guards crashing out the window.

"Hello, Isabelle," he said, voice still thick with a snarl.

"Do you think I won't do it?" The blade pressed in a little more, and Cora felt her breath freeze in her lungs.

When Hayes only stared back, she hissed, "Damn you."

The rest of the guards seemed frozen, unsure of what to do until the royal inspector gurgled, "Get him off me, you stupid bitch."

Hayes snarled, his attention snapping back to him. The she-wolf's mouth tightened, and then she shifted her grip on the dagger in an instant, smashing the pommel across his face.

Cora shrieked in fury, hating the stunned look in his eyes and how his knees buckled. Before she realized she was moving, she was

by his side, kneeling on the ground and shaking his motionless body, heedless of her dress while blood gushed. "You brutes! You horrible, horrible brutes!"

When a hand reached for her, she acted without thinking, aiming her revolver at the face of the goon who had tried touching her. "Get back. I'll shoot whoever comes near us."

He scoffed but didn't try again. Then her gaze darted to the Frosthound guards. They all remained by the closed doors, those strange masks revealing nothing of what they thought while watching, but Cora saw one tilt their head a little, as if noticing something the rest had missed.

There was no time to think about it, because the Saxby diplomat cleared her throat and addressed her. "Miss Marshall. It would be best to give him the gun."

"Like hell."

Her answer was met by smiles from all except the Saxby she-wolf —Isabelle—who hovered beside the coughing, sputtering inspector. Cora was so mad she couldn't decide who to shoot first. They had all dropped their guards, standing flat on the soles of their feet, daggers holstered. Hayes still didn't move.

Just as her gaze swept over them all once more, the royal inspector pushed through the ring of goons, still bleeding from his nose. "Don't be a fool. Hand over the gun and you'll be free to leave. We're only going to kill him."

Cora fired. It was a perfect shot in the shoulder, and the look on his face was almost as satisfying as his howl of pain. Smoke appeared from the wound as he screamed again, clutching at his shoulder.

"Silver bullets," she said to the shocked faces surrounding her. "I thought ahead. Now back off or I'll start taking heart shots."

The goons all pulled back into a knot of confused bodies, circling their inspector while he continued to shake and swear. Beads of sweat appeared on his forehead as he panted, "Antidote."

"No." That came from the Frosthound she-wolf. Her partner said nothing, just glanced at the other guards. They slipped from their positions in response, surrounding the Saxbys.

Realizing all the wolves were distracted, Cora murmured Hayes' name to rouse him. When that didn't work, she pressed a handkerchief against his head. He was bleeding too much to tell where the wounds even were. "Please. You've got to get up."

"It's silver," gritted out the royal inspector between his teeth. His hand trembled against his shoulder, fingers constricting. "It's poisoning me."

"You were warned about what it meant to fight in here," said the female guard, still impassive.

Cora tried shaking Hayes, gaze jumping between him and the other wolves. Fresh tension filled their movements.

As the Saxby guards moved aimlessly around the royal inspector, seemingly helpless without direct orders, he staggered toward the Frosthound she-wolf. "And what if she shoots you next, you crazy bitch?"

The words were barely out of his mouth before her partner lunged, impossibly fast. The dagger in his hand winked just before slicing through the royal inspector's neck.

Cora squeezed her eyes shut but still heard blood splattering on the floor. Yelps of shock overwhelmed a nasty gurgling sound. When she peeked through her eyelashes again, the Frosthound stood over the inspector's twitching body, his knife now bloody.

Then a Saxby guard went for him. The Frosthound she-wolf was already there with her own knife, which had a longer, curved blade that gutted the other wolf with ease. She cut through two more while her partner grabbed the Saxby diplomat, who whined and writhed until he slammed her against the doors and held the blade to her neck. "Enough words. Let's see if your pack still remembers how to act like wolves."

Cora didn't miss how his gaze remained on the female guard, though, or how the rest of the Frosthounds circled carefully, not yet attacking. There was no need to; the she-wolf had already killed the last of the goons, too fast and precise for their sluggish brutality. Then she removed her mask, revealing a face lit with excitement. Her next act was to pull off the leather jacket of her uniform, leaving her in a backless, black shirt. Two skulls glowed between her shoulder blades, one wolf and one human. Their grins matched her own as she faced Isabelle.

The other she-wolf looked terrified, backing away despite the diplomat's whining. Then she bowed her head. "Your Majesty."

Cora swallowed hard. She didn't know much about wolf packs, but it was easy to guess that she was looking at the Frosthound alpha-queen, notorious for surviving longer than any other duelist even as she worshipped her Lady Death.

"Come on," said the alpha-queen, yellow eyes bright. "It'll be a fair fight. I killed your comrades. No one will stop you if you wish to avenge them."

One breath. Two. Then Isabelle shook her head and glanced away from the nearby bodies.

The alpha-queen made a disgusted sound and turned away, kneeling to the bloodied ground with the dagger still clasped in her hands. Then she bowed her head in prayer.

The male guard shoved the diplomat away unharmed. "Looks like the meeting's over. You've got ten minutes to leave."

The implication of what would happen if they didn't was clear enough. As the remaining Saxby wolves slunk out of the room, Cora shook Hayes again, starting to panic. "Hayes, please. We're about to die."

"No." That came from the alpha-queen, who had slipped up unheard. "You're not."

Up close, the faint scars cutting through her left eyebrow and right collar bone were visible. Her black hair was soaked with blood. Yet the frenzied gleam had left her eyes, and behind her, most of the Frosthounds had relaxed enough to begin carrying away the bodies.

After a moment, Cora nodded and holstered her gun. "I can't get him to wake up."

"He will soon enough. In fact, I'd give him some room. The last thing he remembers is fighting. The moment he grows conscious, he'll attack whoever is in front of him before his eyesight even clears. Do you want a bloody nose?"

"No, but..." Cora reluctantly inched back. "He needs help."

"Here." That came from the male guard who had acted as the alpha-queen's partner.

Cora didn't miss the glance his queen gave him when he approached, or his sardonic look in response as he added, "I didn't let anyone insult you. Do you really think I'll let this one hit you?"

That drew a small smile from the she-wolf before she urged Cora further away. Feeling helpless, Cora stumbled to her feet, her gaze never leaving Hayes as the other wolf crouched beside him.

Just before the guard reached out, Hayes jerked awake, the gold of his eyes both furious and bewildered. The guard easily dodged his clumsy swing and steadied him as he staggered up, stepping away when Hayes snarled in response.

"Hayes," cried Cora, hating how blood streamed down his face.

The sound of her voice helped him focus, and his eyes constricted to pinpoints when he saw her next to the alpha-queen.

"It's all right," she said quickly. "They're not hurting me. And the Saxbys are gone. And they're not really guards. Well, not all of them. They're actually—"

"Thane and Cimorene Frost," managed Hayes, looking none too steady.

At that, the male guard took his mask off as well, tossing it to the side without care. He had the look of an alpha-king, harsh and vicious despite the amusement clear in his words. "Even with a concussion, you're the smartest of the Saxbys. None of the others saw what was right in front of them."

Hayes ignored him, instead shaking his head as if to clear it. Then he moved for Cora, growing steadier with each step. "You're bloody."

"It's not mine. It's mostly yours." Then she pressed her handkerchief against his head again. When he started to duck away, she huffed. "Oh, don't be silly. We're not in danger. We'd already be dead if they really wanted us to be."

He let her touch him, but his gaze jumped among the pools of blood left in the hallway. The bodies were already gone.

Thane circled back to his queen and said, "The diplomat and the captain of the guards left unscathed. I'm sure they'll tell their king everything."

Hayes didn't react to that beyond a nod, and his voice remained flat as he said, "How much of this was a set up? You're too pleased to be surprised by this."

The alpha-king didn't look offended at all by the question. "The previous meeting truly has gone over. Our engineers are arguing about water management. They'll go until tonight if we let them."

"And pretending to be guards...?"

At that, Cimorene grinned. It made her appear younger and much less serious. "With a meeting like this, we knew there would be spilled blood. I haven't been able to fight since retiring from the ring. Thane would only agree to it if he was my partner."

"And only because it was a soft pack like the Saxbys," muttered Thane, but his eyes warmed as he glanced at her. Despite their bloodied, lethal appearances, the love between them was clear.

Hayes pulled away from Cora to retrieve his hat. There was a hollow look on his face that she didn't like as he said, "I obviously missed a lot, but all I want to know at the moment is why we're still alive."

"It helps that you're polite," said Thane, raising an eyebrow. "And that when you did crack, you went after a Saxby instead of my queen."

When Hayes only nodded, Cora decided to steer the conversation in a fresh direction. "It's not that I'm not grateful to be alive, but... I shot a wolf with silver on your territory. Won't that...?"

"Complicate things?" Cimorene laughed. "The Saxbys expected this to swing their way. They won't know what to do once they learn it's blown up in their faces instead."

"We didn't trust them before," added Thane. "Nothing's changed."

"Why not?" said Hayes, eyes clear again despite his bloodied appearance.

Another shared glance passed between them before Cimorene said, "A year ago, someone came to us with the claim that the Saxby Pack had been receiving financial backing from a human. And before you ask, we didn't pay him what he wanted for further information, so he left to see if anyone else would. Perhaps it was a mere ploy from another pack to make us suspicious of our neighbor. Or perhaps it might explain why the late inspector was so intent on your father, Miss Marshall."

Shock chilled Cora as much as the blood drying on her clothes. "I... I don't know what to say. Father hates wolves."

"And the Saxbys hate humans. It sounds ridiculous, no?"

Then Thane spoke up, his gaze on Hayes. "Ridiculous, and yet you don't look surprised at all. We all wonder what made you break with your pack. I do remember you, you know. Enough to doubt their claims of treason."

"It's always treason to leave a pack," Hayes said, tersely. "Are we free to go?"

When they both nodded, he offered an arm to Cora, who took it out of habit, still struck numb by the possibility that her father had somehow been involved. The sigil on the back of her neck burned horribly.

Thane had already seemed to dismiss them, instead moving close to his queen with a look that held both feral hunger and a surprising tenderness. Cora didn't need to be a wolf to understand how the pair would celebrate winning their fights.

Cimorene, though, watched them both with a thoughtful expression. Before they could turn to leave, she suddenly said, "There's one more thing that should be said. Miss Marshall saved your life and faced death unflinchingly to do so. I felt both in my tattoos. No, I don't expect you to understand, but I hope you believe it. It'd be better for you both that way."

Hayes said nothing either to that or to the guard who led them out of the mansion, and kept his expression closed while telling Cora he was capable of driving.

"But surely your head hurts," said Cora, fidgeting with the handkerchief. The blood on his face had gone sticky and dark, and now she could see the gashes near his eye and on the bridge of his nose left by that horrible she-wolf.

"I'm fine, Miss Marshall. Forget about it." The words were as dead as his eyes.

"You're not the forgettable type, Detective." She tried a saucy smile.

But he didn't rise to her obvious bait, didn't even look over, and she began feeling scared. This wasn't the detective she knew. Cora thought about telling him how this Isabelle wasn't nearly worth spending the rest of his life with, that she was a coward and had the body type to get thin hair and bad skin later in life. That he was better off without someone who so obviously didn't have a sense of humor or an independent thought in her brain.

But she also knew that none of these things would matter to him. Not since he loved her. And so Cora found herself in a position where she could do nothing but wring her handkerchief between her hands during the entire silent ride back, wishing the scrap of fabric could be the necks of the Saxby wolves instead.

"Maisie, what time is it?" asked Cora, absently braiding the fringe of her lace shawl while the maid entered the room with a tray of coffee and cookies.

It was a question Maisie had heard all morning, but her answer remained as neutral as before. "Ten past eleven, miss."

"Oh. Thank you." Cora settled her hands in her lap and looked back at the letter she was supposed to be reading. Now that her chances of being arrested and charged with her father's murder had faded to nothing, his battalion of lawyers, advisers, and estate managers sought her out when a nod of approval was needed. It was all very boring, but she hated waiting with nothing to do.

After reading the same paragraph twice without taking in one word, she realized the futility of pretending everything was fine. And she was braiding her fringe again.

With an impatient huff of breath, she reached for her appointment book and checked it. She had thumbed through its pages nearly as often as she had asked Maisie for the time, even though the entry she sought out remained the same.

9:30 - Detective Hayes.

He had never been late before. Worse, her two attempted calls to his office had gone unanswered. Something must have happened.

She couldn't help thinking of the expressions on those brutes from the day before. The way that she-wolf had so ruthlessly smashed in his face. What if one of them had slipped into city limits? Yes, she was safe with her name and connections, but what stopped them from going after him?

"Maisie?"

She thought she heard the other girl grind her teeth before appearing in the doorway. "Yes, miss?"

Cora quickly scribbled on the back of the nearest letter and handed it over. "I'm going out. I don't know for how long. Tell anyone who asks that I'm off shopping. If I'm not back by tonight and haven't rung you about it, then call the police and give them this address."

Then she picked a coat and hat in record time and left in the car. Normally, she would have been lost in the thrill of speeding along while the engine growled and the wind whipped at her face, but today even those couldn't budge her worry. What if Hayes was dead? She couldn't even imagine how awful that would be.

Perhaps he was too reserved for his own good, and certainly too stubborn, but he was also fearless, and clever, and determined, and she didn't want to see all that reduced to a lifeless body torn apart by savage teeth. The thought of finding him that way left her mouth trembling, and she quickly distracted herself by checking her lipstick in the rearview mirror. If she was about to face a police interview for

finding a body, then at the very least she could look fantastic while doing it.

She knew the address for his office, having found it back when she was still searching for private detectives. It led to one of the industrial sections close enough to the port that brine tinged the air and rust splotched cars. A few gulls wheeled overhead as she turned down a street crowded with offices, cafes, and shops.

It was a nice area, quiet except for the distant echoes from the docks, and nobody even glanced at her as she found the right place— a two-story brick building as bland and well-kept as its neighbors. She didn't see broken windows or other signs of violence.

The address led her to the upper level. There were two nameplates on the door—Hayes' and someone called *J. Feral*. The window revealed an unlit front office, empty of movement even when she knocked.

At the lack of an answer, Cora tried again, surprised at how badly her heart pounded. Then she pulled a hairpin free and crouched before the lock, her fingers deft and sure. Within a minute, she heard the click that meant she had succeeded, and cautiously opened the door.

"Detective Hayes?" She spoke clearly, eyeing the covered typewriter on the front desk. That explained why her calls hadn't been answered; the secretary had never shown up for work. Nearby file cabinets were open and still spilling out paper, and she toed at some of the bigger piles left on the ground, wondering if they covered bloodstains or something else equally nefarious.

Instead, she found a glass. Then an empty whiskey bottle. Her worry melted into relief as she picked it up and glanced over the

label. Cheap and strong, the kind of hooch used only when someone wanted to drink away all awareness. Or heartbreak.

She began opening window shades and turning on lights, now moving with purpose. She no longer expected to find a body bled out, but one that was, not to put too fine a point on it, soused.

The office door marked with *J. Feral* was locked, but Hayes' was open and that was where she found him, slumped over a desk full of files and papers. The blinds behind him were pulled shut, leaving everything in shadow.

"Hayes?" she whispered, abruptly afraid again. What if she'd gotten it wrong? Not death by teeth, but by self-inflicted bullet? He had looked like his heart was cracking in two when they had left the meeting.

When she moved closer, she noticed another empty bottle near his feet, as if he'd knocked it off his desk or dropped it. His jacket and waistcoat were crumpled on the floor, one of his suspenders had been pulled off and the other was twisted askew... but he was breathing.

Carefully, she ran fingers through his hair, deathly afraid of them coming away bloody. But his scalp and skull felt whole, and her dread evaporated into something much more impatient.

"Hayes." She shook his shoulder and received a slurred groan in reply. "Hayes, wake up this instant."

A harder shake, and finally he stirred, pushing up off his elbows enough to blink at her with bloodshot eyes.

"You're hideously late for our meeting," she said, surveying his unshaven face and wild hair.

"Miss—" Then his voice gave out, and he cleared his throat before trying again. "Miss Marshall, I apologize. I—"

"Drank yourself silly," she said, and dropped her purse onto his desk. "I can't say I'm surprised. You wouldn't talk to me at all about what happened yesterday, so you had to get rid of your thoughts in some other manner."

"Miss Marshall..."

"Oh, it's all right. We all make mistakes. At least you don't look too green in the gills." Then she walked past, finding a few back rooms that connected the two offices. They were tiny but obviously meant to allow him or his office partner to live there in a pinch if they couldn't be torn away from their work. "Is this stove working? I'll make you breakfast since you obviously missed it."

Hayes rubbed at his face, leaving his voice muffled. "That's... very nice of you, but I don't want any."

"Nonsense. You'll feel better after eating." She took off her hat and then her coat, dropping them on the cot by the small closet before returning to his office. "To be quite frank, I thought I was coming here to find a dead body, not one pickled on whiskey and buried in papers."

A growl entered his voice even as his face remained buried in his hands. "Food won't do a damn thing for me."

She watched him for a few moments, not liking how he hadn't met her eyes. He was still hunched over his desk, too. He looked... defeated.

Somehow, that was more upsetting than seeing him covered in his own blood, and she found her voice growing soft with words that had hidden in her heart for quite a while. "I know what it's like to lose someone you love. It doesn't seem fair that the world keeps turning while you feel dead inside. The sigil controlled what I said

and did but couldn't touch what I *felt*. I was very miserable, of course, and didn't know how to find any measure of peace."

That riveting gaze of his was now fixed on her, unwavering despite his sick condition. She sucked in a breath and kept on, wishing someone had told her such things when she'd been lost in her own grief. "Eventually, I realized the only way out of something is through it. To just trudge along and use whatever you can to keep going. When my father first put the sigil on me, I couldn't do anything without his approval. It was terrible, and for so many nights, I just wanted to close my eyes and not wake up the next morning.

"But I *didn't* die, so I had to get out of bed, and keep myself clean and fed, and remember how to speak to others, and soon I started the most boring, harmless hobby possible—arranging flowers. It was such a stupid little thing, but I still had something to do, even if it was just changing the appearance of a room. It was a reason to keep moving forward in life." Her gaze had dropped to his desk, but now she looked right into his face, daring him to dismiss it all as nonsense.

He didn't. In fact, he said nothing, leaning there on the desk as if every syllable out of her mouth had drawn him closer to her.

It was his expression that struck her, though, and she found herself placing a hand on his forearm, wanting him to feel the sincerity behind her next words. "You woke up today. So take a shower, and comb your hair, and pick at the breakfast I'm about to make. Because the world is turning, and you're still a part of it."

For a long moment, those wild, gold eyes only studied her, so intense that she felt like the ends of her hair were about to crisp under his attention. Then he nodded and pushed himself upright,

something like life coming back into his movements. "There's probably nothing in the larder."

She gave him a sunny smile. "We'll see."

By the time he was out of the shower, she had coffee, toast, and an omelette ready on his desk. When he reappeared in the office, dressed but still buttoning up his waistcoat, she said, "Is this where you live?"

"Technically, I have an apartment of my own. My job keeps me from using it much." Despite his terse words, he already looked a little better. In the bright light and with his face freshly shaved, it grew clear that his wounds had already healed into one small scar by his eyebrow.

Cora found herself wondering how normal this was for him, and if his office partner was used to it. "Who's J. Feral? Another detective?"

"No, a thaumaturgist and inventor. We work together on cases if magic is involved."

"What about the secretary? I saw her desk out front."

"Mabel is a sixty-year-old battleaxe who knows what it means when I show up bloody. She's not coming in today."

Cora glanced around the office again, finding nothing personal in it. "No photos, no mementos... don't you have any time for fun?"

He shrugged while straightening his tie. "Not many people like detectives, Miss Marshall."

"Oh, no. Not more wallowing in self-pity." Then she sat on a stack of cardboard boxes near the desk, primly crossing her legs. "Let's talk about something more cheerful."

At that, he glanced over, some of the usual humor returning to his eyes. "Like your father's murder?"

She smiled brightly. "Exactly."

"As it turns out, there are new things to go through. The city police finally sent over all their files." He grabbed one of the boxes and set it between them on the desk. Then he sat down, hesitating at the sight of the food.

When he looked back at her, something in his expression had changed. "Thank you."

Cora knew he meant much more than the breakfast. "You're welcome. You seem much better already."

"Wolves recover faster than humans, whether it's from injury or their own stupidity." Then he rubbed the back of his neck, now looking embarrassed. "In my case, you could call it stupidity either way. You saved my life, Miss Marshall."

Her heart flipped in her chest over the words as much as the way his deep voice spoke them, but she tried to sound merely playful. "Cora. I think we've been through enough together to have *some* sense of familiarity. Don't you?"

He shook his head but also smiled, almost reluctantly so. "You're still my client."

She sighed and rose to her feet. "You really are the most stubborn fella I've ever met. All right, Detective, I've never been a good girl, but I suppose I can give you a break and pretend to be proper. Now eat up while I clean all the papers out front to keep your secretary from quitting on the spot."

It really was impossible to read anything in that striking gaze, but as she began to leave, he suddenly said, "Forget it."

"What?"

"Forget about it," he said, and then he really did smile, a genuine one that left her feeling as sweet as syrup. "Instead, why don't we

look through these and figure out what everyone is trying to hide from us?"

"It's much more boring to read your own police file than I would have thought," said Cora, perched once more on the cardboard boxes by Hayes' desk. "Although, I feel very sorry for whoever catalogued all the things they took from me as potential evidence. My dresses alone take up three pages."

Hayes made a noncommittal noise, intent on the folder before him to the point of forgetting his half-eaten breakfast. Then she saw that the pages were marked AUTOPSY.

The realization that it must have been about Tierney drew a soft gasp out of her. Hayes looked over, his gaze sharp yet sympathetic. "I wasn't sure you wanted to know anything from this one."

"I can't say I'll enjoy it, but it's important and I might be able to help."

He flipped a few pages back. "The official cause of death is blood loss from multiple gunshot wounds and wolf bites. Both lead and silver bullets were recovered and matched to the injuries. The medical examiner also notes that there were several fresh scars, indicating he had either recently been attacked or that his body was healing before being overwhelmed by too much damage."

"That poor man. When we had our fling, he didn't have any scars at all. I suppose he could have gotten them since then, but I don't see how. He lived at the house with the rest of the servants. Someone would have noticed if he'd gotten mangled."

"Was he ever given time off?"

"Sunday evenings. That's hardly enough time to recover from a round of bullets."

Hayes nodded and kept glancing through the report. "He liked collecting tattoos, obviously. The autopsy report counts nine, including one left unfinished."

Cora quickly added up all the tattoos she remembered on him. "Then he was getting a new one. The last time I had the chance to see them, there were only eight."

"Might be something to check out. It's obvious he liked intricate ones that took hours of work. That means the tattooist should know him a little."

Cora found herself rubbing at the back of her head. The sigil didn't burn any more than usual, but she still said, "Do you think this new tattoo could have been the source of the magic that changed him?"

Hayes' voice lost some of its remoteness, as if he'd sensed why her thoughts turned in that direction. "Probably not the tattoo itself since it's unfinished."

Cora managed to keep quiet for a few breaths before asking a question that had burned at her since she'd seen Tierney in the mortuary. "What happened to him? Who could have done this?"

At that, Hayes offered a small but not unsympathetic smile. "That's what we're trying to find out."

"I know, and it's fun until I think of how Tierney didn't deserve this by any means. Then it's simply frustrating. I suppose it was foolish to believe meeting with the Saxbys would give us more information. Instead, they were just as baffled, and we didn't learn anything useful at all."

He closed the file. "I wouldn't say that. They lied about a few things."

"Really? Like what?"

"You said it yourself. They were more concerned about your father than Dominic Tierney. If they were only interested in the magic as claimed, then their main demand should have been having the body examined by the pack enchanters."

Cora tried to think of the most logical explanation but quickly gave up and went with the first one that came to mind. "Perhaps the Frosthounds were telling the truth. Perhaps my father *did* work with the Saxbys. It seems so unlike him, but then, he did like making money more than anything else. And his lawyer, Mr. Forrester, implied that Father was trying something new. Do you think that's it? That one of the other wolf packs paid the informant to find out the details and then somehow used Tierney to kill my father? And perhaps he was meant to go after the Saxbys as well."

Hayes didn't look so convinced. "The thing is..."

Just then, a knock came at the front door—three brisk raps followed by the scrape of a key in the lock. A female voice called out, rough with a growl. "Damn it, Sam, I'm not cleaning up this mess. Once I get you up, *you* are."

Cora shot a startled look at Hayes, who sighed and leaned back in his seat. "She must have heard."

"She?" repeated Cora, and then turned toward the doorway as a figure appeared in it, keys still in hand.

A she-wolf, slender despite the bulky thaumaturgist's leathers she wore. Her red hair was thick and unstyled, framing a delicate, pointed face in wild waves, and she couldn't be any taller than Cora herself. Her eyes, though... they were what dispelled any notion that she was someone fragile or weak. They were a wolf's through and through.

The she-wolf fell silent and looked at them both, sharp and direct. Then, to Cora's surprise, she grinned without showing her teeth. "Thank God. You found someone else to take care of you."

Hayes ignored the comment. "Miss Marshall, this is Jane Feral. Jane, this is Cora Marshall. Be nice to her."

"I'm never nice," said Jane, eyeing Cora with a slight smirk. Then her gaze flickered back to him. "I heard about what happened and knew you'd drink yourself into a stupor. That's the perfect thing to do with a head injury, by the way."

Hayes cleared his throat. "I'm fine, Jane. How'd things go with the Mange hostage?"

"He ate all my food and won $300 from me playing billiards. Believe me, he went home happy." Then her attention switched back to Cora. "How'd you get in? Did he give you a set of keys?"

The she-wolf certainly seemed prickly, but Cora saw no reason not to answer her honestly. "I know how to pick locks."

"Strange habit for a fine lady."

"Oh, I used to trap myself into rooms all the time as a child. One of the servants finally grew tired of rescuing me and taught me how to get out."

Jane raised an eyebrow. "Looks like you know how to cook as well. And I've already heard you're a crack shot."

Cora offered a bright smile. "Then you know much more about me than I do about you."

"Fair enough. I left the Saxby Pack at the same time as Sam. I've made a living supplying raw materials for other thaumaturgists or making custom enchantments, but I'll also work on his cases whenever needed. We exiles must stick together." Then Jane reached over to take a piece of toast from Hayes' plate.

He pulled it out of reach and resumed eating, although not without a wry glance. "I trust her with my life, Miss Marshall. I think we're at the point where you'll have to do the same, because we need Jane's expertise on a few things in this case."

It stung to hear him address her so formally even while he used Jane's first name with such ease, but Cora was practical enough to realize now wasn't the time to pout. "I'll take all the help I can get."

The she-wolf's eyes glittered with amusement, but before she could respond, Hayes spoke her name with enough of a growl to suggest he knew she was about to be rude.

Jane looked unabashed. "You're being very protective. Anyway, I left my findings on your desk yesterday while your face was being smashed in, so I'll assume you never saw them. The samples I took from Dominic Tierney's body indicate magic much more complicated than a spell. It's most likely bio-thaumaturgy."

Hayes swore under his breath, food forgotten.

Cora hesitated, not understanding what those flat words conveyed. "Miss Feral? I'm embarrassed to admit it, but I'm hopelessly stupid when it comes to anything magic-related."

It was a perfect target for a sharp comment, but Jane only said, "At least you admit it. Most people don't and waste my time. A person under a spell is separate from it. They might be controlled or affected by the enchantment, but it can be broken and they will go back to being exactly the same as before. A spell is created and cast. Think of a net trapping fish. They're two separate things. Does that make sense?"

When Cora nodded cautiously, the she-wolf continued. "Bio-thaumaturgy changes a person permanently. Fuses with them, if you like. And instead of being cast, it's created and then transmitted, usually through an injection, but sometimes absorbed through the skin or a superficial cut. Personally, I'm glad the results indicate this is what Dominic Tierney was under. It requires much more experience to create something successful compared to any hobbyist playing with a book of spells. Experience, experimentation, and privacy, since it's strictly illegal."

"Which means a lot of raw materials sent to a remote location," said Hayes. Then he glanced at Jane. "Been shipping materials to anyone who fits all that?"

The she-wolf considered. "Three, all using fake names. I'm sure the addresses can't identify them either, although never discount human stupidity. Clayton Dollar, Lily Pad, and Admiral Antwerth."

Hayes was already writing it all down. "Might get something out of it."

"Doubtful. The last alias alone sounds like a child's name for a stuffed toy."

"He's a rat terrier," said Cora, unable to keep the excitement out of her voice.

They both stared at her.

When the silence stretched on, she repeated herself. "Admiral Antwerth is a rat terrier. He was Freddy Davenport's beloved pet dog. I used to play with him quite often. Your customer must be Freddy!"

"Why am I not surprised you know Frederick Davenport, and on such a personal level?" said Jane, the smirk back on her face.

Cora was too delighted to be affected by the she-wolf's derision. "He fits everything. He's rich and owns a huge amount of land in and outside of the city. We should question him."

"He'll never be interrogated by a wolf," said Jane. "He sees us as inferior creatures."

"Yes, but I can talk to him without raising any suspicion."

Cora glanced at Hayes and felt her hopes deflate, seeing the answer in his expression even before he said, "That's not a good idea."

"Why not? I'd be coy about it."

Hayes shook his head while rising from the desk. "I know you would, but we've talked about this. No sleuthing on your own. If Freddy Davenport has anything to do with this, then he's a dangerous man, and seeing you alone might be just what he wants."

As Jane rifled through the files on the desk, seemingly losing interest in the conversation, Cora tried again. "I can't believe Freddy is the brains behind this situation. I *know* him."

"And you're sure he couldn't possibly do such a thing," murmured Jane, flipping open a file and scrutinizing its pages.

Cora huffed. "I'm sure he couldn't be an experimental thaumaturgist. If Freddy is a part of this, then I think he's supplying the space for those who are, and maybe the protection of his name and connections as well. We're completely alike, you see. Too impatient to make elaborate plans and much too silly to understand anything requiring hard thought."

Hayes stepped close to her, his voice serious yet warm. "Miss Marshall, you're not silly."

The words were almost enough to soothe the increasing feeling of being left out, but then he added, "In fact, when people think you are, you're shrewd enough to use it against them. Who's to say Davenport is any different?"

"But..." Cora groped for words. "We can't ignore this lead."

"We're not. Give me a few days to track down the people behind these other names and to figure out how to get us both in front of Freddy Davenport. This isn't the kind of thing to rush into."

"Yes, I suppose you're right," said Cora, but couldn't help feeling dissatisfied. Out of the corner of her eye, she saw Jane tuck a few folders beneath her arm. "I just feel like I can be more useful."

"Believe me, you won't miss anything interesting. Do you want me to take you back home?"

"Oh, no, it's all right. I drove here." Cora didn't feel like smiling, but she wore one while glancing at Jane. "It was nice to meet you, Miss Feral."

"I'm sure," said Jane, sitting behind the desk to grab another file.

Hayes followed her to the car outside, and Cora found herself hesitating, feeling like there was more to be said even as she settled behind the wheel. "And you're sure you're all right?"

He smiled a little, that warm, wry one she was beginning to crave. "Thanks to you. I'll call when I find out anything."

Then there was nothing to do except drive away, and she did, unaware that he watched her until she disappeared from sight.

When he returned to his office, Jane raised her eyebrows. "I like her. I'm sure you remember I despised Isabelle."

"I was wondering why you were gentle with her."

"She killed Warren, for one. I can't tell you how many times I've dreamed of doing in that bastard myself. And she looked after you today, which means I didn't have to. She might be a tad easy to rile, though. Did you smell her jealousy the moment you used my first name?"

When he didn't respond, the humor faded from the she-wolf's voice. "Since she knows how to get in here, we need to be careful. If she had looked at the wrong papers, she might have discovered you're trying to take the sigil off her. Anything she knows, it does as well, and the only reason it allowed you to learn of its existence is because you're working for its benefit—trying to find her father. If it thought you were a threat... well, any binding magic has self-defense mechanisms. Miss Marshall would find it extremely painful to be near you. Or would just have her brain fried completely. It depends on what her father wanted."

Hayes grimaced. "Can you get it off her?"

"Maybe. I could give you a firmer answer if I knew the sigil's maker."

"I'm working on it."

Jane nodded. "Is that the only thing you're working on? I noticed you kept her away from the files about her father's servants as well. When you noticeably left out *what* part of her memories were taken, I did my own investigation. You're trying to find the man she was going to elope with, aren't you?"

"You're unusually interested in this."

At that, Jane grinned. "You want to change the subject? Let's talk about that new scar beneath your eye. I'm guessing it's from Isabelle."

Hayes' jaw tightened. "I can't say I'm interested in talking about that, either."

"I am. She escaped back into Saxby land. Even though the Frosthounds have taken responsibility for the deaths during the meeting, the details are already circulating thanks to her. Who would have thought a spoiled heiress would also be a sure shot?"

Then Jane studied him carefully. When he said nothing, she added, "The last time you saw Isabelle, you wouldn't talk for days. Yet here you are, already functional and able to think about other things. Maybe Miss Cora Marshall is doing some good for you."

"Jane. Let's get back to business."

"Fine. Avoid it like you avoid all other matters of the heart. I've already given you a list of all the black market thaumaturgists I know. What else do you need?"

"Just work on what you can to destroy the sigil. I'll comb through Isaac Marshall's information and see if any of the names you've given me match."

"Is that going to be the rest of your day?"

"Not if I finish cleaning up the mess I made. I want to have a word with Miss Marshall's friend, Violet Granbury. Now that

Freddy Davenport's name is in the mix, she's been bumped up a lot higher on my list of people I want to talk to. They've been friends for years. She might know something."

Cora really didn't like feeling this way, and it only grew worse when she pulled into the driveway of her house. No, not her house. Her father's. Her wretched, awful father. The sigil felt quiet, hardly warmer than her skin, but she hated the fact that it was there, and that its dormancy hadn't quite erased feeling confined.

Inside, she paced through the rooms before flinging herself into the chair in her father's study. Then she picked up the phone, dialing a number she still knew by heart.

Violet answered on the third ring. "Yes?"

"Vi? It's me, Cora."

"Darling, I know who you are. We've only been dearest friends since forever." There was the sound of her taking a puff on her cigarette. "What's wrong? You've got the throb in your voice that means you're unhappy."

"I wouldn't say that, exactly. I'm just... bored."

"Wasn't shooting a pack yesterday exciting enough?"

"It was just one wolf. You can't believe what the newspapers say. And maybe 'bored' isn't the right word." Cora hesitated, trying to understand the feelings boiling in her heart. "I'm beginning to think I don't have a chance. That he really does just see me as a client."

"So, that's it. For the first time, you understand how it feels when a man isn't interested. Or in your case, a creature. Poor ducky. Come

over and tell me all about it. I'm in the middle of a massage, but don't let that hold you back. Enrico doesn't speak a word of English."

Violet's house looked much the same as when Cora had last seen it—a dour stone mansion with many narrow windows that, as a girl, had always reminded her of peering eyes. Ancient trees offered privacy from neighbors and roads, and Cora pulled into the gravel driveway without fear of being seen by nosy people who might have recognized her.

When the maid showed her into the right room, Violet exclaimed from her position on the massage table, lifting round sunglasses from her face while a man worked over her legs. "My goodness, you do look rotten. I'm bursting to hear everything."

And she really did seem interested, silent yet attentive as Cora paced the room and recounted the day. In fact, it was so unlike her that as soon as Cora finished, she glanced over and said, "Oh, I know, I know, it sounds ridiculous. Poor me, so used to being the center of attention that I don't know what to do with myself when I'm not. But please, no smart remarks."

"I never kick a girl when she's down. There's no fun in it. Besides..." Violet dismissed the man with a wave and reached for a cocktail waiting nearby. "It really is an unpleasant thing to realize."

"It's not just that. It's more that I could feel myself being shut out of things. And he seemed so *comfortable* with Miss Feral. I suppose it made me realize just how proper he's always been with me." Then Cora settled by the nearest window and began plaiting the tassels on the drapes. "You really are a dear to listen to all this. Even I think it's silly."

"Oh, sweetie, you keep insisting I have things like a heart and conscience simply because we've been friends since childhood. I keep telling you, the only heart I have is this little one right here." Violet ran fingers along the gold locket gleaming against her chest and then rose from the table to join her.

The dark silk of her robe highlighted the pallor of her skin and the purple hollows beneath her eyes. Just as Cora was about to ask if she felt sick, the other girl said, "Do you really think Freddy has anything to do with this mess?"

She sounded interested, as if the 'mess' in question were a simple scandal instead of the disappearance of her father and the death of his driver.

Cora shook her head. "I don't think he's the brains behind it at all. He's much too much of a man who lives in the moment. I think he's unintentionally involved, that's all. I just wish I knew how."

At that, Violet smiled and took another drag on her cigarette. "Then I've got good news for you. He's having a party tonight. One of his 'philosophy meetings.'"

"Oh, those." Cora couldn't muster much enthusiasm in her voice. "I don't know, Vi. When you've been to one orgy, you've been to them all."

"The point, you wonderfully silly thing, is that he's called me up to see if I can coax you to go. He's been *aching* to see you. Why not take the opportunity to ask him some questions on the sly?"

The initial burst of excitement in her heart faded as quickly as it had appeared. "I agreed I wouldn't investigate anything on my own."

Violet stared at her through wisps of smoke, as if she couldn't believe Cora was being serious. "Cora Marshall, afraid to go against

someone's will? That was the only way you communicated with your father."

"I know, but Detective Hayes is trying to help me. All he's asked for is that we trust each other with the truth. I'm not afraid of him, Vi. I just don't think that it'd be very honest of me to break my promise."

"Darling, if he's not about to fuck you, then who cares what he wants?"

When Cora just played with the tassels, refusing to look up, the other girl sighed. "I can't believe you're acting so defeated. To hell with the wolf. If you think it's a good idea to look into Freddy, why not do it?"

"He'll be very cross with me," murmured Cora, feeling more and more torn.

"When has that ever bothered you before? If there's one thing you've never been, it's a coward."

After a moment, she looked up, unable to hide the heat in her voice. "It's such a strong lead to go on. I can't just ignore it. I *won't*."

As Violet smiled, Cora added, "Will you be at the party as well?"

A pang of disappointment went through her when the other girl shook her head. "I'm not feeling it tonight, sweetie. You'll have to make your triumphant return all by your lonesome. I'm sure you'll love it. And I'm sure I'll hear all about it in tomorrow's papers."

Freddy's house was modeled after the very latest fashions, a massive wood and glass structure overlooking the ocean. The moon hung high and half-full as a servant took the car from Cora. She glanced at it while smoothing down her mink coat, still feeling a tinge of guilt over what she was about to do. Laughter could already

be heard, as could the jazz band, playing a song that just begged people to try out the jitterbug.

Inside, people sparkled against the geometric decor, remote as statues, yet Cora sank into the seething mass of smoke and smiles without the slightest hint of nerves. She was too used to this to ever feel out of place, even when knowing glances were cast her way and followed by exaggerated whispers into ears.

She slipped into the same superficial greetings as the rest of them and met ingratiating compliments with ones of her own. Her white dress stood out against the glitter, drawing all eyes toward her as she circuited the rooms.

In truth, it wasn't her favorite dress, not by any stretch, because she knew once she descended into the private, lower rooms where Freddy held his "philosophy meetings," it would be torn, wrinkled, and stained. Yet she also knew that wearing it would catch Freddy's eye much faster. White had been out for two seasons, and no one else wore it.

Her calculation paid off. She'd hardly spent five minutes in the billiards room before Freddy parted himself from a group of people, a smile already lighting his face as he approached.

Strange, how a year away from his parties had given her new eyes. She seemed to notice everything about his appearance as if for the first time, notice it and file it away in case it later proved important.

Freddy Davenport was always older than people expected, considering his behavior and way of life. In his late 30s, he nevertheless looked tall and trim, and was always immaculately dressed. He could never have been called handsome—his face had the florid coloring, weak chin, and rabbity eyes of the Crescent City upper class male—but he never wanted for company. His fortune

attracted girls who wanted a taste of living rich, and his devil-may-care charm attracted those who already knew the weight of money.

"If it isn't the loveliest creature I've ever cast eyes on, back at last." Then he took her hand and kissed it, his exaggerated motions mocking the old-world gesture.

Cora smiled, but a part of her still remembered how he had been as quiet as the rest when her father's disappearance had first become known. "How are you, Freddy? I missed you."

"I felt terrible until I saw you were here." His hand settled against her bare back, guiding her through the crowds. "I tried breaking the world speed record with one of my cars today. It blew a gasket instead."

"How awful."

"Isn't it? It cost a mint. It might as well be called a tin can instead of a Duesenberg."

The conversation continued in that vein until they reached a private corner away from the music and hubbub. Then his expression lost some of its blitheness. "I've missed you awfully, Cora dear. It was no damn easy thing to take when Vi told me you wouldn't come to last week's party. Wouldn't, not couldn't."

"Everything has been such a whirlwind since Father disappeared," said Cora, letting her voice fall serious. She searched his face for the slightest hints of guilt.

He shrugged. "Yes, it's rotten luck, all that. But it's over now, isn't it?"

"I'm no longer being accused of his murder, if that's what you mean, but he's still missing and presumed dead."

"Is that why that detective is still hanging around?"

She blinked, startled. "How did you know? Has he contacted you?"

"Gossip moves faster than even my speedboats, darling. And I'm hardly going to let myself be interrogated by something one step removed from my hounds. How would I know anything about your father?"

Cora put a teasing note into her next words despite her flare of anger at the insult toward Hayes. "You know a lot of things, Freddy. You're friends with everyone."

"Are *we* still friends?" His hand slid further down her back in clear disinterest of their conversation.

"I'm here, aren't I?"

"Yes, you are." His voice slid into that thick, suggestive tone that he used whenever he was about to get wicked. "Coming downstairs tonight?"

There was no repulsion at the thought, but no thrill, either. Instead, she felt a sudden throb of pain somewhere in her chest, an ache over how empty it felt to be sordid. Suddenly, she thought she understood the tiredness she'd glimpsed more and more on Violet's face.

"Will it be worth it?" she said, trying to sound coy.

"I guarantee it."

It was a clinch. These secret meetings were always the same. By the end of the night, Freddy would be drunk enough to ramble endlessly, and she would be able to easily ask him questions.

Despite that knowledge, for a moment she nearly backed out. The excitement of learning new information and adding another link to the case had gone rancid. Yet the bitterness of leaving the party without a shred of evidence that she had been right about

Freddy's involvement was too much to bear. "All right. What are we waiting for?"

Freddy only smiled and led her to his study. There was a door hidden behind one of the bookcases, and he opened it with the practiced ease of having done so many times before. Cora kept close as they stepped inside, the smells of cigarettes and sex washing over them even before the moans became apparent.

It looked much like all the rest of Freddy's orgies. A lot of people appeared outright bored whether they were in or out of their suits and dresses. A few were in the middle of carnal acts, but more seemed content to simply watch. The elite of Crescent City hardly knew how to feel delight anymore, and that extended to sex as much as anything.

To her surprise, Freddy didn't stop at any of the couches or rugs, instead walking her to the back where a small hallway led to a door he had to unlock. "Freddy, how many secret rooms do you have?"

"Tonight, only this one matters." Then he opened the door, revealing a stone stairway down that must have been hundreds of years old.

"And what's down there?" She thought she caught a hint of smoke and chanting.

"The true elite. Out here..." His hand waved at the room of people watching and writhing together, "is mere pleasure. Down here you will find *ascension*."

Her skin suddenly prickled. Something about the look in his eyes seemed... ominous. "Freddy, what on earth are you talking about?"

"You'll understand everything before the very end," he said, as they began walking down the steps. "I promise."

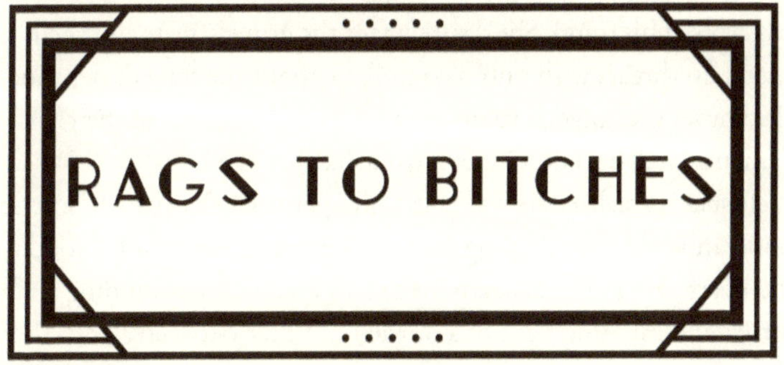

CHAPTER ELEVEN

Ragbag Way was no place to be at night, but Sam wasn't concerned. The shadowy alleys and shops that thrived where city limits met no man's land expected desperate wolves struggling to live without a pack, and it had been years since he had been that.

He smelled addicts hiding rusted knives, prostitutes with their cheap perfume and bone-deep weariness, and a fresh body outside a nearby bar. There was also the familiar cocktail of human sweat, fear, and calculation from those who thought they were safely hidden in the shadows while he walked beneath the glow of streetlights. Those who couldn't see his eyes thought he was a cop; those who could shrank further back in caution, sensing his confidence.

It wasn't bluster. He still knew Ragbag well, and didn't even need his nose to find the tattoo parlor that Dominic Tierney had used for his final, unfinished piece. The dead man's bank account could only reveal the cost, not the place, but Sam had found other tattoo artists who'd recognized the work and told him where to go.

Now he was here, too familiar to feel afraid and too aware to feel comfortable. Unbidden, the thought of Cora Marshall in a place like this crossed his mind. She'd surely face the grimy streets and their uncertain threats with only a complaint about the state of her shoes. He'd never met anyone so undaunted while being out of their element. Hell, he'd never met anyone like her at all.

Just as he realized he was half-smiling, the air sharpened, burned wood and cold ash mingling with the faintest traces of ink, blood... and death. He swore beneath his breath even before rounding a corner and catching sight of a burned-out hole between a peep show place and a pawn shop.

Nobody stopped him from stepping into the remains of the tattoo parlor, but he doubted he'd find much. The lingering cinders smelled and felt old, which meant anything left unburned would have been long scavenged. He circled around the scorched foundation, thinking. The poor bastard who had burned with his parlor wouldn't have agreed, but this was a better lead than anything gleaned from an interview.

Ragbag Way witnessed murders every day, but not with fire. The buildings all leaned together like drunks, and there were too many people crammed inside them with no way out. To burn something, anything, was as good as setting yourself alight. A knife in the back or hands on the throat left a body, but what did that matter? No one who lived in Ragbag had to hide their deeds. Only an outsider would burn an entire shop to make sure nothing remained.

Sam glanced around, feeling eyes on him even as nearby windows remained dark or covered over with signs. He could try combing through the street to see if anyone would talk, but there was a better source of information waiting just two blocks away.

The moon glowed brightly in the sky when he reached the house, an old brick structure as worn and stately as an unearthed statue. It looked the same as ever, standing three stories high yet surprisingly narrow compared to the surrounding apartment complexes. When he saw light winking out from the pulled curtains of the ground floor windows, he continued to the front door and knocked quietly.

Within moments, it opened, revealing one of the few figures in Ragbag feared by all: Minnie Wilkes. She was an old woman now, white-haired, frail, and limping from arthritis, but that didn't quell rumors about her being a strong enough mind reader to boil the brains of anyone she disliked. Whether it was true or not, her house was left alone, and so were any lodgers who were given the upper floors.

Sam gave her a smile—a real one. "Hello, Minnie. Did I wake anyone?"

"No, but we didn't expect you until next week." She pulled him in to kiss him on the cheek and then added, "Come in, you devil. I'll make some coffee."

As he followed her toward the kitchen, taking care not to set off the squeaky floorboards, the grief hit his nose hard enough to make each breath sting. He jerked toward the source out of instinct and realized it was coming from the second bedroom. A she-wolf, her scent still shocked and raw. Then he caught hints of the pup with her, its scent barely formed from being so young. A newborn still in its swaddling.

He knew who they had to be and what must have happened to them, and nearly snarled in frustration.

"Careful, you'll wake them," said Minnie, sensing where his attention had turned. "The girl has barely slept from looking after

the child, and she doesn't trust anyone yet. Sit and talk with me instead. You're here on a case, aren't you?"

He explained about the tattoo parlor while she filled the percolator and set it up on the stove, but his attention flickered all around the kitchen, taking in its clean yet worn state. Once she joined him at the table, he finished with, "The sink sounds like it's leaking. Has anyone taken a look at it?"

Minnie laughed. "Aren't you busy enough without fixing an old house for an old woman? Now, let's see. I didn't know Stickler, the tattooist, too well. He had a petty little mind. Not a planner by any means. But you'd see all sorts show up as his clients, and sometimes he bragged about his connections through them."

"When did the parlor burn down?"

She thought about it while reaching for her basket of knitting. "It must have been a month ago. And before you ask, yes, I felt him die. It was quick as a flash, and happened at least half an hour before people noticed the fire. Ah, that's just what you wanted to hear. Are you close to solving everything?"

"No, but I might be putting some of the pieces together. I have Jane testing samples from Dominic Tierney's unfinished tattoo. If she can pinpoint it as the source of infection for whatever this strange magic is, then the tattoo artist being killed and burned proves that the people behind this hoped to cover their tracks from the beginning." Which meant they were used to underhanded dealings.

Minnie must have caught his unspoken thought, for she gave him a sly smile and said, "It's happened again just tonight, you know. A fire. Someone's shack over on Flash Alley. The police responded this time, even the police captain himself. They've been there for nearly two hours."

It was a strange sort of excitement, hoping to find fresh clues from the newly dead. Sam had met many detectives on and off the city force who grappled with the feeling, believing it turned their hearts to stone. Humans always worried about becoming inhuman, one of the many puzzling things about them. He was far more concerned about what he could *do*, not what he was. Looking too deep within would drive a fella crazy, especially if what he saw around him was bad enough.

When he did nothing more than get up to pour them both some coffee, Minnie looked surprised. "I thought that would send you up and running."

"The cops move slow when it comes to arson. It'll be another hour before their enchanters let anyone investigate the site. You're much sweeter company than Captain Dempsey."

"You and your charm."

For a few minutes, he drank his coffee and watched her knit. Her needles flashed in the warm lamplight, their movements as steady as a metronome. "What are you making?"

"Booties for the baby."

"How are they?" He kept the words as neutral as possible—pure habit, since she would undoubtedly catch his flare of anger.

At that, Minnie studied him, the faded blue of her eyes growing further unfocused. Most mind readers caused a headache when sinking into someone else's thoughts, but not her. It was why she was so feared—she was powerful *and* unnoticeable, even when diving deep for nuances. Humans hated how she could find their secrets in the blink of an eye, but any wolf used to the power of scent and all it revealed took her talents with much better grace, and Sam just finished the last of his coffee while her gaze sharpened again.

"So, you already knew. I wasn't sure since someone else set things up. But then I heard you punched Warren at that meeting, hard enough to knock out his teeth."

"What I knew was that two wolves fled the Saxby Pack and came to you. Two, when there should have been three. Even with the Saxbys refusing to admit anything, it's easy to guess what happened."

She sighed, casting a glance toward the kitchen doorway as if making sure they were alone. "It was bad luck, not a betrayal from Brom. As far as we know, no one found out his part in this, and he's still safe. Some royal guards happened to be patrolling when the girls tried crossing into city limits. Edith was still weak from having the baby, but managed to pass him to her sister, who had already gone over."

And then the guards found her and killed her.

Leaving the words unsaid didn't make them any easier to take. Sam dimly realized he was squeezing the mug hard enough to crack it, and relaxed his fingers in one slow, deliberate movement.

"Did you know her?" said Minnie, her voice gentle. She had too much tact to search for the answer to such a question.

His jaw ached from teeth that had nothing to maul. "No, but I knew her mate, Theo. We trained as guards together. He was executed last week for treason."

When he said nothing else, she sighed. "You're doing the best you can, Sam. Nearly thirty wolves have been rescued this year alone, and from packs all over the city. Not only that, but they had places to sleep and safe jobs to start rebuilding their lives. You did that."

"I know."

"You know, yet you're as angry as ever. Don't shake your head at me. You lived under my roof for two years. I can read your mind like

a book, and it's the most driven one I've ever encountered. You're always intent on doing more no matter what the cost."

"I have to, Minnie. It'll get even worse," he said, and watched her eyes widen as she caught the first hints of why. "Wolves are only peaceful when a few powerful packs cow the rest. It's been eight years since the Orphos and the Lamonts fell, and no one's managed to reach their level of dominance. The violence spilling over to human land adds even more pressure. Every pack is paranoid and running out of money and resources. Desperate to win out against the others and finally end this."

"And how will running yourself ragged help with any of that? You built this rescue network. Now trust us to bear some of the load."

Despite the grim conversation, he smiled a little. "I thought you'd stop scolding me once I moved out."

"If anything, you need more of it now. Your mind has buried itself in work. When's the last time you had a decent meal?"

"This morning," he said, aware it was useless to resist thinking about Cora. He wasn't able to do it even without a mind reader snooping around. Then he got up to wash out his coffee cup, ignoring the flicker of surprise on Minnie's face. The sink *was* leaking. "Is the tool bag still in the front closet?"

"Stubborn boy," said Minnie, shaking her head.

"It won't take long to fix."

And it didn't. It wasn't even ten when he left, making his way through streets that gleamed like oil beneath the harsh light of the moon until he picked up the smells of smoke and electricity. And irritation.

Police had set up barricades and lights around a sagging apartment complex where one of the windows looked burned out. Scorch marks licked all the way up to the roof. A ghostly, blue glow suggested the police enchanters were busy at work inside. The rest of the force waited outside by the barriers, milling about with obvious impatience.

When Sam picked out the familiar silhouette of Captain Dempsey, he veered in that direction.

The moment Dempsey saw him, he gave a growl that would have made a wolf proud. "No. Not tonight. I haven't had a smoke for three hours, and I'm not taking any of your bullshit, Hayes."

"Hello to you as well." Sam paid enough attention to the captain's scent to make sure he wasn't about to snap and then stopped beside him. "Let me guess, the enchanters don't want to risk contamination from any other sources of fire. Including cigarettes."

When Dempsey just growled again, he added, "How much longer will it take?"

"Who the hell knows." The police captain rolled an unlit cigarette between his fingers before tucking it behind his ear. "Why are you here? I'd have thought you'd be busy enough babysitting the Marshall girl."

"She's smarter than you think."

"No. She's clever, not smart. Clever people race into deadly situations because they're sure they can get back out. Smart people know better and stay cautious."

Just then, one of the enchanters came over—a senior enchanter, Sam realized with some surprise. "Captain? It's all clear. We've finished our spells and located the fire's starting point. There isn't a body. It's arson, not murder."

The entire area flickered with matches as nearly every man there lit a cigarette in response, Dempsey fastest of all.

Sam waited until the man sighed out a lungful of smoke and then said, "Why are you here? It's not often that the big guns come into Ragbag."

"The burned apartment belongs to someone we've had our eye on for a while. Harold Beaumont, caught a few times in his youth for illegal experiments with magic. We're sure he belongs to a ring of black market thaumaturgy."

Sam fell still, recognizing the name from the list Jane had given him. "Do you know anything else about him?"

"He has connections with a lot of the city's elite. They trust him more because he came from a prestigious family, whether he does better work than a back-alley enchanter or not. His birth name was Granbury. Harold Granbury." Dempsey took another drag from his cigarette and added, "If you're going to pester me with questions, just come on up with us."

Yet when he turned toward Sam, he found the wolf had already disappeared into the night, silent as a shadow.

The parlor maid at Granbury Manor was used to turning away visitors when Miss Violet was in one of her moods. She wasn't used to doing it with a wolf, especially one that told her with one glance of those strange-colored eyes that he knew she was lying to him. She tried again, trying to keep her composure. "I'm very sorry, sir, but Miss Granbury is in bed for the night. You'll have to see her in the morning."

Sam nodded and then stepped past the maid, ignoring her gasp of shock.

"Sir! I'll call the police."

"That's fine." His instincts told him they'd be needed.

He didn't wait around to see if the maid was bluffing, instead finding Miss Granbury's bedroom. He knocked in silence, feeling tight and trapped in his suit.

"Go away!" shouted a female voice on the other side. Liquor, tears, and anger filled the air.

Then he caught traces of Cora's scent and opened the door without a second thought, ready for anything. The room was dim, lit only by the fire in the hearth, but he quickly caught sight of Violet Granbury standing by the bedside table, a cocktail in one hand. Her other held something much more dangerous.

For a moment, they only stared at each other—the wolf hiding behind the manners of a man, and the woman smiling behind a shiny, snub-nosed revolver. She raised an eyebrow, riveting even as the contents of her glass slopped over her silk nightgown. "I could have shot you."

"You could have tried." He kept his voice even while watching her set the gun back on the table.

Her response was to walk over to the nearest window. The curtains hadn't been drawn, revealing the luminous moon, and she looked at it instead of him while collapsing onto the window seat. "Whatever you want, I probably can't give it. At this time of night, all I can do is fight or fuck."

Deceit was thick in her scent, but not the kind that meant she'd try going for the gun again. He began exploring the room, searching for where Cora's scent was strongest. "I apologize for being this rude, Miss Granbury, but you've been dodging my calls for days."

"Of course. How could I possibly have anything of interest to say? Go pester Cora. She'd certainly love it more than me."

"I like exploring every angle."

"Is that what you call it?"

At that, he glanced at her again. "Riling me up won't work."

She dropped her chin into her hand, her smile sharp despite the unfocused look in her eyes. "Oh, I don't think so. You're bristling with every word that comes out of my mouth. I never knew male wolves were as sensitive as men when it came to being teased. Or as clueless when it came to girls in love. Oh, don't look at me like that. I'm not breaking her promise to keep a secret or anything horrible like that. I simply know her and have since we were children. She's clueless about everything, including her heart."

Then Violet stared out the window, the moonlight draining the color from her hair and eyes. "We both lost our mothers early on, you see. It gave us a sort of bond even as we grew up and discovered what jealousy felt like. She was always such a silly little thing but really quite innocent in her own way."

Sam moved in close enough to run his thumb over the nearest curtain's tassels. Cora's indecision lingered over parts that had been neatly braided. "You're talking about her as if she were dead. But you saw her earlier, didn't you?"

The eerie beauty faded from the girl's face as she got up again, stepping out of the moonlight to reach for a pack of cigarettes. When she held one up in a clear signal, Sam withdrew his lighter and lit it for her, keeping his expression blank.

"What a gentleman," she said, smiling again. It wasn't a pleasant one, but there was a certain curve to her lips that most men would recognize. Then she shrugged her shoulders enough to send her nightgown slipping lower. The nuances of her scent changed.

In silence, Sam pocketed the lighter. When he reached out again, her grin widened.

His fingers caught the gold heart dangling from her thin necklace and popped it open, revealing a cache of white powder inside. "Nasty stuff. Anyone on it is hopelessly hooked. Tell me where she went, or I'll make your life hell by cutting off your supply."

She slapped his hand away, red spots appearing on her cheeks. "You flea-bitten bastard. There's no way you could—"

He finally stopped smothering the growl that had burned in his throat from the moment he'd recognized Cora's scent. "Enough of the smart talk. Where is she?"

But Violet didn't seem to hear him, instead flinging herself away to pace around the room, ripping the necklace from her throat and then throwing her cocktail glass after it. "How? How does the little bitch end up captivating each and every man who so much as looks at her? I hate her. I hate what she's given for being her."

"Does that include Freddy Davenport?"

She panted while looking at him through her disheveled hair, fingers still curled into claws against her arms. "I don't know why you bother asking questions when it seems you already know the answers."

Then she straightened up, a sneer transforming her expression into something demonic. "Yes. She's with Freddy Davenport right now, becoming the precious key to a ritual he's tried to unlock for years. Even though she doesn't know anything. I'm the one who's been there with him from the beginning, who became the brains behind it all. Hiding his ceremonies beneath naughty, private parties —do you think he could have come up with that? Do you think he could ever build something so magnificent? He doesn't even have the

money to pay off the right people. Yet now that we're down to the final rite, he's turned to *her*."

"The final rite for what?" When she didn't answer, his voice thickened into a snarl. "For what, Miss Granbury?"

She stared at him, all life gone from her face. "For ascension. A god from another dimension will be summoned tonight, and beautiful, precious, perfect Cora Marshall is Freddy's offering to it."

CHAPTER TWELVE

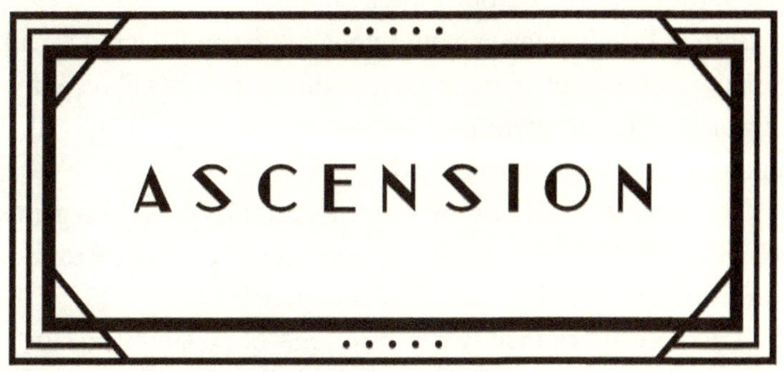

"Freddy, is this really necessary?" Cora tugged at the manacles pinning her hands above her head. She had been chained to one of the stone pillars scattered throughout the room, and could hardly see anything from the many candles placed around her. Their frenzied glow and greasy smoke made her eyes burn, and she squinted while adding, "It all seems a bit... theatrical. Don't you think?"

Somewhere in the darkness, he laughed. "It's essential, Cora dear. Some things require great care."

"Oh." She hoped she sounded satisfied instead of doubtful.

In truth, she was beginning to think none of this would be worth it. She couldn't even make him out among the others. There must have been at least twenty people there, all wearing red robes with hoods that covered their faces. She wasn't sure how any of them could see, which was perhaps why they merely waited among the life-sized statues circling the room, as motionless as the carved marble itself. A few could be heard panting, though, as if very excited.

"And... why am I the only one without a robe? Or for that matter, the only one without a stitch on at all?"

At that, Freddy stepped within reach of the candlelight. He had shed his suit for a ridiculous white garment that looked like a puffy bathrobe more than anything. "Because you are extremely special. A guiding light in the unformed darkness."

"You're too kind." She took a close look at his eyes, which glinted strangely. "Freddy, are you sure you're all right? You don't seem like your usual self, even for these kinds of parties."

"I'm more myself than you've ever seen," he said, moving over to one of the robed figures, who balanced a shallow, gilded bowl on one hand and held a fine-pointed brush in the other.

She turned her head to follow him, using the movement to hide her fingers as they plucked a hairpin free and began working on the nearest manacle. She spoke again to hide the sound of its lock clicking open. "I never understand a riddle for an answer. All I know is that this isn't your usual idea of a fun night."

"Sweet, simple Cora," he said, with real affection. Then he took the bowl and brush from the figure and approached her.

She decided it was safer to keep up the charade while she was still chained in place, and kept both hands in the manacles while he dipped the brush into the bowl and painted something on her throat. It smelled like blood, and worse, it was still warm. The figures around them shifted, hunching strangely inside their robes.

Before she could do more than make a disgusted noise, he said, "I'm still your good old Freddy, who loves his cars and boats and always adds three sugar cubes to his coffee. But some time ago, I came to realize none of it made me happy. Haven't you felt it, the boredom of having done everything? It's an emptiness I've seen in all

our eyes while we drink and smoke away our time. Then one man showed me how there's so much more than this world and its undercooked pleasures."

The brush had been moving along her body the entire time, painting strange symbols with that strange liquid, and Freddy finished with a final glyph in the center of her forehead as he added, "Your uncle was a very wise man, Cora."

"Uncle Alfie? I'd call him a lot of things, but not that. Especially after he went a little batty and started a..." Then her voice faded. "A cult. Freddy, don't tell me this is..."

He had already walked away, and now paused before each of the marble statues to stare into their faces. "A continuation of what he started, yes. I kept it going after he passed on. I had to. The gods must be tended to in their fretful slumber. And I paid tribute to those who came before me whenever I could, including commissioning these. They cost a mint, but I wouldn't have it any other way."

The other manacle was rusted. Cora worked on it carefully, not wanting to break the hairpin. Frankly, she was barely paying attention to what Freddy said. At this point, she just wanted to get out as quickly as possible.

Then she realized he was painting a symbol on the forehead of a statue, just like he had with her. Furthermore, it was a statue *of* her, as naked as she was now, even though all the rest were swathed in the same silly robes that Freddy wore. She didn't know what the implications were, but they felt disquieting all the same.

So did Freddy's next words. "You'll hear their whispers soon, darling, and once you do, everything will grow clear. The crawling

chaos will reach out and show you its true meaning of comprehension."

As she picked at the lock, feeling it start to give, Cora watched the cultists break their positions to light more candles, revealing a stone archway built into the wall across from her. There was also a throne off to the side, but before she could really study it, Freddy looked over. "Are you listening?"

Her fingers froze. "Oh, yes. I'm all ears. Comprehension doesn't sound very fun. What else do the gods reward you with?"

He smiled, the one he always used while feeling particularly smug. "Power and protection. And to their most devoted followers, ascension. Alfred showed us the way, and now we've finally built up things to where we can do it. I'll be the first, and just had to bring out the old man to show him that his efforts weren't in vain."

Then Freddy shifted enough to let her look beyond him to where the others had gathered to bow. The candles flickered and then brightened, revealing the throne in full. A wizened figure had been placed on the plush velvet, hardly more than a skeleton and some skin.

Cora's voice rose into a shriek. "You dug him up?"

"He was never buried." Freddy moved for the archway, then, his hands spreading in the air as if basking in invisible light. "That was a lie to keep your father unaware of our plans."

"My father?" She lunged up against the chains, straining to see after Freddy even as the cultists returned to her. "Did you—"

"No more questions. It's time."

Then hands caught her shoulders and face, pinning her still even as the manacle clicked open. The fingers felt cold and clammy against her skin as they forced her to look at the archway while

Freddy intoned, "The blood of our beloved leader has dried up, but yours will suffice as his closest kin. There's no use fighting, darling. He's had this planned since you were a child."

As soon as the archway began glowing, Cora pulled free of the manacles and scratched at the cultists holding her. Her nails caught the hood of the nearest one and ripped it off. She shrieked and renewed her thrashing at the sight of lumpy flesh and nubby horns where there should have been a face.

They fumbled in silence despite her kicks and blows, trying to hold her without smearing the symbols on her skin. More than one bled thick, dark blood down the brighter red of their robes. It was a nightmare of features, all caught in glimpses as she struggled. Pulpy tentacles where a hand should have been. Eyes slotted like a goat's. Two tongues in one mouth, each caught between the teeth in determination while their owner tried to keep her still.

Then Freddy approached, frowning slightly in the same manner as when he lost at billiards. An irritation over the presumption of the other person not giving him what he wanted. "Be a dear now, Cora. There's no reason to—"

The rest of his words were cut off as she grabbed the nearest thing —an iron candleholder—and clubbed him in the head. When he crumpled into a motionless heap, his followers froze and stared at him uncertainly. It felt almost as satisfying as turning the candleholder on *them* until they flinched away and let her go.

Then the archway brightened into the strength of sunlight, and all the cultists shuffled for it, hands and tentacles and hooves raised high as they began chanting in a language she didn't recognize.

Cora didn't waste time watching anything else, instead running for the stairway up to the door. Her clothes had been left in a pile

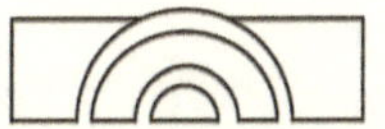

beside the first of the steps, but she stopped only to grab her revolver from its holster. As she checked to make sure they hadn't emptied its chamber, fresh light flared, erasing the entire room. Even when she flinched and threw a hand in front of her eyes, its sheer intensity lit her skin into something translucent, revealing the blood beating through her veins.

The chanting grew increasingly wild as hot winds whipped at her hair. The ground beneath her began to shake. Then the light flickered, offering glimpses of the archway and what could be seen through its mouth.

It looked like a dark, endless void, and yet somehow that absolute blackness writhed to the rise and fall of what sounded like broken flutes. Cora blinked, deciding her dazzled eyes were seeing things, and continued for the stairs. She had the revolver cocked and ready in case a cultist came after her, but they all seemed lost in the sight before them, bodies contorting into impossible shapes while their voices disintegrated into moans and cries.

The stairway was long, long enough that falling from the top would mean sure death, but the strange light still surrounded her like a malevolent presence as she reached the door. It wasn't locked, opening as soon as she turned it, but her relief melted into shock when it revealed the same shining nothingness. It couldn't have been possible. There should have been a room with normal people having a normal orgy. There should have been a way to escape.

When she stretched out a hand, wondering if she'd somehow been drugged or had started hallucinating things, a tentacle lashed out from the whiteness, snaking around her wrist. She shrieked, trying to pull away, and then shot herself free.

A hollow roar filled the air as the wounded tentacle snapped back and disappeared, and even as Cora slammed the door shut again, panting, all light flickered and faded. Her skin prickled at the sudden silence, and she slowly turned around to face the archway.

The cultists had collapsed, the fabric of their robes pooling around their bodies like blood. The room had returned to something dimly lit by candles. And the archway... the archway had disappeared. How could that be?

A wet, sucking sound caught her attention, and she aimed for it without thinking. Shadows rippled and unfurled, and then she realized the archway hadn't disappeared but had merely been hidden behind a hulking mass. A moving mass. A living creature. Even as she gasped, appendages slithered into the light cast by the nearest candles.

She didn't even know what to aim at. There wasn't any sign of a head or eyes. No arms or legs. Grey flesh oozed out between grasping tentacles of all shapes and sizes, some thick and hollow-seeming, and others long and whip-like. And there were so *many* of them, covering the creature's entire bulk.

The creature explored with two of its longer tentacles, feeling everything within reach. From her remote vantage point, Cora felt safe enough but made sure to keep very quiet while it probed at the tile floor and iron candle stands.

It ignored the seizuring bodies of the cultists, instead feeling along the pedestals of the statues, something about its movements seeming confused or unsure. Then it reached the one sculpted to look like her. A tentacle brushed over the symbol Freddy had painted on its forehead. Within a breath, all its nearby appendages reached out, carefully wrapping around the statue.

"Oh, my," murmured Cora, realizing it was able to perceive the glyph.

The entire mass of flesh shivered and split open into a blubbery, toothless mouth. Then the tentacles ripped the statue off its pedestal and shoved it in whole.

Cora screamed, and screamed again when the creature spasmed as if swallowing. The nearest feelers reacted to the sound, squirming along the bottom of the steps. She fired off two rounds, exploding one, but the rest kept searching, leaving slime behind. Then a long, thin tentacle whipped out, missing her by inches to smack against the door. Only her hand over her mouth kept her from shrieking a third time. She inched down the steps while it explored the ceiling.

The creature seemed to be blind, and she moved as silently as possible while trying to keep away from its many arms. Once she made it off the stairway, she searched for any nearby fabric to scrub the symbols off her skin. Some part of her realized she was panting with nerves, but she avoided making any other noise until she stepped over a prone cultist and felt a hand latch onto her ankle.

She kicked back, muffling yet another scream, but the scuffle was enough to send the creature rocking in her direction with a gurgle. She fought with the cultist's grip and finally went for a headshot while writhing shadows fell over her.

Too late, she thought desperately, expecting the pressure of tentacles.

Instead, she heard an explosive shot. The appendages reaching for her burst into grey slime. Before she could do more than flinch, another shot rang out, taking more of the creature with it. The wounds forced it to shrink back from her with an inhuman screech.

This time, she twisted to look up the stairs and felt her heart leap into her throat. Hayes was there with a shotgun, eyes bright gold even in the surrounding darkness while he took the final steps down to her.

"Hayes!" She had never felt so relieved in her life. "I tried to get out, but when I opened the door, nothing was there. It was just—it —"

"I know," he said, shortly. "It's warping space. We can't get out until it's dead."

While the creature repositioned itself, bleeding sluggishly, he shrugged off his suit jacket and gave it to her. "Here. Can you use a shotgun? There are more shells in the pockets. Work it over in places I can't reach."

"What are you going to do?"

He was taking off his tie and shirt as well. A bead of sweat ran down his neck, but he otherwise seemed calm. "Bleed it out. Maybe it doesn't look like it, but it's just flesh."

"Hayes, you should have *seen* what it did to a stone statue. It'll strangle you to a pulp." When he just shook his head, already focused on the writhing creature, she caught his arm, feeling her breath catch. "I'm sorry. I got us into this."

At that, he looked over with his wry smile. "Don't worry about it, Bunny. I've done this before."

Then a shudder went through his body, and she realized he was changing form. She didn't know how to describe it. Plays and pictures always made it out to be something grueling on the body, but all she saw was a flicker of movement that seemed effortless, like when a bird took flight or a cat jumped. Even with the severity of the situation, she couldn't help marveling at how big he was, certainly

larger than any dog she'd seen. His thick fur was a smoky grey where it wasn't white, but his eyes were just the same color while he gave her a final glance, as if making sure she was ready.

When she nodded, he ran at the creature, which now groped at the walls as if to tear them down. She hissed in a breath, steadying her nerves, and then reloaded the shotgun.

The creature hardly seemed to notice him until he bit into the thick tentacles close to its body and ripped one off with a jerk of his head. Cora winced against the roar that followed, and again when the other nearby tentacles lashed out at the source of pain. Hayes was already gone, ducking around to the other side and tearing into grey flesh. The creature was too soft and pulpy to withstand such brutality. Even the merest glance of Hayes' teeth left slime gushing to the floor.

It rocked in frustration, tentacles grabbing the bodies of cultists and flinging them hard enough to break the stone columns and crack the ceiling. Dust and chips of granite scattered through the air, but Cora kept focused and began shooting. She used most of the shells on the upper half of that mountain of flesh, which was well away from Hayes and his routes of attack.

By the time her shoulder throbbed from the shotgun's recoil, most of the creature's mass had been reduced to lifeless splatters on the archway and floor. Its remaining appendages flailed at Hayes without coordination. His fur was covered in its blood but he didn't even shake it off, too intent on getting yet another bite in.

Finally, the creature heaved toward her, most of its tentacles gone, oozing slime everywhere. When it roared, she used the last shell to shoot it right in the mouth. The splatter reached the ceiling. Hayes

ripped at the final, twitching feelers, but the creature had already slumped, its visible skin starting to bubble.

Cora didn't realize what was happening until Hayes raced back and nosed her to hide behind the nearest column. She could hear the creature sizzling like fat dropped into a hot frying pan. She curled herself up into a ball, burying her face into Hayes' thick fur as a final, ear-splitting shriek shattered the air. Light flared brightly as a star, and for a heart-stopping moment, she wondered if they were about to die. Then a cold nose pushed against her neck, nuzzling where her pulse pounded until she stopped shaking.

When the light faded again, she could hear herself panting. Then she realized her fingers were clutching skin instead of fur. Shoulders, actually.

"Are you all right?" murmured Hayes against her ear, his voice rough.

She nodded, for once without words. A wave of warmth filled her, starting from the touch of his fingers and spreading throughout her body. She couldn't remember the last time someone had been genuinely concerned about her.

A little voice deep in her mind insisted that she must have felt such attention once before, that the memories had been burned away by the sigil, but the rest of her knew that this was truly a new feeling, and it was hard to speak through it.

Just as he moved enough to look into her eyes, she said, "Strangely, I don't think I've ever felt better."

He blinked, as if that wasn't the answer he expected.

When they stepped out from their shelter of stone, she found that the archway had crumbled. An especially large chunk had crushed the throne. The broken bodies of the cultists remained, but

all the blood and slime from the creature had disappeared. Only a scorched stain on the floor indicated where it had been.

Cora rubbed at her face, trying to make sense of it all, and then realized there was ash on her forehead. When she checked her arms, she saw that the symbols on her skin were now mere smudges of charcoal.

Hayes was back in his trousers when he rejoined her. "I just tried the door. Everything's back to normal. Ready to go?"

Just as she was about to ask how he had found her, they both heard a groan. Someone else had survived. What was more, Cora recognized the voice.

"Freddy?" she said, and watched him crawl free of some rubble.

"Oh hell," he moaned, weaving while pulling himself up. His eyes remained dazed while his hand rubbed at the side of his head where she had clubbed him. "What happened? Did he reject you? He couldn't have. You have the sacred blood."

She scoffed. "Freddy, you louse. I can't believe you were going to sacrifice me to that... that *thing*."

As soon as the man started toward them, Hayes growled.

In response, Freddy grimaced and smoothed a hand over his disheveled hair. "Let's make this easy. Name any sum you want in return for the girl and your silence."

"Freddy, you should stop talking," murmured Cora, recognizing the kind of stare Hayes gave him.

"Sky's the limit. Whatever she's paying you, I can triple it." Then he stepped close enough to offer a handshake.

Hayes grabbed him by the front of his robes with one hand and socked him in the jaw with the other. Freddy's head snapped to the side, and he was unconscious even before Hayes let go.

"You really are something," said Cora, watching Freddy drop to the ground again. "Do wolves ever get tired?"

He returned to her, still moving too smoothly to seem human. "Sometimes, Miss Marshall. Let's get out of here before we start asking each other questions. The cops will be here any minute."

She nodded and turned with him toward the stairs, but couldn't help insisting, "Cora."

Half a beat of silence passed before he relaxed enough to smile. "Bunny."

She grinned back. She could live with that for now.

Freddy's mansion looked very different in the harsh light of police lamps. Cora watched as officers roped off the property to keep reporters from sneaking in and party guests from sneaking out. There were more inside, their flashlights sweeping through the rooms.

No one had been allowed to leave, and she could hear quite a few people who were unhappy about that, arguing with any officers they could find while trying to hide their faces from the reporters' cameras. Cora couldn't understand why they bothered; information always had a way of leaking out, and she felt sure printing presses were already stamping out shocking headlines and unsavory details for the rest of the city to read in the morning.

That fact no longer disturbed her. Frankly, she had other things on her mind, and it was quite nice to sit there in the back gardens, tucked away from all the others. An officer had given her a blanket against the crisp night air, but after that, she'd been left alone. The sweet smell of roses and the gentle light of the moon cleared her senses, and she knew there was no reason to delay things. "All right. I'm ready."

Beside her, Hayes glanced up from examining a shallow gash on his forearm. He wore only his undershirt, trousers, and shoes but didn't seem to care about his shocking state of undress. "To give a statement?"

"Oh, not that," she said, already distracted by him. He had always appeared sleek and powerful in his suit, but now he was downright virile. The breadth of his shoulders and the strong muscles in his arms and chest were apparent with the slightest movement.

With effort, she returned to her original intention. "I'm ready to eat humble pie for breaking my promise and investigating Freddy on my own. I knew better but did it anyway, just because I felt left out of things earlier today. I'm sorry."

To her surprise, he smiled a little. Despite the lingering wildness in his eyes, he didn't seem nearly as remote as he had in his office. "And I knew better than to pick a fight with a bunch of wolves itching to kill us both, or to get blackout drunk right after. Seems like I'm ahead in the mistakes department."

Relief rushed through her. "I could try to make it even."

When he just shook his head, she added, "I really thought you were going to lay into me."

"Can't say I see the point. You've already told me why and apologized." His focus returned to his injury, and he licked it clean before adding, "I'm not saying I'll keep quiet if you do it again, but... Jane knows how to provoke people. She prides herself on it."

Then he began bandaging the wound without any sign of pain. The muscles in his arms flexed while he worked.

Cora decided there was no way she could pretend disinterest. "When did that happen?"

"I broke through a window to get in."

She moved closer, noticing a faint line near it—a similar cut long healed. "For such a smooth-talking fella, you sure have a lot of scars."

As he tied off the bandage, she saw a much nastier one beneath his collar bone, its shape suggesting a knife blade that had gone in deep. The teasing left her voice. "That one could have killed you."

Unthinkingly, she reached out. He didn't move away when her fingers gently brushed the scar, or when she said, "Hayes, what happened?"

For a moment, she thought he wouldn't answer. He looked at the officers milling around the heavy bulk of Freddy's mansion, at the distant chaos of headlights in the front driveway, and finally at the stars glimmering beyond as if debating with himself. When he spoke, though, there was no hesitation to the words. "After I left the pack, I worked as a pit fighter."

"You... you what?" she stammered, aghast. "But that's *awful*."

His careful expression warmed into amusement. "So, you've seen pit fights."

"Not willingly. George DeHart dragged me to one."

"George DeHart? The famous actor?"

Cora huffed. "Believe me, he only shines onstage. He's a hopeless gambler, and the one night we spent together was nothing but him indulging in every bad habit he could think of. Our last stop was some seedy club that had its own underground arena for fights, and he bet on one. Both men survived, but I've heard that some of those fights won't end until there's a death."

Then she shivered, trying not to imagine Hayes' lifeless body against a grimy floor.

Her hands picked at a frayed edge of the blanket until he caught them with one of his own. "Don't worry about it, Bunny. I went in knowing what to expect. It's dangerous, but it makes better money than a factory and is one of the few jobs in the city where wolves are in high demand. We heal fast and we'll fight anything."

The words soothed her as much as the heat of his fingers. "No wonder you knew what to do with that tentacle creature. But why didn't you tell the police you'd seen things like it before?"

She received an answer, but not from Hayes.

"Because, Miss Marshall, pit fighting is illegal." Captain Dempsey waited a few feet away, having slipped up unnoticed. Even with the brim of his hat tilted over one eye, he looked exhausted, and his trench coat was smudged with ash. "I'm sure he had no idea until well after he'd left for a better job."

"None at all," said Hayes, unfazed by the man's appearance. He gave Cora's hands a gentle squeeze before resuming checking his own for injuries. "Especially since I'd seen some of the police commissioner's closest friends in the audience."

Dempsey cracked a grin. "Don't say that too loudly. He might show up tonight. This one's big."

"Arrests?"

"Mm-hm. Lots of people have done bad things."

Cora gasped. "You can't put any blame on Hayes. He was rescuing me. And Freddy's lying if he's saying Hayes attacked him. *I* was the one who knocked him out."

"Oh yeah? Did you also break his jaw in two different places?" Then the police captain shook his head. "Don't make a fuss. I didn't

mean you two, although it's true Davenport is already talking. I have to say, Sam, it would be nice if we could understand him a little better."

"He can still write." Hayes sounded amazingly calm, but when a stray flashlight beam passed over him, his eyes glowed just like a wolf's. He flexed his fingers, still studying his knuckles, and then bit at one to pull out something embedded in the skin. He turned and spat it out.

"Was that a tooth?" said Cora, watching him.

The police captain's sigh was answer enough. "Just tell me what happened."

Cora tried her best to keep things short and to the point. Dempsey wrote it all down without comment, but once she finished, he said, "You got lucky. You not only survived but broke your case wide open. Davenport's confessing to everything."

"What?" she said. Out of the corner of her eye, she saw Hayes look up, fully alert.

"He wanted Isaac Marshall out of the way to make sure he could use you for this ritual. He's already fingering people connected to the cult, including the black market thaumaturgist he used."

"Harold Beaumont?" said Hayes.

Dempsey nodded. "He admitted to burning down Beaumont's place to cover things up, and another place in Ragbag Way before that. It was a—"

"Tattoo parlor."

"I don't understand any of this," said Cora, glancing between them. "You're talking like it's all wrapped up, but I hardly even know what happened."

Hayes glanced at her, but it was the police captain who answered. "Davenport's followers are humans who modified their appearance with bio-thaumaturgy. It's a common activity with cultists who want to look more like their gods. Harold Beaumont is the thaumaturgist Davenport hired for all the cult work... and for transforming Tierney."

The answer only further confused her. "Those people looked nothing like the drawings of Tierney. And he changed back afterward. They didn't. I saw the bodies as we left the room."

Dempsey shrugged. "It was mere cosmetic work for the cultists. Your father's driver had to be an assassin without realizing it. They infected him by bribing a tattoo artist who was working on him."

Cora looked back at Hayes, wanting to see his reaction to these revelations. "You're not surprised at all. Did you already know about this?"

His voice remained low and even. "I knew the pieces and saw a way they could fit, but that's not the same as a confession."

"Well... what did he do to my father? The body wasn't found."

"Might be some time before it is. You mentioned he had your uncle squirreled away."

"Yes." She shuddered to think of it, relaxing only when Hayes ran a comforting hand along her shoulder.

Dempsey noticed her shiver as well. "Don't worry about it, Miss Marshall. He's not getting free. Even if your father remains missing, there are plenty of other murders to charge him with, and all the evidence is overwhelming."

"Then he did this quite often?"

"You were in just one of his secret rooms." The police captain turned slightly and pointed at a clump of bushes near the side of the

mansion. There was an officer hunched there, sweaty-faced and shaking. "See Robinson there? He was the first one to find the underground levels and what was in them. He's been puking his guts out since. We've found years' worth of missing people."

"My God." Cora covered her mouth with a shaking hand. "I mean, he seemed raving mad just now, but I never thought..."

"Obviously not, since you walked right in there with him," said Dempsey, voice dry.

Her mind couldn't stop spinning, but at last she said, "Well, it's all over, isn't it? I'm free to go home."

Dempsey scoffed. "Over? Things are just beginning."

Then the sound of an argument grew clear. Two figures approached. One was Jane Feral, eyes glowing in the dark like Hayes' while she carried a heavy leather bag. As she walked, she paid attention to everything except the man beside her, a thin, sour-looking police enchanter.

It was his voice that really carried. "You can't come any closer, I tell you. The girl may be contaminated."

"Then why is the police captain and my office partner already here? And I wouldn't try holding me back. These leathers are designed to nullify all magic. I'll spark out your tools."

The enchanter sighed and turned his attention to Dempsey. "Captain, I tried."

"It's all right, Byrd. I know how persuasive she can be. Miss Feral, delighted to see you again. What the hell do you want?"

"Nothing to do with you. I had a brief, confusing call from my office partner to get here as fast as possible with my tools." Then Jane's gaze jumped to Hayes, and she arched her eyebrows. "What'd you do, you idiot?"

"Jane." His tone was deathly serious. He said nothing else but cast a significant glance at Cora, who was already bristling for his sake.

The she-wolf's gaze followed his, settling on Cora's forehead. All the humor drained from her expression.

Something wordless passed between her and Hayes before he rose to his feet and stepped toward Dempsey and the enchanter. "Captain. A word?"

Cora craned her neck, wanting to catch their conversation, but just then Jane moved in front of her and opened her leather bag. "Finding it difficult to take your eyes off him?"

"Oh, I..."

"Don't bother struggling for an answer. I already know it. The symbol on your head is the truly interesting thing." The she-wolf sketched it in a small notebook and then pulled on some gloves. "Did it smell like blood when he painted it on?"

"Yes. How did you...?"

"Humans pretend they're experts in everything, including the arcane. In truth, wolves first dabbled with the occult, and we remember a lot more than they've ever discovered. May I?" Then Jane touched the remains of the symbol and drew back to rub the ash between her fingers, studying it intently. "The rest can be washed off whenever you have the chance, but this one needs to be erased immediately. It's a guiding mark that any of the outer chaos gods would recognize."

"Is that what that... thing was? A god?"

"Not quite." The she-wolf pulled out a vial of clear liquid. "Now don't move."

Cora had never been good at sitting still, and fidgeted with the folds of her blanket while Jane dampened a cloth and carefully rubbed at her forehead. It felt like alcohol but without the burn.

She didn't expect Jane to talk while working, but to her surprise, the she-wolf spoke after a few moments of silence. "So, how many people did you shoot this time?"

Cora took the question at face value in an attempt to remain polite. "I don't remember. Much of it already seems like a blur. We used most of the shells on the creature."

"I'm surprised Sam hit it at all. These days, he takes most of his shots on a billiards table."

At that, Cora flushed. "He didn't miss once. He also tore it to pieces all by himself, even though it was larger than a car."

Jane's only response was to grin and say, "All finished. Use soap and hot water to take off the rest."

When she pulled the cloth away, Cora saw that the ash had bubbled into something dark and sticky, reforming the symbol on the fabric. Just as she winced in disgust, the enchanter's voice rose. "What are you doing?"

Jane didn't react beyond sealing the cloth in a glass jar, and she remained beside Cora as the other three rejoined them. "Getting a few answers from Miss Marshall."

"That was evidence of an illegal summoning," said the enchanter, glaring. "Tampering with it is cause for arrest."

Cora had seen plenty of men throw tantrums and had no interest in watching another one. Instead, she tried to catch Hayes' attention, hoping for a hint of what he'd spoken about with the police captain.

Just as he winked at her, Jane held up the glass jar. "Let's not be petty. I haven't destroyed anything. I merely transferred it from her skin to keep her safe."

The enchanter took it with a sullen mutter.

Dempsey had watched in silence, occasionally flicking ash from his cigarette, but now he studied the symbol on the cloth and said, "Is that what drew the god through the portal?"

The enchanter sniffed. "It wasn't a god. It was an avatar of a god. It's a notable difference. In this dimension, it's only flesh, yet it can affect others. Frederick Davenport was lucky to be unconscious when the portal opened to let it through. The other cultists weren't and went irreversibly insane. What I'm concerned about is how this girl had the same experience and yet remained rational."

When Cora realized he meant her, she smiled vaguely, distracted by the awareness of Hayes replacing Jane's spot next to her. "I've always been lucky."

"Lucky? To witness another dimension?" The man stared at her. "There are people who have studied the possibilities their entire lives in the hopes of catching even one glimpse."

"Frankly, it wasn't all that grand. That pulpy, tentacle creature was awful and I've never seen anything like it, but the portal itself was just a lot of blackness. And flutes. I remember hearing flautists. They weren't very good. They couldn't keep a tune at all."

"Couldn't keep a—" Now the enchanter sputtered. "Do you even know what you were part of?"

The police captain cut him off. "Let's get to the point. Does she need any diagnostic spells performed on her?"

Cora didn't like the sound of that, and liked the enchanter's answer even less. "Of course. She could be contaminated. We can't

trust her word in the face of a situation that all but melted the minds of the other witnesses."

The back of her head started throbbing, and she realized the sigil might be discovered if she agreed to it. More than that, it still had enough control to keep her from doing so. She breathed deeply, trying to keep calm despite the sharp pain that wouldn't fade until the sigil was safe. "I don't see how that's necessary. The creature never even touched me. It ate a statue by mistake. I still can't believe Freddy was going to feed me to that thing."

"That wasn't what it was doing," said the enchanter, darkly.

"It swallowed the statue whole. I saw it."

"Yes, but it wasn't feeding. It was an avatar of a very particular type, and its purpose wasn't to commit carnage."

Cora frowned, hurting too much to make out the implications, but a flicker in the police captain's eyes suggested he'd understood just fine. Then he cleared his throat. "Believe me, Miss Marshall, it'd be better for you this way."

The pain in her head sharpened into something blinding, and she knew her voice sounded higher than normal as she said, "I'd really rather not do this."

"No one can force you to." The sound of Hayes' voice cut through some of the agony, and so did the warmth of his hand lightly catching her arm. She looked up at him in a silent plea, hoping he would see the struggle in her eyes.

His own brightened in response before he glanced over at Dempsey. "What are the other options?"

The police captain sighed and turned to the enchanter.

"There aren't any."

"That's a lie," said Jane. "Unless a master enchanter somehow doesn't know that extradimensional contamination quickly presents itself. Usually within the day."

"Yet also up to three weeks," snapped the enchanter. "She'd have to remain isolated from others for that long. *Freelance* thaumaturgists can take risks, but registered enchanters have to follow the rules."

Jane smiled, showing all her teeth. "It's not a risk, it's a formality. Sam and I would smell the change in her scent if she'd been implanted with something. She's clean."

Cora was beginning to feel nauseous from the pain. "If there's going to be this much fuss, then I'll simply lock myself in my bedroom. The servants can leave me food at the door."

"No good," said Dempsey. "We'll have to search every inch of that house."

Her voice rose. "Again?"

He shrugged. "You were part of this rite. Hell, you were its star. No one's saying you wanted to be, but there might be important evidence of Davenport or one of the others setting you up."

It was getting harder to think, as if the sigil sensed she was losing the argument. "All right, then I'll stay at Vi's house. Violet Granbury. She's my best friend."

There was a sudden silence.

Then Hayes moved closer to her and murmured, "Miss Marshall..."

With that return to formality, she knew his next words would hurt no matter how gently he spoke them. Her breath hitched as she stared into his eyes, their gold heavy with a terrible sympathy.

"Miss Granbury was in on this. She was part of the cult and knew what would happen."

"No." Cora almost laughed. "No, that's ridiculous." Then she looked at each of their faces, and her voice thinned to nothing.

"She left a note confessing her involvement," said Dempsey. When Cora flinched, he almost looked sorry for it, and his usual sarcasm was absent. "I'm sorry, Miss Marshall. She set you up and then took her life."

Cora released a trembling breath, sure she was about to shatter into pieces. "How could she?"

Dimly, she was aware of Hayes moving close enough to hold her, and of tears burning hot against her cheeks. The whole world had blurred over. His voice rumbled against her ear, hard in a way that warned off any further arguments. "I'm taking her back to my place. You know where it is, Captain. Any questions?"

"No." The police captain still sounded grim. "Get her out of here."

The sigil's agony eased by the second as he guided her away, but the hurt in her heart remained. "Thank you," she managed, unable to say anything else.

He pulled her a little closer, chasing away the chill of the night. "It'll be all right."

All she could think of was Violet's bright, sharp smile. "Right now, it doesn't feel like it."

"I know, Bunny. But it will."

CHAPTER FOURTEEN

Cora had to admit that solving the case wasn't nearly as satisfying as she had imagined. In fact, as her reflection in the mirror proved, it was downright awful.

The thin light of the nearing dawn emphasized her red-rimmed eyes and the dried mascara trailing along her cheeks. Her complexion looked both blotchy and washed out, and even her hair had frizzed out of its usual finger waves. She was certainly glad that the drive back from Freddy's had happened while it was still dark, and that Hayes had simply shown her to a bedroom and told her to take as much rest as she wanted.

Her sleep had been fitful, as if her brain was too full to fall quiet. Now she sat on the upholstered bench placed at the foot of the bed, staring out the window at a nearby pond. It was a lovely view, but she hardly even saw it. Freddy, a demented cult leader who sacrificed people. Violet, involved in it all and still so cool and calm about sending her right into the thick of things.

In a way, it did make a terrible sense. Freddy simply wasn't smart enough to keep such an illicit existence secret. He had always displayed his follies with a smile, depending upon his charm and family name to carry him along without consequence. Yet Violet... yes, she was shrewd and tactical in every way. She enjoyed playing with people's expectations, and always claimed she loved enemies more than friends because it was more fun using them. Apparently, that sentiment hadn't been the world-weary mask all Crescent City socialites loved to wear but instead cold, plain fact.

Cora felt her lower lip tremble and quickly dashed the thought from her mind. She was sick of crying, and it wasn't helping her feel better in any way. Good things had to have come out of the night before. She just needed to think them through.

People would finally stop accusing her of her father's murder. All the reporters and newspapers now had plenty of other figures from high society to chase after. And perhaps she was to remain in isolation for no good reason, but the time would be spent with Hayes.

This final realization was enough to chase off some of her gloom. It also stoked an inclination to explore what she had been too distraught to take in before. She'd never been in a lone wolf's home. He certainly had masculine tastes when it came to the bedroom, which had mahogany furniture that looked very stark against the cream walls. The closet was small and empty, so she wrapped herself up in the ratty police blanket and moved for the door.

There was a note taped there, written in Hayes' sharp, bold hand:

I went out to get a few things. Look around wherever you want and use whatever you need. I'll be back soon.

She took him at his word, searching through the rooms for any hints of his life beyond being a detective. They were few and far between in the small parlor, which was devoid of personal touch, and the kitchen, which looked like no one ever cooked in it.

Just as she peeked into the main bedroom, keys jingled in the front door's lock. Her heart leapt into her throat until it opened and revealed who was there.

Jane Feral raised her eyebrows while dragging Cora's entire overseas luggage over the threshold. "Don't look so disappointed. I just came back from your house. I asked the servants what you'd need for a few days and they packed all of these. Half feel like they weigh more than I do."

Cora tried to regain her composure. "Thank you. That's very kind."

"It was Sam's idea, not mine. The police have finished searching your house, so if there's something missing, blame them." Jane released her grip on the handles to reach for a bundle of papers tucked beneath one arm. "I also grabbed the morning mail and whatever else was waiting on your study desk."

Cora could only thank her again, adding, "I really do appreciate it. It's a lot of trouble to go through, whether it was your idea or not."

The she-wolf glanced around the small hallway, taking it in as carefully as Cora had. "I have to say, Miss Marshall, you're resilient if nothing else. Most people wouldn't have faced last night and come out still willing to see the best in others."

When Jane walked past her, Cora followed. "To be honest, most of it already feels like a blur. And I really don't understand why I have to be isolated at all."

"Do you understand *anything* that happened last night?"

Cora thought for a moment. "Hayes has incredible stamina. He didn't slow down once while tearing up that repulsive creature, and then right afterwards he knocked out Freddy like it was nothing. I had to use an iron candlestick to do the same thing."

Jane stared at her for a moment, as if she wasn't sure whether Cora was serious. "We're wolves. It's normal for us. Let's put that aside for now. Freddy Davenport is the leader of the cult your uncle started. Last night, he summoned an avatar of their god. You already seem confused. Is it about the avatar? Think of it as a physical manifestation of the god. Something that is living flesh able to interact with our world."

"It looked more like a clumsy blob made of tentacles to me," said Cora, unable to keep the doubt from her voice.

"It still successfully came through the portal. That fulfilled half of the conditions needed to bring about the actual rebirth of the god into this world. The other was you."

At that, Jane paused and looked at her expectantly, obviously waiting for her to put two and two together and voice the answer.

Cora felt like a child facing her stern governess once more. "Because I'm related by blood to Uncle Alfie?"

"That's why they thought you were the best option, but in truth, any woman with a working uterus would have been fine."

"With a..." Then Cora's voice rose into a shriek. "You—you mean that thing was going to impregnate me?"

"Now you're on the trolley," said Jane, sounding satisfied. "It took you long enough."

"My God. I should've hit Freddy a few more times for good measure. Would I have even survived giving birth?"

"You saw the father. What do you think?" When Cora only shuddered, Jane added, "Maybe I should have waited to shock you. You don't look too good. Have you had anything to eat or drink?"

"Not since yesterday morning." So much had happened since then that there hadn't been any time to think of food, let alone sit down and eat some.

"There won't be much to choose from." Jane headed for the kitchen, obviously aware of where to find it. "Sam's idea of a meal is frying hot dogs in whiskey and ketchup, and that's when he bothers keeping anything here. That's why he's gone out, to get the basic goods needed in a functioning life now that he has a guest."

With everything else still spinning in her mind, Cora decided to ask the impertinent question that had lived in her heart since she'd met the she-wolf. "Why do you always seem so pleased with me and yet so hard on him? My past experiences have been quite the opposite when it comes to meeting another woman in a man's life."

There wasn't an immediate answer. Jane found a tin of coffee in one of the cabinets and checked it, taking much longer than needed to see it was empty. Her eyes were a pure yellow, harsher than Hayes' gold as if warning others about her sharper nature, but right then they looked muted with old grief. "Because I want him to be happy. Orphans are common in wolf packs and are raised together. That's the closeness you sense between us. We're like brother and sister. He's the only family I've ever had."

Cora nodded, feeling her reserve thaw into hot sympathy. "I'm sorry. My mother died in childbirth. You wouldn't think you could miss someone you never knew, but you do, don't you? Every day."

The she-wolf took her in with her full stare. "You're truly genuine, aren't you? Want to know the most tiring thing about

living among humans? It's smelling the lies beneath their false little words and trying to act like I haven't noticed. If a wolf pack survives on loyalty, then human society runs on deception of all shapes and sizes. A constant stream of self-delusion to keep away the crippling fear of being prey."

"I suppose none of us realize how well a wolf can smell."

"No, or think through what that means. For example, it's easy to track exactly where someone's been." Then Jane cast a significant glance toward the main bedroom.

"Oh. Then he'll know that I..."

The she-wolf nodded, her gaze now glimmering with amusement. Before Cora could do more than flush, she added, "I suppose you've been embarrassed enough in the last twenty-four hours. Come on. I'll show you everything and then he'll think it was my idea."

"Oh, well..."

"It's not far from the truth. It's been some time since I've visited. I want to see how badly he's been doing at having a life outside of work."

It was hard for Cora to contain her curiosity as Jane turned on the lamps inside the bedroom. It was as clean and well-kept as the guest bedroom, with similar furniture. As Jane prowled around, shaking her head every now and then, Cora drifted over to the dresser, which had a few books on it. They were the type of dusty tomes that her father kept in his study, but when she picked one up and opened it, she found the middle of the pages had all been cut out to hide a red rectangular case.

"Oh," said Cora in shock, well-used to the sight of morphine kits. She knew if she opened it up, she'd find a syringe, hypodermic needles, and vials waiting to be injected.

Jane came over. "Repurposed for anti-silver. He always keeps some within easy reach."

As she put the book back, Jane opened the first set of drawers and pulled out lumpy, grey fabric still cradled in the brown paper it had been mailed in. The address was in shaky, old-fashioned handwriting. "Looks like Minnie made him some more socks. She was our first landlady after we left the pack, and I know Sam still visits her regularly. Her late husband had been a wolf, so she was much kinder to us than most humans."

"I suppose we shouldn't be doing this," murmured Cora, torn between the guilt of rummaging through Hayes' personal things like a cat burglar and the excitement of learning things about him.

"Do you think he didn't study *you* just as carefully?" Jane moved on to the wardrobe, which was the same mahogany as the rest of the furniture. A few suitcases were stacked on top of it, but the she-wolf ignored those, instead opening its doors.

Cora studied suits hanging from their hangers on the right side before Jane exclaimed and reached for one of the shelves on the left. "Looks like he added to his collection."

She pulled out a jar half-full of bullets. They were misshapen, as if they'd already been used. A few had the heavy gleam of silver.

Shock ran through Cora once more. "He's been shot that many times?"

"To be fair, some of these were from back when he was a pit fighter."

Cora glanced over the neatly arranged clothing, troubled by what they hadn't found as much as what they had. She was beginning to understand Jane's point; there wasn't a hint of Hayes beyond his work life. She'd known plenty of men who had been utterly obsessed with their career, but they still had family mementos, or a silly hobby like collecting stamps, or even just a fish tank to look after.

Then her eyes caught the wink of gold between two folded shirts. Without thinking, her fingers brushed it and then plucked it free.

It was a pocket picture frame, the type that hinged shut to the size of a cigarette case. One side was empty, but the other held a photo of Jane and Hayes, both years younger and wearing dark uniforms. Jane looked as serious as ever, but Hayes... Hayes was *smiling*, a big, boyish grin that looked at odds with his formal appearance.

"This photo..." she murmured, unable to take her eyes off it.

Jane leaned in as well. "Ah. One of the few signs that I have any sentimental feelings. That was the day we both began training for our professional places within our former pack. Inspector and researcher, respectively."

"He seems so happy."

"He was, yes."

When the she-wolf offered nothing else, Cora turned to her. "What happened? Why did he leave the Saxbys? I can't believe he did anything bad. I just can't."

The she-wolf studied her intently, expression inscrutable. "A pack's definition of 'bad' is different from a human's. The truth is, we both fled at the same time for the same reason, but it was worse for him than for me. He'll tell you when he's ready."

Then Jane took the frame back from Cora, returned it to its place, and closed the wardrobe's doors. "Speaking of, he's likely to return soon. If you need anything else, ask him. I've been up for thirty-two hours and need some sleep."

"Thank you. Really."

The she-wolf just nodded and moved for the front door, but her voice drifted back to Cora. "He's starting to remember happiness again, you know. I can smell it. It's whenever he looks at you."

Before Cora could say anything, the front door opened and closed, leaving her alone. She could feel herself smiling, *really* smiling, at least until she unconsciously turned toward the wardrobe —and its mirror. She no longer had the haze of shock to soften the blow, and let out a gasp at her sorry state. "He certainly wouldn't if he saw me like this."

She unpacked her suitcases long enough to find her toiletries and a silk robe. The bathroom was as modern and neat as everything else in the apartment, but she barely noticed it while scrubbing herself clean until her skin stung. Then she drained the tub and refilled it with steaming hot water, intending to soak.

Jane's guess proved true; Cora barely had time to sink in with a sigh before she heard the sharp click of the front door's lock once more. Anticipation left her breathless as she settled into a pose that didn't show any more skin than one of her dresses—yet. Then she used a sponge to pour water over herself, raising her voice above the splash. "Hayes?"

"Miss Marshall." Despite the long night and early hours, his voice sounded clear and alert. "Already awake?"

"Yes. I've always been an early riser. Come right in."

"It sounds like you're taking a bath."

"The tub's walls are very high. Believe me, I'm more decent now than I was last night, and you didn't seem to mind then." Cora casually scrubbed at one forearm with the sponge, and made sure she was still in that position when he appeared in view.

Frustratingly, he still wore his hat, tipping it to block even a sideways glance her way. "Those were unusual circumstances."

For a disappointing moment, she thought he was about to leave. Instead, he shifted enough to lean against the doorway. Settling in. "I can smell that Jane's been here. She didn't press you too hard on anything, did she?"

Cora smiled at the protective undertone to his words. "Not at all. She was very nice. I finally understand why I have to be isolated, although I have to disagree that I'm in any danger. That thing never even touched me."

"It's just common protocol for the city. People get nervous when transdimensional beings rip the fabric of reality. They want to make sure nothing's left behind except some oozing remains. It's why the surviving cultists are being isolated as well, even though the creature wasn't after them."

"Hmm." Cora lathered up her other arm, making sure the water splashed invitingly. "Does that include Freddy?"

"Sure does. He can't buy his way out of this one. The city needs to make an example of the wealthy not being above the law."

"And since *I* turned out to be innocent, they'll use Freddy instead." Her gaze dropped to the sponge in her hand, all thoughts of coaxing over Hayes' eyes abruptly gone.

His voice grew gentle. "It's all right to feel conflicted about it. It's hard to get rid of what you felt for someone, even after knowing the horrible things they did."

"Oh..." She looked up again. "If he appeared before me at this very moment, I'd just slap him silly. It's more that... it's very strange to think of how I missed him and all the rest throughout the year my father controlled me. Yet as soon as I came back, this happened."

Then she squeezed fresh water over her face. "But I refuse to keep crying about it. My cheeks are puffy enough already."

At that, he straightened up from the doorway, not quite turning in her direction. "Miss Marshall, you're the most beautiful girl in the city. I said it when we first met, and it's just as true now."

Oh, she had it bad. Plenty of men had said such things to her, but her heart had never melted like now. It took all her control to remain merely playful. "I thought we'd moved on to 'Bunny.'"

She caught a hint of his smile before he stepped inside, still using his hat to block his view. To her surprise, he then sat next to the tub with his back to her but angled enough to keep their faces close. Most men would have looked uncomfortable or downright silly sitting on the floor in their fine suits. Not him. He looked even more handsome and rugged, and also seemed perfectly at ease, as if he could lunge up in a moment with the same swiftness he had shown as a wolf. With a sigh, he said, "Let's wait until you're back in clothes."

"Still insisting on boundaries?" she teased, pretending nonchalance while lifting one leg under the guise of washing her foot.

"Still needing them. Now more than ever." He turned just enough to look into her eyes. In the early sunlight, his were a bright gold. "You must know how you affect me."

At first, she couldn't believe he'd broached the subject. "Well, I wasn't completely sure. There are lots of reasons why a fella might

insist on staying proper. And I'm not very experienced with facing indifference. Usually, I stoke just the opposite reaction."

He laughed a little. "I can believe that. But despite what the pictures and plays say, private detectives stay professional with their clients."

Both legs back in the water, she shifted enough to really face him. Even with what Jane had told her about wolves easily sniffing out the hidden parts of a human heart, she didn't feel an inch of embarrassment or shame. "Am I still your client, though? Last night, everyone seemed very sure that it's all wrapped up."

"Freddy finished confessing while you slept. Apparently, the year you were close to your father's side and out of reach is what pushed him to pay the thaumaturgist he used for cult work to concoct something to transform Tierney. He didn't want to wait any longer."

"I still don't understand why Freddy would do it that way. It seems so risky and complicated compared to... well, I don't know. A bomb, like police initially thought."

Hayes nodded shortly, and she had the feeling he wasn't quite satisfied, either. "He said it was the best way to get close to your father without somehow harming you. The transformation was triggered by the full moon, so he used his connections to make sure your father would be traveling at the time. He also admitted to hiring thugs to kill the two lovebirds we interviewed. He was scared that whatever they witnessed might hold enough clues to link back to Tierney and then him. He didn't realize the body had survived. It wasn't supposed to."

"That does match with the hint Roy gave me. Remember? He said a human had ordered the hit." Cora squeezed more water over herself, but absently. "Then it's all over? The case is really closed?"

The amusement returned to Hayes' expression. "Not for Captain Dempsey. The Saxbys will want their pound of flesh from good old Freddy. And even with his confession, the police will need to comb through all his property and connections to build *their* case. The trial will be its own circus. Our case, though... yes, Freddy's confession has solved it. I'd feel better if I could interview Davenport myself, but it's unlikely to happen. His lawyers arrived this morning."

"Then... then I just have to wait through this silly isolation and I'll have my life back." She could hardly believe it. Her entire body felt like it was glowing from the mere thought.

She looked at Hayes with a shining smile. He still seemed calm and amused, but there was a heaviness to the gold of his eyes that surprised her. He almost looked sorry that it *would* be over. Before she could ask what was wrong, he said, "What's the first thing you're going to do when you're back home?"

"Oh, I'm not even thinking about that. It's dizzying enough just feeling the weight off me. Besides..." She paused to run the sponge along her collar bones. The water trailed down, and she was gratified to see his gaze almost follow it. "It'll be just as much fun staying here until that police enchanter is convinced I'm safe. But... Hayes? *Am* I still your client?"

He nodded. "I said our case was solved, not closed. The police weren't the only ones after you. I want to make sure the Saxbys are also satisfied with Freddy Davenport confessing to everything."

Cora sighed. "Drat. I suppose that's very sensible, and sense is something I've never had. Although I can't promise to stop tempting the unprofessional side of you."

He was smiling again, if wryly. "It's all right. I'll enjoy it."

Then he rose to his feet, looking toward the doorway again. "Want some coffee?"

"I'd love some."

"It'll be in the kitchen whenever you're ready."

"What about you?"

"I'll be in there with my own cup. I need to finish going through the transcript of Davenport's confession."

Strange, how the idea of them quietly reading together delighted her as much as if he *had* pulled her out of the tub and taken her right into the bedroom. She tossed aside the sponge with a sigh, sure that the day ahead would make up for her lousy night. "I'll be right out."

CHAPTER FIFTEEN

Captain Albert Dempsey couldn't remember the last time he felt this relieved over a case wrapping up. The sun had been shining for over an hour and he was still in the ritual room of Freddy Davenport's "mansion of madness," as people were already calling it. He had seen too much to feel sick by what his men were turning up, but he was tired. Exhausted, in fact, but word had come in that the police commissioner himself was about to appear. Al knew he'd demand answers, especially the ones they didn't yet have.

At least the bastard couldn't protect his friends this time. The city was ready to boil over, and the commissioner was the type of man to save his neck over another's. Davenport and his cultists would be hanged as proof that the rich and powerful also faced consequences for breaking the law. Al hoped the common man savored it, because it wouldn't happen again anytime soon.

Just as he lit a fresh cigarette, the commissioner's voice echoed from the stairway. Everyone else in the room immediately straightened his uniform and posture, trying to look as crisp as possible. Even the enchanters, normally so intent on their work that they wouldn't respond to a question shouted in their faces, paused to make sure their bandoliers hadn't slipped out of position. Al remained as he was, aware that nothing would save him from looking like a wrinkled mess.

Lights had been brought in, exposing every inch of the room, and all eyes were on the commissioner by the time he reached the final step, already frowning at the crumpled white dress and shotgun shells near the tips of his polished shoes. "We haven't started bagging evidence?"

Commissioner Keene had a politician's voice, big and booming. He didn't speak so much as punch holes in the air. In appearance, he was just as intimidating, short but thick in the neck and chest, and with a face built to scowl. His waxed mustache gleamed as brightly as the gold buttons of his uniform, and right then it bristled as he spoke against the resounding silence to his first question. "Well?"

Al kept quiet, knowing Master Enchanter Byrd would have to explain.

The enchanter rose from the dead cultist he had been examining. "Commissioner, we weren't yet expecting you, and our analyses are still—"

"Shut up. I don't need the details. Tell them to Johnson." The commissioner gestured at the man who had arrived with him, a young, neatly dressed fella who looked nervously at the body near Byrd.

Al couldn't blame him. The commissioner's assistants always suffered bizarre and untimely deaths. One had died from fireworks that exploded too early during the city's anniversary gala. Another from being kicked by a police horse during a parade. The latest had

choked on his damn sandwich. City enchanters constantly tested for signs of a clever curse but never found anything. The only certain fact was that being Keene's assistant was an unusually dangerous position.

When Johnson was drawn away by the enchanter, Commissioner Keene turned his frown on the nearest officer. At that, Al decided his men had already had a rough enough time and walked over to join them. "Morning, Keene. Breaking in a new one?"

"Don't waste my time, Captain. What the hell is going on? Last night, I was told this was just another playboy taking things too far with his coked-out sex cult. Now the mayor is not only getting calls from every high-powered lawyer seething over his clients being put into cells like common criminals, but the Saxby Pack is demanding at least three people who were involved."

Al glanced around the destroyed room and the many bodies it held, wondering if the commissioner was that oblivious to what he stood among. "The playboy was Frederick Davenport, and his cult worshipped an ancient god that could end this world if roused."

"Freddy Davenport has long been known for his debauched ways, and there are ten other cults in this city with the same goal."

"Yeah, well, he brought something through." Then Al pointed at the broken archway. The sigils were clearly visible even through the dust and scorch marks. When the commissioner paled, he added, "Every elite name is attached in some way, including Cora Marshall's."

Keene's expression changed yet again. "How was she involved?"

Just as Al was about to answer, movement flickered from the corner of his eye. Nothing more than a figure stepping around a fallen column, but still concerning. He knew every cop and

enchanter in the room, right down to the way they walked. This was a stranger. If a damn reporter had somehow snuck in...

He breathed out a lungful of smoke to cover his slight glance over. Then he bit back another breath, this one a sigh. It was Jane Feral, cool and collected as if she had every right to be there. He let it go for the moment and refocused on Keene. "They were trying to have their god reborn into this world. She was chosen to carry it."

The commissioner swore. "This is a nightmare. Was she implanted?"

"No. Our enchanters cleared her half an hour ago. They've mapped all the residue left in the room. *That* kind wasn't present. She's safe and out of this investigation."

"Tell that to the Saxbys. They want her, Davenport, and a man named Harold Beaumont."

"He's a black market thaumaturgist." Then Al spent the rest of his cigarette explaining how it all connected back to the Isaac Marshall case. He stayed put while speaking, aware of the enchanters' need for concentration.

The commissioner, however, moved among the various bodies and shattered rock, expressionless and strangely silent. His assistant followed like a dog, once flinching when a broken statue further crumbled and pelted him with chips of marble. Enchanter Byrd fidgeted whenever the two men passed by dead cultists that were surrounded by glowing wards—a sign they hadn't been checked and cleared of lingering magical effects—but didn't dare stop them.

Al waited with growing suspicion. Occasionally, he spared a glance for Jane Feral. The she-wolf made no attempt to interfere with his men, hands behind her back as she studied the bodies that were uncovered. Up to something, no doubt, and he probably

wouldn't even get a hint of what her motives were. When her gaze briefly met his, he gave her a sardonic nod and received a close-lipped grin in return.

Just then, the commissioner spoke up, now by the crushed throne near the archway. "Has Isaac Marshall been found? No? What about Harold Beaumont?"

When Al shook his head again, Keene turned to his assistant. "Johnson, give me the shorthand on the Saxby Pack."

The assistant cleared his throat. He still looked like a scared rabbit, but his words came out smooth and clear. "A long-lived dynasty that has fallen in recent years. Their king is in his twentieth year of rule, but the pack remains unstable from a broken treaty with the Sinclair Pack five years ago. Traditionally, their wealth came from gold mining, although there is some suspicion that these veins are now depleted. They are considered to be a small threat against individual humans. Desperation and weakening status among the other packs have left them with a higher than normal disregard for city policy."

Al looked over at Jane Feral again, aware that her sharp hearing would have caught the man's words. She seemed uninterested, instead speaking with one of the enchanters scraping samples from a gilded bowl that had smashed and splattered its contents.

"Did you hear him, Captain?"

Despite the impatient tone to Keene's words, Al refused to jump to attention like a schoolboy that had been caught out. For the commissioner, these were facts. For him, they were a few cold words that couldn't approach the slaughtered bodies he and his men had to bag up and take off the streets. "I'm not sure I agree about the 'small threat' part."

"You're missing the point. There are *three* parties demanding immediate answers: the public, the mayor, and this pack."

Al walked over to the commissioner, knowing the man hated being towered over. Rumor had it that he wouldn't even let his wife wear heels. A small part of his mind argued that it did no good to rile Keene up, but the rest of him realized the commissioner never came to a crime scene unless he was about to use it. Twenty-three years on the force and it still made him angry when political maneuvers nosed their way into an investigation.

He hid it from his voice as he said, "The newspapers will satisfy the public for now. We're sending every piece of information to the mayor as we learn it. That leaves the Saxbys, and we've held them off for this long."

The commissioner's frown deepened as he was forced to look up at Al. "That's no longer the goal, Captain."

Al could already guess the answer but asked anyway. "What's the new one?"

Keene pulled out a cigarette case and opened it in a silent offer. The filters had the gleam of true gold. When Al shook his head, the commissioner took one for himself. "Didn't you hear Johnson? The Saxbys are desperate enough to tip over into sheer aggression. We need to satisfy them to keep the peace."

"You're talking about handing over the three they want."

"Not all three. Just one. Davenport is out of the question. He's committed too many crimes. Harold Beaumont isn't a bad pick, but he hasn't been found."

"That leaves Cora Marshall, the only innocent person involved."

Keene scoffed. "I doubt Miss Marshall was all that innocent. It's common knowledge that she and Davenport were very close. And

for God's sake, who lets themselves be chained to an altar unless they've already agreed to be the sacrifice?"

"You've never interviewed her," said Al, unable to keep the dryness from his voice. "She's clueless as a rule."

"The Saxbys don't believe so."

Al had already smoked his cigarette to a stub but couldn't resist taking a final drag. It was better than telling the commissioner that this idea was the worst one he'd heard all week. Saying so wouldn't do any good; the mayor and several other city officials wanted the Saxby situation resolved before it riled up the other packs. If that meant giving over Miss Marshall, well... in the end, Crescent City always ate its own.

Unbidden, his gaze jumped over to Jane Feral, who had casually moved out of Keene's sight. She glared right back and then gave him a tight shake of her head.

Before Al could react, the commissioner's tone hardened. "Where's Miss Marshall now?"

"With Sam Hayes, and he's not about to hand anyone over to his former pack."

"Perhaps he can be convinced, Captain."

In other words, get a few men from the force to rough him up until he gave in—and kill him if he didn't. Al sighed, as much from sticking his neck out as for doing it for those two. "Frankly, Commissioner, even I'm not convinced. She's the only survivor of the ritual who hasn't gone insane or hidden behind a lawyer. We'll probably need to question her again. Our enchanters still aren't sure how the creature might have affected this room and the people present when it appeared."

Keene reddened, but when Al remained unflinching, the other man turned away, glaring at the nearest dead cultist. The sheet didn't quite cover the body, with a cloven hoof and a tattooed hand sticking out from the white fabric. Anger filled both the commissioner's voice and steps as he circled the glowing wards around it. "Byrd. Why isn't this room decontaminated? It should be easy enough to tell what's normal magic and what's residue from something out of a different damned dimension."

At that, Byrd hurried over, looking nearly as nervous as the commissioner's assistant as all three gathered close to converse. Al took the opportunity to walk over to Jane Feral.

She didn't even give him a chance to speak. "Don't be an idiot. It's a terrible idea and you know it."

"Morning to you as well."

"Captain," she hissed. "They'll kill her. Anyone can see she had nothing to do with this. The Saxbys only want her to soothe their pride over what happened at their meeting with the Frosthounds."

"Maybe, but it's not my idea, so yelling at me won't work."

"You're the only city official who bothers talking to lone wolves," she replied, the flash of her eyes revealing just how infuriating she found that. "Which is ridiculous, seeing as Sam and I can and have done much more for the city than any of the packs."

Al just shrugged and started to flick his cigarette away.

She stopped him. "Maybe you truly are brainless. Don't contaminate a room of unknown residue. I'm surprised they're letting you smoke in here at all."

"They said it was safe as long as I stayed away from the wards." He crushed the butt beneath his shoe instead and added, "Listen, I don't disagree with what you've said. God knows you're both pests

when you're helping out. I can't imagine what you'd be like as enemies."

"Don't patronize me. Just convince the commissioner to hold off the Saxbys."

"Miss Feral, it's not like I can change his mind with a snap of my fingers."

She grimaced and glanced past him. He didn't like the way her eyes suddenly widened, or how her expression relaxed into a nasty grin. "Perhaps it's a moot point. He's about to kill himself, anyway."

Al turned in time to catch the commissioner finishing his cigarette and letting the butt drop. It rolled through the wards unnoticed by Enchanter Byrd, who still stammered through an explanation. The moment it reached the body, it sparked unnaturally.

"Keene!" yelled Al, already reaching for his revolver.

Just as the commissioner looked over, the sheet twitched. Then it bulged.

"What the hell—" began Keene.

Tentacles exploded from the fabric, dripping slime and blood as they groped in the air. The sheet shredded, revealing flesh swelling up and out, absorbing the original body and spreading over the protective wards like pulsing tumors. Enchanter Byrd turned ashen and fumbled at his bandolier. Keene's assistant screamed.

Al called at the officers closest to the frozen commissioner, who could only stare as the tentacles loomed over him. "Pettis! Mitchell!"

His men were well-trained, reacting despite their horror to grab Keene and haul him out of reach as the first of the appendages whipped out. The air around them flared when they tried wrapping around Byrd, setting off his defensive enchantments. The smell of

scorched flesh grew suffocating as the tentacles burned and writhed, lashing out in all directions. An uninjured one caught the next closest figure—Keene's assistant. He screamed as it hauled him up into the air.

Even as Al's brain wanted to quit in shock, his instincts kicked in. He aimed and shot, severing the tentacle. A throbbing noise, less a howl than a sheer sound wave, filled the room as Johnson dropped back to the ground, his head and back taking the force of the fall. Before Al could even breathe out in relief, three more tentacles emerged from the wounded one and grabbed Johnson once more. This time, they immediately pulled him in among the masses of flesh.

"Cease fire!" said Keene, all smoothness gone from his voice as his assistant disappeared except for muffled screams. "Hold your fire or you'll hit him. Byrd, get your men in there."

More appendages slammed into nearby enchanters, flinging them at those farther away. Al felt a bead of sweat run down his neck. Goddamnit, the thing somehow *knew* who could threaten it. It was sentient.

Then the pile of flesh convulsed. The screaming stopped. With all the enchanters down, there was no way of saving Johnson, and bullets were all they had left.

"Take it down," he said, sure his men would follow his order over the commissioner's. Then he took the first shot to erase any final hesitation. Within moments, gunsmoke joined the chaos.

Their bullets peppered the creature, spraying dark slime and shooting off tentacles. It shuddered from the loss of its limbs, and for a moment Al hoped they were weakening it. Then the tumor-like

masses constricted, and a new bubble of flesh emerged into the open, bringing Johnson out with it.

Or at least, parts of Johnson. Mostly his upper face, although Al could see what looked like the poor bastard's spine pushing through the glistening surface of the shapeless mass. There was no way he could be alive, but when his eyes rolled toward the nearest officer, Al realized the damn thing wore him like a mask.

The officer screamed in response. Al knew the sound of a man ready to lose his mind, and swore under his breath when the officer stumbled backwards, dropping his gun.

The air rippled with sudden heat. Then red light shot past Al's right side, spearing the creature. Lightning crackled over every inch as it seizured. He risked glancing back and saw Jane Feral on the floor, grimacing as if she'd been thrown there. There was a weapon he'd never seen before near her, some kind of bulked-up submachine gun.

"What is that thing?" he yelled, while his men continued shooting.

"One more shot will stop it for good," she managed. "Use it."

No time for other questions. He holstered his gun and grabbed it, quickly finding the scope and trigger. He aimed just as two more officers in the creature's view dropped to their knees, both clutching at their heads.

"Not my men, you son of a bitch," he muttered, and then fired.

This time, the creature actually *boiled*, sizzling as if the light evaporated the very water from its blood. Flesh collapsed, twitching erratically. Al roared at his officers to cease fire with a voice he hadn't used since his military days. Silence fell, broken only by the drip of slime.

As the smoke thinned, Jane moved up beside him, gingerly rubbing her shoulder. "It's down. If any of your enchanters have regained consciousness, they can finish it off properly."

"You're explaining everything later," he snapped, handing the weapon back. Then he moved for the three officers that had been affected by the creature's attention.

Two already stood again, unsteady but clear-eyed. The last man, who had also been the first affected, still rocked and trembled on the floor. The enchanters who hadn't been knocked unconscious all crowded around the commissioner to make sure he was unharmed, and Al didn't bother hiding the rage from his voice. "Is Byrd still unconscious? Then I'll give the orders. Contain those goddamn remains and wipe out whatever magic is left."

He crouched before the officer, dismissing the commissioner's stutter of rage over being ignored. "Pettis. Pettis, look at me."

The man—kid, really, since he was barely twenty—stared at him without seeing. "I saw it. It went right into my mind and started showing me things. It's... it's..."

When the officer's voice grew hysterical, Al interrupted him, keeping his own calm and steady. "It's dead meat, so relax. Everything's all right."

"No, you don't understand. It knows me. It *knows*."

Al sensed what the kid was about to do and grabbed his hand before it could reach his holster. Pettis didn't fight back, instead just sweating and shaking. Probably in shock.

"Take his gun away and get him a blanket," he said to the nearest officer and then refocused on Pettis. "Listen to me. Who's talking to you right now?"

"Y-you. Captain Dempsey."

Al nodded. "That thing is gone. There's nothing else it can do. And if it tries coming back, we'll turn it into another splatter on the floor. Even gods die in this city, and anything out there is nothing compared to the shit we face every day as its sworn officers. Understand?"

The man was still shivering, but awareness had returned to his eyes. "Yes, Captain."

"Good. Now get up so the enchanters can check you over."

Al rose to his feet with the officer and let them guide him away. The kid would probably be all right. He hoped so.

"Dempsey!"

At the sound of the commissioner's voice, Al turned and found Keene right in his face. Despite everything, it was hard not to smirk at how slime stained his fine suit, or how fury strangled his next words. "Find out everything you can. *Everything*. I want Harold Beaumont and anyone else involved in this cult to be swinging by the end of the month. We're nailing every bastard to the fullest extent."

"What about the Saxbys?"

A loud squelch interrupted them, and they looked over in time to witness the mound of flesh shrink and collapse under the work of the enchanters. The mass holding what was left of Johnson popped with a final spray of slime. His face slid to the ground, staring in their direction.

The commissioner growled. "They can chew on bones for all I care. They aren't taking a single thing from us."

Watching the man stalk off almost helped against his growing headache. Almost. Al rubbed his forehead and then reached in his pocket for a fresh cigarette. Instead, his fingers found a note.

If you still want to talk (and believe me, we need to), I'll be at the Red Rose Cafe. Don't keep me waiting.

—*J. Feral*

Al was tempted to send a few officers to get her and take her to the station; the coffee was much better there. Then he sighed and found the police detective who had been assigned to the case. "Nichols. Take over. I'll be back in an hour."

The cafe was like countless others he'd been to, where the waitresses were tired and even the coffee tasted greasy. A few other patrons had the yellow eyes of wolves, but it wasn't hard to pick out Jane Feral with her red hair and thaumaturgist's leathers. She sat at a corner table by the window, ignoring the cup by her elbow in favor of reading the morning paper's headlines.

He took the opposite seat without greeting her. "It's illegal to carry weapons modified with experimental magic. I'll have to pull a few strings to keep you from being arrested, and I'm not sure I want to."

"That's gratitude for you," she said, absently. "If I hadn't been there, the commissioner's stupidity would have left at least half your men dead. Blood, gold, and fire—that's what that particular god demands as tribute, and his cigarette satisfied all three. Funny how things work out, hmm?"

Al rubbed at his eyes. They were starting to grow bleary. "Miss Feral, right now I'm a bad target for being taunted. I'm too exhausted to react to anything besides the cold, hard truth."

"What makes that the exception?"

He pointed at the coffee. "Are you going to drink that?"

When she shook her head, he took it and drained it halfway with one swallow. It was terrible enough to jolt him back into full

alertness. "Because people lie so much that it always surprises me when they're honest."

At that, she met his gaze. Wild eyes scrutinized his face with the ruthlessness of a born predator, but he suddenly had the feeling that she was unsure. Maybe even nervous. "What that assistant told you about the Saxbys... does the city know anything more than that?"

"My branch doesn't. Why?"

The she-wolf grimaced and leaned back in her seat. "Sam trusts you. I used to think he was being stupidly optimistic like always. Now, I'm not so sure."

"Do you ever give compliments, Miss Feral?"

"Have you ever met someone who really deserved one?" she shot back. As quickly as she bristled, she settled down again. "All I meant is that your loyalty obviously lies with the city. Or at least, that's what I believed. But I could smell your contempt for the commissioner, and your fear for your men. You really think they're more than just living bodies to command."

"Don't get too soft toward me. I'm still a corrupt official willing to pull strings as needed."

"Yes, but not always for yourself. I'm willing to gamble on that." She stared at her folded hands for a moment. He didn't miss how her knuckles had gone white with tension, but her voice sounded as crisp as ever as she added, "Wolves know loyalty and all it can hide. Humans aren't the only ones who can keep secrets... or find themselves in a position to reveal some.

"What the late, lamented Johnson said about the Saxbys was true enough, but there are details you should know about that broken treaty. The youngest Saxby princess was supposed to be married to one of the Sinclair princes. It came out too late that the prince was

deranged, violently so. He killed her. Both packs went to war, but the Saxby king also blamed his advisors for not finding out the prince's true nature beforehand. He ordered them to be executed."

Al raised his eyebrows. "Is this why both you and Sam ended up living among humans?"

"Sam's reason, anyway. I was just a tag-along."

"Why do you want me to know this? You heard the commissioner's change of heart as well as I did. Cora Marshall is now safe. Nothing's going over to the Saxbys."

She cocked her head at him. "Because of Harold Beaumont. I examined that room very carefully, and the way he built his enchantments is entirely different from the samples I took from Isaac Marshall's driver. And the materials I supplied show the same bizarre schism. It's like—"

"You're the one who shipped him the materials?" interrupted Al, sharply.

"Through completely legal means, and I didn't realize it was him. Technically, they were purchased through an assumed name that turned out to be Freddy Davenport. I had no idea until I walked into that room this morning and analyzed the magical residue."

"Lady, it's like you're *trying* to get arrested."

"No, what I'm trying to do is get it through your thick head that Harold Beaumont spent most of his career working for humans and then somehow discovered the kind of knowledge that only wolves have had." She stared at him as if gauging whether he understood her yet, and then added, "The creature that Dominic Tierney turned into resembles a badly made version of the myths some packs have about berserker wolves of old."

Al had seen the witness sketches of Tierney in his transformed shape. The lupine features were impossible to deny. "Are the Saxbys among the packs who believe in these myths?"

He knew the answer by the frustration that seeped into her expression. "No."

"Then what makes you think they're behind Harold Beaumont's familiarity with it? He could have learned about this through some old book, or from a lone wolf he knew. His type gets their hands on every form of magic possible because they live from commission to commission."

Her mouth had tightened into a thin line, but she didn't disagree with him. He kept his next question gentle to avoid turning it into a dig. "Do you have any evidence that the Saxbys are involved beyond Tierney running through their territory and killing some of them?"

"No." The word was both grudging and defeated. "All I can say is that there's always more happening than they let on."

Al shrugged and finished the dregs in his cup. "That goes for everyone. But you've caught my interest. If you find out more, tell me. That is, if you're not too busy looking after Cora Marshall. I heard you packed her suitcases earlier this morning."

The she-wolf seemed slightly mollified by the fact that he was taking her seriously, but still rolled her eyes. "It was a favor for Sam. Until I can break out in my own field, I have to make do with helping him."

As he pulled out enough change to pay for the coffee, he nodded at the newspaper in front of her. "You might be interested in the third page. The city is holding an open contract for a new submachine gun that will be issued to the entire police force. They want something that will drop a wolf as easily as a human without

the expense of silver bullets. Yours was accurate, and electricity is an interesting idea. The recoil needs work, though. I'm not surprised it sent you flying back."

When she turned to the right page with obvious interest, he almost laughed. "Not afraid of betraying your own, huh?"

"Captain, I was hardly loyal even when I belonged to a pack," she murmured.

Just before Al turned to leave, she glanced at the opposite page and then grinned. "Oh, this is fantastic."

"You're looking at the wrong page."

"No, I'm not." Still smiling, she folded the paper open and then offered it to him. He scanned the biggest headline.

SOCIALITE TELLS ALL IN SUICIDE NOTE

"Your boys aren't very good at keeping evidence out of the reporters' hands," said Jane, her glee obvious. "Violet Granbury's note has been printed in full, and it seems she didn't hold back on anything... especially for our Miss Cora Marshall."

Al sighed, but the she-wolf wasn't waiting for a reaction. Instead, she quoted the note aloud even as he read it in silence.

"I want to make it very clear that Cora Marshall had nothing to do with any of this. The idea of her taking credit for what I spent years to achieve makes me sick. The little fool doesn't have the brains, the determination, or the daring to bring an end to this miserable world, and it was on Freddy's insistence alone that she was chosen as the vessel for his beloved god, even after she started seducing subhumans. I guess that's the reward for spreading your legs for every man in town—you end up good for nothing else."

Al handed the paper back, aware that the department would probably receive a letter from Miss Marshall's lawyer before the day was out. "If we're lucky, she didn't see it."

Jane grinned again. "This was the same edition in the bundle of papers I gave her this morning. If she's like every other human and insists on reading the paper over breakfast, then she'll find it halfway through her first cup of coffee. I just hope Sam is in the same room when she finds out."

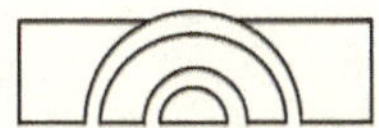

CHAPTER SIXTEEN

"Violet, you snake!" The words were underscored by the crinkle of newspaper pages being strangled in a tight grip.

"Miss Marshall?"

"You *rat*." Now they were being torn apart.

"Miss Marshall."

"You two-faced, pinch-mouthed, spiteful little shrew!" Cora threw the ragged paper to the floor. Then she snatched it up to read the final lines of the article, ignoring the flicker of movement across from her as Hayes rose to his feet.

"And if you see this, Cora dear, let me add, 'congratulations.' Having the favor of a god must feel wonderful after being rejected by your pet detective. You're once more the center of all attention. Love and kisses, ducky."

Her shriek rattled the coffee cups in their saucers. When she tried ripping the newspaper into even smaller shreds, Hayes caught her hands. "Easy. Try to calm down. She wrote that just to rattle you."

"It certainly worked! It's bad enough she tricked me into becoming a sacrifice for a disgusting blob. Now she's insulting me from beyond the grave, and *everyone* can see it." Cora flung herself back in her seat, cheeks stinging with heat. Her heart pounded like it was about to pop.

In front of her waited a grapefruit half she'd picked from the array of food on the table. She shoved it aside and went after a box of donuts, devouring two in the time it took Hayes to draw his chair next to hers. When he pulled his plate over as well, she grabbed the sandwich on it—a huge thing stuffed with fried eggs, cheese, and ham—and took the biggest bite she could manage.

Grease ran down her fingers as she swallowed, but she took a second bite that was just as ferocious. It was then that she grew aware of his attention. "I always eat like a man when I'm furious. All self-control flies right out the window."

Hayes shrugged. "I never understood having a piece of fruit for breakfast. That's not a meal. It's a garnish."

"Try telling that to my tailor." She took the sugar bowl and emptied it into her coffee. Then she gulped it all down.

For several moments afterward, she panted for breath while the urge to scream and throw things faded beneath the shock of so much grease and sugar. "I can't believe reporters got their grubby little hands on her note. I'm sure they'll go for her diary next. She always kept one."

Her fingers remained tight against the coffee cup until Hayes once more coaxed them to relax against his. "Even if the police keep the rest out of reach, you're front and center as the one victim of the cult who survived. When Davenport and the others go to trial, you'll be the most important witness testifying about them. It's

unfortunate, but the newspapers won't leave you alone anytime soon. Last night's ritual was the topic of conversation wherever I went this morning."

She sighed, the warmth of his touch melting her anger. "It's not really the lack of privacy. At this point, it feels normal for strangers to know more about my life than I do. As for Violet, well, she always had to have the last word. *Always.* I'm just fed up with people thinking I'm dumb and useless. I don't like it, you know. I really don't. But once I realized no one ever took me seriously, I learned how to use it to my advantage. It almost made their assumptions fun... at least until Father disappeared."

Then she glanced up, aware of the answer even before she asked the question. "It's going to happen again, isn't it? All these people will comb through my life and question whatever they find in the most condescending way possible. And I'll have to sit there with a smile when all I really want to do is tell them off. Or at least strangle them with their ties."

"At least one thing will be different. You won't be facing them alone." He studied her glum expression and then added, "Tell you what. Since we'll both be busy and stuck inside today, how about something to look forward to in the evening?"

"Like what?" she said, already brightening.

He smiled a little, that reluctant one she loved seeing. "Your choice. Think of something we can do tonight. Something fun."

It was impossible to hold onto her frustration when he was so close to her, so steady and sure and flat-out irresistible. "I can think of one thing already, but we've agreed to stay professional."

"There's your sparkle," he murmured.

Now her heart beat like a drum for a very different reason. Then the phone rang, its shrillness impossible to ignore, and Hayes squeezed her fingers a final time before pulling away. "Sounds like the rest of the city has woken up."

She sighed and poured a fresh cup of coffee, this time adding a normal amount of cream. "Yes. I suppose it's time to notify everyone where I am. The lawyers alone will be in fits over last night."

They were. Not fifteen minutes after she phoned to tell Maisie where to direct callers, her father's lawyers arrived. With their stooped shoulders, dark suits, and balding heads, they looked as dour as vultures while crowding together in the small living room. There hadn't been time for her to change out of her peach nightgown and silk robe, but they knew her well enough to ignore that fact. Only Mr. Forrester gave her a paternal frown, warning her of an impending lecture.

She tried fending it off by greeting him and then immediately adding, "I hope your head is feeling better from our last meeting. I've heard migraines can last for weeks."

"It's fine," he said, curtly. Then he glanced over into the main bedroom where Hayes paced while on the phone. "My God, Cora, I can't believe you're staying here."

"Why not? It's a very nice place, and the view outside is wonderful. Are the ducks still in the pond? I was watching them earlier."

"I meant being alone with the wolf. And to be in such a state of undress in front of him! It's a shocking business."

"Not as shocking as nearly being sacrificed, and I survived that just fine," she said, keeping her smile bright. Despite herself, she also looked over at Hayes. He turned enough to give her a wink, the

wryness in his eyes suggesting he was well-aware of being the subject of their conversation.

Her smile grew genuine as she refocused on Mr. Forrester. "Besides, he's been frustratingly professional since the day we met, so there's no need to scold me like I'm your daughter. I'd much prefer that you scold me as your *client*."

"He is, Miss Marshall," said one of the other lawyers, his long face crinkling in consternation. "We don't want to give Frederick Davenport's team any further examples to discredit your character."

Mr. Forrester raised a hand. "Let's not get ahead of ourselves. First things first: composing a statement for the police. Mr. Brix will take charge for now."

Cora muffled a sigh, realizing things were about to get very boring.

She recounted the night as clearly as possible while they took notes. They were thorough yet impersonal; even questions about her exact history with Freddy remained as bland as their expressions. When their attention shifted to composing the statement, she knew she'd be ignored for a while and began pondering Hayes' idea. It was difficult to think of a good time that involved staying at home. She was far more used to enjoying the glitz and glamor offered throughout the city.

Her mind didn't return to the men before her until Mr. Forrester handed over a pen and the statement. After she read and signed it, the lawyer said, "That's all we need at this time. If anyone tries to interview you, direct them to me. Do you have my number? Good."

Just then, Hayes walked into the room. Mr. Forrester turned to him and added, "That goes for you as well."

Cora bristled at the man's frigid tone, but Hayes' easy expression didn't change. "Relax, Mr. Forrester. I'm as concerned about her safety as you are."

"I should hope so." Then he and the other lawyers rose from their seats. "We're walking a tightrope here. Davenport's defense will try anything to shift the blame from him. It really would be better if you were under police protection, Cora. Staying with a wolf has too many implications."

It was a sentiment later repeated by the police detective and enchanter who were her next visitors. By that time, she had been able to style her hair into soft finger waves and wore a cream dress striped with gold at the collar and waist. It was a breezy and appropriate look, as well as one of her favorites, yet she felt far less comfortable facing them than she had with the lawyers. Notably, Hayes took the phone off the hook and settled next to her while the two men introduced themselves and sat down. His presence kept her from fidgeting with her diamond bracelets.

Detective Nichols had the dull neatness of an accountant and was unremarkable in every way. He spoke without aggression or kindness and read through her statement with the same neutrality. "This will do. We may require a follow-up interview later. There's only one other thing to discuss at this point: you're clear of contamination."

She blinked. "Oh. That was very fast."

The other man cleared his throat. Cora recognized him—and certainly his pompousness—from the night before. It was that master enchanter fella. Byrd. He looked pale, even unwell, hands twitching slightly as he said, "An incident this morning expedited matters. All enchanters on the force were reassigned to this case, and

with the extra manpower we've been able to identify and map out all magical residue."

Cora nodded but was more interested in the bruise by the man's temple. It hadn't been there before. "Are you quite all right?"

The man reddened. "Of course."

Hayes also looked him over. "No, you're not. What happened?"

Byrd drew himself up. "It's nothing worth going into. All you need to know is that Miss Marshall hasn't been… compromised by the creature."

Then Nichols folded his hands, resting them on Cora's statement. Unlike the enchanter, he showed no sign of nerves. "It's the only reassuring thing we learned. In fact, I strongly recommend you accept police protection. Immediately. The magic in this case is baffling, and we have yet to find Harold Beaumont. He's a dangerous man who has repeatedly unleashed unknown magic, and there's no telling what he might try next."

Cora shook her head. "Thank you, but I feel very safe here."

"Nothing gets through the wards protecting this place unless I want it to," said Hayes. They were mild words, but his expression made it clear that he wasn't about to argue.

Nichols' voice turned dry. "Yes, we're aware that Jane Feral is quite the enchanter."

A scoff from Byrd suggested he didn't agree, but the police detective wasn't finished. "Now that we're through with Miss Marshall, are you willing to answer a few questions?"

Hayes remained easy in his seat. "Sure."

Cora understood both of their glances. Her part in the conversation was finished, and she could escape. Relief fought with

curiosity while she rose from her seat, and she made sure to leave the door to the guest room slightly ajar so she could listen in.

Unfortunately, the apartment was large enough that their words were indistinguishable. All three had that brisk, flat tone that men often took with each other when speaking as professionals, and she soon found her thoughts drifting in a different direction while she unpacked her suitcases. It seemed likely that she would stay with Hayes until Harold Beaumont was found. The idea was thrilling, and so was listening to his deep voice, so confident and decisive compared to the skeptical drawl of the police detective and the pinched interjections from the enchanter.

Strange, how comfortable she felt here. All her old friends would have reacted to the plain bedroom in shock and the lack of servants in outright horror. Then they would have complained about going without the luxury and coddling they expected as part of life.

Well, she thought it was wonderful. Hanging up her clothes in the small closet and setting out her cosmetics on the simple table was satisfying in a way she couldn't explain. She felt... tucked right into Hayes' life without being pressured to fit perfectly.

She had never lived with anyone besides her father, and they had always done their best to ignore each other whenever humanly possible. Perhaps that was why it was so hard to think of a fun idea for the evening—there had been nothing to enjoy at home. If anything, *fun* had meant getting away from it. To shop, or watch the latest play, or stay out at parties until night gave way to dawn.

Now that she thought about it, it had all been some form of erasing loneliness. The dry, dusty type that permeated her father's house. The raw, throbbing type that could appear even at the most raucous parties.

She didn't often examine herself and couldn't say it felt comfortable. But it did put her in a distracted mood, enough so that the slam of the front door startled her. She looked over just as Hayes knocked and stepped inside the bedroom.

The tension in his shoulders stayed out of his voice. "They're gone."

"Is everything all right?"

"It's fine. They'd rather have you under their watch, but I got them to agree that you could stay here."

She sat on the bed beside her suitcase, aware that there must have been much more to their conversation. "The lawyers advised police protection as well. You're the only one not pushing me to accept it. Why? Is there some danger I don't know about?"

For a moment, he hesitated. The gold of his eyes darkened into something grim, even angry. "Let's call it bias on my part. Once you see one organization at its worst, you distrust all the others. Besides, they couldn't prevent a suicide note from falling into the wrong hands. What might happen to an important witness?"

Perhaps the words should have left her frightened, but she hadn't lied to the police detective—she truly did feel safe with Hayes. She pushed herself upright and approached him, putting a teasing note in her voice. "Then I guess we're stuck together."

He nodded, still on edge. "We probably won't get any other visitors today, but I'd guess the phone will start ringing off the hook once I put it back in place. Is there anyone you want to talk to?"

She glanced at her remaining luggage. "No, I'll be busy enough unpacking."

He hadn't exaggerated about the amount of calls. Most seemed to be from lawyers representing various people connected with

Freddy's cult, all of them hoping to interview her or Hayes. Others were thaumaturgists or researchers dying to hear a firsthand account of a transdimensional being. And of course, there were the journalists.

He was still stuck on the phone when she finished her last suitcase and went into the kitchen to make a fresh pot of coffee. As she put the percolator on the stove to heat it up, her eyes roamed over the pristine pots and pans hanging against the wall. Then an idea popped into mind, and she began checking the larder. The percolator finished at the same time she did, and she was still smiling while taking a steaming cup to Hayes.

By this point, he had set up at the small desk near the window, jotting down notes while he listened. He hung up without a goodbye and glanced at her.

"Coffee?" he said, appreciation clear in the word.

"You were starting to sound tired." Then she handed it over.

He took it with a smile but still looked surprised. "You seem very comfortable in the kitchen."

"I suppose I am, yes." She hadn't really thought about it. A girl of her wealth and position had servants to do everything, which meant she wasn't expected to know anything. "I'm not sure how... wait, I do remember."

A flash of insight filled her mind, like recalling fragments of a dream. "I pestered the servants to teach me basic housekeeping, because I expected to do it all on my own as a... a wife. As his wife."

The lover she had planned to elope with. The lover scrubbed out of her life down to his name, down to her being able to make coffee without realizing the significance of it. Silence fell, and she felt herself flush. Not from revealing this glimpse of her past devotion,

but because doing so might have changed the easiness between her and Hayes. He said nothing yet watched her intently.

She put on a smile, determined not to let it spoil things. "Anyway, I'm glad I can remember whatever they managed to teach me." Before she could add anything else, the phone rang again. She groaned. "It's really been going all day, hasn't it?"

"Half of it is directed from my office," he admitted. "It should quiet down in the evening. Speaking of... have you thought about what you want to do?"

"Yes," she said, her smile widening. "You'll soon find out."

It wasn't exactly a surprise. Even though he was trapped in his bedroom, the chop of a knife against the cutting board and the smells of tarragon and shallots quickly filled the apartment. She had no trouble finding her way around the small kitchen and soon fell into a rhythm of preparing ingredients, shaking the sizzling pans, and tasting to check the seasoning. She couldn't remember the last time she'd enjoyed herself this much without sex playing a part.

Typical of a man, there was no sign of table settings beyond plates and utensils, but she was able to arrange the food nicely on the kitchen table. A glance out the living room window revealed night had fallen.

Hayes was still on the phone when she walked in. The hoarse note was clear in his voice while she sat on his desk and primly crossed her legs. She waited until he hung up before saying, "Don't you think you've done enough work for one day, Detective?"

He smiled wryly, rubbing a hand against his five o'clock shadow. "What do you suggest?"

"My fun idea. Jane told me you don't get a home-cooked meal very often, so I made us both dinner."

"I noticed a lot of good smells out there." He obligingly followed her out and sat at the kitchen table. She set the plate before him with a flourish. "Filet mignon with *béarnaise* sauce, potatoes *noisette*, and stuffed artichokes."

She was quite pleased with the results considering how long it had been since she'd cooked with careful technique. The beef was sliced thinly and drizzled with the sauce, the potato balls were perfectly round, and she'd even remembered how to hollow and cut the artichokes into the shape of swans.

Hayes stared at the food, clearly impressed. "I haven't had a meal this fancy since my time at court."

It was the first time he had mentioned his old life in the Saxby Pack without sounding bitter or guarded, but Cora decided not to point it out. As she brought over her own plate, she said, "I learned from Henri Toussaint, but really, it's more about the presentation than anything. If you break it right down, it's still just steak, spuds, and greens."

"Henri Toussaint? You mean, the famous chef?"

Cora nodded. "We met and quickly moved beyond being strangers, although I can't say what possessed me. He was bad-tempered and unbelievably fussy. When I pointed out those flaws, he claimed I couldn't handle a day of what he gave to his underlings in the kitchen. I like a challenge, so I bet him that I could last a week and if so, he'd have to teach me how to cook without *one* insult in the process. He had to eat his words, and I went from not knowing how to boil water to understanding the five so-called 'mother sauces' like the back of my hand."

Hayes laughed, finally losing the professional mask he'd worn all day.

As they began eating, she couldn't resist using the syrupy tones that wives on the radio always used on their husbands. "So. How was your day?"

It worked. He answered her playfulness with his own. "Uneventful. Yours?"

"A little dull compared to the night before, but the company has been much better."

"I'm better than a god, huh?"

She loved seeing him come alive. Perhaps it was fun to tease his self-control, but coaxing out his unguarded, boyish smile made her heart outright flutter. "You're certainly more handsome. And really, it's a marvel to watch you work. You handle things better than most businessmen I've known."

"I have a lot of experience from my former position in the Saxbys."

It was another mention of his past that held no bitterness, and Cora decided to risk learning more. "Back when we first met, Captain Dempsey told me you were the royal inspector."

A wry glint appeared in his eyes. "Between him and Jane, you must've learned everything about me. Yes, that was my final place in the pack. I started off as a guard at sixteen, transferred to the investigative division at twenty, and became the royal inspector at twenty-four. I left two years later."

"And then became a pit fighter," she murmured, gaze moving to where that nasty scar on his chest hid beneath his shirt.

"Just until my career as a private detective took off."

"Lady Hawthorne's murder. Her mother didn't believe it was suicide, and you proved Lord Hawthorne killed her instead. I couldn't believe you managed it."

He shrugged. "It was a straightforward case. Humans aren't used to a wolf finding clues with their nose. I smelled him on the body immediately. The hard part was cracking his false alibi."

She leaned forward, food forgotten. "But that's what I mean. He had powerful friends everywhere. I'm sure some must have threatened you."

"Sure, but that's the nice thing about living among humans. There's no one I have to answer to and there's nothing to intimidate me with." A moment of silence passed before he added, "Is that case why you chose me over all the other private dicks out there?"

She thought about giving him a coy answer, but he sounded truly curious. "Well, yes. When public opinion turned and I was seen as a conniving killer, not one person I knew took my side. And believe me, I reached out to plenty. I suppose I realized how cowardly humans are and that a wolf, at least, wouldn't be afraid to fight. But I didn't expect us to be so..."

As her voice trailed off, she waved a hand in the air, unsure of how to even describe how exciting, how *good* her life had become despite the nasty circumstances.

"I know," he said, quietly. The words brushed over her like a caress. "It's the same for me."

It made her feel as sweet as syrup, and she didn't even mind when he moved onto the neutral topic of stopping in at his office tomorrow to collect any mail. Obviously holding onto his resolve to stay professional for dear life. She didn't try returning to personal topics, well-aware her presence would continue to crack his reserve. She only hoped he would give in sooner than later. Just because she understood his point in avoiding improper behavior with a client didn't mean she *agreed* with it.

When they finished eating, he shook his head and looked at her. "That was the best meal I've ever had. How about I do the dishes as a way to say thanks? I'll pour us some drinks afterward. Maybe we can find something on the radio."

"All right," she said, hardly able to hold her excitement. "I'll freshen up in the meantime."

The servants had packed her array of perfumes along with the rest of her toiletries, but she decided against wearing any, remembering the sensitive noses of wolves. She refreshed her makeup and changed into a lace-edged chemise and a silk robe. Both were a delicate pink in color that contrasted nicely with her black thigh-high stockings and garter belt. The final touch was a pair of heeled slippers.

Out in the living room, she arranged herself on the couch in a lounging pose that always worked very well on men. When he came in with two empty glasses, she was pleased to see that he couldn't resist glancing her over. "You're not going to make it easy on me, are you?"

She shifted slightly as if moving into a comfier position, one that happened to arch her back and push out her chest. "Not at all."

He walked over to the small bar that was next to the radio. "What do you want?"

"Any scotch or whiskey will do. If you can believe it, I've never been fond of cocktails. I much prefer the taste of plain alcohol."

He turned on the radio while adding ice to the glasses, flicking past two stations and pausing on a program announcer to pour the liquor. Cora gasped, forgetting all about her seductive pose to shoot upright and twist toward the radio. "Don't switch it! He's just said that Murder Time will be on next. It used to be my favorite show."

"Can't say I've ever listened to it." He brought the drinks over and sat beside her, taking a sip from his before loosening his tie.

She took her glass and thanked him, but absently, instead caught up in the theme music. "It's an hour-long show where each episode is a different murder mystery. Obviously, you try to work out the killer's identity as the play goes along. Just before the resolution, there's a thirty-second intermission for you to make a final decision before the ending reveals everything. I listened to it religiously as a girl."

Hayes nodded. He looked less interested in the explanation than in her, the gold of his eyes warm and relaxed. "It sounds straightforward enough. How many of the mysteries would you solve?"

"I always felt I was quite good at it." Then she flashed him a smile. "Up for a battle of wits?"

"What's the prize?"

"Bragging rights."

"All right."

She was too excited to sip at her drink in an alluring manner, instead using the whiskey's strong burn to clear her head as the program began. The premise was simple enough: a rich man was poisoned on the opening night of his new restaurant. His lovely, unfaithful wife and cash-strapped business partner were among the suspects. Although the wife insisted her affairs were only spiteful rumors, she *was* seen arguing with her husband on the night of his murder, to the point of storming out and returning shortly before he died. Witnesses couldn't agree on the timeline of her movements, with some insisting they'd seen her after she was supposed to be back in the restaurant.

When the music for the intermission played, Hayes said, "The eyewitnesses should be interviewed again. Maybe it was poor lighting. Maybe they remembered incorrectly. There are a lot of innocent reasons why a witness might be wrong. One might have even lied about it to protect the girl... or blackmail her. The partner seems more likely. He was the one who inherited all the businesses and was also the beneficiary for the dead man's life insurance policy. Always check the name on that. It ends up matching the killer and explaining their motive for so many murders."

Cora had been thinking carefully throughout the show. "If an eyewitness saw the wife at a time where she *did* have an alibi, then who's to say there isn't someone posing as her? Or—what if she has a twin sister?"

"A twin sister no one knows about?" Hayes sounded baffled.

"Why not? She mentioned having a foster father at one point. Perhaps the twin was adopted by someone else. Maybe she resents her luckier sister and wants to ruin her life, right down to framing her for scandals and murder!"

When Hayes started to respond, she flapped a hand at him. "Shh, it's starting back up."

Five minutes later, Cora smiled triumphantly over the show's ending theme.

Hayes looked torn between confusion and amusement. "How did she know what her sister would wear that night in order to mimic her appearance and poison the husband?"

"You obviously aren't a woman. It's vital to know what everyone will be wearing at an event like that. You don't want to be caught dead in the same dress or furs as another girl. What if it looks better on her?"

"All right, but how would she get an exact replica of the outfit right down to the jewelry?"

"Where there's a will, there's a way."

He shook his head and smiled—his real one. "Guess there's no point in being a sore loser. I concede. Were you always this good at solving the murders on this show?"

"Fairly. I do wonder if it didn't give me an itch for detective work. I've certainly enjoyed being your assistant." She smiled back, realizing how they had moved closer to each other throughout the program, so close that the heat of his body gave her as delicious a burn as the lingering traces of whiskey.

As the radio's noise shifted into music, she couldn't help asking, "What about you? When did you become interested in investigating crimes? What made you devote your life to it?"

He didn't tense up at the question, and she wondered how long he had expected it. "I like helping people, especially the ones who have been wronged. It's easy to grow hopeless in a world like this, but I can't live that way. I have to think that I can make a difference against all the corruption and greed that drives a lot of crime."

Then he looked out the big window at the nightlife glittering beyond. One hand toyed with his empty glass, but he didn't seem inclined to get more. If anything, he looked frustrated instead of dejected, eyes sharp as he took in the glittering lights of Crescent City.

Cora watched him, for once without words. His shirtsleeves were still rolled up from washing the dishes, and the top button of his collar had been undone sometime throughout the evening. Little details, but they added to the sudden intensity she felt from him. He was a wolf without a pack, hiding all but the most polished parts of

himself to live among humans. Did he ever get a chance to rest? Did he ever have a day without frustration?

She reached out and brushed his bare forearm, wondering if he would pull away. He didn't. Instead, he turned toward her, those wild eyes absorbing every inch of her face.

"You don't just try," she said, softly, hoping he would sense the truth of her next words. "You succeed. People talk more and more about you and your cases, you know. They want to sneer, but what can they say besides calling you a wolf? As if that's an insult compared to what *we* are. We're all bored children playing with expensive toys because we're too scared to grow up, or face being hurt in life, or even just admit how useless we are."

They were now so close that his mouth was inches from hers. She felt like she could lose herself in the gold of his irises as he said, "Don't include yourself. You're none of those things. In fact, you're the most remarkable woman I've ever met."

Why was she always breathless around him? It was as if the slightest action on his part showed her how a full heart sweetened the smallest moments in life. Oh, she'd known plenty of charmers who could make a girl feel good, and plenty of seducers who drew out the chase to make the resolution all the more thrilling. But they were all like fireworks—a big, bright bang with nothing left afterward. A brief distraction reinforcing the emptiness she felt the rest of the time.

Suddenly, she realized this all was much more than teasing him for the reward of his attention, and much more than the surprise of being treated like she was worth listening to. What she felt had a name—love.

Shock left her staring down at her glass. She wasn't sure she knew what to do with love. It hadn't been part of her life growing up, not with a dead mother and a father cold as ice. And as an adult, her only experience with it had been burned from her mind. Was this really another chance at feeling it? At *being* loved in return?

Still speechless, she looked back up and saw an intensity in his expression that matched the one whirling in her heart. For the first time, his face lost all hints of professional reserve. He wanted her. He wanted her *badly*. The moment stretched out, hot and tenuous, as if a single word might break it.

"Hayes…" she murmured, heart aching for release.

At the sound of his name, he moved in, as silent and sudden as the wolf he was. His mouth found hers, hot and urgent. Then his hand caught her chin and angled it to deepen their kiss. As soon as she gasped against his hunger, his tongue slipped in.

Her body throbbed in pure excitement as her hands ran along his chest and shoulders, thrilled by the hard muscles and impatient strength. Each shared breath felt electric, and when he growled at her fingers sliding down past his lean stomach, she moaned in response. Without breaking off the kiss, he used his weight to pin her beneath him.

Just as his hand found the sash of her robe, the phone rang. She groaned in disappointment as he broke off, swearing under his breath. Shivers ran over her inflamed skin as he got up to answer it.

"What is it?" he said, voice rougher than normal.

Cora watched his expression change. A different kind of tension filled his next word. "When?"

He didn't say anything else before hanging up. For a few moments, he only stood there by the phone and stared at it, rubbing the back of his neck.

"Hayes?" She pushed herself into a sitting position, realizing something was wrong. "What is it?"

At that, he looked over. His voice sounded very flat. "Freddy Davenport is dead."

CHAPTER SEVENTEEN

Jane Feral had searched through the police archives for nearly an hour before the shouting began. She didn't pay much attention. For one thing, it was on the main level above. For another, it would likely distract Mr. Newland, the police archivist. The human was as precise and dusty as the file cabinets and stored evidence he looked after. If he found her, there was no chance he'd let her stay without written permission.

Just as she found the right files, an alarm blared from somewhere within the room. Jane flinched, resisting the urge to cover her ears against the piercing noise. Harsh fluoride lights flickered into life. Then came the heavy, metallic thump of doors locking into place.

At the first hint of human panic, she shrank back into the nearest shadows, remaining perfectly still as Mr. Newland hurried past. The man patted sweat from his forehead with a handkerchief while the alarm rose to a new pitch and pulsated in an obvious countdown. Jane watched him disappear into the special collections room just before its door slid shut. The glyphs etched into its surface brightened into the color of flames.

Above, muffled shouts moved in all directions. It was easy enough to guess that someone had either attacked the station or tried escaping from it, and the archives had been locked down to protect their contents. Excellent. She now had plenty of time to read without disruption.

Jane checked her bandolier to make sure her safety charms were active and then returned to the file cabinet to collect the folders. They were of varying ages, some battered from being thumbed through so many times, and a few fresh enough that she could still smell the people who had handled them. Only the name on the labels was the same: Harold Beaumont.

The police hadn't exaggerated about following him for years. It took her several trips to transfer all the files to the nearest reading desk. Sam would have laughed to see how few she could carry at a time; physical strength had never been one of her talents, and she hated exercise too much to try changing that. Gunfire rang out as she switched on the desk lamp, but her focus had already narrowed to Beaumont and all that the police had on him.

His first brush with the police had been when he was twenty-two and still known as Harold Granbury. He had been caught stealing bodies from a cemetery. Since the graves had all belonged to the unidentified dead, and since Harold was a bright university student from a renowned family, he had avoided any serious charges for his 'tasteless joke.'

That had changed when he did it again, this time from his family's mausoleum, and was found to be using the bodies as raw material for experiments with bio-thaumaturgy. In response, his

family had publicly disinherited him. Friends in high places had helped lighten his prison sentence to under a year, and afterward he had changed his name to Harold Beaumont and began life as a freelance enchanter. He had never been caught again due to lack of evidence, but police suspected he'd played a part in many black market magic cases that remained unsolved... especially the ones that suggested a certain madness at work.

For Beaumont *was* a madman. What was impossible to see in the dry police reports grew crystal clear once Jane began studying the notebooks and ledgers collected from his apartment in Ragbag Way. His work might have been considered brilliant if it had been practical enough for those who demanded reliable results in return for their money, but no one would ever call him sane. His jumps in thought and blatant disregard for what was impossible gave him an edge over professionally trained enchanters, who all crafted their magic in the same manner. He was willing to try anything if the client offered enough money.

He was also an alcoholic; as smoke-stained as these papers were, she could still catch traces of cheap whiskey. A few were even stained. Despite this, Beaumont was surprisingly neat and detailed with his records, keeping them for every commission he'd ever had and even cross-referencing the research materials he'd used. Each commission had a number instead of the client's name, but he had made the mistake of dating them, and Jane quickly flipped through the pages, her interest deepening into an excitement she only felt while hunting.

Sam had done his part in finding Isaac Marshall's secret ledgers to pinpoint when the sigil had been placed on Cora Marshall and how much it had cost. It was all Jane needed to find Beaumont's notes for

that commission. As the gunfire above intensified, she began copying his words and adding her own notes in the margins. If she was about to battle wits with a madman, then she intended to collect all the information possible.

Her attention didn't waver until her ears registered total silence. Then she noticed the crick in her back and stiffness in her limbs, and knew hours had passed even before checking her watch. The doors might open soon. The lights were already back to normal. Carefully, she tucked away her notes and replaced the files, her gloved fingers making sure nothing was out of order. Disappointment bit at her while she worked, and she wasn't sure how to tell Sam that she had learned everything about the sigil, could even replicate it now... and yet, she wasn't any closer to getting it off Miss Marshall.

By the time all the doors unlocked, releasing Mr. Newland, she was back in the shadows, waiting patiently to see whether it was safe for her to emerge unnoticed. Fresh air washed into the room along with all the smells from above. Gunpowder, of course. Burning wood and hot metal from spent bullets. And... magic. She stiffened at its familiarity. Several of the nuances were exactly the same as back in Freddy Davenport's ritual room. Beaumont's work yet again.

Just as she risked taking a step toward the exit, one of the labels on a nearby cabinet caught her eye.

SUBHUMANS.

Curiosity won out over anger, and she slipped over to it instead. Captain Dempsey kept insisting that they knew very little about the Saxby Pack, and she wanted to see how true that was. It didn't take long to find the right file, or to see that both she and Sam were included in it as "former members." Just as she began reading, a voice spoke from behind her shoulder.

"Find anything useful?"

She snarled from being caught unaware, and snarled again at the sight of Sam standing there, obviously amused. "Damn it. You and your guard training. I didn't even hear you come in."

He glanced around at the endless shelves and filing cabinets. "Your scent has filled the room. How long have you been in here?"

Despite her lingering annoyance, she was gratified to see that a day with Miss Marshall had left him looking less grim than usual. She couldn't recall the last time she'd seen him smile—*truly* smile. "Hours. Why?"

"Then you don't know why the station is shot up."

"Not a clue. Do you?"

"No one is willing to tell us."

"Us? Look, take off the scent scrambler. I'm tired of asking questions."

For a moment, she thought he wouldn't. But then he removed his wrist watch and set it on the nearest shelf. As soon as the enchanted object lost contact with him, his scent grew clear. So did another—Miss Cora Marshall's, all over his skin. The implication was as obvious as the frustration in both scents.

Jane grinned at him. "You couldn't even last a day. Why'd you stop?"

Sam shot her a look. "The phone rang. It was Dempsey telling me that Freddy Davenport had just died. By the time we made it over to the station, it was locked down. They didn't let us in until after sunrise."

"You should have gone back home and finished where you left off."

"Jane," he growled. "I got lucky that something stopped us. It would have been a mistake."

"Hmm." She picked up the watch, absently checking the enchantment to see if it needed repairs. It didn't but had a new scar on the wristband. There was probably a new one on him, too.

"I disagree," she said, without looking up. "You only need to worry about the sigil deciding you're a threat to its purpose of finding Isaac Marshall. Other than that, it won't care what you do. In fact, it might help to be unprofessional with Miss Marshall. You would appear to be like the previous men in her life—interested in that and that alone."

He shook his head. "Not all of them. One was going to marry her."

"If he exists. You've been searching for him from the start." Even as the words left her mouth, she caught a new thread in his scent: resignation.

"Roland Archer," he said, quietly. "Worked on the estate as an assistant gardener."

All her hopes to get him to stop being stupid and admit his feelings for Miss Marshall suddenly felt as fragile as cracked glass. "What? The last I heard, you were still looking through Isaac Marshall's paperwork for any servants who left during the right time frame."

"I narrowed it down a while ago. The head gardener remembered when Archer left and why: he'd received an inheritance from a distant relative and hoped to restart his life with it. I later confirmed it with the relative's lawyer."

"But are you sure? *Really* sure? The timing could be mere coincidence."

He paced along the shelves of stored evidence, revealing his tension. "I found a minister that Archer contacted as part of the elopement plans. Yesterday, he finally called back. He remembered the situation well enough. The marriage would've been done quickly and secretly—in the dead of night, in fact—because the bride came from a wealthy family that knew nothing about it and wouldn't approve."

Then Sam stopped and faced her. "Jane, it's him. Roland Archer is the man she fell in love with."

Jane sighed, wondering whether it was worth pointing out that it didn't matter what Miss Marshall had felt about this man since those memories had long been erased. "Obviously, she can't know about this until the sigil is no longer a concern."

"Agreed. So how close are we to getting it off her?"

Now it was her turn to fidget, and she knew he noticed. "I don't have anything encouraging to say. Isaac Marshall had several conditions for the sigil, and they included that she couldn't even think about removing the sigil, much less hire an enchanter to do it. If someone found out about it, she had to direct them to him, presumably so he could buy their silence."

"And if anyone tries to take it off her?"

There was no way to soften the answer. "Then the sigil must immediately terminate itself and any part of Miss Marshall's mind that might recall it. With no further specifications, it seemed Harold Beaumont took that to mean Miss Marshall's brain should be absolutely fried."

"Goddamn it," muttered Sam, unable to keep the heat from his voice. "And there's no way around it?"

"I can't give you false hope. He was quite thorough in his research and showed special interest in what doctors are doing with lobotomies. I'll try whatever possible to neutralize the sigil, but before you ask, I don't know how good our chances are. I'm still deconstructing how he crafted it. In the meantime, we need to remain careful that no one discovers the sigil. Help her keep her secret, Sam, because if she ever realizes you're trying to free her, so will it."

He nodded, wordless once more. His eyes remained hard with repressed fury.

Jane hesitated, wondering if she should try to distract him. She had always been terrible at emotions outside of provoking them. "However, I have been wondering whether we should reveal more about the pack."

Then she almost bit her tongue at the stupid slip. *The pack.* She had never felt any particular loyalty to the Saxbys despite being born and raised as one; Sam had certainly been much more dutiful and earnest about his role in the pack and what he could do for their king. Yet it was she who unthinkingly spoke as if they were still part of the Saxbys. He never made that mistake.

He was also much kinder than she, and instead of pointing out her word choice, he merely said, "Which parts and who to?"

She brandished the Saxby file still in her hand. "I think we should enlighten Captain Dempsey about what happened to us."

"Going soft on a human, huh?"

"Of course not. But I dislike the fact that the Saxbys are being seen as an innocent party in this situation, and the police captain is the only one willing to listen to a wolf."

Sam took the file from her and glanced through it. When he remained silent, she added, "We both know they must be involved. Their bluster about wanting justice for the Saxby wolves killed by Tierney is a laughable excuse. At least, it is to us because we know better. The humans seem willing to accept it. If they're so desperate to remain involved in this case, then they must have played a part in it.

"At the very least, I'm sure they're the ones who passed on information for Beaumont to use in making his version of berserker wolves. He has no notes for the bio-thaumaturgy used in Tierney's transformation. More than that, none of his other enchantments reuse elements of it, even when he modified the cultist's bodies. No enchanter creates from scratch every time. We build upon what's already worked. But trying to explain this sounds like a desperate attempt to blame the Saxbys unless we reveal the things they've done before."

"Because none of their myths include those of the berserker wolves. And a wolf pack known for their rich mining deposits would never need to sell information to humans." When she growled in frustration, Sam raised his eyebrows. "So, you've already brought this up with Dempsey."

"Barely. I told him about the death of Princess Liana and what Alpha-king Saxby did to his advisors in response. I *didn't* include the fact that he knew the Sinclair prince was insane and covered up the information because he hoped for that outcome. Or what your part in it was."

She fell quiet as fresh anger burned in Sam's scent. Not toward her; it was the same rage and helplessness that had lived with him from the moment he had realized the level of corruption in his pack.

That he had been loyal, blindly so, to a king willing to let his daughter die if it meant declaring war.

In a softer tone, she said, "What I told him only made the Saxbys seem more like victims instead of what they really are: a pack willing to try stupid plans that fail."

"Fail? They got exactly what they wanted." Sam flipped through the pages in the file with that distracted manner he took on whenever keeping his emotions in check.

"I don't see how. The alpha-king not only lost his daughter and saw his pack reduced by half, but their strongest ally was pulled into the mess and lost everything for it. And although the Sinclair Pack was destroyed, the Saxbys were too weak to take over their territory."

"I doubt that was the goal." Then he looked up at her with the cold, shrewd expression that had unnerved even the other royal advisors of the pack. He was always so easygoing in his manner that it was almost a shock to witness how fierce and pitiless his assessments truly were. "The alpha-king's plan only failed if you think he wanted the land. He didn't. The feud with the Sinclairs had long been over personal grudges, not greed. Winning meant everything to him, and that war not only got rid of the Sinclairs but the Bacas as well."

"The Bacas were our strongest ally. We celebrated for weeks when Princess Lorelei mated with their king. I had to wear my formal uniform each day. It was terrible."

"He was willing to lose Liana. What's one more daughter? The Bacas expected gold in return for their military support. Once one dried up, so would the other."

"And our mines had been dwindling for years." It all made sense as he laid it out, so much so that Jane almost felt embarrassed for not

seeing it sooner. "All right. So the alpha-king got what he wanted. Can we say the same about this situation?"

Sam considered. "The answer depends on why the Saxbys are so anxious about Isaac Marshall. Are they hoping he's still alive, or do they want to make sure he's dead?"

Just then, Mr. Newland appeared from behind one of the shelves, his spectacles flashing beneath the harsh lights as he shook in indignation. "What are you two doing down here? You certainly don't have permission."

Sam offered the folder. "Just curious about the official opinion on us. I've been waiting for hours to speak with the captain. Is he free yet?"

The man took the file and checked it for missing pages. "If you want a conversation with Captain Dempsey, try going upstairs. Now will you please leave?"

It wasn't a conversation. It was a full-blown argument, audible even as Jane waited out in the hallway while Sam and the police captain went at it in his office. She wasn't alone; Cora Marshall and what looked like a retinue of lawyers stood there as well. So did a few police officers, who seemed edgier than normal while guarding them. Miss Marshall greeted her, sincerely so. The lawyers didn't bother, instead casting suspicious glances at the fresh bullet holes in the walls. Repairmen already worked on shattered windows.

"So. What happened?" said Jane, to no one in particular. Sam was stubborn as hell and Dempsey didn't sound ready to back down, which meant she'd have to learn the answer from someone else.

One of the officers glanced at her, but it was Miss Marshall who answered. "They won't tell us. Whatever happened, it was quite the firefight. There are spent bullet casings everywhere and of different

calibers. I don't understand why so many shots went into the ceiling, though."

Jane could smell the officers' surprise and felt some herself over the shrewd observation. She really couldn't tell how much of Miss Marshall's bubble-headed personality was a mask and how much was a life of being expected to do nothing and know nothing. "Very astute of you. Notice anything else?"

The girl was also good at deflecting sarcasm. A spark of fight in her eyes was the only sign she'd understood it. "Well... Detective Hayes' voice doesn't rise at all when he's angry, does it? It just grows deeper. I haven't met many fellas like that. Usually they sound like children throwing a tantrum."

Jane didn't miss how one of the lawyers all but rolled his eyes in despair.

Just then, the door to Dempsey's office slammed open. Then the police captain stalked out, snarling over his shoulder as Sam followed. "We need her. She's the only one left."

"Police protection won't be any safer," growled Sam. "If anything, Davenport dying here in the station should reinforce that."

The police captain scoffed while lighting a cigarette. Despite the exhaustion in his face, Jane noticed how steady his hands remained. "Let me tell you what happened to Freddy Davenport. His lawyer met him at his request, just as he has twice before without an issue. Only this time, Davenport took the man's pen and stabbed himself in the throat. Repeatedly."

"Suicide?" said Jane, already suspecting it was the wrong answer.

The police captain turned his glare on her. "No. An enchantment."

Jane raised an eyebrow and glanced up. "Did it make him crawl on the ceiling like a lizard?"

"Not him. His hand." In the silence that followed, Dempsey took a long drag. His voice continued to seethe as he added, "We took the body to the morgue. Despite being dead, one of Davenport's hands managed to strangle the morgue attendant and then sever itself using autopsy equipment. All hell broke loose once it reached the main levels of the station. It choked out two more men and felt up a secretary."

"So it had some form of sentience." Jane examined the bullet holes again. "And could travel over any surface."

"Like a rat. And it hid just as well. The station was in lockdown for hours while we searched for the damn thing. It was trying to escape."

"An enchantment that didn't want to be examined," she murmured, feeling the first spark of possibility light up her thoughts. "Who finally shot it down?"

"The captain," replied one of the officers. "In one try."

Dempsey waved the comment away. "That's beside the point. What's important is that more of this unknown magic killed Davenport. Not only that, it used a figure he trusted. We can't take any more chances. Miss Marshall has to be put under our protection and isolated until we find Beaumont and nullify his goddamn spells."

Jane's gaze flickered over to Sam. A muscle jumped in his jaw as he listened in silence, and she knew they both thought the same thing. The first police enchanter who examined Miss Marshall would set off the sigil's defenses. In trying to protect her, they would certainly kill her instead. Then again, trying to explain the situation

would mean trusting multiple people to keep a secret successfully. Jane didn't think that would last more than an hour.

One of the lawyers cleared his throat. "If our client agrees, we are willing to work with you to iron out the details, Captain."

All attention fell on Miss Marshall, who hesitated. She didn't seem frightened so much as concerned for Sam, who was still obviously irate. "It doesn't sound like something I'd enjoy, but I suppose if I have to..."

"You don't," said Sam, his voice still closer to a growl.

"She does," snapped Captain Dempsey. "Which you'd realize if you looked at this situation as a professional instead of a lovesick puppy."

"Captain," Jane interjected, recognizing the dangerous way Sam fell still. "May Sam and I have a brief discussion with you? We're concerned about the Saxbys and how they might react to this news."

It was an outright lie, but with Miss Marshall in plain hearing, she didn't dare reveal the true reason.

The police captain shot her a look that suggested she was pushing it, but after a moment he threw open the door to his office again. "This better be worth it. Hanover, find a chair for the lady in case this takes a while."

As soon as the door closed behind them, Jane raised a finger to her lips. "We need total privacy for this conversation. Miss Marshall can't overhear."

Dempsey's eyes narrowed, but he tapped one of the glowing glyphs on his desk without comment. The walls around them shimmered slightly with ghostly light. "All right. No one outside will hear us even if we start up a fresh shouting match. Now get it

through your thick head, Sam. This has grown too big. You have to move out of the way."

Sam scoffed. "You swore you'd play fair if I did. You got us over here by claiming the details of Freddy's death were too sensitive to trust to the phone. That has nothing to do with putting Miss Marshall under city protection—the same city that was ready to hang her."

"That *was* playing fair. Again, look at things professionally. I know you're smart enough to see the signs once you do."

Jane growled softly, sensing Sam's increasing rage. No wolf liked feeling trapped. She just hoped the captain wasn't stupid enough to keep goading him.

To her surprise, Dempsey seemed to sense the danger in Sam's lack of a response. The anger didn't leave his voice, but he did sit behind his desk to give Sam some space. "I don't care about whatever you and Miss Marshall are doing or not doing with each other. It's irrelevant. I'm talking about getting too damn protective over your client to see things clearly. You want to know what happened in between chasing down that hand? The commissioner told me to call you with orders to turn over Miss Marshall to us. He also told me to ignore whatever happened next. He's not the only city official tired of this case. They want you out of the way, and they have their own men ready because I never let them use mine."

Sam didn't react, but Jane felt her fangs ache. "Let's be clear here. Are you saying the other city officials are willing to kill Sam?"

The question left her under the full weight of the police captain's gaze. His scent was muddied by his constant smoking, but right then she caught his frustration and regret that it had all come down to this. "Sure. What consequence would come of it? You two have the

combined arrogance of an entire wolf pack without the safety of belonging to one. Did you really think you wouldn't step on any toes?"

Jane didn't answer, hot bitterness filling her full over the fact that wolves without a pack would always be seen as weak.

Dempsey turned back to Sam, who had also remained silent. "In your *professional* opinion, would you be more helpful to Miss Marshall as a body that'll never be found, or as someone who can work on her side unnoticed while all the attention is elsewhere?"

When Sam did finally speak, he sounded calm and flat, all internal struggle smoothing into a firm decision. "Trust me, Al, we understand our position in human society. It's more than that."

Then he glanced at Jane.

She understood. There was no other choice. They had to reveal the sigil's existence, and it would be safer if she did it. If the police captain broke their trust and the sigil became widely known, it was better to have the enchantment identify her as an enemy, not him. "The truth is, Miss Marshall *is* in danger. Can you keep a secret, Captain?"

"No."

"Too bad, because you need to know this one. There's a spell on Miss Marshall. It's been on her for over a year and was meant to invisibly control her. If your ham-handed enchanters poke and prod her for hidden magic, they'll trigger it and kill her."

Dempsey rubbed at his head. "Who put it on her and how did you two find out about it?"

"Her father, and now that he's disappeared, it desperately wants to find him. Because of that, it let Miss Marshall tell Sam about its

existence and purpose. I don't think she realized how unusual that was. I don't think she's able to realize much about it at all."

"But she's aware of it?" Then the police captain's expression changed. "You're talking about a goddamn binding sigil, aren't you? And Isaac Marshall was the one who controlled it. Why didn't it fall apart with his death?"

"Why would it? He was trying to prevent scandal, Captain. That would include the public learning that he did such a thing to his daughter."

Dempsey swore and leaned back in his seat, absently staring at the far wall while he thought. The cigarette in his hand burned unnoticed.

Sam had been pacing around the room, but he now stopped and faced the police captain. "So. Will you help keep our secret, or will you be the cause that kills the final prominent figure in a case that's already being called 'the crime of the century?'"

Just then, a brief knock sounded on the door, followed by it opening. Jane arched an eyebrow as Cora Marshall entered with a determined expression. "I'm sorry for the interruption, Captain, but I think you've yelled at Detective Hayes long enough. If you're going to make such a fuss, then fine, I'll go into police protection."

For a moment, the police captain only rubbed at his temple while staring at her. "Believe it or not, Miss Marshall, I'm open to a compromise. You can't stay with him, but considering the recent chaos, a safe house might be better than the station."

Jane sensed Sam relax a fraction, but both their gazes remained on Dempsey, even when Miss Marshall said, "What?"

"We don't know what Freddy Davenport was about to discuss with his lawyer, only that it triggered magic our enchanters failed to

detect. Rather than risk the same thing, I'd like you to stay at one of the private nursing homes we have connections with. Sometimes we send witnesses there if they're in danger. I'd say this counts."

Miss Marshall glanced at Sam, obviously unsure.

"It's the best we're going to get," he told her quietly, and then gave her a faint smile.

Jane almost shook her head at the amount of trust visible in Miss Marshall's expression as she nodded. How the hell had the girl survived this long when she was so openhearted?

If the police captain also noticed it, he made no comment as Miss Marshall turned back to him, her voice growing brisk. "Well, I have heard of those places. They're more like private retreats, aren't they? I've had quite a few friends go to some to settle their nerves."

Dempsey nodded. "You'll have your own room, but you can't leave it or have visitors of any kind. There'll be a guard outside the door to make sure."

"Not even Hayes?" Miss Marshall sounded stricken.

Jane bit back a grin and glanced at Sam, who gave Miss Marshall a reassuring look before focusing on the police captain. "What about the police, the commissioner, or even Miss Marshall's own lawyers?"

Dempsey stared back for a moment as if to say, *I know what you're really looking for, you son of a bitch. A promise you can hold me to.* "No one can see her, and no one can cross my orders. She has to be completely isolated until we find Beaumont."

"Well, I suppose it only makes sense," said Miss Marshall, accepting it with another firm nod. "I accept as long as I can take all my luggage. I'm not wearing whatever shapeless gown and dreary robe they offer."

"Why would you need—" Then the police captain cut himself off. "Fine. Whatever you want. We'll make sure your bags are brought over."

"I'll do that while the lawyers work out the details," said Sam, his fingers already brushing Miss Marshall's arm.

"I'll send a few men along to help," said Dempsey, the look in his eyes promising that any objection would be ignored.

Jane followed them out long enough to share a parting glance with Sam. The last glimpse she caught of them was Miss Marshall smiling at him while tucking her arm into his, and the way he couldn't resist moving closer in response. God, she hoped he would at least tell the girl how he felt about her.

Uninterested in dragging around Miss Marshall's suitcases a second time, she instead walked throughout the station, taking in the damage. The bullet holes made an interesting pattern, suggesting the hand had zig-zagged to avoid being shot. No one she asked would talk about what they'd seen, although apparently only the morgue attendant had been choked completely to death. The two officers just had marks around their necks. The secretary had already quit.

Once more, she found herself wondering whether this bizarre enchantment might be the key to solving the problem of the sigil. Most enchantments were crafted to self-destruct if their creator didn't want others to be able to examine them. Yet Harold Beaumont had decided to have his merely scamper away...

"Enjoying yourself?" Dempsey's sardonic tone cut through her examination of dark blood left on a broken window.

She ignored his question to ask one of her own. "Have you ever seen anything like this?"

"No. Have you?"

She shook her head. "What happened to the hand?"

"We have it in our lab. It's being studied right now."

"Then it's still alive? Intact?"

"Intact enough to scratch at its glass jar, anyway."

Jane fully turned toward him, hoping he'd hear the urgency in her voice. "I need to see it. Right now."

"Our enchanters will send along anything they learn."

"That's not fast enough. Please, Captain."

He sighed and checked his watch. "All right, but let's make this quick."

The police laboratory was nicer than the Saxby Pack's, and *much* nicer than her own cramped little space. Jane glanced over the equipment with envy, but most of her attention remained on the cluster of enchanters Dempsey led her towards. They all surrounded a steel table that held a large glass jar lit from all sides.

"Give us a few minutes, boys," said the police captain, sending them away with a jerk of his head.

They left in a cloud of sullen mutters, but Jane had already forgotten about them, instead completely absorbed in the specimen before her. It was a hand all right, but a terrifying version of one. The fingernails had sharpened into claws, and the skin over the knuckles had split, oozing a blackish-purple slime. The palm had a large bullethole, but that didn't prevent the hand from jumping and twitching like a spider, crawling all over the glass in rage.

"Ugly little bastard, isn't it?" murmured Dempsey.

"Ugly? It's the best thing I've seen all day." Then she looked over at him with a grin. "It transmuted itself."

"What?"

"The enchantment that killed Freddy Davenport transmuted itself. Your men will find no hint of magic left in his body. All the bio-thaumaturgy and spells on him pooled into this hand. That's why it severed itself, so that it could get away."

"Back to Beaumont?"

"Of course not. To leave you unable to pin anything on him. He's been caught by you once, Captain. Do you think he ever wants to face a conviction again? Most enchanters fear that competitors will study their work and steal from it, but that isn't Beaumont's concern at all. He's paranoid and fears being caught above all else. I bet every damn one of his enchantments has this condition put into it. If it's about to be examined, it'll tear itself away and disappear. I need to see the archives again. Right now."

The police captain eyed her. "What do you mean, 'again?'"

She could feel herself glowing with excitement. "If I'm right, then I can modify this clause. Turn it into something less... destructive toward the human host."

"And why would you want to do that?"

She raised her finger. "Client confidentiality."

His grimace acknowledged that he understood she meant the sigil.

She could have left things there, and normally would have. Perhaps it was the euphoria of the moment. Perhaps it was the mere fact that he actually listened to her ranting. Regardless, she found herself asking, "Where are you from, Captain?"

"Why do you want to know?"

"Mild curiosity. Sam got you so mad that an accent slipped into your voice. There isn't one, normally."

At first, she thought his answer would only be a long-suffering sigh. "I was born in the country. Rosewood, if you want to get specific."

Ah, one of the forests further out than Corpsewood. Also, one that had rural packs. "Then I'll assume you knew about wolves before coming to Crescent City."

"Sure did. It was one of the reasons why I relocated here after the war. I didn't realize city packs were nothing like country wolves. Ten times as neurotic and amazingly passive-aggressive for creatures with fangs. Hell, I didn't even know most city wolves can't shift form."

"The war? I'm learning all sorts of things about you today, Captain."

He scoffed and lit a fresh cigarette. "Seems to me you should be concentrating on other things. How's that gun prototype coming along?"

"Swell. How about your investigation into the Saxbys' potential involvement in this case?"

"Non-existent."

Jane gave him another smile, pleased to kill two birds with one stone. "Then let me give you a few more details to help you along…"

CHAPTER EIGHTEEN

Cora couldn't repress a pang in her heart at the sight of her luggage being carried out of Hayes' apartment and into the unmarked cars parked in the street. She hid it with a pleasant expression, fluffing up her thick stole to give herself something to do while Hayes spoke quietly with the two policemen, both out of uniform. No one looked happy, and she couldn't say she felt any better.

In fact, she found this new arrangement to be downright silly. Why should she be in danger from Harold Beaumont? Unlike Freddy, she didn't know the enchanter or where he might be hiding. But she *did* know what powerful men were like when they wanted their way, and it was obvious city officials were scrambling to stop the chaos caused by Freddy and his cult. Now she would have to stay at one of those dour women's retreats until they decided she was safe. As if she could be safer under police protection than with Hayes.

Just then, he walked over to her. His shoulders were visibly tense, and he spoke in that flat tone he used when hiding his anger. "I'll drive you there. They're going to escort us."

In the car, he growled briefly when the shorter, stouter officer signaled at him that they'd lead the way. "I'm sorry things turned out like this."

"So am I, but there are worse things than being bored." She looked out at the heavy traffic, already feeling better now that they were talking about it. "I say we take this as a chance to find Harold Beaumont before anyone else. If you can't reason with someone, embarrass them instead. And being stuck in a room can't stop me from working as your assistant sleuth."

He nearly smiled at that, but it was obvious he was still on edge.

"I... hope you don't regret anything about last night," she said, feeling surprisingly hesitant. She'd been considered a bad decision by more than one man, but a good cry and a round of shopping always melted her indignation. Normally. That wouldn't be the case if she saw the same cold light in Hayes' eyes, and she knew it.

For an agonizing breath, he remained focused on the road ahead. Frustratingly, the brim of his hat slanted over too much of his face to glean anything from his expression. The crush of traffic, complete with insults, honking horns, and rumbling engines, created a cacophony that somehow made their little space all the more private while she waited for an answer.

Just as her fingers began worrying at the pearls sewn on her purse, he reached over and squeezed her hand.

"No, Bunny. I don't regret it," he said, his deep voice softening until it brushed her ears like velvet.

Her heart threatened to break open and gush everything it held. Not only her feelings for him, but also her urge to break the arrangement with the retreat. She wanted to shake off the escort car and drive somewhere they couldn't be found. She wanted to continue what had been interrupted last night. A brief touch between their gloved hands was no longer enough, especially since this might be their last conversation for quite some time.

As if sensing her thoughts, his voice turned brisk. "So. Beaumont. What are your ideas on finding him?"

It was an obvious change in topic, but even she had to agree it was for the best. "Well, if he's still able to cast magic, then he must have access to supplies. While you and Captain Dempsey were trying to outshout each other, I pestered one of the officers into telling me a few things. Beaumont's only known laboratory has been burned down, so he must be working from whatever place Freddy gave him for the cult-related enchantments."

"Why would Freddy Davenport give him a separate lab?"

"That was always Freddy's way. He had lots of hobbies and kept any middlemen needed for them at his beck and call. He had a repair shop built into his car garage and another in his boathouse. They were fully staffed at all times. It used to confuse people, you know, since he had a reputation for being careless, but it's really very straightforward. He had obsessions and put everything into them."

Hayes nodded, falling silent while navigating the car through a rough patch of traffic. Cora glanced out the window as the road curved away from the cramped businesses and waves of foot traffic. Signs became replaced by wild grass and tangled blackberry bushes. It was nice to get away from the hustle and noise of the city, and yet it meant she was that much closer to the retreat.

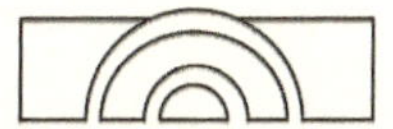

Unwilling to face the future, near as it was, she quickly added, "I told the police all this, but they don't believe Beaumont would hide on Freddy's land. 'Who would hide in the home of the man trying to kill him?' Even though they admit he's likely a madman."

"Even a sane fella would see it as a sound option. Right now, Beaumont is the most notorious figure in the city. The property of a man locked up, powerless, and facing death is much safer than trying to blend in with the public."

For a moment, she almost forgot to feel sad. "Then you agree with me."

He smiled—*really* smiled. "Let's just say the police aren't the only ones trying to find every piece of land that belonged to Davenport."

As salt tinged the air and the trees on either side flattened into marshland, she asked, "That Admiral Antwerth alias that bought materials from Miss Feral—what was the delivery address for it?"

"A storage unit that was traced back to Davenport. He would have hired someone to pick up the shipment and take it to Beaumont."

"And how much of Freddy's estate have the police searched through?"

Now that the traffic had faded to a few cars, they moved at a good clip. Hayes seemed more at ease, relaxing in his seat and leaving just one hand on the wheel. "The mansion where he performed the rite and a lighthouse that's been unused since he closed his family's shipping lines. They know he has more property, but there's no telling how long it'll take them to go through it all."

Cora nodded absently. "Freddy always bled money and was quite willing to sell off businesses and land that had been in his family for

generations. I think we should look at his finances to compare what's been sold with what's left. If he held onto anything that would have made him a lot of money, then it's suspicious."

"Could also be a patch of land that nobody would want to buy."

"Oh, that's an easy guess. Bullfrog Pond. It's been dried up for generations and is too close to no man's land for anyone to want it. Freddy once used it for his airplane hangar, but he stopped flying planes years ago." The excitement left her voice as she remembered she couldn't track down this lead with him.

Then Hayes glanced at her, some of his usual humor back in his eyes. "How about a bet on it? You say he's on a prized piece of land, and I say he's in a dried mud patch."

She smiled at the reference to their night before. "What's the prize?"

"Bragging rights."

"Deal." Then she realized they were stopping near a cluster of buildings. The smell of brine remained heavy in the air. "Oh, no. Are we here?"

Hayes remained in the car with her while the officers also parked and got out, looking around. "Not exactly. They're worried about us being followed."

"By Beaumont?"

"Even reporters would be bad enough. Whatever they find out, so will everyone else."

Cora made a noncommittal noise, still studying their surroundings. The damp air and bold gulls perching on every car and roof suggested that they were very close to the ocean, but there were too many buildings to see anything. Well-kept houses mixed together with hotels, shops, and restaurants, but all were so close

together and narrow that Cora knew they had to be in an older part of the city.

Hayes made eye contact with the taller officer in an unspoken signal. Then he said, "We're walking the rest of the way. They'll come back for your luggage after you're inside and safe."

"They seem so serious. Are they really expecting trouble?" It looked like a quaint, harmless tourist town to her, but she checked her thigh holster before getting out with him.

There were enough pedestrians that they blended in while crossing the street toward the town's bank. It was a stately old building, several stories high and with massive columns flanking the entrance. Several people were going inside and coming out, but the officers wordlessly guided them around the side instead. Cora couldn't help being very aware of how loud her heels sounded against the old-fashioned cobblestones compared to the fellas' silent steps.

When the shorter officer raised a hand, she casually brushed at the folds of her skirt, ready for anything. Instead, he just knocked on a polished steel door painted white to match the marble wall.

The man who answered looked as staid and droopy as an aged bulldog. His grey hair glinted in the thin sunlight while he motioned them inside, and he sounded neither alarmed nor interested while shutting the door behind them. "This way."

The room was well-lit but very plain compared to the bank's exterior, with only several steps leading up to another steel door. Cora bit back a gasp of surprise when the man grabbed the polished wooden handrail and pulled, lifting the entire staircase from the floor. Cogs groaned against each other as the facade continued to rise, revealing an entrance to a secret tunnel.

"What..." she started to say, but the taller officer interrupted her.

"Better take your shoes off, lady. It's soft dirt and rock from here on out. You'll roll an ankle in those heels."

Cora gave him a bright smile. "I'm sure I'll be fine. I walk everywhere in these."

When the man looked ready to argue, Hayes stopped him with a brief but deep growl.

The other officer shrugged. "You'll be the one carrying her if she twists something."

The tunnel's mouth was just big enough for them to duck through, and it was a short, two-foot drop down to its dirt floor. The taller officer went first and immediately slipped. By the time he had finished swearing and stumbling back up, Hayes had gone through without incident. He offered a hand to Cora, but she merely smiled again and jumped down beside him, landing easily.

"I'm very flexible," she said breezily, while the officer glared and slapped dust from his suit.

Both policemen remained quiet while they walked through the worn brick tunnel, and Hayes didn't seem inclined to talk, either. Cora noticed how his earlier tension had disappeared. In fact, he was downright relaxed compared to the officers, who looked ready to pull their guns at the sight of a rat.

Finally, just to chase away the oppressive silence, she asked, "Why does this tunnel exist?"

Hayes sounded amused. "It was built before the turn of the century. Many prestigious clients used it after finishing their business at the bank."

"And what was on the other side?"

"A brothel."

"Oh. I never realized they were once legal."

At that, the shorter officer answered. "They weren't."

The tunnel ended with a short wooden staircase. The taller officer went up first. Hayes kept himself between her and the door but still looked calm. At the man's call of all-clear, they went up as well.

All that met her curious gaze was a gravel pathway surrounded by uncultivated bushes and clusters of cypress trees. In fact, she didn't see any buildings at all.

"The brothel burned down fifty years ago," murmured Hayes. "Now it's wildland used to give the retreat some privacy."

For several yards, she remained quiet, aware of her growing nerves even as birds chirped cheerfully and sunlight sparkled among branches. Both policemen looked relieved, even eager that the journey was nearly over. And Hayes... well, he had resumed wearing his professional mask, making it impossible to guess what he thought.

Then a flicker of movement near a large cypress on her right caught her attention, and she glanced over in time to see a man pull back out of sight. No, not a man—even from that distance she had caught the glint of gold eyes.

Shock burst through her just as Hayes squeezed her arm to get her attention. The shake of his head managed to convey both a warning not to alert the officers and reassurance that it was all right.

Her surprise only intensified, and she used the act of slipping her hand through his arm to furiously whisper, "You knew he'd be here?"

At his slight nod, she added, "Because you *told* him to be, didn't you?"

His gaze remained on the officer in front of them. "Did you really think I'd trust the police to handle this?"

"But you've never mentioned working with other—"

Before she could finish the sentence, both officers stopped by a ridge of pine. The shorter one glanced at Hayes. "This is as far as you go, buddy."

Cora looked past the man and caught glimpses of a white building, simple yet imposing. Beyond it waited the glimmering ocean. They had reached the retreat.

In an attempt to remain lighthearted, she said, "I suppose I can't receive letters as well as visitors."

Hayes looked guarded again, eyeing the officers and their obvious impatience. "You might be able to write them."

She forced herself to let go of his arm, aware of how her pulse raced. "Be careful. I'll hold you to that. Although I'm sure your days will be much more interesting than mine."

He gave her a small smile, but his expression remained serious. "I won't try to contact or visit you. Not for any reason. If anyone or anything suggests otherwise, don't believe it."

She nodded. "Then... I suppose this is goodbye."

The gold of his eyes darkened a little, and he lost that crisp tone for something warmer, something private. "No. It's an, 'I'll see you soon.' Hang in there, Bunny."

She held onto his words while the receptionist checked her in and the head doctor greeted her personally. He was a thin, mild man who only said that he hoped she'd enjoy the stay, and that while nothing could be given to her from the outside, they'd do their best to accommodate her otherwise. Cora gave a suitably polite response, hoping she didn't look as reluctant as she felt.

A nurse showed her to the bedroom. It was bright, airy, and as luxurious as any hotel room she'd been in. These types of places usually were, since the women who visited them were rich and sick from indulgence instead of disease. Cora wasn't surprised when her luggage arrived only after it had been searched for bottles of morphine and caches of cocaine.

Unpacking didn't take too long. The robe and gown offered for patients actually recovering from injury or illness were just as dreadful as she'd imagined, and she quickly shoved them to the far end of the closet, which was much too small to hold all her clothing. It was something that would have annoyed her normally, but instead she thought back to how Hayes' closet had been even smaller. How she hadn't minded it at all. She checked her watch. He probably wasn't even back in the main districts of the city yet. Hardly half an hour had passed.

The large window had a bench built into it, allowing the patient to sun herself. It could also be opened to allow in the scent of the rose trellis below. When Cora looked through the pristine glass, she saw a sedate garden and some green lawn where a few patients walked or performed other types of gentle exercise. The ocean looked so near and yet also completely out of reach, and watching the glimmer of its waves made her feel even worse.

She tried reading a few books but quickly grew bored. A call button brought in a nurse no matter what time of day or night it was, but she resisted the urge. There was nothing really wrong. Merely, she didn't want to be here.

She managed to wait until after supper before asking a nurse for writing materials.

"I'm sorry, Miss Marshall. You aren't allowed pens or pencils."

She supposed she couldn't make a fuss over that when it was how Freddy had died. "What about drawing crayons?"

It wasn't the prettiest letter, but she was still able to write it.

My dear Detective,

It's funny to think that the last time I wrote to you, it was to ask for a consultation. I am much more confident now that everything will turn out fine. Perhaps that's ironic, since I'm just as caged now as I was then. But don't worry, this isn't a "poor little me" letter. The staff and room are very nice, and so is the view. And frankly, the last thing I want to talk about is staying here.

I thought of something else related to Beaumont and Freddy's death. What was Freddy about to reveal to his lawyer? I think the time of his death is as suspicious as its manner. From the moment he woke up surrounded by the ruins of his ritual, he began confessing all his deeds and didn't stop. So why kill him when the cat was already out of the bag? Maybe there was something more he knew...

Just some thoughts to add to the ones we had earlier. I'm sure you're already working on our bet. And Hayes, I know you're very serious about your job, but try to have some fun as well. Sometimes it's as if you've forgotten what that even feels like.

The words from Miss Marshall's latest letter ran through Sam's head while he waited in his car, unnoticed by the pedestrians passing him by. He'd always had a good memory, but this was more than that. He could imagine her voice right down to the syllable, just like he could pick up which optimistic sentence hid annoyance and which held true excitement. The bare traces of her scent lingering on the sheets of paper drove him mad. He wasn't just missing her; he was goddamn miserable.

But he was used to the feeling and knew how to bear it as one scar among many picked up since his life with the Saxbys ended. He remained easy in his parked car, avoiding suspicion by reading a newspaper as if waiting for someone. Not too far from the truth; he kept all his focus on the people scurrying in and out of the radio station across the street, searching for one in particular.

His eyes itched from the enchantment that darkened them into a human brown, but the small irritation was worth it. No one looked at him twice, and the police car that passed by left him alone.

A few minutes past noon, a new flood of people emerged from the radio station. This time, one of them was the man he wanted to see. Roland Archer, out on his lunch break. Sam studied the human, feeling his muscles contract with the urge to change form. Instincts were instincts—his wanted to treat Miss Marshall's lost fiancé as a rival. And wolves didn't like rivals.

Archer was a tall, lean man of twenty-five who had started working as a servant while still a teenager. His father, a piano maker, had died young, leaving the family business in ruins and his loved ones destitute. Sam had found a few of Archer's former employers and those who remembered him had nothing bad to say. He'd been quiet and reliable. The other servants had said the same thing, only adding that he played the piano like a professional.

Then, a little over a year ago, an unexpected inheritance from a distant relative had allowed him to move into a good career of performing and composing music for one of the city's radio stations. All in all, Sam had a solid summary of Archer's life but still knew nothing about the man himself. For one thing, he wasn't sure why Archer had let Miss Marshall go without a fight. Money wasn't the reason; the inheritance had been genuine, not a pay-off from Isaac Marshall in return for forgetting about his daughter.

So now here he sat, telling himself he could hunt this human for answers like it was just another job.

When Archer crossed the street and disappeared around the corner, Sam waited a few breaths before getting out of the car to follow him. His scent was clear and unremarkable. Just one more healthy if harried human among many.

Sam tracked him to a cafe bustling with the lunch crowd. Cold beer, sizzling beef fat, and melted cheese filled the air, but he only

ordered coffee while settling into a corner table. Archer had chosen one of the stools at the counter. The place was too noisy to hear anything he said, but Sam was more interested in his interactions with others.

A shadow fell on him through the window beside his table. Sam glanced over, already suspecting who it'd be. He held back a sigh as Jane glared at him, her eyes a bright, human blue. His self-control felt strained enough without Jane shredding at it to try and get her way.

As soon as she took the chair across from his, she hissed, "What are you doing? The Saxbys are meeting with city officials in under two hours. We should be there."

He waited until the waitress came over with his coffee and left again. There were two cookies on the saucer, but he ignored them and drank from the cup, intent on keeping a clear head. "I've got something else planned."

"This?" Her voice dripped with disgust. "If anything, I thought you'd be looking into the leads on Freddy Davenport's properties."

"Searching either Bullfrog Pond or Mallow Manor will take hours. And you know what I'm talking about. You gave me the enchantment this morning. This is just to pass the time."

Her eyes widened, the act emphasized by their disconcerting blue. "I didn't think you'd go through with it. I know Brom is your friend, but that plan is a death sentence."

He shrugged, seeing no reason to argue about it. He loved Jane like a sister, but she was always sure of being right—and in the worst ways possible. "How'd you track me here?"

"I noticed an eye color enchantment was missing. Mabel said you'd gone out on something related to the lovely Miss Marshall's

case. Since she's been safe in the retreat for the past three days, there could be only one reason you'd hide as human."

Then Jane glanced over to where Archer sat, eating a ham sandwich. "Is that him? My God. She has terrible taste in human men. I suppose he's not bad-looking for one of them, but comparing the two of you would be pitiful. What was that nickname you picked up in guard training? Back when you tried having a life outside of work?"

"Jane," he said, already feeling tired. "I'm in no mood for this."

"This isn't how I saw my day going, either. But I don't understand why you're doing this. She's good for you. You haven't been drinking. You're getting more sleep. Some days, you even look happy. So why let her go? Considering the other men from her past, this human likely wasn't a positive figure in her life."

"That's what I'm trying to find out," he said, ignoring the rest of her point.

Like many people, Jane liked to grab a few details that fit together and then craft an entire narrative out of them, no matter what other information or evidence appeared afterwards. That method was no good. It led to tunnel vision, not the truth. He couldn't make that mistake, especially since he had no chance of staying impartial to whatever he found out.

Sure, he knew how Miss Marshall made him feel, and could make excuses all day for why he shouldn't tell her about Archer. But doing so would be worse than a lie. It would be using her trust for his own gain.

"You know, she doesn't even miss him."

"Because those memories were burned away," he said, shortly. "And despite that, she still feels grief over what she lost."

"But how do you know she'd feel happier having him back over having a future with you?"

He growled under his breath, crumbling the cookies into nothing while not-quite watching Archer. "I don't. I don't know anything solid about this man. But I have to find out, and I have to tell her what I find."

"Why?"

"Why?" he repeated, mostly in disbelief over her genuine confusion.

"Yes. Why let her know? Her grief is nothing more than a ghost of memories she can never get back."

"Jane, everyone else in her life has lied to her. I won't do the same."

"But this is different. It'd be a good lie. Like... claiming someone died peacefully instead of screaming in agony. Or that kindness is rewarded in this world. It's the type of lie that gives the heart peace and hope."

He shook his head, aware of how many cases he'd seen that had started from lies made with good intentions. "You're not changing my mind about this. I need to be honest with her."

At that, Jane arched her eyebrows. "Oh, we're talking about honesty, are we? Then prove it. Tell Cora Marshall how you really feel. Tell her how she's gotten you to sit up and take notice of life again instead of rotting away behind your desk or barely surviving dangerous situations. Stop pretending she's just another case and admit that you're in love."

When he didn't respond, she studied him. Then she added, "You won't, will you?"

He knew his silence was answer enough.

"Don't tell me you still pine for Isabelle."

It was such a bad shot in the dark that he laughed despite himself. "Jane. That's been over for five years and you know the reason why."

"Then explain."

He sighed and leaned back in his chair. The truth burned mercilessly. "If he's a decent fella who can give her a good life, then she's better off with him. That's what it comes down to."

Her attention turned into scrutiny. "Ah, that's what this is. You aren't resigned at all. You're desperately hoping he *is* a scumbag, just like her other old flames. Have you found anything so far?"

"No."

"Are you hoping to?"

"Yes," he gritted out.

Just then, Archer checked his watch and rose to his feet, preparing to leave. They both watched him nod a quick goodbye to his waitress while she cleaned water glasses. Her gaze slid over to his spot on the counter and then away again at the single penny left behind.

As they followed him outside, Jane's tone grew sardonic. "He's a bad tipper. Do you think that's enough to condemn him?"

"At least one of us finds this funny." Sam's gaze remained on the man as they kept behind by about three or four pedestrians. Archer wasn't going back to the radio station. Instead, he headed for the open market where stalls offered street food, trinkets, shoe polishing services, and other odds and ends.

Despite the noon hour nearly being spent, the place was still bustling, and Jane had to duck in close and raise her voice to make herself heard. "I don't find it funny. It's infuriating. If this human turns out to be an upstanding citizen and you bring them back

together, you'll lose your only chance at being more than a sad son of a bitch who gets drunk every night, and I'll once again be the only one who thinks to look after you."

Those last words ended in a growl, and then Jane suddenly stopped and faced him, passing a hand over her face to terminate the enchantment on her eyes. They flared bright and fierce as she stared at him. "What's your definition of 'decent,' by the way? Someone not in exile from their pack? Someone not ashamed of what they've become? Maybe we both bristle when being called dogs, but you're the only one who believes it's true."

His self-control finally snapped. He snarled, feeling his teeth sharpen enough to flash at her. "Lone wolves don't fit in this city. Look at what a successful life among humans means. Fighting for their amusement. Cleaning up their scandals. One of us even turned to prostitution."

"I've heard he's also the richest," said Jane, the arch of her eyebrow suggesting she missed his point on purpose. "He bought his second house last week. I can't even afford a second pair of working leathers."

"He has money, not stability. And not safety."

A flicker in Jane's eyes told him his point had finally hit home, but her voice remained as fed up as his. "Leaving the pack doesn't mean we have to be alone for the rest of our lives. You love her, Sam. Shouldn't that be enough?"

He nearly growled again, but other pedestrians were already casting nervous glances their way, and this wasn't an area used to wolves.

When his body language softened, so did Jane's, and she glanced over to where they'd last seen Archer. Then she stared. "This might be a wasted conversation. He's buying flowers."

Sam turned in time to catch Archer taking a bouquet of irises from the vendor and thanking the man with a nod. Both he and Jane fell silent while following Archer out of the market. It didn't take long for his path to end at a prim brick building divided into large apartments. An old woman on one of the ground-floor patios looked up from her knitting and then waved her handkerchief at Archer, who smiled and brandished the flowers before entering through the iron gate.

Sam looked away, not needing to see anymore. He had scrounged up enough information on the Archer family to recognize her as Alma Archer, Roland's mother.

Jane sighed. "Well, he's not an orphan. I guess he does have something over you."

"Goddamn it, Jane," he muttered, but without any anger. The miserable pit in his stomach had nothing to do with her.

"He might still have a new sweetheart. Or a horrible character flaw. Are you going to talk to him?"

"There's not enough time," said Sam, turning away. It wasn't a lie, but he also knew he was too wound up to talk to the man and keep it impartial. "How about you? Do you want a lift to where the Saxbys will meet with city officials?"

"It would sure beat taking the bus. It's going to be at—"

"The Telladay Conservatory."

"Has anyone ever mentioned how you're too good at your job?" In a different tone of voice, she added, "Are you sure about this plan of yours?"

He nodded. "The alpha-king himself will be at that meeting. So will most of the royal guard. It's the best chance to break into their quarters without being swarmed."

"If you say so. Here's some extra antisilver." She began to reach into her pocket.

He stopped her. "Keep it for yourself. You might need it."

She scoffed. "They're meeting with humans."

"After avoiding any interaction beyond their diplomat. Just be careful."

"You too, you idiot."

It didn't take long to drop her off a few blocks from the conservatory, but he didn't linger. The danger ahead helped him focus, and by the time he arrived at Minnie Wilkes' house, he was back in control.

Even so, she shook her head at him and said, "An argument muddles the mind too much to read it clearly. It'd be better and faster to tell me with words. The room is ready, but I still don't know who to expect, just that Brom is involved. Was he caught? Did they find out he's your contact?"

"No. Things are getting worse for the Saxbys that aren't part of the court. The alpha-king is breaking more and more of what keeps a pack whole."

When she waved at him to take a chair, he took it but remained on the edge of his seat. "It's the royal guard. They're doing whatever they want unchecked, especially against the regular pack guards. A few days ago, one took Brom's mate for his own."

Minnie knew enough about wolves to be shocked. Her eyes widened further when she caught a hint of the rescue plan from his

thoughts. "And just you and Brom are sneaking in? My God, Sam, it's suicide."

"So is crossing an alpha-king's order, and I survived that," he said, smiling faintly.

"At least take Joey along as an extra body."

"Joey is on a different job." He wanted someone to keep an eye on Cora at all times while she was stuck in that place.

When Minnie nodded reluctantly, he cocked his head toward the stairway to the second floor. "I know Eve has her hands full with the baby, but I need to ask her a few questions that could make this easier."

The young she-wolf's scent was full of hatred toward him. Her eyes glittered with it as well while she sat beside the crib and gently rocked it. They hadn't met before, but she knew he'd been part of the royal court, and that was enough. On his end, he was surprised by how much she looked like her sister—the same dark, curly hair, amber eyes, and stubborn chin. He still remembered how he and the rest of Theo's friends ribbed him for always falling tongue-tied whenever the pretty Edie passed by.

"What do you want?" she murmured, keeping her voice quiet to avoid waking the baby. He didn't miss the protective way she kept herself between him and the crib. Even though she kept her gaze away from him in reluctant deference, he knew that if he made one sudden move toward them, she'd fight to the death over the pup.

"I'd like to ask a few questions. You don't have to answer if you don't want to."

Her expression grew skeptical, but she nodded.

"I'm trying to rescue someone else later today. Someone your sister might have known. Her name is Holly."

She jerked. "Holly's in trouble? What happened? Is it that bastard Lowell? He's been after her for weeks even though she always tells him no, that she loves Brom."

When the baby began to fuss, the she-wolf bit her lip and dropped her voice back to a murmur while soothing her. Sam waited until the baby fell quiet again. "Brom and I need your help."

The anger had changed in her scent. Now she looked at him with doubt, not suspicion. "I don't understand. What can I do?"

"The night you escaped from the pack... who chased you?"

"Royal guards. I saw their uniforms."

Sam knew he had to be delicate with this next question, and that it would still hurt her. "Minnie said you were bloody when you arrived here. Was any of it from the guards?"

Eve drew in a sharp breath. "Yes. One caught me by the hair through the fence and I... I stabbed him. It was only his hand. I wish it had been his throat."

"What'd you stab him with?"

"My paring knife. It's all I had." Then she reached into her sweater pocket and pulled it out, smart enough to realize he wanted to see it. The blade was small yet sharp, and flecks of blood dappled it and the wooden handle.

When he pulled out his handkerchief, Eve said, "Are you taking it?"

"No. I just want some of the blood." He could feel the weight of her gaze while he rubbed the stains clean. When he offered the knife back, she took it in silence. Enough anger had left her scent that he now smelled the worry threading through it.

It stirred up his own anger, the fact that her first reaction to a fellow wolf was fear instead of trust, but he kept his voice calm. "Thank you, Eve."

She nodded, unsmiling, and turned back to the baby.

As Sam rose from his seat, he watched her trace one tiny hand until it clasped her finger. "What's her name?"

The she-wolf glanced back, and for a moment she looked so much like her sister that he thought he faced a ghost. "Theodora. It's what Edie wanted."

He nodded, sensing she would hate any acknowledgement of the grief rolling through her scent. His steps were silent against the floorboards while he left the room and went back downstairs, feeling like something inside him was about to snap. He'd gotten what he'd hoped for, but that didn't make him feel any better. If anything, he was glad of the danger and bloodshed ahead. They would chill his thoughts to a hunting focus.

He reached the agreed-upon location on time—a spot where Saxby land bordered an abandoned warehouse set on human territory. It was an area often unpatrolled, with nothing but uneven, silty land and some sparse trees.

One of the shelves inside the warehouse had been wiped clean, with two folded uniforms set on it—a regular guard's and a royal guard's. Sam saw them a moment before one shadow stepped away from the rest.

Brom didn't have his usual smile, and the amount of anger in his scent was enough to sting the eyes and nose like smoke. "Sam. Everything's gone smoothly so far. I have twenty minutes before I'll be missed."

Sam nodded, already taking off his tie. "Good. One break on our end: I'll be able to pass off as a royal guard."

Brom hardly seemed to hear him as he paced, every movement filled with rage. Sam wasn't sure how the hell he'd held himself together this far. "Brom, you need to stay calm."

"Two days," snarled the other wolf. "He's had her for two days. Just walked into our home and took her while I was on duty. When I went to the Captain of the Royal Guard, she told me that crossing him would be treated as treason to the crown. I know you loved her, Sam, but if I see that bitch today..."

Sam shook his head. "She's not here. Neither is Lowell."

"You're sure?"

"Right now, they're on human land." When Sam smelled his disappointment, he looked up from removing his cufflinks. "Listen to me. We're getting Holly out, but you have to keep a cool head until we're in there. If we slaughter on the way in, we'll alert others. Save it for when we're leaving."

There was a flicker of acknowledgement in Brom's eyes, but his edginess continued to thicken the air while Sam finished changing. He had never worked as one of the elite royal guards, but a uniform was a uniform, and wearing one felt both familiar and strange.

It was a small emotion, easy to push away, and his nerves felt steady as he turned his attention to his bloodied handkerchief and the vial Jane had given him. Its contents were clear but bubbled slightly while he pulled out the cork and poured them on the handkerchief. The sting of magic filled the air.

Brom watched in silence as he cut the pad of his thumb and pressed the fabric against it. His muscles immediately cramped, a sign that the magic was slipping into his body. The spell was built

upon his ability to change into a wolf and back, but Jane had warned it wouldn't be nearly as comfortable. For nearly a minute, he shook and sweated while the transformation took place, hearing Brom growl softly at his obvious pain.

When it was over, he straightened up and wiped his forehead. "Well? Who did I turn into?"

Jane's work was excellent; even his voice had changed, and Brom stared at him in open surprise. "Gil."

Sam nodded, already feeling steadier. "Another lucky break. He's also with the king."

Then he holstered his gun and checked his daggers. A royal guard's uniform came with spells designed to suppress their scent, taking care of the last thing that might betray his true identity. "If there's anything out of place, now would be the time to say so."

A trace of the other wolf's renowned humor returned. "Let's put it this way. You're so convincing that I'm fighting not to stab you."

Sam laughed. "That's the friendliest thing I've been told all day."

"I believe it. You're still living with Jane, aren't you?"

Their dark humor faded when they stepped back on Saxby territory. The plan was simple: under his guise as a royal guard, he would walk directly into their quarters, a building that was part of the royal court and therefore off-limits to regular guards like Brom. He knew the layout of the rooms from visiting Isabelle, including the underground escape routes built in case of emergencies. Brom would wait at the end of one that opened up near no man's land. From there, they could travel through forest until they reached human property.

A glance was all they shared before splitting up. Sam remembered Gil as being surly and uncommunicative even with his friends, and

so he ignored all other wolves he passed except fellow royal guards. Even those only received a brief nod.

It all looked the same, so much so that it felt like stepping back into the past. How often had he walked down these jade and obsidian halls to surprise Isabelle during her times off duty? Both infuriating and impressing her that he had slipped in without being caught.

But he wasn't the same wolf, and it wasn't Isabelle he now sought out. There were several she-wolves in the royal guard, but all he had to do was follow the scent with fear in it. His nose led him to a room on the second floor, and from there it was easy to find a door with Lowell's name on the nameplate.

Each door had a combination lock, something he had expected. He had brought his picks along and could even shoot it out if the situation grew desperate, but he found himself trying Isabelle's old master code that allowed her to enter the room of any guard below her. To his disbelief, it still worked. Five years and she hadn't changed it.

As soon as he shut the door behind him, the fear filling Lowell's apartment exploded into desperation. He scanned the sparse furniture of the small living room and then the closed door that would lead to the bedroom. "Holly? You won't believe this, but I'm working with Brom. We're getting you out of here."

There was only a slight scuffing noise in response, and he knew her well enough to wonder what the hell she was about to attack him with. Carefully, he tried the door and found it blocked. He gritted his teeth and threw his full weight against it, breaking through.

She immediately began screaming, shrinking back against the opposite wall. There was a letter opener in her hand, its dull metal

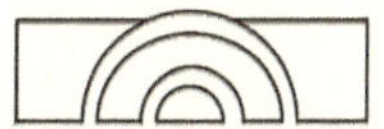

blade shaking as she pointed it at him. Sam took in her appearance while shoving aside the chair and desk she had put against the door. He couldn't see more than a bruise on her cheek, but the collar of her blouse was torn and her eyes were frantic.

He took a step toward her. "Holly? Holly, I'm here to help."

The words had hardly left his mouth before her hand moved, darting up to press the letter opener against her throat. She was panting, ready to jab it into the veins and arteries throbbing against her skin in her panic.

A quick glance at his watch warned him that there wasn't much time to convince her who he was.

"To hell with it," he muttered, and bit his tongue to draw blood and break the spell hiding his appearance. Shifting back felt like taking a huge breath after struggling underwater. The world wobbled and snapped back into place even as Holly gasped.

"Sam!" Her hand dropped back to her side.

He held up a finger to his lips and then gave her one of his silver-edged daggers. "Brom's safe. Just keep quiet and follow me."

Aware of how dicey this was about to get, he glanced along the hallway before leading her toward the stairs that would take them to the underground storage rooms. They made it to the first level before running into a royal guard coming out of his room. Sam dimly recognized him, and from the flicker in the other wolf's eyes, he recognized Sam as well.

"What the hell..." was all the guard managed before Sam lunged. He grabbed the other wolf by the collar and stabbed up through the tender spot between his chin and his neck, stopping any chance of a howl of alarm. The body slid to the floor, twitching.

"They'll smell the blood," he muttered to Holly. "We better run."

Her only response was to kick off her shoes, grip tight against her dagger. Without them, she was the quieter and faster one, already halfway down the next set of stairs when the shouts began. Sam sheathed his dagger and drew his gun instead, keeping one eye above them as the steps spiraled down. They were almost at the door to the storage level when boots pummeled the stairs. Then a shot rang out, hitting the wall inches from his head.

He twisted and shot back, convinced he was too late for anything but a bullet going into him. Instead, he caught the nearest wolf in the chest, dropping him. The body blocked the rest long enough for him to run down the last of the steps.

Holly was already wrenching at the door. "It's locked!"

He blocked her body with his own while punching in Isabelle's code. The door clicked open just as another guard jumped over the railing and landed near them. Sam shoved Holly through and out of the way and then grabbed the guard's wrist when he tried to aim with his gun.

A mistake in how it left his body open, and he knew it even before the guard's other hand flashed with a dagger. An explosive jolt up through his stomach took his breath away. The searing agony of silver spread everywhere, contracting his muscles, but he managed to twist his grip until the gun pointed at the guard's face. A twitch of his finger and it fired.

They fell to the ground together. He was shaking, sweating, feeling like every vein in his body was about to pop from the silver poisoning, but somehow he crawled free and through the doorway before more guards could reach him.

Holly slammed the door shut and then leaned over him, panic etched into her face while she pressed hands against his stomach to

try and stop the blood. On the other side, someone threw their weight against the door, making it shudder. Terror flooded her scent, but she wasn't about to leave.

"Keep going," he said, forcing one hand to reach for the pocket where he'd put some antisilver. "Go to Storage Room 5. There's a door hidden behind the wooden crates of absinthe. It'll lead right out to Brom. I'll catch up."

"You're too noble, Sam. It'll kill you one of these days." She undid the pocket button for him and pulled out the capped syringe. "Do you want me to do it?"

He shook his head and used his teeth to take the cap off. "If you won't leave, then take the gun. Aim at the door in case they break through before I'm back on my feet."

The door jumped and shuddered while he jabbed the needle into the side of his neck and injected the antisilver without ceremony, hoping his hand wasn't shaking enough to break it off. His heart sounded too loud in his ears, blotting out whatever Holly said to him next. Damn it. It might've been too late to recover.

One breath. Another. Then the lights above him stopped swimming. The raw agony slowly eased to a dull cramping that he could breathe through, but he still felt blood soaking through his uniform. No time to let himself heal—now he could hear again, and the guards were punching in codes, trying to find one that would open the door.

With a final hiss of pain, he rolled up to his feet. Sweat soaked his collar, but his hands were steady again as he took the gun back from Holly. "Come on."

She remained beside him while they found the right storage room and slipped inside. He paused long enough to shove several of the

crates against the door, ignoring how they grew splattered with his blood. Holly pried open the door with her nails, desperate again now that freedom was almost within reach.

He made sure she was fully in the tunnel before he aimed at the crates by the door and fired a few times to shatter bottles and set the absinthe inside on fire. It would be enough to keep the guards from following them. The entire room was full of wood and alcohol.

It must have been some time since the tunnel had been checked on, for only half of the lights set into the ceiling worked, leaving them in gloom while they traveled through it as quickly as possible.

He suspected the effects of silver poisoning hadn't entirely left his system yet, because even though the ground beneath their feet was smooth cement instead of uneven dirt and rock, he still found himself sinking into memories from only a few days before. Of walking besides Miss Marshall—*Cora*, her name was Cora, but he avoided the intimacy of her beautiful first name even in his thoughts—and trying to act calm and collected when he wanted nothing more than to knock out those idiot policemen and hide her away from the schemes of her city. One of those gut-deep urges that came to him whenever she gazed up into his eyes, scent full of her longing...

"Look. Sunlight."

Holly's voice brought him back to the present, and he tried to breathe in deeply. His lungs responded well enough, and he held her back with a wave of his hand before knocking on the steel door set in the ceiling.

He was ready with his gun by the time it opened with the tortured squeal of rusted hinges. Then Brom reached through, bloodied yet whole and unharmed. "Holly!"

Despite the chaos and terror of their flight, it was the sound of his voice that dissolved her expression into tears. As soon as Brom pulled her up and cradled her close, she began crying against him, fingers digging into his shoulders as if she'd never let go again.

Sam turned away to give them privacy, taking it as a chance to shut the door and glance over two nearby bodies. More royal guards, probably ones that had been unlucky enough to patrol this part of the territory line.

Then he checked his wound. It still bled sluggishly, but the blood was bright and clean. He was out of danger.

He'd just finished reloading his gun when Brom spoke again, this time sounding grim. "How close are they?"

Sam looked up. "We need to keep moving. Eventually, they'll alert someone who knows about this tunnel."

They reached no man's land without trouble, but he didn't feel safe until they were through the forest and onto the vacant lot that backed up to a nightclub. A man sweeping up broken glass quickly looked away from them. If there was anything Sam appreciated about humans, it was their willingness to turn a blind eye to whatever wasn't their problem.

After what they'd escaped from, the dangers of Ragbag Way felt laughable. No one wanted to go after a group of bloodied, bristling wolves, and Sam parked in front of Minnie's house without fear of coming back out to find it missing.

Minnie met them at the door. Brom and Holly received a gentle welcome, but her smile turned into a sigh at the sight of Sam covered in blood. "Oh, Sam. Let's patch you up in the kitchen. No arguing, now."

By the time he'd showered and let her look at the wound, it was a ragged gash surrounded by bruising. She shook her head while bandaging it. "It'll scar."

He shrugged and glanced over as Brom came down the stairs. Minnie had given them the second floor. Anger continued to pulse throughout the other wolf's scent, but he was steady again. Able to think.

Brom sat in one of the empty chairs, shoulders tense. "She's resting now. Thanks, Sam. Without you..."

"I know," said Sam, sensing his struggle for words. "Don't worry about it. We beat the odds without losing anything for it."

Minnie scoffed while tying off the bandage. "Yes, you did. You lost a lot of blood. Get some rest for a few days. Stay here if you need to."

"Not yet. There's something else I need to do." Sam reached for his shirt and pulled it on, relieved to feel only a slight pull from his wound as he began buttoning it up.

"It can't wait?" said Minnie, not even hiding her exasperation.

"No." Then he shrugged into his shoulder holster and checked his gun out of habit. "Jane went over to watch the Saxbys meet with city officials. Something tells me it won't go well."

CHAPTER TWENTY

Captain Albert Dempsey hated wearing his dress uniform. The black wool felt stifling in the conservatory's humid atmosphere, and the gold braiding and white gloves highlighted his smallest movement. At least he didn't have to carry a smallsword like the police commissioner.

Commissioner Keene looked irritated as well, tapping his fingers against the gold pommel of the aforementioned sword while the enchanters finished the last of the wards that would protect him—in theory. Al already had all of his in place. They made his skin prickle a little but were otherwise fine.

When the commissioner continued to glower, Al couldn't resist asking, "No assistant today?"

Keene turned his glare on him. "Even I'm not above superstition on a day like this. Whenever an alpha-king wants to meet with city officials, it's always a cover for something else. He's been sending his lackeys to pester your division for weeks, so something must have changed for him to show up and demand an explanation. And to list us out by name! The sheer gall."

Beside Al, Detective Nichols cleared his throat. Al recognized it as a nervous tic, as was the man's dry recital of facts that they all already knew. His voice gathered them together like a handful of cards. "Myself, Master Enchanter Byrd, Captain Dempsey, and you. Everyone in a position of authority for the Isaac Marshall case."

"And how would they know that?" demanded the commissioner, removing his peaked cap to wipe sweat from his forehead. "The mayor and the rest of the council are convinced someone is leaking information from your division, Captain. That's treason."

Al didn't see the point in responding to a tantrum, but Nichols stiffened. "It's just as possible that it's someone in your office, Commissioner. Or yours, Byrd," he added, causing the enchanter to wring his hands even harder.

When Keene grew red in the face, Al shot Nichols a look that said *cut it out*. Then he said, "I know the council is suspicious of how my division interacts with the two ex-Saxbys. Like I've explained many times before, it's better to stay friendly with them. Lone wolves are an easy way to collect information on all packs."

The other man waved away the comment. "Well, it ends today. Whatever these wolves want, they're using tactics that might embolden the others. Out of concern for the safety of our city, we can't allow this to go on. The Saxby Pack is in for a rude realization."

Then he glared at Al a final time, as if waiting for a protest. Al just shrugged. He knew what they had all been told to expect during the meeting, but he also knew that despite the commissioner's indignation, they were *all* under suspicion of accepting bribes from the Saxby Pack in return for information. Which meant there was

probably a lot that had been decided by the mayor and council that he didn't know. Goddamn, he hated politics.

Just as he reached into his pocket for a cigarette, a new figure entered the room, silent and stark against the ostentatious orchids that surrounded the glass table where the meeting would take place. Al felt himself smile for the first time that day as Captain Inge Falk greeted them all.

They knew each other from the war, and he had fought hard to get her promoted to head of the tactics division when the commissioner had balked over a foreign woman taking such a vital position. She looked hard and intimidating in her uniform, and her broad face rarely showed emotion. Despite living in the city for over twenty years, she still had an accent that gave her words a cold precision. "Everything is ready."

Keene didn't look reassured. "Are you sure? Have all the buildings in the five-block radius been cleared of citizens?"

At Captain Falk's crisp nod, Al asked, "What do you want us to do if they get aggressive?"

There was a brief gleam of amusement in the woman's eyes, but she was much too proper to answer with a joke. "The wards will protect you from bullets and blades. If anyone touches you, they will receive a nasty shock. By then, my men will be taking action."

"And you're sure they won't be sensed?" said Keene, glancing around the room. "Them or the magic used to hide their presence?"

"They're already in place. Do you see them?"

Al was the only one who didn't look around. The technology was based on the kind of camouflage tactics he and Falk were both familiar with, using the environment to hide a human body and

their weapon. In this case, magic took it to the next level of masking scent as well.

"No," said the commissioner, grudgingly. "What about their aim? The plants won't obstruct their view?"

"We're using heat to sight, and wolves have a different temperature than humans. Don't engage them if they attack."

"Easier said than done," muttered Nichols, but the commissioner was already speaking.

"Just make sure you keep all hell from breaking loose." Then Keene pulled out one of his gold cigarettes and returned to his seat, still sulking over the fact that he had to be there at all.

Al noticed how the commissioner kept sweating. Some of it could be blamed on the heat, but his gut told him there was more to it. The man should have been used to dealing with wolves, even alpha-kings or queens. It wasn't unheard of for some to briefly visit human land, especially for ritzier events. They *were* royalty, after all, and expected to access all the luxuries of the city as such. Keene had surely rubbed elbows with one or two during an opera's intermission.

So what the hell was it?

Even as he continued to eye the commissioner, Falk cleared her throat, drawing his attention. "There are a few more things we need to clear you of, Captain. If you would come with me?"

The arch of her eyebrow suggested this was more than mere formality. The feeling in Al's gut deepened as he nodded, lighting his cigarette.

The Telladay Conservatory glittered behind them as she led him across the street toward the stately opera house on the other side. It was odd to see empty sidewalks and dim windows in nearby

buildings. Once inside, their feet sounded overloud against the marble floors and stairways.

It took three flights of stairs to reach the roof. Out in the open air and away from others, Captain Falk relaxed enough to laugh. "I thought you'd be puffing by now. All those years behind a desk with nothing but cigarettes to keep you company."

"I like to think of myself as a hound at heart, not a lapdog. I'll keep working until I'm dead." Al scanned the statues, nooks, and stone flourishes that comprised the rooftop bannisters. "So. Why are we here?"

"I thought you would like to see the sniper ready in case of emergency. You might be fascinated by the advancements made in the rifles." Then she led him over to where her man was situated. His clothing mimicked the color of the stone, and he didn't look up when they approached.

Al sensed the kid's growing unease as they both studied him. Maybe he knew what their positions in the war had been; maybe he was just nervous from two high-ranking officers watching him. Either way, Al decided to give the kid a break by turning to look out on the city instead. "They make them a lot fancier these days. I can almost hear all the magic buzzing from it."

A grimace from Falk told him she agreed. She had always liked the sturdiness of an old-fashioned bolt action rifle. Her own in the war had been her grandfather's. As they began following the perimeter of the roof, she said, "Times aren't desperate now."

"But just as dangerous?" He knew they would be talking with care from this point on, every sentence offering up a hidden meaning. Falk wouldn't reveal things to him that she wasn't

supposed to—not openly, anyway. She had her own neck to look after.

The other captain fell silent for a moment. "Did you think you would survive the war?"

"I never tried to guess the future. Taking each day as it happened was always enough."

She nodded. "It's one way of thinking. Not the way I see things, perhaps, or how I carry out the decisions handed to me."

Al didn't respond, aware that she was about to hint at something very important. As she considered her next words, his gaze fell from her face.

Their uniforms were very similar, and he easily found a slight outline over her heart, imperceptible beneath the black wool except to those who knew exactly what it was: a copper pocket frame. He'd seen it once, some time after they had become friends. One drunken night, she had opened it up and showed him what was inside—a picture of her with her husband and children.

Despite sharing a bottle of the strongest hooch he'd ever had, the words had flowed out of her with perfect clarity. She had been away to see her sick mother when the war broke out, just a farm wife in a country village. She had returned to find everyone harvested by the mech-enchanters, her family included. Within a week, she had joined the military and was placed in one of the sniper divisions, determined to take as much revenge as possible.

Al had seen her unguarded rage that night, and hadn't been surprised when she had accumulated over 300 confirmed kills to her name by the time the war ended. Many others thought he and Inge had been lovers, but their closeness had been that of friends. He'd

never seen her show interest in anyone ever, and he had never seen her without that photo tucked against her heart.

Iron Inge, they'd called her, but he'd known it was fury that had driven her, not any sense of duty. It was what would give him a fighting chance now against any bullshit that the city was planning for him and others at the meeting.

Just then, she turned to him. "Do you remember the wartime question every soldier was asked?"

"Sure. 'Are you prepared for a closed casket funeral?'" With the enemy forces harvesting brains to build more war mechs, it had been common practice to completely destroy the head when possible. "Why ask that?"

"It's become relevant for you again."

His voice sharpened. "My chances of surviving are that slim? If they are, I know it's not because of the Saxbys."

"It's a fragile situation, and suspicions run sharp. No one likes your friendliness toward the wolves, Captain. No one trusts it. Your men uncovered the information that the Saxbys regularly betray others. A stab in the throat when a friendly handshake is offered. Yet some still wonder if you've risked that."

Al sighed out a lungful of smoke. "The irony is that I've never played nice with others, wolves or human. Merely *fair*. So what are they expecting?"

The other captain shrugged. "Don't let yourself be taken by the wolves. It's one possibility I was told to prepare for—the Saxbys attempting to carry off a human for their own interrogation tactics. With the border to no man's land so close... well, it's not an unlikely scenario."

"Especially if the human was willingly taken away? So. The sniper won't protect us, just make sure we can't tell the wolves anything. No wonder Keene is sweating bullets." Despite the lightness to his voice, irritation seeped through him. He didn't like being thought of as someone who would take bribes at the first opportunity. God knew he had refused them often enough throughout his career. "Tell you what, if it comes to that, have your boy shoot me in the right side of the head. It's less obstinate than the left."

He could see Falk wanted to smile, but she resisted with a shake of her head. "You never change, Al. Be careful. Aside from your detective, no one in that room will trust you."

They were walking back to the stairway now, taking in the last glimpses of the view of the city. "My reputation is that bad, huh?"

"Rumors are swirling with how friendly you are with the two exiled Saxbys."

"More like they won't stop poking their muzzles in my damn cases."

"I see." Captain Falk's voice turned sly. "Then you won't mind if the she-wolf of the two is killed in any crossfire?"

It took Al a moment to understand the implication. "Are you saying she's in that damn conservatory?" he snapped, glaring out at the shimmering building. From that distance, its spherical shape was apparent.

"Yes. She's trying to hide herself through magic, but my men are using heat-sensitive scopes. She's watching from the spiral staircase that leads to the upper walkway."

"Damn it. Hold back on telling anyone else. I'll get her out."

From the way Captain Falk chuckled, he knew she'd enjoy watching.

When he returned to the conservatory, he ignored his seat at the table for one of the trees near the first metal steps up to the walkway. The conservatory was all one massive room, but the various plant species segmented it as thoroughly as a formal garden, giving him privacy from the others. He pretended to study the orchids nestled against the smooth bark while blowing a lungful of smoke upward.

The action was rewarded with a cough above him. He looked up at the steps spiraling above his head, finding where the smoke curled around what looked like empty space, tracing the silhouette of a crouched body.

"Goddamn it, Feral."

When the figure made no movement, he stepped closer to the stairway. "Are you going to make me smoke you out?"

There was a moment of hesitation before she flickered into view. She didn't look repentant at all, instead glaring as she coughed again.

"What the hell are you doing here?"

She shrugged. "I want to hear what they'll say."

"Too bad. This meeting is confidential. You're not supposed to know it's even happening."

"For once, it's not your department's failing. We gathered the information on the Saxbys' side."

"We? Are you telling me Hayes is here, too?"

"No. He's busy with something else."

In his mind, that made things even worse. He could trust Sam Hayes to handle himself in a tough situation. He'd seen and worked with the wolf enough to know he had good self-control under pressure, remained tactical, and read people well enough to stay alive.

He couldn't say the same about her. So far, his only experiences with Jane Feral was that she believed she could handle anything by being the smartest one in the room.

He jerked his head toward the doors. "Scram. I'm not playing around today."

"Neither am I."

"If you don't get out, I'll arrest you."

Some of the humor faded from her eyes when she realized he wasn't about to let her stay. "No one will notice. I'm not about to try anything."

"What is it with you two? It's like you're so used to living in danger that you forgot how to play things safe. You're an ex-member of the pack. Neither side is going to allow you to listen in on this."

"But—"

"I'm telling you, stay out." At her obvious frustration, he added, "Look, maybe I can get you in with the enchanters. But you'll be stripped of your gear and can't leave their sight until this is over."

"I won't interfere," she insisted. "You know me well enough to trust me. All I want is to—"

"No one cares what you want. You're a loose end."

He saw hurt flash through her expression, but she only gave him a stiff nod.

Something told him not to trust his eyes at the sight of her leaving out through the back entrance while being escorted by two officers. The feeling continued to itch at him while the Saxbys arrived.

Alpha-king Saxby wasn't the first royal wolf he'd ever seen and looked typical for wolves of his status. Stone-faced and grey-haired. Ruthless eyes. In good shape for being in his late forties. Not a fancy

dresser, but his suit screamed understated wealth. Al hadn't been able to find out anything personal about the alpha-king, but his history as a ruler suggested he held onto grudges and didn't care about the cost of an action as long as it fell on someone else's head.

Al's takeaway was that he faced a wolf used to having the world spin however he wanted. A delusion that could maybe be used against him once they all started talking. Then he glanced over the royal guards surrounding their king. Twenty of them, all in their own version of a dress uniform. The amount of gold on them was staggering. Even their daggers looked gilded.

"No weapons," said Captain Falk, her tone flat and unshakeable.

"This wasn't told to us," said one of the guards.

She gestured toward one of her men, who was already opening a sheaf of papers to a precise place. When he offered it over, she said, "It was part of the agreement drawn up and signed by all members of this meeting, including your king. Now. No weapons."

As the wolves reluctantly handed over their daggers and revolvers, Al shared a glance with her. He knew they were thinking the same thing. A lot of wolves were trained in hand-to-hand combat since they couldn't carry weapons while shifting form. From what the city's sources had gleaned, the captain of the royal guard was particularly good at it.

He could believe it. She was young and unscarred but had a hardness to her eyes he'd seen in many suspects sitting across from him in interrogation rooms. She didn't view the people around her as anything beside objects to use or destroy.

Just before Al joined the other city officials at the table, he muttered to Falk, "Is that pain in the neck we talked about still with your men?"

She understood that he meant Jane Feral. "Yes. The enchanters, specifically. Good luck, Captain."

Once they were all seated, orchids surrounding them in bursts of color and many of their faces already shiny with sweat from the humidity, the commissioner thanked Captain Falk before she left and then began his usual introduction.

Al barely listened, having long heard enough of the man's oily voice and oilier placations. Instead, he studied all the wolves before him, trying to figure out their possible soft spots. In a way, he looked forward to this. It had been a while since he'd interviewed someone who hadn't already been questioned. He enjoyed the game of getting people to talk, especially the ones who hated or feared him on sight. It wasn't just hunting for clues but also finding the right tactic to get them to open up. Sometimes it was sympathy, sometimes it was anger. Something told him these wolves would be easy to rile.

As Master Enchanter Byrd took his turn in babbling to the wolves, Al's attention switched between the alpha-king and the captain of the royal guard. He had a hunch there was something between them. His division had done a lot of investigation into the Saxbys, scraping up information that many wolves thought humans could never find, but he always paid attention to his gut, too. What he noticed now was how only the Saxby captain had no fear in her eyes. Sure, she came off as a cold bitch, but every living thing held an instinct for survival. She wasn't afraid to be there and she wasn't afraid to be near her alpha-king. She didn't feel she was in danger at all.

Then the alpha-king himself spoke up, catching Al's attention. "All we want to know is what's going on. The city has stonewalled us from the very beginning. You wouldn't send over the body of the

creature that invaded my land and killed my guards, each human you blame as the ultimate culprit ends up dead and unable to be questioned, and now you claim you can't find the thaumaturgist responsible for this strange magic."

"It's a complicated case," said Al, wanting to protect Nichols from the wolf's wrath. "But we've sent copies of everything in our files over to you."

"Then your division isn't well-organized, because we've never received them."

Al kept his voice affable. "I sent them myself. Try again."

The alpha-king's eyes glittered. He didn't like being challenged at all. "Try again at what?"

"At giving a reason for why you wanted this meeting. We've shared everything with you. What do you expect to get out of this?" He really was interested in the answer. Truth or lie, he'd be able to use it for more insight.

After a moment, the alpha-king grudgingly said, "It's recently come out that Miss Cora Marshall is nowhere to be found, and the city isn't distressed about that. We're very curious as to why."

Al didn't quite nod toward Nichols, but his men knew him well enough to pick up his slightest movements during interviews. Nichols sounded calm as he said, "Every other major name in this case has ended up dead. We didn't want the same to happen to her. We're also close to finding Harold Beaumont."

"Assurances aren't good enough. The city's actions can't be seen in a positive light."

Nichols' voice sharpened. "What are you suggesting?"

"Incompetence or a cover up."

When the alpha-king's gaze fell on Al, he mildly said, "A cover up for what?"

At that, the Saxby captain scoffed. "It's known that your department in particular is very friendly with the exiled wolf calling himself Sam Hayes."

Al didn't miss the extra dose of venom lacing the name. Goddamn, Sam could be stupid. "We're friendly with most of the private dicks in this city. It's normal procedure if they stay by the book and don't interfere with our cases. More than that, he was hired by a private citizen to look into Isaac Marshall's disappearance independently. You want to tell me how to avoid someone investigating the same suspects, scenes, and witnesses?"

The commissioner cleared his throat. "Let's avoid getting into arguments. We came here ready to share all the information we know about the transformation of Dominic Tierney and its cause. The police enchanters have concluded their findings on the magic behind this situation. It's a bio-thaumaturgic serum created by the freelance enchanter Harold Beaumont. The serum was given to Mr. Tierney at a tattoo parlor. The artist had been bribed by Frederick Davenport, who wanted to assassinate Isaac Marshall out of a need to use his daughter for an illegal arcane ritual."

The alpha-king sighed, frustration clear on his face. "So you've said. Yet you've never offered evidence for any of the links in this chain."

Al raised his eyebrows. "Have your boys come to a different conclusion?"

"We find it odd how Marshall's daughter is connected to this case at every level and yet has been dropped as a suspect."

"Why do you think she's in on it?"

"For one thing, having the sense to hire Sam Hayes. He's highly antagonistic toward his former pack and king. He'll never come to a conclusion that favors us... even if it's the truth."

All shrugged. "I don't know anything about his view of the case. We're here to talk about the city's, and we found out interesting things about Beaumont's serum and its origin."

At his glance, Enchanter Byrd cleared his throat. "Elements of the serum draw from ancient magic. We've been able to track it to a strain of curses that survive through generations. The legends of berserker wolves aren't entirely false. It's documented that several packs have a heritage involving these wolves. Sometimes, there are even throwbacks."

The alpha-king scoffed. "Those are myths to scare pups into behaving for their nanny."

Al decided to poke at the wolf. "Even myths can have a basis in reality. Your old enemies, the Sinclairs, were rumored to have trouble with it. I'm surprised you didn't recognize the look of the creature tearing your guards apart. Historical accounts point out the throwback problem affected the royal family every few generations."

Al watched the wolves all fall very still. When the alpha-king said nothing, Al looked at the captain of the royal guard. "You used to be Princess Liana's personal bodyguard, didn't you? How did the Sinclair prince she was supposed to marry end up killing her?"

"He slit her throat," she said, voice cold.

Al glanced at the commissioner to see if he was done with the charade. When he got the silent answer, he sighed and braced himself for a potentially nasty response. "All right. Now let's hear the honest answer."

The she-wolf's flat tone turned murderous. "Do you think I would lie to my king about his daughter's death?"

"No. No, I think you both knew exactly what would happen. Lovers often share a lot."

Al expected a reaction. He just didn't expect it to happen so damn fast. All the guards lunged for him. The alpha-king disappeared behind a wall of uniformed bodies, giving Al a final glimpse of the wolf's furious expression. Then there was a fist heading for his face.

He ducked and used the wolf overextending his reach to shove him away. The commissioner's voice rose in frantic tones. Al's hand twitched toward the jacket of his uniform, but by then Falk's men were already at work.

No bullets in such an enclosed space. The conservatory's board members had also insisted that their precious plants couldn't be put at risk in any way. Instead, darts were used, silver-tipped to drop the wolves. If any of the humans were caught, it would hurt less than a bee sting and be harmless. It worked... until it didn't.

For Al, it happened in a silent explosion of smoke. The protective wards on him flared hot enough to give his skin the uncomfortable itch of sunburn. They disappeared just as quickly, reduced to smudges of ash against the black wool. Even as thick, scentless smoke washed over him and all the others in the glass room, he swore under his breath, recognizing what had happened.

One of the wolves must have activated a spell scrambler. Everything magic-related had been nullified, including the invisibility spells on Falk's men as well as any wards the city enchanters had cast. He and every other human inside the

conservatory were on their own. And from the sudden screams and splattering sounds, it wasn't going well.

Just as he realized the wolves would be able to scent and track every human in the conservatory, a gunshot rang out. Then the commissioner screamed. Al felt the old calm come back to him as he unbuttoned his uniform's jacket enough to pull out the gun that had been holstered snugly against his ribs. He could probably find the way out without tripping over too many bodies, but that wasn't where the man's voice had come from. It was from deeper into the conservatory, like he was either lost or being dragged to the back entrance.

Falk's men would be watching that area, too, but if the smoke was this thick everywhere, then he wasn't feeling good about their chances of spotting the commissioner. He also didn't feel good about the silence around him—it meant the fighting was over and the human officers inside were all dead. Were all the wolves? Maybe not, since they didn't have to speak to communicate or hunt.

The thought kept him light and cautious with each step through the blinding atmosphere. He listened as carefully as possible even after finding a trail of blood to follow. The commissioner's voice continued as a series of groans and whimpers. He had been through similar situations in the war, with smoke or fog so thick he couldn't see his damn hand in front of his face, much less the enemy trying to kill him. The trick was not to panic and to be ready to shoot in any direction.

Plants brushed him like ghosts as he eased his way to the other side. The orchids had been replaced by thick-fleshed carnivorous plants and a stream feeding trees covered in vines. The smoke was

thinning enough for him to catch sight of the commissioner being dragged by the Saxby she-wolf while he clutched at his bleeding leg.

Al's first shot got her in the back. She went down with a snarl, barely more than a shadow writhing on the ground. He stayed cautious while moving for them, reaching the commissioner just as Detective Nichols appeared out of the thick smoke, gun also drawn.

"Cuff her," said Al, kneeling down beside Keene. Then he realized Nichols was aiming at *him*.

"Ah, hell," he sighed. "So the informant *was* from my division."

"Sorry, Captain." The other man looked as steady as ever. "I was hoping to keep you out of it. Now put down your gun and slide it over."

No time to feel things like betrayal or anger. Al did as he said, keeping his movements slow. By then, the she-wolf was jabbing herself in the neck with a syringe, breathing easier within moments. When she rolled to her feet, the air was clear enough for Al to see the hatred in her eyes as she glared at him, but she only turned Nichols and said, "We'll take them both."

Nichols nodded and then gestured at Al again. "You're not a coward, so you won't run off like the commissioner here. Help him so we can move faster."

Arguing wouldn't do anything, so Al ignored the commissioner's attempt at words as he hauled him upright and steadied him, taking the weight off his injured leg. He didn't expect any leniency from Nichols or the she-wolf as they began moving, Nichols behind them and the she-wolf ahead. The blood running from the commissioner's leg splattered with each painful step. Their progress was cripplingly slow, and the smoke was thinning by the moment. The doorway was

yards away, a square of bright light surrounded by blossom-filled vines.

"It's looking clearer out there," muttered Nichols. "You said the smoke would last long enough to make it over the border."

"It should," came the terse reply. "Unless there's someone trying to..."

Al watched as the she-wolf stiffened and looked toward her left. "Keep going," she said, voice tight. "I'll catch up."

While she disappeared deeper into the conservatory, Al calculated the angle of the doorway. The air outside was also smoke-filled, but they probably all looked like dim shadows by now, and he knew Falk and her paranoia. She was just the type to insist on magic-free weapons as backup. If the city had okayed her request, then there was just a chance... a better one than expecting to survive being tortured by wolves. He kept compliant until they were barely a foot away from the entrance. Then he kicked the commissioner's bad leg out from underneath him, trusting the smoke to hide the act.

Keene went down with a scream, sliding out of Al's grip. When Al knelt beside him, Nichol drew closer, ready with his gun and obviously frustrated.

"His leg is bad off," said Al, looking up at Nichols. "He'll bleed out in a few minutes unless I put a tourniquet on him."

Nichols sighed, but the blood streaming out on the tile was impossible to deny. "All right, hurry up."

"You son of a bitch," managed the commissioner, as Al began looping a belt above his knee.

Al ignored the comment, keeping his movements short and efficient to hide the fact that he was shifting position in a way that forced Nichols to move to keep a good bead on him. A shot rang out

from somewhere inside the conservatory. Then a yelp, too animalistic to come from anything besides a wolf. Al watched Nichols, who was looking more nervous by the moment. When a snarl echoed from among the dim silhouettes of the plants, Nichols took an unconscious step toward it, sensing trouble.

As soon as the man stepped within the full light of the doorway, his head snapped on his neck sickeningly in an explosion of blood. He crumpled to the ground with a gaping hole in his skull.

Al moved faster than he had in years to grab the gun from the body, keeping low in case there was another sniper bullet coming. Then he wedged the commissioner against the nearest tree trunk and crouched beside him as Falk's men began shouting warnings that they were coming in. Just as Al was about to yell back about the she-wolf, glass shattered somewhere in the direction of where she'd disappeared. It didn't take a genius to know that she was fleeing. Now that it was almost over, his heart was beating fast and hard. He always hated these in-between moments the most—not in danger and not yet safe.

He didn't relax until they were escorted out of the conservatory and into the organized chaos of the tea shop Falk was using as the base of operations for the city enchanters. As the commissioner was swarmed by them, Al stayed out of the way and smoked, waiting for Falk to come over. The smoke had already been cleared, and fresh wards glowed brightly. When he checked his watch, some part of him felt surprised that only ten minutes had passed since the debacle had started.

When the other captain walked over, he blew out some smoke and smiled a little. "You saved my neck."

"You're very sure it was me."

"I recognize an Iron Inge shot when I see it."

Despite his even words, her voice grew sympathetic. "I'm sorry, Al. I know you care for all of your detectives."

"Yeah, well, life's full of disappointment." Then he straightened up in his seat. "How about yours? How many made it?"

"The four who found Enchanter Byrd and escorted him out. As for the wolves, the alpha-king escaped with two guards. They are now over the border. No civilian casualties from them, thankfully. The other guards are dead except for one—their captain. She's gone missing." Then Falk frowned. "A few spots of blood indicate she's wounded. Did you fight her?"

"No, but someone else tried to," said Al, remembering the look on the she-wolf's face right before she had lunged into the smoke. Then he studied all the enchanters in view and felt his stomach sink. "And I don't think the Saxby captain is the only she-wolf missing. Where's Jane Feral?"

It took five minutes for Falk's men to find a blood trail leading to an abandoned factory just inside no man's land. It was a bad location for escaping; it was surrounded by junk on all sides and then flat land with nothing to hide behind. The Saxby captain must have gone to it out of desperation. From the tracks left behind, the body she had been dragging had been struggling. That meant Feral was probably still alive.

Al turned toward the nearest enchanter. "Whose blood is it?"

"It's not from the Saxby she-wolf," said one of the enchanters, his fingers still glowing with the remnants of his detection spells. "But it *is* a wolf's. Do you think Jane Feral is working with her former pack?"

Al pulled off those stupid white gloves and then his cap. "Just the opposite. Feral is in a world of trouble. If the Saxbys see Sam Hayes as a good buddy of ours, they'll think the same about her."

"The commissioner was clear," warned Captain Falk. "No one is to step out of the city."

"A step is all it would be," muttered Al, staring at the yellow paint running over the stoop into the factory door. It was the border itself. Then he sighed. "What the hell. The commissioner isn't too happy with me right now, so I'm probably fired already."

"Shoo the Saxby captain back onto city land, and you might not be," said Falk. "But only if she's alive. I've just had a *discussion* with the mayor about his disappointment that the guards are all dead. The city officials badly want a living wolf to interview."

"Want me to bring back lunch while I'm at it?" Al was already shrugging off the stiff jacket of his uniform.

Falk just smiled while exchanging the silver bullets in his gun for regular lead. "You have five minutes before the mayor will come looking for you. He's nearly finished with the commissioner."

He knew the drill; as soon as he was back in city limits, they'd swarm to help him. Out in no man's land, he was on his own. He mentally bitched out Jane Feral the entire time it took to reach the warehouse safely. Adrenaline once more honed his senses as he got inside through a broken window. He was ready with his gun while following droplets of blood and then footsteps in the dust. The factory's interior was in bad decay, giving him plenty of cover in the form of rusted machinery and stacks of weatherbeaten chairs.

Two voices grew clear: a thick snarl he barely recognized as Jane Feral and the cold tones of the Saxby captain. That explained why

he'd been able to get inside without being seen; she was already trying to get information out of Feral.

Al inched closer until he was able to see them, angling himself behind a support beam. He'd have to duck out for a clear shot, but for the moment he could take in the situation unnoticed.

Jane Feral was already bloody-faced and struggling to breathe, limp on the floor in a way that suggested she couldn't move. Her bulky enchanter's leathers hid the extent of her injuries, but the agony on her face was all he needed to see. The Saxby captain was kneeling against the smaller she-wolf, one knee pressing into the tender part of the sternum and one hand holding a dagger against her cheek. Her voice was hardly more than a murmur, but Al could still glean the words.

"Since you've never been in a fight, I should make something clear. Being cut by silver isn't the same as other metal. Even if you survive the poisoning, whatever is sliced away doesn't grow back."

Then the knife tip moved to Jane's earlobe. "The ears... the nose... the eyes. I'll start taking them all if you don't answer my questions. After all, all you need to use is your tongue."

Al fired. It was a clean neck shot. He knew normal bullets didn't kill wolves but wasn't sure if one could still scramble their brains.

The she-wolf was back up as soon as she'd fallen, throwing the dagger in his direction. Damn, she was fast. The beam he was behind kept him safe and he shot again, this time aiming for a knee. Not as clean, because she was already moving, scrabbling behind the nearest machine for cover.

Jane Feral was still breathing, left out there in the open. Al risked moving to her, throwing a steel table on its side to give them cover and give him time to assess whether she would survive the fight.

There was too much blood on her to guess by sight. As he quickly began checking her neck and chest for obvious wounds, she seemed to grow aware of him.

"Why, Captain," she muttered, eyes unfocused. "I didn't know you were hiding such passion."

"Shut up. I'm trying to see what's fractured." He moved down to her hips. The mere weight of his hand drew out a shriek in reply. "A few ribs and one of your pelvic bones. I can't move you."

Just then came the sound of bullets dropping to the floor. The Saxby captain had already healed. Al swore to himself and then told Feral, "Don't try anything. Just stay there."

If the bullets weren't going to work, then he'd have to subdue the wolf with something else. He left the safety of the table to grab a nearby chair and threw it at the she-wolf as soon as she slipped around the machine, flexing her bare hands. She obviously wasn't afraid of fighting him, but the sight of a chair flying her way still made her duck back, eyes flashing with fury.

Another couple of chairs sent her scuttling this way and that. She didn't seem to know what to do against things being thrown at her, and Al almost laughed at the idea of never being in a street fight. The fourth chair finally caught her before she could hide behind another machine, and she fell with it, snarling. When Al approached with another chair, she struggled against the wooden legs long enough for her hand to flash to her boot and then back out. Whatever she had winked in the bright light shining through the row of windows behind her.

Shit, he thought, knowing he was in trouble. Expecting a knife to fly through the air at him.

Instead, it was a derringer so small it looked like a toy. It fired, catching him in the left side of the head. He heard a howl from Jane Feral as he staggered from the force. When he straightened up again with a sigh, the Saxby she-wolf's eyes widened in shock just before he smashed the chair into her. She shrieked as the gun fell from her hand. Before she could recover, he caught her by the collar and threw her through the nearest window.

Glass exploded through the air while the Saxby captain tumbled over the yellow line and into the reach of Falk's men. Al watched long enough to make sure they were able to control and handcuff the she-wolf before returning to Jane Feral.

She was still conscious, even pushing herself up on her elbows. "I focused on my pelvis and spine. They're stable now, so just drag me out."

He scoffed. "You're tiny. I'll carry you."

She rolled her eyes but said nothing as he easily scooped her up. She didn't look good, sweating and shivering, but her eyes seemed to focus on his face once he started walking. "You're bleeding from the head. She *did* hit you. How are you talking with a bullet in your brain?"

Of all the things she'd focused on to keep herself awake. "Call it being lucky enough to have a war souvenir. Now shut up and save your breath."

She nodded, still breathing too fast for his liking. "Albert Dempsey. Served in the Cognitus-Argellan War, more commonly referred to as the Tin War. Sniper with over 200 confirmed kills. Received two medals of honor for his service."

"Why are you so interested in my past?"

"Why not? You're interested in everyone else's."

"It's my job."

She didn't have time to answer, because then they were back on city land and being surrounded by enchanters and officers.

Falk, bless her, had one of the ambulances ready to go. "It took you seven minutes."

"Yeah, well, I'm getting old." When he turned back toward the warehouse, he heard her intake of breath. Then he remembered about the headshot. "Don't worry about it. Feral is much worse off. How's the commissioner?"

The answer didn't come from Falk but instead Commissioner Keene himself. "Alive, thanks to you."

He was already standing again, and the mayor was there beside him. The mayor's florid face was beaming while he watched the Saxby captain being escorted to a police car. "Your bravery in saving us from the traitor and capturing one of those responsible for this terrible attack won't go unnoticed, Captain. With a little cooperation from her, the case should finally be solved."

Al decided it was better to say nothing. Unfortunately, Enchanter Byrd did. "Your head is bleeding."

"It's nothing."

"Nothing?" interjected the mayor. "It looks like she shot you."

Al sighed and knocked his knuckles against the metal plate in his head, watching the expressions around him change. "Metal against metal. I'm fine."

"Fine?" Byrd's voice rose several notches. "The impact might have caused internal bleeding. And why do you still have a metal plate in your head? Such a surgical technique was considered barbaric even when it was used."

He pulled out a cigarette, already sick of talking about it. "It's worked fine for the past twenty-five years."

"And bone regeneration has been perfected for the past ten. Captain, it's only a four-day stay in the hospital."

"Four days too long for me."

The mayor shook his head. "No, I insist on the best medical treatment. And when you get out, we'll throw a city gala for your bravery."

"A gala?" He hated parties, especially ones that required his dress uniform.

"You'll be the guest of honor," added the commissioner, his expression suggesting that he knew this would be perfect revenge for Al kicking his injured leg. The two men both looked as pleased as cats.

Before Al could argue any further, a howl of rage came out from one of the cars. The Saxby captain had managed to lock her feet around an officer's neck and bring him down with a twist of her hips. He looked confused more than stunned as she rolled free.

Just as Al reached for his gun, someone roared the she-wolf's name. "Isabelle!"

Al had never seen Sam Hayes look so mad as he pushed through the officers until they faced each other. He wasn't armed, but the tension in his body told Al that the wolf was within inches of tearing into her with his bare teeth. Then he remembered that Hayes would be able to smell Jane Feral's blood on her.

"What the hell did you do?" snarled Hayes. There was blood on him, and Al saw another wolf with stained clothes close behind.

At the sight of Hayes, the she-wolf had stopped fighting the officers. And as they put her into the back of the car, her shoulders

slumped, as if she realized it was all over. "Don't look at me like that. It wasn't my decision. I was—"

"Following orders." The hatred in those words seemed to stun even the Saxby captain, and she said nothing else before an officer shut the door.

Al didn't like the look in Hayes' eyes, and called out to him. "Don't do something stupid. She's under police custody. And Feral's fine."

Sam Hayes glared over, but then Jane spoke his name from the ambulance. She was still bloody-faced but also sitting up gingerly, something that would have been impossible if her pelvis was still broken.

Al lit his cigarette, aware it would be his last one for four days while he was in the hospital. His mood was dark enough to blot out the sun. When Hayes came over, he scowled at the wolf and said, "You had terrible taste in women. I'm glad it's improved. Who's your new pal and why are you both covered in blood?"

The rage was clearing from Hayes' voice. "We caught the Saxby alpha-king and his guards while they were trying to reach pack land. The king escaped. His guards didn't."

Al suspected there had been a lot more to it than that. "I'm guessing you knew Miss Feral was going to be here."

"Yes." Then Hayes stepped closer. "Thank you. You saved her." The look on his face suggested he knew how brutal her death would have been.

Al shrugged and flicked away ash. "She'll be fine. That's the only positive thing to say about this goddamn mess."

Hayes nodded, but his eyes still looked wild. "I heard you're being called a hero of the city."

"I know. What else could go wrong?"

Just then, they both heard a male voice shout for Hayes. The panic in it was clear. A male wolf in street clothes tried to push his way through, snarling at the officers who were edgy about so many sudden appearances of wolves.

When he saw he had their attention, he simply raised his voice instead. "Sam, she's gone! The girl's gone. No one went into her room, but an officer stopped by and spoke to her guards. Then she gave them the slip. I tried following her, but she stole a car, and... I lost her."

Al had enough experience with binding magic to guess that the goddamn sigil on her must have activated. From the look on Hayes' face, he was thinking the same thing as he turned back to Al, new tension filling his movements. "Where were your boys searching for Harold Beaumont?"

"Mallow Manor. Before I left for the meeting, I had gotten word that things were looking promising. The cellars had been turned into an obvious laboratory." Then Al sighed. "If Beaumont is still alive in there, try to keep him that way. I've had a bad enough day already."

CHAPTER TWENTY-ONE

Cora glanced in the rearview mirror and bit her lip in anguish while her foot pressed harder against the gas pedal of the stolen car. The retreat had already disappeared from view, and it didn't look like anyone followed her. The sigil burned like a brand, forcing her ever onward.

She shouldn't have eavesdropped. At the sound of footsteps approaching the door to her room, she had hurried over, bored and eager for any news. She'd gotten it. Nobody had come inside, but she'd recognized the head doctor's voice while he murmured to the officer outside. Not all the words had been clear, but the urgency behind them was unmistakable.

"Keep a close watch on her. I've just received word they found the crazed man's secret laboratory. It's at one of Davenport's properties. The country manor, I believe. They already uncovered evidence related to her father, and, well... let's keep her isolated for now in case of some last act of magic triggered by these discoveries. Allow no one inside, not even members of my staff."

The vague intimations had ignited the sigil in a way she hadn't felt since Father had disappeared, crushing all willpower with a blinding headache until she gave in and became a puppet to its command: go find him.

Her fingers didn't feel like her own while she gripped the steering wheel, strangling the fine leather in frustration. Her attempts to be noticed and caught by the guards or staff members had all been fruitless, and now here she was, barrelling down the road. She even knew exactly where to go.

The only country property Freddy hadn't sold was Mallow Manor. One of the places included in her bet with Hayes. *Hayes.* Cora's heart throbbed just thinking about him, but she wasn't hopeful enough to believe he'd find out about her escape in time. The sigil was hellbent on bringing her back to Isaac Marshall, and now it finally had a lead on where to go to begin tracking him. She could feel how the nasty little thing tightened its control with each breath, replacing pain with numbness now that she obeyed it.

It had been years since Cora had visited the manor. Old Man Davenport had still been alive then, and had regularly held hunting weekends for his friends. Cora's father was among those, and she had spent many hours exploring the estate instead of standing with the other wives and daughters while the men shot at pheasants.

The manor itself looked much like she remembered, dour and heavy in the way that only a home filled with generations' worth of relics and furniture could be. Police officers surrounded it while enchanters and detectives worked, oblivious to everything except their pursuit of finding and collecting evidence.

Unfortunately, there were also reporters and spectators cordoned off to either side of the driveway. Cora kept her gaze fixed on the

manor ahead, even when the first shouts of recognition were followed by the flash of cameras in her face. The sigil throbbed in time with her heartbeat while she parked and got out, keeping her steps brisk as if she was meant to be there.

Inwardly, she felt like she had stepped right into hell, but there was no turning back, not even when the officer at the front door held up a hand at her approach. His uniform looked as neat as his blond hair beneath his hat, and his closed-off expression suggested he wasn't about to be swayed from his duty. "Miss, you can't go in. This is a crime scene investigation."

A surge of relief quickly evaporated beneath the weight of the sigil. It pushed words into her mouth and choked her when she tried holding them back. She swallowed hard but gave in before the officer noticed her struggle. "I'm Isaac Marshall's daughter. I was told he might be here, and if he is, I demand to see him immediately."

The officer eyed her and then called inside for the nearest higher-ranked man. An enchanter responded, a tall, gaunt fella who Cora dimly recognized as being one of Enchanter Byrd's underlings. As they murmured to each other in between glances in her direction, her hands convulsively strangled the handle of her purse.

The sigil didn't want to wait, and she found herself speaking again. Her tone came out cold and dismissive, mimicking her father's idea of proper behavior. "This is ridiculous. What is your name?"

"Enchanter Leary, Miss Marshall." The man sounded unimpressed by the imperious words but took a step closer to study her. "Who called for you? You're supposed to be with an escort at all times."

"I fail to see how those questions are relevant. All I want to know is whether my father has been found. I'd like to speak with Detective Nichols. He's in charge of the case against Mr. Davenport, isn't he?"

"He's away on other business. Now, Miss—"

Her next words grew frigid even as the sigil seemed to burn away her skin. "I won't be put off. What did you learn about my father?"

The enchanter hesitated. "All right. Come with me and I'll show you what we've found. You're about to be disappointed, though. It's merely some personal belongings that *may* belong to your father. We needed to reach out to you anyway for confirmation, so at least this will save time for everyone involved."

"But you haven't found him?" She wanted to cry in relief. The sigil grew subdued, its presence fading into something that felt hot and angry, like a fresh bruise.

"No. The body we discovered has already been identified beyond all doubt. It's not your father."

The enchanter led her into a kitchen crusted over with grime and rotting food. Flies buzzed around their faces, but the smell was a much worse experience, and she was relieved when they began descending rickety wooden steps down to the root cellar. The natural darkness quickly gave way to the artificial lights. The air took on the stench of old earth and then an odd, clinical odor. Something like... formaldehyde.

When Cora realized they were about to enter Harold Beaumont's secret laboratory, she asked, "Are you saying you've found Mr. Beaumont?"

"Well, what's left of him."

Before she could ask what exactly *that* meant, they reached the bottom stair. A squat wooden doorway gaped ahead, revealing

concrete floors and plaster walls covered in all sorts of pipes, tubes, and wiring. Voices echoed in a confusing rhythm. The flashes from police cameras were constant.

Then the enchanter stopped her with a sigh. "Are you sure you want to come in here, Miss Marshall? We haven't yet taken away the body, and it isn't a pretty sight."

The sigil gave her no choice. "I insist."

Inside, the lighting turned bright and sterile, shining off of the maze of metal tables and glass instruments. Papers were scattered everywhere. Flies zipped by in a frenzy.

The police stood out very starkly in their dark uniforms, but Cora's gaze instead jumped to what most of them surrounded. It was the kind of chair typically used for medical or dental exams, able to be positioned at various angles. At the moment, it reclined back like a chaise. Trays of tools and mirrors had been set up all around it. The officers and enchanters blocked much of her view... but not everything.

Blood had dried in a large pool around the chair. A stiff hand, still wearing a medical glove, hung toward the floor. A scalpel waited inches away, too crusted over to glint.

"My God," said Cora, her revulsion genuine. "What happened to him?"

"It was a madman's death. He tried to perform an appendectomy upon himself and bled out. He's been dead for a few days."

"That's *awful.*"

Her horrified voice drew the attention of a nearby man while he loaded files into an evidence box. His plain suit and youth suggested he was a junior-level detective, without any real authority, but he

approached them with a frown. "What is she doing here? No one was supposed to bring her out of hiding. Orders from the captain."

"I had to come as soon as I heard there was news of my father," replied Cora, trying not to sound bitter even as the sigil throbbed against her scalp.

Enchanter Leary cleared his throat, but the other man didn't give him a chance. "You brought her down here? It's an active investigation."

The enchanter's stooped shoulders straightened in indignation. "If this case is expected to be solved as quickly as possible, why not save time whenever we can? Miss Marshall will need to identify any possible belongings of her father. If she can do it right now—"

"That's not the point, Leary."

"And you're not the lead detective of this case anymore than I am, Grayson. Now's not the time to pull rank on me."

The argument continued from there. It was clear to Cora that without the presence of Captain Dempsey or another figure experienced in directing a group, the well-oiled machine behind investigating a scene quickly began to grind. Even as relief threaded around her heart from the possibility that she might be sent away, the sudden hiss of a welding torch caught her attention.

On the far end of the room, a man worked on one of several locks set into a steel door. The sigil urged her closer despite the sparks. When Enchanter Leary walked over, now red in the face, she said, "What does he expect to find inside?"

"We don't know, but this property needs to be fully examined. If there's a locked door, we have to break through it. Now, please, if you would just come over here and look at this. As soon as you answer, we'll take you back outside and into safety."

"Good," said Cora, able to speak that much of her mind.

The enchanter took her to a table where boxes of bagged evidence were neatly stacked. Within moments, he offered one such bag over to her. "Don't take it out. Just look at it and tell us if you recognize it."

The sigil's pulse shot into a frenzy until she felt dizzy. "It's Father's signet ring. I'm sure of it. You found it here?"

"Yes. We've been examining Harold Beaumont's lab notes. Some included materials for enchantment use, and your father's ring was one such example. No, don't press me for more information. I'd rather wait for someone with more authority to tell you anything else."

Before the sigil could force her to argue, a murmur started up back by the entrance. A handful of words, repeated among everyone present until they rushed toward Cora and the enchanter like ocean waves. The expression of every person who heard them changed from tired, intent, or grim to complete shock.

"The captain's been shot. He's in the hospital. It was some wolf bitch and Nichols. *Nichols.* The bastard two-timed us with the Saxbys."

As soon as Cora heard the pack's name, she dropped the ring back on the table, heart racing. Her next words were her own, and they rang throughout the room. "Was anyone else hurt?"

The junior detective, Grayson, responded, but not to her. His face looked very pale, but he sounded furious. "Someone get her outside and make sure she's watched over until an unmarked car can take her back to the station. We don't know who they'll come after next or what's safe right now."

Cora knew a refusal was out of the question. The entire atmosphere had changed. She found herself escorted by four silent officers through the back of the manor and into the isolation of the formal garden, which was severely neglected. Some part of her noted that Freddy must have sent away all servants when Harold Beaumont had taken over the manor for his work. The rest of her still spun in shock. The sigil throbbed uneasily against her scalp, unsure of what to do, and she found herself pacing along the shaggy hedges and overgrown rose bushes, staring at the distant road that could take her away from this terrible place.

Then she heard a voice that made her heart sing. "Get out of here. I need to talk to my client."

Hayes was bloodied and missing his hat, but he looked as unfaltering as ever while ducking between two hedges to approach her and the officers. They blocked him. "Sir, stay back."

The bright gold of his eyes blazed at them. "I'm unarmed."

"Stay *back*. No one gets close to her, especially a bloody wolf. If you argue, then we'll move past the talking stage before you can blink."

Cora tried to sound reassuring even though she wanted to just melt into his arms. "Hayes, it's fine. I'm all right, and I don't care what they hear. Are you hurt? There's so much blood..."

"Saxby blood," he said, shortly. "The alpha-king made some stupid decisions today."

Then he scrutinized every inch of her face before adding, "What about you? Who got you out of the retreat?"

"I did it myself. The guards and staff all believed I'm a little feather-head helpless at doing anything. It was extremely easy to take a hairpin and stick it into the cord of a desk lamp in my room, which

shorted out the entire wing of the building. Climbing out the window and down the trellis in the middle of the chaos took less than three minutes."

Despite the watchful officers, he smiled faintly. "Always so clever, Bunny."

The sweetness of his pet name for her sharpened the agony of her next words. "Hayes, there's undeniable evidence that my father was here."

She didn't need to say anything more. She could tell by the way his expression changed that he knew the sigil had been involved. Then he looked past her at the manor's entrance, jaw tightening as she added, "It *is* Harold Beaumont's secret laboratory. And he's in there, dead."

"I know. I can smell it," he murmured, turning back to her. Every line in his body suggested tension. "We need to leave. Now."

"Sir, again, she's not going anywhere," said one of the officers.

"Unless I'm being detained, then yes I am," said Cora, already turning toward the gravel path that would lead to a back road out of the property. Then she found herself surrounded by bristling officers, neatly cut off from Hayes. "Stop this. I'm his *client*."

"Miss, we've just learned of a situation involving the Saxbys, and let me tell you, no wolf is taking off with a human right now."

From the way Hayes' pupils contracted, he was trying very hard not to snap. "You don't know the full story. I'm no longer with the Saxbys, and Miss Marshall needs to be somewhere safe. Immediately."

"Please..." began Cora, sensing the growing agitation from the officers.

Then she heard it. A voice just at the edge of her senses. A commanding baritone she had argued with many times. The sigil flared into life, and only the ring of officers kept her from running toward the sound. Even as her fingers clenched into fists, tears filled her eyes as she realized what must have been behind that steel door in the lab.

As Hayes swore beneath his breath, she spat out a word she'd hoped to never speak again. "Father."

A figure emerged from the same back entrance she had used to reach the garden, already wrapped in a blanket and flanked by enchanters. Her father looked unshaven and slightly disheveled, his fine suit now wrinkled as if that was all he had worn since his disappearance, but he didn't seem bewildered or in shock so much as vaguely irritated, shaking off people and their questions.

When his voice rose above all others, it was in a calm command, not a desperate shout. "I'm cold, filthy, and have been without sustenance for days from being trapped in that damn cell without contact. Once I've been driven home and given a chance to address all three of these issues, I will answer questions."

He hadn't yet seen her, but with each passing moment, the pain from the sigil grew worse, swelling into a pressure in her head that felt dangerous. She couldn't stop looking at him, and only her sheer force of will prevented the sigil from opening her mouth in a scream.

Then she heard Hayes growl just before smoke billowed all around, taking away her sight. It was so thick that she couldn't even see the officers circling her, but in the next moment someone grabbed her arm and tugged her into a flat-out run. She didn't know which way her father was, which meant the sigil didn't, either. Her mind spun from the tiny bit of slack created by the confusion.

By the time she recognized Hayes' hand against her arm, they had moved far enough from the smoke to see each other's faces. "Did you do that?"

"Jane's work, technically," he said, keeping them to the soft grass so that their steps wouldn't sound against the gravel pathway nearby.

Despite the pressure in her head, she laughed. "They probably think you're kidnapping me. They didn't even trust you to begin with."

His answer was a mere scoff while he continued guiding her away as quickly as possible. From the shouts of the officers, they weren't going to let him off if they caught him.

"Where are we going?"

"Somewhere that's not here."

Her hope shattered within the next breath, because her eyesight had cleared enough to realize they were nearly at the road—moving *away* from her father. The pain from the sigil turned blinding. "I can't. I can't leave him."

The urge to return forced her to wrench her hand away from Hayes. When she resisted turning toward the manor, the agony left her bent over and panting for breath. Suddenly, she tasted blood and realized there were trails of it trickling from her nose. The sigil was ready to move beyond mere pain if she continued to fight.

"Goddamn it." Hayes caught her chin. "Cora? Cora, listen to me."

The sound of her name in his voice somehow gave her the strength to look up at him, gasping as the sigil's control increased into something skull-cracking. She couldn't speak, shaking while staring at him in desperation.

"This isn't the end," he said, his eyes as intense as his words. "No matter what your father or the sigil makes you do."

She felt close to fainting but managed to say, "He hates wolves. Oh, go before he sees you. He'll make you hurt much more than me if he knows how much I... I..."

He stopped her agonized words by running a thumb over mouth. "I know. This isn't the end. I promise you."

Then he released her, and she had to turn away from him, each and every muscle in her body compelled to move toward her father. She felt sick and dizzy, unable to speak while wiping her face clean with a shaking hand.

Officers found her just as the final wisps of smoke cleared, and her last true thought was the hope that Hayes had gotten away. She couldn't respond to questions beyond a shake of her head, all focus trained on her father, who was about to get into an unmarked police car.

When he saw her, faint surprise filtered into his expression. "Cora. How did you..."

"We've been trying to find you, Father," she managed, hating how happy she sounded despite the nausea settling into her stomach. The sigil burned beneath her hair in slow, steady pulses, pleased to be back with its master. "I suppose there's a lot to explain."

"Never mind. We'll discuss it later. Right now, I'm tired. Let's go home."

When her body moved like a marionette to obey the order, she wanted to scream. Instead, she felt herself smile. "Of course, Father."

CHAPTER TWENTY-TWO

Jane Feral had never been in a hospital before. She studied its spotless corridors and busy staff with interest while handing her business card to the nurse behind the reception desk. "I'm here to see Captain Albert Dempsey. He was admitted three days ago."

The woman looked like a battleaxe of a nurse, broad and grim and pragmatic, and when she stared at Jane's yellow eyes and then the box of chocolates beneath her arm with open suspicion, Jane remained as polite as she could manage. "I heard he's had visitors since yesterday, especially for work-related reasons."

"That's an understatement. He's been acting like he's in an office instead of a hospital. Let's see some formal ID, please. Anyone can have a business card printed."

Jane supposed the request was only fair, considering the captain had been shot by a she-wolf, and handed over her city-issued license for being a practicing thaumaturgist. She always hated showing it because of the red bolded letters declaring AMATEUR as the answer to which academy she had been taught at, which was the worst stigma a freelance enchanter could have.

The nurse took down the information without comment. As she returned the license and a visitor's badge, she said, "He's out on the grounds for recuperating patients. Go back out and take the side path leading around the east wing of the hospital."

"Thank you." Jane was confident of finding her way; she had already caught his scent, including the nuances. It was healthy, free of infection or pain, and filled with irritation.

Despite the gray pajamas and robes every patient wore, it was easy to pick out the captain. He sat by himself on a veranda that overlooked the lawns and courts set up for gentle exercise. Away from the main hospital and its odors of disinfectant and illness, the air took on the freshness of sun-warmed grass, but Dempsey watched other patients with the expression of someone who would rather be anywhere else.

When he saw her and all but rolled his eyes, she grinned. "Good morning, Captain. How does it feel to have an entire skull again?"

"Rotten. They got me through the operation just to kill me with boredom." His hair wasn't combed back like usual—she guessed patients weren't allowed pomade or other extraneous items during their stay—but he was neatly shaven and looked otherwise like himself. Fully recovered.

When she took the other chair at his table, he sighed. "Why are you here?"

"I have a get well gift for you." Then she set the box of chocolates between them.

He eyed it and then her. "I didn't think you paid any attention to social niceties, Miss Feral."

"You *did* save my life, Captain." She thumbed through the pile of newspapers on the table but had to admit to herself that she was more interested in him. "Thank you."

When he realized she was sincere, the skepticism left his expression. Enthusiasm didn't replace it, but he still pulled off the lid to glance over the delicate truffles nestled in their paper liners. Jane realized she was studying him with too much care, but it was hard to look away.

She had expected to find a man shaken or at least out of his element from a near-death experience and subsequent surgery. Or worse, suffering from aftereffects. Instead, Dempsey didn't seem diminished at all. She told herself that the relief stealing through her heart was merely because he was the only human who listened to her and was in a position of power to do something about it.

Just then, he looked back up at her. "Can't say I have a sweet tooth, but I appreciate the gesture."

"Maybe the bottom layer will be more to your liking."

When he lifted the gold cardboard sleeve that separated the chocolates from what waited beneath, his expression changed. Then he pulled out the matches and one of the cigarettes she'd packed in there and lit it up in record time. He breathed out a lungful of smoke, and all the tension left his face. "Christ, I needed that."

"I assumed as much." Jane finally chose a newspaper and began scanning the front-page articles. Unsurprisingly, they were all about the discoveries at Mallow Manor. When it became clear the captain wasn't about to speak, she began reading one aloud.

"Questions remain after the bombshell reappearance of Isaac Marshall. The renowned businessman went missing weeks ago and was feared dead by many, including his only daughter, Miss Cora

Marshall. Sources close to the police maintain that Mr. Marshall is recovering well after being found captive in a secret room on property belonging to notorious playboy Frederick 'Freddy' Davenport, whose list of confirmed depravities grows with each passing day.

"Miss Marshall is staying close with her father while he recovers and is quoted as being 'very relieved' to have him safe and sound and back at home. Herself a near victim of Freddy Davenport's diabolical occult practices, it remains to be seen whether further light will be shed on high society's unraveling secrets."

She glanced over at the captain, who listened without interest. "There's more, but it's just a bland rehash of what we already know about Freddy and his friends being very naughty in their mansions."

"What's your point?"

"I have several, in fact."

Then a nurse approached their table, carrying a phone with a long cord so that it could be used out on the veranda. "Captain? There's another call for you from the department."

The tone of her voice made it clear that this wasn't the second or even the third.

Dempsey didn't look surprised. "All right, I'll take it."

The woman frowned at the cigarette in his hand, but he noticed and shot her a look that sent her away in silence. He still sounded annoyed when he spoke into the phone. "What is it?"

Jane ate one of the truffles while the captain listened to the other man on the line. "Why are Grayson and Leary working on the same part of the case? They hate each other. Send Grayson to find and interview any neighboring farms or homes near the manor. He needs the experience."

She couldn't quite make out the response, the words reduced to muted murmuring, but Dempsey began rubbing at his forehead. "An official warning from what? Yes, I'm aware of our dress code and its requirements. What I meant was, how the hell is Grayson breaking it? No. Find him and have him call me."

When he hung up, Jane took a second chocolate and said, "Having to manage your minions long-distance?"

"The kid's up to three warnings because he won't shave his face. He just got hit with another complaint about it."

The phone rang just as the nurse was halfway to their table to take it back. She rolled her eyes and left again while Dempsey answered. "Yeah? We'll go into your argument with Leary later. Just tell me why you're walking around like you don't own a razor. That's it? It's a common problem. Put hair conditioner on five minutes before you shave. It softens the stubble enough to keep you from scraping your skin all to hell. Yeah. I'll be back tomorrow. We'll go over the rest then."

When he hung up, Jane couldn't help smiling. "Did you just have to explain to one of your men how to properly shave his face?"

The captain's response was to sigh out another smoke cloud. "Grayson didn't have a father growing up, and his mother sure as hell couldn't teach him how to handle a rough beard."

Jane studied him. She didn't often pay attention to her emotions and most of the time thought she would be better off without experiencing any at all, so it was hard to understand the strange tug at her heart at that moment. "You truly care for your men, don't you?"

He eyed her, wary once more. "And?"

"It's just an observation." She glanced out at the vivid green lawn, unsure of why she wanted to continue speaking about it. Unsure of what to even say. "A lot of humans assume wolves in a pack act as one mind. That there is a closeness and trust and loyalty that connects us all from birth. If that's true, then it's only to a lucky few. For the rest, it's a fantasy. An illusion. The alpha-kings and their queens are spoiled children who never grew up, and the rest of us are their toys. I think if more of them cared for and protected their own as deeply as you do, then the packs of Crescent City wouldn't be so thoroughly broken."

Her gaze remained on a group of patients playing a friendly game of croquet until he responded, his voice slipping toward something gentle. "Having met your former king, I'm going to take a wild guess that you're speaking from personal experience."

"Mm. Plenty of it. I'm very sad you weren't able to break a chair over *his* head as well. Speaking of, how did you know Isabelle is his lover?"

Dempsey shook his head. "You were back in the conservatory for the whole meeting? I told you to stay out."

"And I ignored you. I thought that if they used magic to attack, I could reverse it. And I slowly was, at least until Isabelle caught me out."

"Why wasn't your equipment fried along with our enchanters'?"

"Do you really think a wolf pack desperate enough to work with humans has any talent left in their midst? I was the brain behind Saxby magic, and when I left, no one could replace me. My enchantments are five years out of date, but they have nothing better. And I was already clever enough at that point to make sure any spell I created could never be used against me."

Nicotine seemed to have brought back the captain's sardonic humor, because he only laughed. "Humble as ever, Miss Feral."

She still had the newspaper in her lap and now folded it, following the original creases with careful precision. A decision crystallized in her mind, one that felt right and yet made her stomach flutter. "Jane. I think we're beyond a surname basis now. Don't you?"

The man was always good about avoiding direct stares with her and Sam, which most humans forgot about while dealing with wolves, but she still felt the weight of his attention in the short silence that followed.

"You always talk fancier when you're nervous, you know that?" When she glared at him, he grinned and added, "All right, Jane. You've buttered up my ego long enough. Why are you reading news articles to me when we both have inside views of the case?"

Despite being in a private setting, Jane still glanced around. "Our views have been at odds before. The city initially viewed Isaac Marshall's disappearance as a murder and was ready to charge his daughter for it. Now Mr. Marshall is alive and well, and the scope of your investigation has widened to include much of high society, a renegade thaumaturgist, and the Saxby Pack. I'm very curious about the city's plans, considering how most of the major figures in this crime are already dead."

The captain raised an eyebrow. "Maybe ours widened, but yours should still be razor-thin since it's only focused on one person."

Jane nodded. "Cora Marshall. I doubt the papers are right about her feeling 'very relieved' right now. Although, that's better than reporters finding out about the sigil controlling her. I trust *your* ability to keep it secret, but I can't say the same about the rest of the

department, especially if your investigation uncovers some of the clues ours has."

"Like Isaac Marshall's hidden ledgers? Or how Harold Beaumont wrote his clients' name in code but didn't alter dates or payment amounts in his notes? Give us some credit. It's our job to find things."

Her expression must have tightened, because he added, "Relax. We'll prove there was an illegal transaction between them, but not yet. This is a sprawling case, and our enchanters are already overworked from analyzing every piece of magic Beaumont did for Davenport's cultists."

When she sagged in relief, he studied her carefully. "You really think that thing would kill her at this point? It got what it wanted. She's back with her father, and he's the type who thinks he's untouchable to the rest of the world. He gave an interview through his lawyer and then dismissed my boys like they were servants."

Jane leaned toward him, pitching her voice low in case the nurse tried to return for the telephone. "Remember Freddy's hand? Now imagine that same demented imagination filling Isaac Marshall's requirement to prevent Cora Marshall from revealing the sigil exists and is controlled by him. I've looked through his notes very carefully and have been able to deconstruct all the elements of the enchantment. Even if her father is willing to let the binding of his daughter become public knowledge—which I doubt, since illegal magic is one of the rare crimes the upper crust can't bribe away— Harold Beaumont was obsessed with escaping detection. The sigil will kill her and rip itself free. Within a few days, it will rot to nothing, leaving no evidence of the magic he created. I assume Freddy's hand no longer exists."

"Disintegrated after that first day like it had been dropped in acid." Then Dempsey sighed. "So, you want breathing room to work out how to save Miss Marshall."

"Please." Jane meant the word to come out crisply, but instead it sounded very tired.

The captain stubbed out the butt of his cigarette and immediately lit a fresh one. "I'll see what I can do. No promises. Are you confident about getting it off without killing her?"

"Let's say I'm confident in my progress. I just don't know how much longer it will take to complete and test a reverse spell. Believe me, I've been asked again and again for a clearer amount of time. I can't give it." Despite herself, a sour note had entered her voice.

Dempsey noticed. "Sam's not taking it too well, huh?"

"I saw his face when he received the letter from Isaac Marshall declaring his services were terminated. He looked ready to kill."

"Well, tell him to hold back. I don't want to see him in one of the cells when I arrive at work tomorrow. Besides, Miss Marshall is a tough nut. I don't see her cracking underneath her father." Then the captain's voice turned brisk, professional. "I'll keep an officer on watch outside Marshall's home, and they'll be followed when either of them goes anywhere. With how this case has been, the mayor is paranoid about ending up with more dead bodies."

Then he paused, as if waiting for her to protest. She didn't. She and Sam felt the Saxby Pack might not have its tail fully tucked between its legs. Maybe city officials weren't the only humans they wanted to attack... and if other people stood guard, that left more time for them both to work on saving Miss Marshall.

When she remained quiet, Dempsey finished with, "Aside from that, I'll focus our resources on the other figures involved... for now."

Aware that it was the best he could do, she nodded. She had given her first name, but he hadn't offered his. Better play it safe. "Thank you, Captain."

He studied her again. She had to admit the attention wasn't unpleasant. "Al. Never Albert."

Despite the mammoth task ahead of her, she smiled. "Al."

Someone knocked on Cora's bedroom door just as she removed cucumber slices from her eyes, which were puffy from a night of crying. The vases of lilies and chrysanthemums on her dressing table gave the air a funereal quality, but arranging flowers had been the only thing keeping her sane since returning home with Father, and she stared at the white petals while Maisie entered with a quick curtsey.

"Good morning, miss. Your father wants to see you in his study once you're dressed."

"Thank you, Maisie."

A small frown at her reflection was the only sign of her struggle against her hands mechanically choosing clothing her father considered proper: a long-sleeved knit dress in a hideous shade of brown and sensible shoes with the lowest heel possible. She knew it was useless to fight the sigil but refused to simply accept how it could take control of her body over the slightest things.

The resistance left her with a headache by the time she reached her father's study. The sigil pulsed contentedly in his presence as she stopped in front of his desk. "Good morning, Father."

"Cora." Her father was in the middle of writing letters and didn't look up. He had gone grey early in life and now his hair was completely silver, glinting in the lamp light. With some surprise, she realized all the window curtains were drawn, as if the bright sunlight would be too much for him.

Without looking up from his work, he said, "You'll be going without me to all our social appointments. I'm not feeling well."

He did look sickly, she had to admit. Her father had always been an imposing, distinguished man, but now his skin had a grey pallor and the pen in his hand moved with less force than usual. Inwardly, in the small part of her mind that remained free to think however it wanted, she wondered if he had contracted an illness that might kill him. She hoped so. It was a shocking thought, but she wasn't sorry for it at all.

Just then, his gaze flickered up from the letters. "Did you hear me?"

The sigil pulsed painfully until she answered. "Yes, Father."

"And do you remember what the appointments are?"

"Yes. Visiting with Mrs. Crainshaw and her daughter, going to Mrs. Einhorn's luncheon, and finally the opera tonight."

"Good. Explain to them all my absence as needed. That's all." Then her father bent his head toward his work in silent dismissal.

There was nothing to do except return to her room. The sigil burned steadily against her urge to scream and throw things, and at last she sat on the bed, glaring at the flowers around her. Over a month of living like this, and it hadn't gotten any less infuriating.

Her father was like a block of granite, slowly crushing her life into a model of his old-fashioned propriety.

Oh, she knew why she had to visit all the fuddy-duddy family connections today even without him. He wanted to build a good reputation for her with those willing to pretend that the recent scandals still shaking the city could be left in the past. Worse, it would possibly work.

She didn't know what the newspapers claimed and couldn't read them to find out. But she was very aware that out of the sprawling mess created by Freddy and his cult, she and her father were seen as the only innocent figures involved. It left her in a positive light with Father's old-money friends, all of them proud of being as stiff and unchanging as statues. And now she was forced to act like them, one command at a time.

Well. She had never given in easily, and wasn't about to start.

Her determination spurred her into fighting the sigil throughout her day despite a growing headache in response. As with all her previous attempts, it proved impossible to win against the nasty little thing, and by the time she was settled into her father's private box at the opera house, she was both furious and fuzzy-headed.

The singing didn't help with the pain, and it was only the sigil that kept her smiling during the intermission when she mingled with the other members of the audience. She wasn't allowed to drink or smoke, and the sigil also smothered a groan of frustration from her when Mrs. Portsmouth, one of Father's old friends, caught sight of her and came over.

"How are you, dear? You're looking well. So much more composed these days."

The other woman appeared unchanged, hiding her bulky body beneath layers of beaded chiffon, and sounded the same, too, her voice as loud and squawking as a parrot while she dove into a mostly one-sided conversation.

Frankly, it was the most depressing moment of the night to realize she was dressed as modestly as the other woman. Perhaps even more so, seeing as her gown and shawl were a bland taupe compared to Mrs. Portsmouth's raspberry. For the first time that night, Cora gave up and let the sigil guide appropriate responses from her mouth. Her thoughts thickened into a mindless fog that always seeped in whenever she wasn't actively fighting the sigil and its full strength, and she wasn't sure how much time had passed before one word brought her back.

Wolf.

"I'm sorry?" she said. Her own query. Her own focus on what the other woman had just said.

Mrs. Portsmouth frowned slightly, looking toward the bar where a large crowd had gathered to order drinks. "I said that it's unfortunate you had to seek out dealings with the type of creature one would really rather not know. I don't blame you for the circumstances that forced you to that decision, but it's terrible how every wolf now must think you're friendly with their kind. That one has been staring at you in the most audacious way for the past five minutes."

Cora's heart jumped in her chest at the same time the sigil flared against her skin while she looked with Mrs. Portsmouth, expecting a familiar figure that she was still able to visit in her dreams. The sigil relaxed a fraction of a second before disappointment replaced her hope.

It wasn't Hayes. Instead, it was the alpha-king and alpha-queen of the Frosthound Pack, standing together in much the same way as when Cora had last seen them, bloody and amused while surrounded by savaged bodies. They *still* looked amused, chatting with the few people who weren't giving them a cautious berth. Cimorene's black hair was pulled back into a bun like most of the other women, but she wore a tuxedo as tailored as her king's, the outfit turned into something more feminine by plunging down in a daring neckline and matched with two-toned brogues customized with high heels.

It was she who watched Cora openly, her interested expression sharpened by her bold red lipstick. Alpha-king Thane murmured something to her while glancing around the room, sardonic humor brightening his gold eyes whenever a human started back from their presence.

When Cora's gaze met the alpha-queen's, the she-wolf nodded and then approached, passing through the crowd with ease. Mrs. Portsmouth just had time for a scandalized gasp before Cimorene was within speaking range. Her voice sounded as cool and collected as Cora remembered. "Miss Marshall. So many things have happened since we last met."

The sigil didn't seem to know what to do in the face of a wolf with ambiguous intentions, and so Cora was allowed to sound a little like herself as she replied, "They have, haven't they?"

"And now you're back with your father." The arch of Cimorene's eyebrow could have meant anything.

"Is this really necessary?" interrupted Mrs. Portsmouth, with a frown.

"Not for you, no." The alpha-queen looked unoffended by the stiff glare, merely motioning Cora to move away with her. When the older woman huffed, the she-wolf added, "We'll remain within sight, never fear."

They found privacy on a velvet bench large enough for two. The alpha-king moved closer to them, his attention on the people around them even as Cimorene's focus seemed to fully narrow to Cora. "I won't waste time. Do you remember when I said you were ready to die to protect your detective? That you in fact saved his life?"

Cora felt the sigil start to pressure her to demur that her connection with Hayes was long ended, but before she could do more than open her mouth with a heavy throb in her heart, the alpha-queen shook her head. "I'm not interested in polite excuses, so you don't need to give me any. I want to clarify because it's important you understand. The tattoos on my back warn me when Lady Death is near, whether for myself or another. They allow me glimpses of the future... at least when it comes to a life's end. There was danger around you both that day. It's still there for you."

"I—but everything's over. Isn't it?"

"Don't be so sure. I can't tell how individual fate plays out. Only when someone is on a path that promises death. For all the bodies borne from your father's disappearance, there are still more that will be connected." Then the alpha-queen nodded and rose to leave.

"Wait." Cora heard her voice rise in panic and spat out the next words before the sigil had a chance to constrict her throat. "What about Detective Hayes? Is he also..."

"In danger?" finished Cimorene. "I haven't seen him, so I can't answer you. It's interesting, though. When we first led you both

onto our land, I sensed how one of his possible paths was suicide. That path disappeared when you saved him."

Cora felt a knot form in her throat as she stared at the alpha-queen, speechless.

Cimorene studied her for a moment longer and then nodded in goodbye. "Remember my warning. Enjoy the rest of the opera."

Then she moved away with her king, soon disappearing among all the bodies and cigar smoke.

"My dear, are you all right?" Mrs. Portsmouth's voice sounded theatrically concerned after the alpha-queen's assured tones. "Whatever was she talking about?"

"I'm not sure," said Cora, in all honesty. "She left me confused more than anything."

Then, aware of how little time was left before the intermission was over and she would have to spend hours back in her seat in that stuffy box, she turned to the older woman and added, "Would you excuse me? I think I'd like some fresh air."

"Are you sure? All by yourself?"

"I won't be alone. There's still an officer watching over me for protection." Then Cora made her final excuses and slipped away, aware of the sigil throbbing against her scalp.

An attendant opened the door for her, and then she was outside in the cool night air. Cars rumbled down the street, erasing any sense of privacy. The sigil burned its ever-steady beat as she walked without thought, following a desperate urge to slip away for just a little while. Her mind spun over the alpha-queen's words while she moved toward the dim buildings of businesses that had closed for the night, eyes still dazzled by the bright lights she'd left behind.

Then hands grabbed her. One clamped over her mouth and the other snaked around her body, pinning her arms to her sides. Her scream came out as a muffled squeak while she was dragged backwards into a nearby alley, the darkness barely pierced by moonlight.

Even as she writhed against her attacker's grip, a second figure appeared before her with a brief growl. The hands against her tightened. Before she had time to realize anything more than they were wolves, the one holding her bit into the side of her throat.

She shrieked, her shock matching the sigil's as it flared against her scalp until her entire skull and neck burned. It wasn't the pain that made her cry out again but the feeling of *movement* under her skin, slithering toward the bite in a way that left her shuddering against the grip holding her still. The wolf in front of her stepped closer, eyes glowing.

The pressure of the bite changed. Something dark and rancid slid over her dress, leaving a trail of blood and slime until it dropped to the ground with a wet slap. Before her eyesight could clear enough to take in what had just happened, the wolf holding her quickly dragged her to a waiting car. She came over her shock enough to try to struggle, but found herself pulled into the backseat with her kidnapper.

Before she could do more than scream and scratch at any part of the kidnapper within reach, the car's front door opened and the second figure slid in behind the wheel, ripping off what Cora now saw was a leather thaumaturgist's mask. "It's out and caught in a specimen jar. She's safe."

Just as Cora gasped, recognizing Jane Feral's flat voice, the hand against her mouth shifted to cup her chin instead. "I'm sorry, Bunny. We had no other way to rescue you."

"H-hayes?" she managed, her terror evaporating into lightheadedness as Jane started up the car and joined the flow of traffic. Despite her body's sluggish shock, she forced herself to twist toward him. In the flickering illumination of the street lights, his eyes were the same bright gold she remembered, fierce and intent on her face.

She immediately burst into tears, clinging to him. "Did I hurt you? I'm sorry. I didn't know it was you."

The feeling of his arms settling around her now felt like the sweetest sensation possible. "Believe me, I was glad you fought back. If you suspected who I was, this whole plan would've failed."

Her hands kept tracing his shoulders, neck, and jaw out of fear that this was a mere dream she would wake up from. When he pulled off his gloves to wipe the tears from her cheeks with bare fingers, though, the heat of his touch reassured her it was all real. She began shivering, now crying out of sheer relief. "I can't believe it. The sigil..."

Hayes seemed more intent on pressing a handkerchief against her neck, which already felt merely tender, and it was Jane who responded to the uncertain words. The she-wolf looked slightly disheveled and flushed from wearing the heavy mask, but her expression was one of complete triumph. "We took it out of you. This little charade was a way to make the sigil believe you were about to die. From my research, I knew that it would panic and escape from your body. And it did."

Then she reached into the front passenger seat for a moment before holding up a glass jar. A slug-like creature inched against the glass, leaving behind a trail of slime and blood.

Cora's shriek made the car windows shake. "That was in me?"

"I was hoping for a 'thank you,' not ruptured eardrums."

"Jane," growled Hayes, pressing closer to Cora as she fell limp against him once more, staring at the jar until Jane returned it to the front passenger seat.

The she-wolf sighed, but her expression remained smug in the rearview mirror. "The sigil didn't look like that while it was attached to you. It was merely a tattoo. I modified its escape mechanism so that it would turn into a separate entity rather than take over a part of your body. It's a clever idea, isn't it? And I was able to pull it off.

"Without getting too technical with my explanation, let's say it was impossible to put any spell on you without the sigil sensing it before it could take effect. So I enchanted Sam's teeth instead. His bite sent the sigil in a panic and introduced my reverse spell in one swift act. I could have put the enchantment on my own teeth, but he didn't trust me to bite you without puncturing anything serious. Your wounds should have healed to raw points on your skin, by the way. Don't glare at me, Sam. Check for yourself."

Cora blinked at Jane while Hayes pulled his hand away as if to look at her neck. Most of what the she-wolf said barely made sense to her, and the rest flew out the window when Hayes started licking at the bite. The heat of his tongue felt as intense as the sigil's had been, but instead of burning her, it soothed.

When she gasped, Jane's gaze flickered to the rearview mirror. "We have slight healing properties in our saliva. Nothing very noteworthy. How *are* you feeling, Miss Marshall?"

"I'm not sure," she said, as Hayes growled softly against her skin. She had the feeling the sound was meant as a rebuke to the sudden sly tone in Jane's voice, but against her skin it felt thrilling. "I haven't been allowed to feel at all since Father came back."

"That's all over," said Hayes, his voice still rough.

"I'm so glad," she murmured, shifting until their faces were inches apart. Her nose was stuffy from crying, her hair felt like it had frizzed out of its finger waves in some areas and gone stiff from dried blood in others, and she wore an ugly, unflattering dress in front of him, but for once she didn't care about her appearance. He was staring at her with an intensity she'd never seen, and at the moment, she wanted nothing more than to kiss him and feel his heat fill her throughout.

His mouth caught hers, teeth still sharp as if he hadn't gotten rid of his anger. She could feel his frustration from the past month in every slide of his tongue, but she only felt a bubbling delight and melted into his rhythm until she forgot to breathe.

"You probably shouldn't make her pant. She's going to be weak enough as it is."

Cora groaned when he pulled away, but she had to admit the inside of the car spun a little while she gasped for breath.

"More?" she whispered against his mouth.

She felt him smile. "Later. I better let you recover first."

"I suppose that's only sensible." After she resettled herself against him, she gingerly touched the back of her neck, still in disbelief that the sigil was finally, blessedly gone.

The awareness of what had happened widened until she suddenly remembered about the officer tasked to watch her. "The police

department assigned a man for my protection. He might have seen you pull me into the car."

Hayes' fingers lightly brushed her cheek, as if he couldn't resist touching her. "I dealt with him before you came out of the opera house."

Cora accepted it with a nod, but Jane suddenly said, "You didn't do anything too nasty, did you? Captain Dempsey is very protective of his men. He'll be mad if you hurt him."

Hayes' gaze remained on Cora's face. "Why worry about that?"

Jane rolled her eyes. "I'm still trying to get that open contract for the force's new submachine guns, remember? It's hard enough to stay in the city's good graces as lone wolves, especially now."

"I punctured his car tire, that's all. I didn't want him following us. The city had their chance to protect her and failed."

"Where are we going?" said Cora, half-wishing the car ride would never end. It felt too wonderful, snuggling up to him there in the dark.

"A place where you can recover," he said. "Jane and I know someone who is a mind reader. Her name is Minnie Wilkes, and she'll be able to sense what long-term effects the sigil might have left behind. She's the best person to help you heal and get back on your feet. We'll be there in another half-hour."

"I can't go back to your place?"

"No. Neither can I. Once the city realizes you slipped their watch, my office will be one of the first places they look. I don't want anyone else knowing where you are tonight. Once you're ready to decide what you want to do, it'll be a different story."

Cora nodded but couldn't say she was all too interested. She was exhausted, shaky, and so glad to be back in his arms. In her mind, the

only important question to ask was, "Will you stay at Minnie's, too?"

"Tonight, anyway." Then his voice took on a teasing note. "You're still my client, Bunny. I need to look after you."

CHAPTER TWENTY-FOUR

Cora didn't realize how weak she felt until she tried getting out of the car. Her knees wobbled as soon as she stood. The stars spun slightly.

Just before she collapsed on the pavement, Hayes caught her. "Easy. It took a big enchantment to destroy the sigil."

"I feel amazing, though. Honestly. My head is light and... and *free*. I didn't realize how my every thought was so heavy before."

"You still need to recover." Then he lifted her up in his arms and began carrying her.

There was a scoff from Jane, who had gotten out of the car but remained standing by it. Drunken shouting drifted from one of the surrounding dim buildings, but the she-wolf didn't seem concerned. In fact, even with blurring vision, Cora could pick out Jane's smug expression as she said, "Face it, Miss Marshall, you're about to be fussed over. I'm sure you'll survive."

The sky continued to slide like spilled ink while they went up the narrow stairs to the front door. Before Hayes had a chance to knock on it, it opened. Cora caught a glimpse of a tiny old woman, her faded shawl and white hair glowing from the lamplight within. "Up to the third floor. The first bedroom is ready for her. Quickly, now. The world is probably spinning for her."

The old woman wasn't wrong, but Cora still felt unbelievably free. The absence of pain or control left her sinking into anything she managed to sense, no matter how innocuous. How the muscles in Hayes' shoulders flexed against her arm, which she'd managed to hook around his neck. The very steadiness of his breath. The faded flowered wallpaper, worn wooden bannisters, and carpeted stairways that briefly made up the world before it widened into a room. All of it proved what she was still afraid to believe—that she was free of her life with her father.

"Here we are." Hayes carefully eased her onto a small bed.

For a moment, she only sat and rubbed at the back of her head while her dizziness subsided. Lamplight warmed the cream ceiling and rose-colored wallpaper. There was a small window near the bed, its curtains drawn for the night, and the fire in the hearth had already burned down to a bed of coals that would keep the room warm.

The last thing she noticed was an old-fashioned flannel nightgown draped over the foot of the bed. Hayes also eyed it before his gaze jumped to her bloodied, disheveled gown. For the first time that night, he seemed uncertain.

Cora flashed a smile despite the lingering shivers throughout her body. "I can do that much myself. Though if you wanted to help, I certainly wouldn't mind."

His expression turned wry, and he was still smiling while turning away to stir up the coals in the hearth. The set of his shoulders made it clear he wouldn't face her again until she had changed.

She really was weak, fingers slow and trembling while they slid off the gown. Jane's enchantment must have done something to clean itself up, because even though the clothes were stiff with dried blood and slime, her skin was absolutely spotless. Cora was glad, because even the simple movement of pulling the nightgown over her head left her body throbbing down to the very bones.

Well, if she was about to pass out, there was one thing she needed to do beforehand. "What time is it?"

Hayes glanced at his watch and returned to her while she sat on the bed. "Ten minutes after eleven."

"And does that telephone work?"

"Sure. Why?"

"I want to phone Captain Dempsey and reassure him that I left my father of my own free will. I see no reason to cause a panic over my disappearance when I'm perfectly fine."

"Your scent is already full of exhaustion."

"I know, and I'm very much looking forward to sleeping and waking up in a place that isn't my father's house. But I think it's important."

After a moment, he nodded. "I know the number by heart."

He quickly dialed for her and then handed over the phone. While waiting, she absently ran fingers over her scalp, still marveling at the simple skin there. There was a slight headache forming at her temples, but it felt normal, nothing more than a clear sign from her body that it was overtired.

The captain answered on the second ring, almost growling, "Dempsey."

"Captain! I guessed you'd be working after hours. You don't seem like a man who sets aside any time for a social life."

"Miss Marshall. Are you about to explain why you slipped my man?"

"Yes. I refuse to live with my father anymore. I'm perfectly fine but unwilling to go into more detail about why or where I am at the moment. I don't want the reporters or anyone else to know. I have a lot to think through. And whatever Father says, it isn't true. I wanted to leave him, and I have. This is entirely my own decision."

The captain didn't sound any less irritated. "And are you now with a certain private detective?"

Cora decided it was best to remain coy. "I'm not at his office or home."

"I know that. We already checked."

"My goodness, you and your men really are efficient, aren't you?"

"Miss Marshall, where the hell are you? How are we supposed to stay in contact?"

"My lawyer will be in touch."

There was a brief rustle of paper. "Mr. Forrester?"

"No, that's Father's lawyer, though I expect he'll bluster at you as well. I won't keep you, Captain. Until the next time." She hung up on his sigh. The conversation, brief as it was, had sapped even more of her energy.

Before she could do more than sigh herself, there was a brief knock on the doorway. The old woman from earlier—who Cora guessed was Minnie Wilkes—came inside and studied her. Then she clucked her tongue. "We'll save proper introductions for tomorrow. You're exhausted. It's time to sleep or risk making yourself worse. You've had powerful magic leaching from your life for over a year. If you let yourself rest in bed tomorrow, I can see you being fine in a few days. Keep pushing yourself and it'll turn into a week or longer."

Her head really was starting to throb, so Cora didn't argue, instead meekly slipping beneath the sheets and embroidered blankets.

Minnie then turned toward Hayes, who remained near the bed. "Come on. Out, now."

Hayes shook his head, his expression remaining easy. "Don't worry, I'll let her rest. I'm sleeping in the chair tonight."

There was a brief pause where Cora realized that the old woman must have been reading his thoughts, because without another word from him, she gave in with a nod.

"Get some sleep, girl. If you hear any noise in the night, don't worry over it. You're safe now." Then Minnie left, shutting the door behind her.

Despite Minnie's warning, Cora turned onto her side to watch Hayes pull the chair closer to the bed. "You really are a stubborn fella to keep to that chair."

He acknowledged her words with a grin before settling in. He had already shrugged off his jacket and hat and now loosened his tie.

As he unbuttoned his sleeves and rolled them up, she watched in unusual silence. Some part of her still felt shocked that the night would end very differently than it had started. When she did speak, all the teasing had left her voice. "I missed you so much."

At that, he reached out and caught her nearest hand. "I know, Bunny. I wanted to get the sigil off you a lot sooner. It had to be hell living with your father again."

"I don't care." And she really didn't. When her fingers entwined with his, she added, "That's all over, and I have no concern for my father or what he thinks."

The color of Hayes' eyes remained heavy and warm, but a grim note slipped into his next words. "He might try to punish you some other way."

"He can't. That's why he put the sigil on me. There was no other way to control me. I've never told you before, did I? I don't suppose I could talk about it. Father likes to put on airs, and he's very good at making money, but his side of the family faced ruin by the time he met my mother. It was her money that allowed him to build himself up, and when she found out she was going to have me, she had some set aside in a trust that only I can touch. It gives me a very generous amount per year, easily enough to live on."

"How are you sure he can't touch it?"

"She set up the trust with Allagash & Crown."

When the answer drew out a low whistle from him, she knew he understood the significance of the prestigious bank. Then he said, "So your mother came from old magic."

"Yes. Only someone of her blood can access the account, which means Father isn't able to touch a single penny, and he knows it. Strangely, he seems more impressed than anything whenever he talks about it. A 'good business maneuver,' he calls it. I do think he loved my mother in his own strange way, but..."

Then she realized Hayes' expression had grown distant yet focused. "Hayes? What is it?"

He shook his head slightly and seemed to come back into himself. "Nothing worth worrying about. It's just interesting to hear."

"Really? I think it's boring. I only cared about Father's money in terms of spending it to get a rise out of him. Anger is still a form of attention, and I suppose I thought that was good enough at the time. Now I want nothing to do with him." Then she drew in a

breath, half in disbelief at how freely she could speak. The lightness in her mind felt dizzying. "Hayes, you really are a marvel. I never thought I would feel like this again."

His eyes warmed once more. "Jane's the miracle worker, not me."

"Jane pays attention to other people only when she has to. If it weren't for you..." Then her hand pulled away to fiddle with his rolled-up sleeve. It was horrible to imagine what the rest of her life would have been like.

After a moment, his fingers covered hers, squeezing gently. "I know. But you're not out of the woods yet. You need time to recover and put your life back together."

"But why here?" She couldn't hide her disappointment. "Why not at your apartment?"

"It's still better if your father doesn't know where you are. Not until it's clear that he can't get at you again."

She was starting to feel drowsy but didn't want to stop talking to him. "I can already think of a few lawyers to help with that. Father never minded burning bridges, so there are plenty all too happy to work against him."

Hayes didn't look surprised but only said, "Relax for now. Whenever you're ready, give me a list and I'll find their numbers for you."

"Are you leaving?" Her hand grabbed at his.

He smiled, that wry, warm one she loved. "Don't worry, you've got my company for the rest of the night. Get some sleep."

She didn't want to. Bed rest seemed like a waste of time when she had just gotten back the chance to be with him. But the pillow beneath her head felt very soft, and the room felt very cozy from the warmth and gentle crackling of the coals in the hearth. Finally, she

gave in to her exhausted body with a sense of not drifting away so much as curling up against the strength and reassurance of his presence.

She didn't even stir when his hand eased from hers to tuck some hair back behind her ear, feather-light and careful, but another figure noticed while pausing in the doorway.

"She's already in a deep sleep," said Holly, her gaze slipping from the bed to Hayes' face. "Good. Brom found out some things about the pack today. He's wanted to tell you all evening."

Hayes bit back a sigh and nodded, still watching Cora. "All right. We'll go into it tomorrow."

The she-wolf's body stiffened. "The human won't wake up for the rest of the night. You can smell it as well as I."

"Tomorrow." Now Hayes looked up at her, his tone warning her not to push it further.

The she-wolf glanced away first. "Very well."

Before she could leave, Jane appeared in the doorway as well and slipped through with her usual sarcasm. "Sweet dreams, Holly."

For a few moments after the other she-wolf disappeared down the stairs, Jane stood next to Hayes in silence, watching him instead of Cora. "She'll be fine."

He leaned back in the chair, relaxing at last. "I know. Thanks, Jane. You crafted something most enchanters would claim is impossible."

She nodded, her expression softening. "The others will keep pushing for your attention whenever possible. They see you as a leader now, especially with what's been happening with the Saxby Pack."

He glanced at her with equal affection. "Finally learned not to say 'our pack,' huh?"

"Maybe I'm merely developing an independent life." She leaned against his chair, her attention now back on Cora, who continued to sleep peacefully. "If you want to thank me, then spend time with her. Not just to look after her but to have fun. The others don't understand. They're too caught up in the idea of returning to pack land. They think you're helping for the same reason. I know better. I'm shocked your heart hasn't imploded from the sheer stress of the past month."

"Trying to replace Minnie's role of mothering me?"

"Just nagging at you to let yourself be happy in these uncertain times."

At that, the humor drained from his expression, and he reached out to trace Cora's face again. "Believe me, Jane, I want to. And for the next few days, I will."

CHAPTER TWENTY-FIVE

Cora woke to muffled voices and the clatter of plates somewhere below. Instinctively, her hand jumped to the back of her head and found only sleep-mussed hair and normal skin. She sighed, all dread melting into relief. The sigil was gone. It hadn't been a mere dream.

The fire had smoldered out and left the room in darkness, but she could see that Hayes' chair was empty. And if she listened hard enough, she could hear his voice among the others, indistinct but serious in tone. Grim, even.

Whatever was wrong, she knew it couldn't be about her. She was clear-headed and free of pain, only slightly wobbly while she got out of bed and walked over to the window to open the curtains. For several breaths, she basked in the bright morning sunshine, unfazed by the decaying factory that made up most of her view. At this moment, everything seemed beautiful to her, and her one wish was to be in her own clothes so she could look as good as she felt. There was a mirror on the small dresser nearby, its surface spotted with age, and when Cora glanced at her reflection, she wished for a hairbrush as well. Just as she started fussing with her appearance, someone knocked on the bedroom door.

Hayes stepped inside carrying coffee and a plate filled with enough eggs and buttered toast for two. He had changed his clothes and looked freshly shaven but already seemed tired. Some of the tension left his body when he saw her. "Minnie told me you were awake. How are you feeling?"

She beamed. "Wonderful. Although I suppose I should still be in bed."

He winked while setting the food on the table. "I won't snitch."

Within a minute, he had moved the table and chair so that they could sit across from each other comfortably. She sank into the easy intimacy of sharing a plate with him, not even minding how the old-fashioned nightgown left her as modest as a nun.

As she bit into a piece of toast, Hayes said, "Minnie will visit later to check your mind for any lingering effects left by the sigil. Are you comfortable with that? Plenty of people don't like the idea of someone digging through their thoughts."

"I always say whatever is on my mind. It's one of my few good habits. Besides, the whole city knows all about me. There's probably nothing left for a mind reader to uncover. To be honest, I'm not thinking about the sigil at all."

He tilted his head, one of those wolfish movements that she loved seeing. "If not that, then what?"

She studied him. His rough desperation from the night before had calmed into his usual steadiness, but the playful glint to his eyes was still missing. He sat in his chair like someone ready to jump up at the first sign of danger, and there was a grim set to his mouth that she recognized.

After a moment, she ran a hand along his arm. When the muscles beneath her fingers relaxed in response, she said, "Hayes, what's happening? You have that certain look that only comes out when you're thinking about your old pack."

"I didn't realize it was that obvious." Then he sighed and finished his coffee. "How much did you hear about the Saxbys while living with your father?"

"Hardly anything. Father wouldn't let me read the papers. All I know for certain is that the Saxby alpha-king met with city officials and attacked them. Captain Dempsey and the police commissioner were shot but survived. I don't know what happened to any of the wolves."

"The alpha-king escaped. The captain of his royal guard was caught and arrested. The others all died."

"But I thought their captain was..." Then she hesitated. She remembered the she-wolf's name perfectly well but didn't want to press on an old scar from his past.

He finished the sentence for her. "Isabelle. She was the one who shot both Al and Commissioner Keene."

"Oh, Hayes. I'm sorry." Her fingers still rested against his arm, and now they moved down to squeeze his hand. She didn't care about politics but wasn't completely clueless about them. No city official would take an attempt on his life lightly. The she-wolf surely faced a noose unless... "Is the alpha-king fighting to charge and try her in his own legal system?"

"No. Even if he did, the city wouldn't acknowledge it. The Saxby diplomat's seat was removed from the city assembly, and a no-trade order has been put in place."

Cora almost gasped. "But that's as good as a death sentence for the entire pack. Everyone knows the wolf packs all depend upon exporting to the city. Even if New Obsidian or another of the city-states could jump in as a replacement, they wouldn't dare break their treaties with Crescent City over one struggling wolf pack."

She now understood his grim manner, but strangely, her response chased some of it away. He smiled a little and said, "You know, all your old tutors who called you a pea-brain should've been in different careers."

Then he added, almost despite himself, "I don't know how you do it, but it's always easy talking to you, even about the hardest things."

They had shared kisses that had already revealed the intensity and passion he was so reluctant to reveal to the world, but somehow those words felt far more intimate. A glimpse of his raw feelings.

"I feel the same way," she said, softly, all thought flying from her head while she looked into his eyes.

The tension that had just started to leave his movements suddenly returned. He glanced toward the door and finished the dregs of his coffee. "We're about to have company."

There wasn't even a knock on the door. It just jerked open with a muffled thump while Jane struggled inside, dragging Cora's suitcases behind her. She was panting. "Why am I always doing this?"

"You could've chosen to watch over her instead," replied Hayes.

Jane scoffed while piling them into a corner. "You mean, stay here? No, thanks."

Cora glanced between them, excitement bubbling over. "You collected my things from Father? I thought it would be impossible without an army of lawyers."

"He doesn't know. The servants said he's sick. That maid of yours recognized me and packed your cases."

Cora shifted in her seat, already itching to change into some prettier clothes, but the sudden sharpness in Hayes' voice caught her attention again.

"How sick is he, Jane?"

The she-wolf shrugged. "There were police enchanters present to check him. They seemed unconcerned and had already ruled out poison, spells, or any other attempt on his life. He might be experiencing effects from the destruction of the sigil. I was focused on Miss Marshall's comfort, not his."

"No, it can't be the sigil," said Cora. "He was sick in the morning."

"What were the symptoms?" said Hayes, his attention now on her.

"Well, he did seem weak. His hand shook from writing a letter. And his skin had a definite pallor. He was shivering and sweating at the same time. But it was nothing too serious. No coughing or labored breathing. And he certainly wasn't confused or delirious."

Hayes only nodded, eyes narrowing slightly.

Cora glanced at Jane, who didn't appear enthused about the information. The she-wolf's next words confirmed it. "Sam, I thought you were going to take time off from thinking like a detective. Let Captain Dempsey's men look after Isaac Marshall. Now that Miss Marshall is free, I don't see why we need to care about him."

"I certainly don't," said Cora, and resumed eating.

The comment coaxed a reluctant smile from Hayes. "All right. If you're going back to the office, Jane, lock up my side for me."

Cora returned his smile, pleased by the implication that he'd stay and keep her company.

He did, leaving only to take the empty dishes back downstairs. While he was gone, Cora quickly washed up. Then she found a peach-colored chemise and paired it with a black-and-gold silk robe that she left untied. She was sitting on the bed and brushing her hair by the time he returned. "I have to admit, I'm still weak, but I feel miles better in my own clothes. I bet if I styled my hair, I could even manage to dance."

He surprised her by reaching out for the soft waves falling over one eye, tucking them back behind her ear. "Maybe wait on the dancing until you're back on your feet. How about cards instead?"

She won twice at double solitaire but had to admit he had her beat at poker. She had never been a sore loser and merely laughed while pushing her pennies over to his side of the table. "And here Jane told me you loved billiards."

"I do. I used to play a lot when I was a pit fighter. It calmed me down in between bouts."

The reference to his past was made without bitterness, but the words still drew her mind away from the new hand he dealt out to her. "What do you want your future to be, Hayes? Now that you're in a better place and have a successful career, what are you looking for?"

"I don't often think about what I want. Whatever I or the people close to me need is more important." He seemed focused on his cards, but there was a trace of resignation in his expression. "What about your future, now that it's free?"

"Well, I've become quite a fan of doing detective work. I wouldn't mind returning to it. But I suppose I should first focus on

cutting all connections with Father. That mostly means hiring lawyers for any legal details and finding my own place to live. And then... living."

"You sound excited," he murmured.

"I am. It won't be like before, and I don't want it to be. I've had enough of the constant circus of my old social circles. Everything was always so busy and yet so empty at the same time."

Then she looked up at him, feeling herself glow. All his attention was on her face, and the intensity of his gaze melted her last bit of restraint. "Do you know what I keep thinking about, Hayes? The day spent with you at your apartment. Despite the strange, terrible things I'd seen and learned just before, I felt so peaceful and right there. I felt like I was home. And I have that same sensation this morning. When I was a child, I had a few experiences with fevers that required bedrest to recover from. They were some of the most boring memories in my life. I always thought I was too impatient to enjoy quiet moments... until we met. I can't remember being so comfortable in someone's presence no matter where I am or what's happening."

"I know what you mean, Bunny," he said, and then sighed. "The past month was rough on me. I didn't realize how much until last night when you were in my arms."

"Hayes," she whispered, wondering how her heart could feel feather-light and overfull at the same time.

The phone rang. He jerked toward it, pupils constricting, but made no move to answer. At his lack of surprise, Cora realized that he had been waiting all morning for a call.

Within a minute, Minnie Wilkes came inside, silent despite her uneven gait. Her expression was as grim as Hayes'. "It's for you, Sam, and you'll want to take it downstairs."

He rose from the chair, turning toward Cora. "I'll have to leave after this call. It might be hours before I'm back. I'm sorry."

She stood as well, unconsciously reaching for him. "Is everything all right? Are *you* all right?"

"I'm fine, Bunny. There's just something I need to do." He gave her a faint smile before moving for the door, but his expression had already hardened by the time he disappeared from view.

In the silence that followed, Minnie appraised her. The slight shake of her head was the only hint of what she thought about Cora's bold state of undress. "Well, you certainly are alert enough for proper introductions. I'm Mrs. Minnie Wilkes."

It was a struggle to remember her manners through her worry for Hayes. "Miss Cora Marshall. You're very kind to let me stay here."

"Sam told me a little of your situation. Did he tell you about what I can do?"

"Yes. You read minds."

"That's right." The old woman had a knitting bag with her, and now settled in the chair before pulling out her yarn. "There won't be any pain, but I'll have to be very thorough to see what the sigil did to your mind and whether it left any traces behind. That means learning a lot about you and your thoughts, girl. Can you take that?"

Cora nodded. "What do I need to do?"

"Nothing. I find it easiest to let your mind wash over mine, so do things as you like." Then Minnie began knitting, seemingly ignoring her.

At first, Cora fell quiet while gathering up the cards, unsure if Minnie needed silence to work. She couldn't help thinking about Hayes and what that phone call meant for him.

Just as she finished shuffling the cards, the thin cry of a baby came from somewhere downstairs.

When she cast a startled glance at Minnie, the old woman said, "You're not the only tenant at the moment. There are four others, including the baby. Has Sam mentioned them yet? No, I'm not surprised. I told him to be careful with over-taxing your mind. They're former Saxby wolves. Eve is the one looking after her little niece. She's good friends with Holly, who's here with her mate, Brom."

Cora felt her interest rise despite how the knitting needles clicked in a steady, lulling rhythm. "Is Hayes helping them adjust to a life among humans?"

"Yes. I'm sure you'll meet them once you're well enough to be up and about."

"I'm hoping that will be very soon. I'm itching to begin living again."

"I think you'll be fine. They took some memories from you, I'm sure of that. But you'll heal from the binding itself."

The rush of relief felt more muted than she'd expected, perhaps because she was still worried about Hayes. "I'm very glad to hear that, Mrs. Wilkes."

The old woman studied her. "Sam will also be fine. It's pack business, Miss Marshall, and he's used to dealing with that."

Cora nodded but couldn't help asking, "Will he be back soon?"

"Have a little patience. You're not his only concern." The words were mild, but Cora heard the reservation in the other woman's

voice. With sudden insight, she understood that Minnie had sensed her longing for Hayes and didn't approve of it.

Yet Cora was well used to disapproval, especially from old ladies, and saw no reason to avoid voicing her suspicions about why Hayes had looked so grim. "Was the phone call about Isabelle?"

Minnie looked up from her knitting again. This time, her hands fell still. "He's told you about her?"

"Well, a little. He's never gone into details, but I met her and quickly realized she must have been very important to him when he was still part of the pack."

"Important?" The old woman laughed, a creaky sound without humor. "Sweet child, she's his mate."

Captain Albert Dempsey once again found himself in his dress uniform. And once again, he found himself stuck with Commissioner Keene while the other man paced and worried at his mustache. Yet there the similarities ended: they waited for only one wolf instead of several, and they were at the police station, in a rarely used office built as an entire second level for the front half of the building. Massive two-sided glass windows provided a view of the entrance and areas open to the public, and Al looked out in silence while the commissioner fumed.

"He's obviously fled. I don't know why you wasted time leaving a message at his office. All the information points to him leaving with the Marshall girl. Her disappearance at the opera and a subsequent call where she refused to say anything except that she had left of her own free will, neither of them at his office or home this morning... do we have people watching the city's border with Saxby territory?"

"Sure do." Al knew the significance of Miss Marshall leaving her father. The sigil was off her and would no longer be a problem to his investigation. It gave him enough patience with Keene's blustering to keep his reply mild. "He won't show up at the Saxbys."

"Oh, no?" The commissioner stopped to look at him. "He's never let us interview him. He blatantly withheld information about his connection to Isabelle Saxby. There are only unreliable sources for the claim that he hates his former pack. What if he's as duplicitous as the rest of the Saxbys? We should have entertained that angle earlier."

Al smothered a sigh and finally glanced away from the windows. "You really think he kidnapped Cora Marshall and took her to his old pack?"

"We're uncovering more and more evidence that the Saxbys were involved in the murder attempt against Isaac Marshall, which makes their past interest in Miss Marshall all the more notable."

"I don't disagree, but Sam Hayes doing that? He's got puppy dog eyes whenever he looks at her. All his evasions have been related to protecting her, including not telling us that he's Isabelle Saxby's mate." And now that Miss Marshall was free, his protection no longer needed to include silence. "No, he'll come to the station as asked."

The commissioner scoffed. "What makes you so sure?"

Al faced the windows again and then tried not to laugh at the timing. "Because he's just stepped inside."

Keene turned and muttered something at the sight of Sam Hayes willingly giving up his guns and dagger to the officers who had stopped him just inside the entrance. Al had told his men to handcuff the wolf only if he resisted being taken to an interview room, but he didn't expect it to happen. It didn't.

As they both watched two officers escort Hayes out of sight, the commissioner said, "I'll lead the questioning."

Al nodded, uninterested in arguing.

They left the office together, but while Keene moved for the room where Hayes would be placed, Al approached the officer who was tagging the weapons taken from the wolf. "Ehrl. Did he ask for a lawyer?"

"No, sir."

That fit with his suspicions about Sam deciding to break his silence and cooperate. Al rubbed the back of his neck, wondering if something would finally go smoothly in this damn case.

By the time he stepped inside the room, the commissioner was already seated across from Sam, sifting through a thick case file. The two officers stood within lunging distance of the wolf, but Sam seemed unconcerned, remaining still and silent. The harsh, overhead light constricted his pupils to pinpoints when he glanced toward Al, expressionless.

Al settled into the nearest corner and lit a cigarette. "Did your secretary give you the full message?"

The question drew a miffed look from Keene, who had likely wanted to let the silence stretch on to fray Sam's nerves. Al knew better than to try that tactic; wolves never saw a lack of conversation as *silence*. Their ears still picked up too much information—pulse rate, the steadiness of a breath, and probably even a mouth drying from fear or teeth grinding in frustration. Keene should've figured out that much from all the times they'd questioned Isabelle Saxby.

When Sam responded, his voice sounded as steady as ever. "She said the police department called to tell me that Isabelle's execution

has been set for six this evening. And that Isabelle's last request was to speak with her mate. Me."

"Do you deny it?" said the commissioner, already jotting down notes with a gold filigree pen.

Al didn't miss how Sam looked at the glittering pen with contempt, but the wolf's tone didn't change. "No."

"Why did you hide this information?" said Keene.

"I didn't. I cut all loyalty to the Saxby Pack when I left, including with Isabelle. I'm just here to clear any suspicions against me."

Al blew out some smoke, deciding to push at Sam a little. If the wolf came here to spill his guts, then he needed to start before the commissioner lost patience. Anger might burn away his terseness. "Does that mean you won't be at the execution? It's your right as her mate."

He knew Sam well enough to all but read the words *don't give me that bullshit* in the glance he got in reply.

Then Commissioner Keene added, "More to the point, why should we trust what you have to say about Isabelle Saxby? She's been much more forthcoming. Much more willing to work with us."

Sam remained more polite with the commissioner. "Look, squeezing information out of people is my job as well. I know all the tricks and don't want to wait through them. I'm here to give straight explanations, and I'll prove their honesty with some truth-teller."

In the silence that followed, he looked between Al and Keene with a trace of impatience. "I'm talking about taking the serum before continuing the interview."

"We know what you meant," said Al, staring. "We're just stunned to hear you say it."

Technically, there were a few options for someone wanting to prove their innocence. Truth-teller serum was one of them—an experiment in using select bio-thaumaturgy. Inject it into a fella and he couldn't lie. He didn't have to talk at all, either, but whatever did come out of his mouth would be honest.

Realistically, truth-teller was a dead end of a technique. It had been around for years but was rarely requested by either side of the interview. The city didn't like the option because statements given under the influence of the serum were inadmissible in court. And the suspect or witness rarely asked for it because anything they said might give detectives enough information to find evidence that *could* be used in court. Sam must have been pretty damn sure about wanting to stay in the city's good graces—and being able to do that once he talked.

Even Keene seemed hesitant over what to say. "It's an option for citizens. Humans. We don't know how effective it is with a wolf."

"There are some documented cases down in the department archives. After all, truth-teller was modified from magic used by wolves."

The commissioner briefly tapped his pen against the file. "Why do this now?"

Sam smiled grimly. "I know Isabelle. If she wants to see me, there's a reason. Her request alone has me in trouble. I don't want our final conversation to add to that."

"It's called a request for a reason," said Al, watching him carefully. "You don't have to talk to her."

"Yes, I do," came the quiet reply. "I couldn't live with myself if I refused to face her."

Truth-teller was injected into the crook of the arm, and it was Master Enchanter Byrd who administered it and stayed to watch for any sign of a bad reaction. The wolf showed no sign of pain or confusion while rolling his sleeve back down, but Al noticed sweat on his face and neck while the magic took effect. The slight buzz from the overhead lamp was the only noise in the room.

Keene thumbed through the file, frowning slightly. With the commissioner's gaze on the table, it was Al who saw Enchanter Byrd nod as a signal that they could start asking questions.

Al finished off his cigarette and then said, "Why the hell are you doing this? You're smart enough to have a lawyer keep us off your back."

Despite the harsh light flooding over him, Sam's pupils had widened until the gold of his eyes was almost gone. His answer sounded steady enough. "There's no reason to stay silent anymore. The city no longer suspects my client of crimes she didn't commit, and the Saxby Pack has collapsed. Revealing its secrets can't hurt anyone."

"Let's start at the most logical point," said the commissioner, glaring at Al before resuming his focus on Sam. "Are you Isabelle Saxby's mate?"

"Yes."

"For how long?"

"Nine years. We went through the ceremony when I became a junior inspector at twenty-two."

The commissioner's pen scratched against the paper before he said, "We're very curious about what having a mate means for a Saxby wolf. It clearly varies among the packs we're in contact with, from the coldness of a legal contract to the belief in soul bonds."

"It's much like your marriage. Instead of a ring, it's a tattoo over the heart using ink made from your mate's blood. And unlike a ring, you can't take it off, only hide it with an enchantment."

Al nodded. Isabelle Saxby had such a tattoo, and the enchanters had wondered at its significance since it glimmered like magic but didn't hold any spells. "Any other differences?"

Sam's voice turned grim. "Divorce doesn't exist if you want to get out. Just death."

Keene raised his eyebrows. "That's not really a problem for you at this point, is it?"

The wolf's stare in response made the commissioner clear his throat and flip through a few more pages in the file.

Al sighed and circled around the room until he fully faced Sam. "We just need to know you won't try anything. The diplomat from New Obsidian finally agreed to be in the same room with wolves, which meant the execution could go forward. Less than an hour later, we learned from Isabelle Saxby that she has a mate. By right, you're allowed to be there, even if the other witnesses to her death are convinced you'll lose your mind and go on a murder spree."

"I won't do anything. I haven't loved her for years. There's no loyalty between us."

Keene tapped his pen again. "What about loyalty toward the Saxby Pack?"

For the first time, Sam lost enough of his self-control to rub his face, looking truly tired. "On her end? I don't know. On mine, I'm trying to help what's left of the Saxbys overthrow their king before another pack takes over the territory and does it for them. They suffered under his rule for years. They shouldn't have to suffer more."

Al didn't miss the distant word choice Sam used to talk about his former pack. "Who's going to be the new alpha-king?"

"That's their decision, not mine."

Even Commissioner Keene couldn't deny the wolf's disinterest, and after shuffling through the papers for another breath, he closed the file. "Very well. I need to speak with others before you'll hear the city's decision about the execution, but I'm satisfied that we can safely fulfill Isabelle Saxby's last request. If you're willing, we'll bring you to her cell at the prison."

"Then it won't be private," said Sam. He didn't sound surprised.

"No," said Keene, his tone threatening against any argument. "Do you still want to see her?"

At the wolf's nod, the commissioner rose from his seat. "A route to the prison has been closed off for restricted use for the day. It won't take more than half an hour to arrive there. Good afternoon, Mr. Hayes."

When Keene turned to him, Al stayed where he was. "I still have questions related to the Davenport case."

"Fine." Then the commissioner knocked on the door in a signal that he was ready to leave.

After the door closed behind the man, Enchanter Byrd looked at Al doubtfully. "Should I administer the antiserum?"

"Sure," said Al, watching Sam's hands shake until he clenched them. It didn't take a genius to realize the wolf was feeling the truth-teller. "Then you can get out of here. I know you'll be running around for the rest of the day."

Half a cigarette later, Al watched Sam relax back in his seat, eyes back to normal. When he said nothing, Al did. "Still feeling helpful?"

"Depends on what you want to know."

"When did you realize the Saxby Pack was involved with Freddy Davenport's cult and Isaac Marshall's disappearance?"

Sam thought for a moment. "Soon after I took on Miss Marshall as a client. I saw how Isaac Marshall's car looked. The fire distorted a lot of the metal, but I noticed claw marks in a few areas. Too large for any wolf's, but unmistakable. Then I interviewed the two witnesses who were chased by Marshall's driver. One of them made drawings that were very detailed. The similarities between them and the accounts of berserker wolves were obvious."

Al nodded. "My men scrounged up the basic information about those and the modern throwbacks. We found out it's a wolf that doesn't change over correctly. He's deformed, some sort of half-man, half-beast creature in appearance. He's also mindless with bloodlust and tries to kill anything that moves. And finally, he's a big, strong son of a bitch that's impossible to control. Sounds like the descriptions of Dominic Tierney."

"Throwbacks also don't change at will. Something can trigger their shift at any moment, and they can't prevent it. Think of it like migraines."

"Except migraines don't end in a massacre."

"No." Sam almost looked back to normal, absently adjusting his damp collar as he added, "But there are some differences. Harold Beaumont's enchantment must have added... traits to what Tierney changed into. The autopsy report mentioned silver bullets didn't drop him, and that interested me. Silver is as deadly to throwbacks as to any wolf."

"Meaning?"

Sam shrugged. "It locked in my suspicions about the Saxby Pack being involved. They needed military strength. Fighters. What's better than an unstoppable creature having immunity against silver?"

Al nodded. It fit with what he'd thought.

Then Sam unexpectedly said, "Has Isabelle talked about this at all?"

"Barely anything. We're hoping she'll open up to you."

The wolf scoffed, expression turning grim once more. "We'll soon find out."

Al drove himself to the prison, not wanting to get stuck with the commissioner again. The crowds waiting outside the high walls were massive; news about the impending execution had spread like wildfire.

Inside was just as bad. Various city aides and enchanters scurried around while he sought out the block that would hold the condemned. He knew the place well enough to find it without trouble, and the guards knew him well enough to leave him alone.

The interrogation room in this section of the prison was much more modern than the one at the station, but that fact was clear only on the other side of the two-sided glass. Both the commissioner and the prison warden were already there, watching Sam Hayes while he sat at the bolted table. The chair across from him was still empty.

The warden, a barrel-chested man with ice blue eyes, nodded at Al. "They're bringing her in soon. It's good to see you, Al."

"Same, Mick." Then Al glanced into the room. "Think she'll be trouble?"

"She hasn't been so far."

Just then, the door into the room opened, and two guards escorted Isabelle Saxby inside. Despite the unflattering prison uniform, the she-wolf looked lean and lethal, sitting across from Sam with complete composure. He remained silent, watching her without expression.

"Hello, Sam," she said, with a faint smile.

He didn't smile back. "Why did you ask for me?"

"I wanted to see you. Why did you come?" Her voice sounded light, playful, as if she wasn't hours from death.

"Isabelle, it's all over. Alpha-king Saxby has barricaded himself with the remaining royal guards and most of the pack's stored supplies. The rest of the Saxbys are trying to kill him and crown a new king. The chance to find out what the plans were with Harold Beaumont's experiments will be lost once you die."

"The humans are satisfied. Why aren't you?"

"Because the city wants to wrap up its case. I want to make sure the Saxby wolves left behind won't have any nasty surprises."

"Noble Sam." Isabelle cocked her head at him. "You could have gone so far if you'd dropped your delusions of keeping a conscience while advising the king. I thought you would. We could have both been happy then."

When he said nothing, just narrowed his eyes at her, she added, "Why should I help you now? There's no benefit in it for me."

"You always wanted the last word. Here's your chance."

"It's tempting," she mused. Then she leaned back in her chair. The chains connecting her hands jingled from the movement. "What do you want to know?"

Sam wasted no time. "Why did the alpha-king focus on creating and controlling throwback wolves?"

"He thought to get use out of the Sinclair prince even after he'd died. The power of such a creature was impressive. Imagine an army of them. Even with our resources so badly drained, we would have ruled the other packs in a year. The Sinclair prince had been skinned like all the rest, so we were able to give Harold Beaumont the pelt to help his experiments in developing the 'berserker serum,' as we called it."

"Why go to humans for help?"

"As much as it pains me to admit it, there was no other choice. Jane is an annoying little bitch, but she was the pack's only enchanter worth anything. How is she, by the way? Surely grateful for that thick-headed police captain coming to her rescue."

Sam's voice didn't quite dip into a growl. "She's very excited to watch you die."

Isabelle just smiled again. "Are you?"

"You won't get me to bite. We're long past our old arguments."

When the she-wolf glanced away, lips moving into a smirk that suggested they both knew better than to believe that, Sam added, "Why use that serum for Isaac Marshall's assassination? It was clumsy and too intricate to be a surefire death."

"He had to die, anyway. Why not use his driver to test the serum? That Freddy Davenport was against it, of course. He sniveled over every little thing. But it was easy for the enchanter to set the transformation to be triggered by the moonrise, and even easier for us to arrange the human to be near our land when it happened."

A trace of remembered excitement had appeared in the she-wolf's expression. In contrast, Sam's eyes had darkened in disgust. "All so you could see what happened when unknowing wolves tried to fight the berserker."

"They were only pack guards. Their deaths offered much more than their lives." Then she refocused on him. "I'm impressed, Sam. You used to take the loss of your friends very badly, even when it was at our king's command. Do you hate him as much as me?"

When Sam said nothing, some of the playful malice left her face. "Will you give me nothing to take to the grave?"

"What do you want?" he said, quietly.

"Something you wouldn't tell me otherwise."

There was a long moment of silence. All mockery had left her face, and all indifference had left his. Then he murmured, "At one point, you were my everything. I won't enjoy watching you die. I can't."

"Because it'll hurt," she said, her words equally soft.

He didn't answer. He didn't need to.

She nodded as if he had and then looked away. "Just like it hurt me to choose the pack's well-being over your life."

"You chose the king's well-being, not the pack's."

"I never saw a difference. Think up a final question, Sam. I've grown tired of this."

"What was Freddy Davenport's reason for working with the alpha-king? Money? We know Davenport was up to his neck in debt."

"Of course not. Why would you..." For the first time, Isabelle looked truly surprised. Then she laughed. "You're still missing links in the chain, and now you're out of questions. Don't worry, Sam. You're smart. I'm sure you'll figure it out even without my help."

A muscle jumped in Sam's jaw, but he said nothing while she twisted to look at the guards in a clear signal that she was ready to

leave. When she faced Sam again, that dark playfulness had returned to her eyes.

"You know, I didn't love him," she said, remaining seated as the guards drew near. "The king. I don't think I ever felt love aside from you, Sam. But power was always more important."

Then she did rise, turning with the guards without resistance and letting them escort her out.

Sam stood as well, keeping to his side of the table, but his teeth flashed as he said, "No, Isabelle. You were always in love, but only with yourself."

She started, as if shocked that he had responded, but then the nearest guard shut the door behind them, leaving Sam alone in the room.

Behind the two-sided glass, Al watched the wolf while the prison warden told one of his men to let him out only when Isabelle Saxby was back in her cell. If he'd had any doubts about trusting Sam to stay calm during the execution, this had flattened them. The wolf had the stiff posture of someone aware they were being watched but looked damn tired.

"He won't be a problem," said Captain Inge Falk, stepping up beside Al. "All he waits for is relief."

Al turned away from the window, taking in how the others were already leaving before glancing at her. Ballistics had proven Isabelle Saxby had killed five of Falk's men during the fight at the meeting. Maybe his old friend looked unflappable as ever, but Al bet she was boiling inside. "Agreed. How are you, Captain?"

"Somber. It's never an easy thing, an execution."

He grinned while they began walking out of the viewing room and down the first of the hallways to the execution wing of the

prison. "Bullshit. I know you've been looking forward to this. You're like a mother hen to your boys, and your bloodthirst is bigger than a wolf's."

Falk almost smiled, but her voice remained crisp. "True. Hopefully, there will be no more delays."

"From Sam Hayes being her mate? Unlikely. You saw him yourself."

"Then you haven't heard." Captain Falk spoke the words just as Al heard the first echo of voices. None sounded happy. "The Frosthound alpha-king and alpha-queen have arrived to witness the execution. The seating plans will have to be reapproved by all."

Al sighed, realizing the hours ahead would be a circus.

He was almost right. The sight of people hurrying around the audience chamber was more reminiscent of the time he had investigated a murder committed during the opening night of a musical revue while the damn thing was still playing. Insanity whirling all around for a single event that would cycle through newspaper headlines for a day and then be forgotten.

City aides shouted orders at sweating, disheveled men who arranged the rows of chairs. Their voices grew oily and compliant whenever they spoke to a higher-ranked aide or one of the diplomats frowning at diagrams of the proposed seating changes. Family members of the victims stood in the lone quiet corner of the room, their black mourning clothes acting as a shield against the chaos. And then there were the wolves, avoiding each other and humans by carefully drifting through pockets of space, never lingering in one area for too long.

Al picked a spot near the viewing window, which currently had its heavy curtains drawn, to wait out the confusion. He had just lit

up a cigarette when one figure broke away from the rest to approach him. Some of his irritation melted at realizing who it was. Jane Feral's eyes glinted with excitement, and unlike the others, she was openly smiling.

"Miss Feral," he said, since they weren't alone.

"Captain." She glanced at the curtains. "I wish we could see the execution room. I haven't heard which method was chosen."

"Firing squad. Only used for wolves since they can't die from being hanged." He studied her, amused at how she had bothered to tie her hair back and oil her enchanter's leathers. "Wanting to look nice today?"

"It *is* a special occasion." In a different tone of voice, she added, "I saw Sam a few minutes ago. You were very considerate to take him off the truth-teller as soon as possible. It's an unpleasant experience for wolves."

He nodded. "I figured going through the interview was bad enough. While we're on the topic, do *you* have a tattoo I should know about?"

"You've seen my entire body, Captain, and more than once. What do you think?"

He almost cracked a smile at that, but just then Commissioner Keene's voice rose to blistering levels, aimed in their direction.

"You. Yes, you, the redhead. Which pack are you with?"

"None. I'm an ex-Saxby," said Jane, not hiding her contempt for his ignorance.

Al watched the commissioner's frown deepen. Before the other man could say anything, he did. "Still struggling with the Frosthounds?"

Keene's mustache quivered in sheer rage. "It's a nightmare. We can't turn them away, but the other wolves all refuse to sit beside them. This execution will not be delayed over pack squabbles."

Al wasn't about to coddle another round of bluster from Keene, but Jane spoke up, her tone suddenly polite. "Sam and I will sit on either side of them. We won't mind."

When they both glanced at her, she added, "The other wolves have agreed to our presence, haven't they?"

The commissioner traced the stiff shape of his waxed mustache, still eyeing her. Then he nodded shortly and disappeared back into the chaos of bodies.

When Al raised an eyebrow at Jane, she said, "I don't want the execution delayed any more than that jelly of a human. Isabelle doesn't deserve a few more hours. She doesn't deserve anything except those silver bullets."

There was a heat to her voice that went far beyond hatred. Al had seen the nasty injuries Isabelle had given her; it had been flat-out torture. But his gut told him there was still more to it. "Sam was almost skinned for being a traitor, wasn't he? And she was the one who put him in that position."

Jane started, confirming his hunch. Her teeth flashed as she said, "Yes. If he hasn't told you the details, then I won't, either. But she knew what would happen to him and still did it. She doesn't believe in anything except herself. So perhaps it's gauche to be this gleeful, but I won't hide it even though it's improper of me."

He suspected that one of these days, he'd find out what the Saxby Pack had done to *her*, and that it would explain why her defiant streak flared at odd times. Until then, he knew a sarcastic response to

this would send her shying away. "Don't worry about it. You'll be surrounded by people who also hate her."

She relaxed a fraction. "Does that include you?"

"Right now, I hate this damn uniform over anything else."

Just as she laughed, a hesitant voice interrupted them.

"Miss... Feral?" A city aide approached, so exhausted there were dark circles beneath her eyes. "We're ready to seat you. You as well, Captain."

"Finally," he muttered, and took a final drag from his cigarette before following the girl.

He had to sit with the commissioner and the mayor but was mostly resigned to the fact, pretending he was too interested in where everyone was being seated to notice their conversation about the diplomat from Xenic being overdressed. The entire front row was reserved for family members of the victims. Falk sat there as well, her rigid military posture at odds with the shaking shoulders and curved backs of those in mourning. A few cried off and on, although they tried to stay quiet about it.

The rest of the rows were divided into three sections. The left held the twelve normal citizens brought in as witnesses for the public, as well as the diplomats from the other city-states. The middle section was for him and the other city officials, acting as both barrier and reassurance against any trouble from those sitting in the final section on the right: the wolves.

When Al glanced in their direction, he saw that most looked stone-faced. It made sense; they were diplomats as well, all from packs that had demanded to witness the trial, sentencing, and now execution for various reasons. All except the Frosthounds, who still hadn't given a reason for their sudden appearance. Al wasn't too

worried. He knew the alpha-queen was from a death cult, and that the king had risked everything to have her. Dropping in on an execution was probably like going to a party for them. The alpha-king was obviously enjoying himself, watching everything with a faint smile that widened at any nervous reaction from the other wolves. His queen remained fixated on the drawn curtains, hands clasped as if in prayer.

Just before Al's attention flickered away, the Frosthound alpha-king offered a cigar to Sam Hayes, who sat to his left. Sam's grim expression didn't change as he shook his head. Then a soft hiss came from Jane Feral, who sat by the alpha-queen. Jane's expression was pure anticipation while she motioned the alpha-king to pass the cigar over. With a shrug, he did. The alpha-queen took it from him and handed it to Jane without looking away from the window. She and Sam were the only ones who seemed to feel the finality of the situation, and they were the first to stiffen in their seats even before the curtains twitched and then opened.

Isabelle waited in a chair placed against a wall, blindfolded and composed. A hush fell over all witnesses.

A calm always came over Al whenever he was faced with death. He didn't like feeling so dispassionate but didn't fight it, either, taking in the narrow slits in the opposite wall where the mouths of the rifles would be positioned. He knew the five men there had all been picked for their aim, and he knew it would be quick.

It was. The glass muffled the deafening blast of five bullets into one sharp *crack*. Most of the witnesses weren't used to executions and jumped from the noise. The wolves were all on the edges of their seats, unblinking at the sight of blood. The silent tension around them seethed in comparison to the sobbing from the front row.

Then the Frosthound alpha-queen bowed her head, and as soon as Al saw her beatific smile, he knew Isabelle Saxby had died.

Al waited until a medic entered the room and checked the body for signs of life before he glanced at Sam. The wolf stared without expression, even when more men stepped into the room to cover up the body and take it away.

Then the diplomat from Xenic rose to his feet with open disgust on his face. "As barbaric as expected. I'll find my own way out."

Al didn't watch the man go. Eventually, he knew they'd fight over an extradition case between the two cities, but right now there were other things to do.

The curtains were drawn shut again, prompting the rest of the witnesses to leave as well. As Al rose to his feet, he remained focused on the wolves. Most representing their packs moved for the exit without acknowledging each other. Jane was among them, looking the wildest he'd ever seen her. When their gazes met, she sucked on the cigar and gave him a grin he already recognized, and he was glad he was off duty for the rest of the night.

To his surprise, the Frosthounds had lingered, with the alpha-queen briefly speaking to Sam. He nodded in reply to whatever she said. Then the alpha-queen turned to her king, who slipped an arm around her waist before they left, sharing his cigar.

The room felt much larger when it was just him and Sam. The wolf remained in his seat, bracing one elbow on his knee while his other hand rubbed at his face. Al studied him for a moment and moved for the hidden door built into the left side of the room. He knocked and waited.

The prison warden answered it, shoulders squared as if expecting trouble. "Everything all right?"

"Sure. It's just us two. Do me a favor, Mickey, and give me that whiskey bottle you keep around in case a witness faints."

The man glanced past him. The caution in his expression faded. "Right, her mate."

Within a few minutes, Al sat beside Sam and poured out a shot.

Sam straightened up to take it from him. "Thanks. I told Jane to go on ahead. She hated Isabelle. There's no reason she should pretend otherwise."

Al waited until he drank it down and then took a shot for himself. "Off the record and out of curiosity, who pursued who?"

The wolf was handling it better than he expected, even managing a wry smile before he answered. "I pursued her."

"Jesus Christ, Sam."

"I know." Now Sam leaned back in his seat, looking at the curtains again. "That's what all of this was about. Wanting to see how blind I was. Trying to see how blind I still am."

"And there's no one prettier you can confess this to?" When the comment drew a side-glance from the wolf, Al laughed. "You really think I don't know you're the one who whisked away Miss Marshall? Or that I don't know how you feel about her?"

Then Al poured a final shot for the wolf and rose to his feet. "You can't get a more definite end than death. Take it, Sam. Go home to your girl."

Cora played with the sash of her robe while waiting through the distant tolling of the city's clock tower. Eight in the evening, and from the quiet of the house, she was the only one up and waiting for Hayes. She thought he'd come back to Minnie's for the night. At least, she *hoped* he would.

The fire in the hearth crackled when she stirred it up, desperate for something to do. At the muffled noise of the front door downstairs opening and shutting, she brightened until she heard a male voice that wasn't Hayes'. Brom, she supposed, and received confirmation a few moments later when a female voice in the bedroom beneath hers greeted him. The house fell silent once more.

Finally, nearly half an hour later, she heard the door again, and this time recognized the tread of the footsteps. Unable to resist, she slipped out of her room and down the stairs barefoot, moving for the soft clink of a coffee cup being drawn from the cupboard.

By the time she reached the parlor, Hayes had taken the chair by the fireplace. He sat on its edge with the coffee cup in one hand, watching the flames while their flickering outlined him in gold. He looked tired and absent, but the moment she stepped into the room, he turned toward her, eyes sharpening with surprise. "You're still up."

She smiled while settling on the floor near the hearth, not liking how the other chairs would leave her unable to face him. "I heard you arrive."

"Sorry. I was trying to be quiet."

"Don't be. I listened for you. I was worried."

Their eyes met for a long moment before he returned his attention to the fire. Then he sighed, and his broad shoulders sank as if burdened by a great weight. "Isabelle's execution."

She nodded, shifting enough to brush a hand over his while he gripped the mug. "Minnie told me after I kept pestering her about why you left. If you'd rather be alone..."

"No." He finished his coffee and set it aside to join her at the hearth, leaving them close enough that she could see the day's worth of stubble on his jaw. "No, I wouldn't."

Her hand found his forearm, stroking along the tense muscle there. Now she could see a tired relief in his eyes, and when he spoke again, she sensed the words had long lived in his heart unsaid. "There's nothing to grieve for. We hated each other for years. But seeing the end took me back to the beginning, too. It's hard to think about when we had just become mates. How our future—and the pack's future—seemed so sure."

"You were in love," said Cora, gently.

He smiled, but it was humorless. "I don't know. It felt like it at the time. Then I found out what she was willing to do and realized I was the dumbest fella alive."

The line of his mouth remained grim as he looked over at her. "The day we met, you asked why I left the pack. Are you still curious?"

When she nodded, he continued. "Isabelle was part of the reason. She was the personal guard of the alpha-king's youngest daughter, who was about to be married to the alpha-prince of a rival pack. I was told to investigate the prince for any flaws and soon found he was insane and had killed others close to him. I warned Alpha-king Saxby, but he told me to forget what I had found. To tell no one. The original plans of marrying off his daughter for an alliance wouldn't change. We were sending her to her death. Her own father *hoped* for it. In a pack, there's no higher word than the king's, but I had to do something. I trusted Isabelle with the truth and a plan to help the princess escape before she traveled to the other pack."

Then Hayes stopped and rubbed the back of his neck. The piercing color of his eyes had nothing to do with the reflected light from the fire as he stared into the flames.

Cora could easily guess the rest of the story. "But she betrayed you. Oh, that—I should have shot *her* instead. And all those Saxbys had the audacity to scold you about loyalty. Rats have more compassion."

Her hand jumped over her mouth after the outburst, but Hayes only laughed a little. "Don't, Bunny. I like your moxie. Anyway, Jane found out what happened and helped me escape the cell I was put in. We both fled into human territory, unable to do anything for the princess."

"Hayes, I'm so sorry."

He shook his head. "The past is the past. If nothing else, today showed me that. Regret gets you nowhere, but I'd be lying if I said it

doesn't still bite at me. Maybe if we hadn't been mates, I would've been clear-headed about her. Maybe I would've trusted someone else and been able to save Princess Liana."

Cora shifted closer, hating how the mere sight of the she-wolf must have been so painful for him. "Your whole life was turned upside down. I think it would be strange if you didn't have any regrets. But you know, whenever I remember something in my life that I wish I'd done differently, instead I find myself thinking of how those bad decisions led me to where I am today. Who's to say where we would be now if even one choice was made differently? You and I would have had no reason to meet. That's one thing, at least."

She was absently staring into the fire when his hand brushed her cheek, coaxing her to look at him. Some of the weariness had left his eyes, replaced with warmth. Her heart beat a little faster, and she tried not to sound breathless as she added, "But that's just the way I move forward whenever I've been a fool. And believe me, I've had plenty of practice."

"I think you spent so much time convincing other people you're a silly, shallow socialite that you began believing it yourself," he murmured.

She sighed, her fingertips now feather-light against his jaw. The air between them felt hot and alive. "And I think you spent so much time fighting the horrible parts of this world that it's the only way you know how to feel good about being alive."

"True, but I've been learning new ways recently." His voice brushed against her mouth as he moved, erasing the final inches of space between them. Her heart felt hotter than the fire beside them.

His kiss was deep and slow before he broke off to bury his face into the curve of her neck. His breathing remained even and steady,

but she felt his bone-deep weariness while his body relaxed against hers. She pulled him even closer until her arms could wrap around him, aware that in that moment, he needed her presence more than anything.

Her fingers moved slowly, soothingly, stroking along the back of his neck and down over his shoulder. When they reached his collar, she grew aware of the heat of his body through his shirt. Again, she wondered how a wolf who walked among humans could stand wearing their stiff layers of clothing. How tiring it must be. How confining.

She found herself loosening his tie. He growled softly, nuzzling the pulse in her throat while she slid the thin strip of fabric away and moved to the buttons of his shirt. Then she felt the grit of ash against her fingers, and looked at them in confusion. There was a smudge on the inside of his collar, too. "What..."

He shifted enough to glance at her hand. His expression grew grim again. "Saxby mates are tattooed with each other's blood over their hearts. When one dies, the survivor's tattoo crumbles into ash."

She pushed open his shirt collar to better see the lines left on his chest. They were smeared but still vaguely resembled a stylized crescent moon. Her heart ached for him. "Your own version of a sigil reminding you of the life you'd lost, each and every day."

"You had it much worse," he said, quietly. "Mine is a symbol, not a binding. I was free to rebuild myself."

"Were you?" She glanced up at him. "Or were you feeling just as trapped by your past as I was by my future?"

His eyes were a dark gold while he studied her, their wildness reminding her of when she'd seen him as a wolf. Her gaze dropped back to the hard muscles of his chest while a feeling of what to do

grew stronger within her heart. Slowly, deliberately, she wiped her hand across the remnants of the tattoo, erasing the lines. He growled, but she sensed it wasn't a warning for her to stop. Then she shrugged off her robe and used the fine silk material to brush off the lingering ash. His heartbeat sped up against her fingertips.

"There," she said, softly. "Now it can't haunt you anymore."

Then came the plaintive fussing of an infant. Cora felt Hayes tense beneath her touch while they both turned toward the doorway. A young she-wolf stood there with a baby in her arms. She stared at them wide-eyed, seemingly frozen to the spot.

"I-I'm sorry," stammered the she-wolf. "She's been sleeping only when I walk with her lately. I didn't mean to…"

Hayes' voice sounded rougher than usual. "It's all right. Goodnight, Eve."

When the she-wolf quickly slipped upstairs again, Cora looked back at Hayes, trying to mask her disappointment at the interruption. "I think I just got you in trouble."

His expression left her breathless. It was as intense as their night together in his apartment, all reserve and formality gone. It told her without a word that he didn't give a damn about being interrupted. And that he didn't want to stop.

"Where?" she whispered, her grip strangling her robe. Would this finally be it? Could they finally be together without any care for tomorrow?

"Your room." Then his mouth was on hers, intoxicating her with each flick of his tongue.

In the bedroom, he pulled the nightgown off her in a whisper of silk, kissing at her neck with the slight hint of teeth. She arched into him, marveling at the strength in the hands exploring her body. In

the darkness, his feral nature came alive, his slightest touch brimming with wordless hunger.

"Hayes," she murmured, ready to melt as his fingers slid up her thigh and over her hip.

"Sam." His deep voice against her skin sent hot shivers throughout. "I've wanted to hear you say my name since the minute we met."

She closed her eyes, wondering why tears welled up behind her lids even though she had never felt this good before. As his lips brushed hers, she sighed, feeling boneless. "Sam."

He was as powerful and virile out of his clothes as she remembered, and her anticipation flared into sheer need. The bed creaked at the slightest touch, so he picked her up instead, easily holding her weight while tasting at every part of her within reach. She panted in time to his thrusts, clinging onto his broad shoulders while his power pushed her ever closer to cherry-sweet release. When it rushed over her, she couldn't help crying out his name and felt him smile against her neck, his hips shifting against hers for a deeper angle that sent her straight into a second one.

Even once she had recovered, his stamina remained, keeping her to a hard, fast rhythm. His hot mouth stoked her lingering shivers, driving her along with him. She didn't know whether to gasp for mercy or beg for more.

"How long do you last?" she managed.

He laughed, bringing his face back to hers. "A while. I'm a wolf."

To her delight, he wasn't exaggerating. They didn't stop until dawn, finally settling together in bed. She felt inflamed and deliciously alive while he pulled her close. His eyes were closed, but

one of his hands continued to stroke along her body, as if he couldn't stop touching her.

She played with the thick hair at the back of his head, studying his face. Even in the dimness, she could already see how relaxed he appeared. "Sam?"

He looked at her, the gold of his eyes catching the last glimmer of light from the fireplace. "Hm?"

"I don't think Mrs. Wilkes or the others will be pleased with us in the morning."

"Believe me, Bunny, it was worth it. And I'll keep them from scolding you."

She smiled, settling in against him. "Cora. I think we're past the point of professionalism now."

His laugh was a rumble against her cheek. "Far past it, Cora."

Cora was very relieved to find that Hayes—Sam—acted as unprofessionally with her in the morning as he had throughout the night. Despite the lack of sleep, she felt bright-eyed and refreshed by the time they both washed and dressed. His freshly shaven face nuzzled against her neck until he could lick at her pulse while she put in her earrings. Her giggling in response was soon interrupted by a sharp knock on the door.

No one opened it, but Minnie Wilkes' voice drifted through. "That's enough now. Get downstairs before you miss breakfast."

Sam kissed her a final time and straightened up. In the morning sunlight, he looked rested yet hungry, eyeing her as if he wanted still more. "I'll go down first to make sure everyone stays civil."

She faced him while putting the other earring in. "Oh, I don't care if they frown at me for behaving outrageously. It's been my reputation for years, and I've heard every comment in the book."

"They can still be polite." His hand traced her cheek a final time before he left, steps silent against the floorboards.

Syrup-sweet satisfaction lingered in her every thought while she finished dressing, but she remained aware enough to choose a subdued outfit. If human women resented heiresses flaunting their wealth, then she-wolves probably weren't much different. Her knit dress was a demure navy blue, stylishly tailored but without any further decoration except some silver stripes on the sleeves and skirt.

Downstairs, she chirped a greeting to Minnie in the kitchen over the sizzling of eggs and tomatoes frying in bacon fat. She found the others in the breakfast room. From their stiff postures and quiet conversations, no one seemed very happy, and Sam had that easygoing yet detached expression he used to keep a discussion calm. It didn't change while he gestured at her to take the chair beside him and then introduced her to everyone.

There was Brom, big and brawny and focused on shoveling scrambled eggs into his mouth more than anything. He had just come back from a night shift at the docks and seemed exhausted. His mate, Holly, was tall but slender, had auburn hair, and pointedly refused to look Cora's way. And finally there was Eve, the young she-wolf who had been so aghast at seeing them together. She still seemed embarrassed to face Cora, instead fussing with baby Theodora asleep in her arms.

It was mostly Holly and Eve who talked to each other, although Brom occasionally tossed a friendly comment Sam's way. Cora decided it was better to keep quiet and focus on the plate of food Sam had gotten for her. When he passed over the cream and sugar for her coffee, though, she couldn't resist smiling. The reserve in his eyes disappeared long enough for him to wink in response.

"You put that much sugar in your coffee?" said Eve, still looking baffled by Cora's very existence.

"I have a terrible sweet tooth," replied Cora, and took a sip. She sensed the playfulness draining from Sam again, but truthfully, she wasn't nervous at all to be the outsider at the table. It was unlikely their comments would be anything worse than the malicious wit that passed as talking with friends among high society.

"So, you're the latest case for our Sam," said Holly, suddenly.

Cora brightened her smile, remembering to keep her mouth closed to avoid showing her teeth at the she-wolf. "Yes. I doubt he expected so many twists and turns when he first took it on. I certainly didn't."

"But it's surely over now. All the human papers have moved onto other topics." The word *human* had a particular inflection to it.

"I hope so. I'd like to move on, too," said Cora, and bit into her toast.

Amber eyes glanced over her face and away again. "That's good. Sam has many other things to worry about."

At that, Sam shifted in his chair. It was a small movement, but Cora watched in fascination as it caused a ripple effect in the postures of the other wolves. It was clear who was the dominant one in the room. "Holly, you're not anywhere as subtle as you think. Don't try speaking for me while I'm right here."

As soon as he looked at Holly, she nodded stiffly and fell quiet.

Brom shoved the rest of his bacon into his mouth, his attitude toward Sam as comfortable as before even though his posture remained deferential. "Holly's just twisted up with nerves. We took control of rooms near to where the king's barricaded himself, but he's stuck fast like a tick. At least we're close to controlling the storage units."

There was a slight growl from Holly that seemed directed toward him. He acknowledged it with a shrug, still eating, but Cora noted how the lapse into silence seemed focused on her. It was easy to realize they didn't want to discuss their pack in front of a human.

Sam also understood, because after finishing his coffee, he said, "Do you need to talk to me before getting some sleep?"

At Brom's nod, Sam turned to Cora. She didn't like how some of the tiredness had returned to his expression, but his voice sounded reassuring. "I'll be back in a few minutes."

Once he and Brom stepped out into a tiny backyard used as an herb and vegetable garden, silence fell around the table. Cora reached for the nearest newspaper to read the headlines, remaining quiet even when Holly and Eve began talking about a play heard on the radio the other night. Oh, she recognized their behavior; she'd known plenty of mothers, sisters, and close friends who had shown similar coldness because a man important to them was interested in *her*. That busybody mixture of protectiveness and suspicion over their darling boy being led astray—nevermind that the darling boy knew full well what he was doing.

Yet she simply wasn't interested in reacting to it. There were better things to focus on, like what the papers had to say about her disappearance from the opera house. Most of the headlines were about Isabelle Saxby's execution. The only article about her was buried on the third page, and it implied she was simply up to her old tricks and had found a famous—or notorious—figure to spend a few days with. Frankly, she was glad. It gave her more breathing space to figure out her new life.

Minnie came in from the kitchen with her own plate of food. When she settled down at the table, she studied Cora with an

expression that was more resigned than critical. "Well, girl, how are you this morning?"

Only a slight hint of irony marked the words. Cora, well-used to disapproving old ladies, remained cheerful. "Outright wonderful. You've been very kind to watch over me, but I feel fully recovered."

"You seem well enough," the other woman acknowledged. "Although, you need some awareness of what setting off on your own will mean. More... caution about the seriousness of escaping your father."

"I thought a lot about it yesterday. I don't see any reason to fuss over it this morning."

The response drew a slight shake of the head from Minnie.

Cora was very pleased to see that, because it meant she was still good at her mental defenses. Keeping her voice airy, she added, "Instead, I've been thinking about last winter's fashion, particularly the use of oversized buttons to break large blocks of color. There were so many coats, blouses, and dresses that had them. It will take all day to run out of examples. I'm sure I'll dwell on nothing else."

It was the first time she had seen Minnie surprised. "You know how to loop thoughts against mind readers? Goodness, girl, I see Sam wasn't exaggerating when he said you had hidden talents."

"Yes, but he didn't know that. Or at least, I never told him. He might have sleuthed it out when first looking into my case. I was very good friends with a man named Cornelius Arbot, who was from Aquila. You know how that city is. It's said that everyone there has such strong telepathy that some don't even know what their own voice sounds like. Cornelius always spoke very well, though, and taught me a few techniques to protect my mind."

"Yes, since coming into the city, we constantly read in the papers about your many good friends," muttered Eve, who now gently rocked the baby while finishing her last slice of toast.

It was tempting to see if she could stoke the two she-wolves into outright bristling with merely one impertinent remark, but Cora knew it wouldn't lead anywhere good. Instead, she looked at Minnie and said, "I'll open my mind back up if you prefer. I just don't think you *would* with the types of thoughts running through it this morning."

"You're a brazen little thing," said the old woman, but grudging respect laced her voice. "Do as you like. I can tell your mind is in fine shape and form, and that's all we needed to know."

Just then, Sam and Brom returned inside, Sam saying, "Tomorrow at dawn. It's going to be a short visit. There's a lot for me to do here, too."

His voice sounded dispassionate and hard, and Cora was dying to learn more. As soon as he appeared in view, he focused on her, still a little grim. "Everything all right?"

"I was about to ask you that."

He nodded and glanced at Minnie. "Is she well enough to go out?"

"Oh, I'd say so," said the old woman, dryly.

"Really?" Cora felt herself light up. "I was hoping I could. I even took a chance earlier and made an appointment with a lawyer. It's at ten today."

"Let me know when you're ready," said Sam. "I'll take you."

Soon, she found herself beaming in the passenger seat while he drove her through the city. Whenever he wasn't using both hands on the wheel, his free one clasped hers, his touch warm even through

their gloves. Despite the misty day, the buildings, people, and other cars all appeared so vivid to her gaze. Her thoughts still wheeled at the sense of freedom.

"Well, that wasn't so bad," she said, cheerfully. "I was expecting a tongue-lashing about improper behavior."

Out on the road and in the fresh, briny air, he looked more relaxed but wasn't yet smiling. "Minnie's better than that. She just said I wouldn't be allowed to stay overnight until you move out."

"Oh, no." She couldn't help sounding crestfallen.

His hand squeezed hers. "It's fine. Her next words were that you *are* well enough to move out. At this point, your father's the only thing to worry about."

The idea of being back in Sam's apartment made her giddy, but she tried hard to focus on the new turn to their conversation. "Has he given a public response to my disappearance yet? I'm sure he's very suspicious and confused by now. He probably even thinks I'm dead somewhere."

"If he does, he's not showing any concern. He hasn't left his house and continues to refuse phone calls, but public perception of him remains sympathetic. He's seen as a lucky survivor of Freddy Davenport's cult plans who is slowly recovering from his ordeal."

"Hmm. I'm sure he's had Mr. Forrester amass whatever important people he thinks are necessary to lay low and avoid scrutiny. Well, that's all right. I'm about to find my own."

They reached a stoplight, leaving Sam free to look at her. The wryness had returned to those beautifully wild eyes. "Speaking of, who's this lawyer you're about to see?"

"Mr. Otto Snaith. His family was nearly ruined by Father a decade ago. I thought it was safest to see someone who would feel

absolutely murderous toward Father and therefore wouldn't back down from such a formidable figure." Then she thought for a moment. "And if I like Mr. Snaith, I'll talk about the sigil as well."

When Sam raised an eyebrow, she said, "What Father did to me is bound to be found out anyway, isn't it? Just now, you said the *public* perception of Father is that of an innocent man. You didn't say it's what the police think."

For the first time since he'd left her bedroom, his real smile returned. "Clever Bunny."

She grinned back before he said, "Your father hired Harold Beaumont to create the sigil. The police have his ledger of illegal enchantments and are slowly working through it. I don't know how close they are to finding the entry for the sigil, but whenever they do, they'll be able to connect it with your father just like I did."

Cora nodded. "I see no reason to avoid helping them along, but I still want a lawyer to iron it all out first."

Despite his history with her father, Mr. Snaith proved to be very neutral in manner. A thin, drab man with wire spectacles that flashed in the harsh lighting of his office, he carefully listened while she explained her intent to cut all connection with her father and live independently. Then he answered her questions, most of which boiled down to how well a restraining order would work against a powerful man like her father, and what other types of lawyers she might need if the situation grew complicated.

She liked his explanations enough to decide to trust him further, and before he could wrap things up, she cleared her throat and said, "There's one more thing, Mr. Snaith. I thought I should mention this, and if you aren't able to help me, then maybe you could refer me to someone else. I've explained about wanting to stay away from

my father's control, but I suppose you couldn't know that I meant it literally. Up until very recently, I truly was under his control. Over a year ago, he had a binding sigil put on me. It took this long to escape it."

The lawyer's body language changed. He had been very stiff and proper up to this point, but now he outright froze at her words. His eyes, which were enlarged by his spectacles, stared at hers unblinkingly, and she was suddenly reminded of a short yet intense fad that had rippled throughout the elite of the city: keeping a praying mantis as a pet. She had never done it, but many of her friends had, and she'd been amazed at how the little creatures seemed so indifferent and still until sensing prey. Then they moved like lightning, catching and eating unlucky insects head-first, those enormous eyes now ruthless and knowing.

Mr. Snaith wore such a look now. Isaac Marshall, using illegal magic on his own daughter. Isaac Marshall, revealed as the kind of monster among the city's elite that would be shown no mercy. His downfall would be spectacular.

"Why don't you start from the beginning about this?" he said at last, and actually smiled.

She was smiling as well by the time she left his office. It brightened at the sight of Sam, and as they walked out of the building together, she said, "He was very helpful and very confident that I'll be safe from my father and any tricks he might pull to make my new life miserable. He's not the type of lawyer who helps with police interviews—in fact, he warned that I might have a whole team of lawyers by the time this is through—so I gave him your office number for anyone he wants to refer me to. I hope you don't mind since I don't have my own phone yet."

Sam nodded, settling a hand against her back as they joined the flow of pedestrians. "Not at all. Is he sending the bill there, too?"

"Bill?" she said, absently, too caught up in the excitement of spending the rest of the day together. "Oh, I haven't hired him yet. He'll get back to me once he has a representation agreement for me to look at."

"He's a lawyer and still wants to be paid for today. As soon as you stepped into his office for a consultation, he started charging by the minute."

"Oh. That's why he kept looking at his clock. I thought he was bored by my explanations. I was trying to be thorough." The realization left her frozen on the sidewalk. "I didn't even think about money. I've just always signed my name whenever necessary."

Then she looked at him in chagrin, embarrassed by the oversight. "And here I thought I was doing a good job of things."

At that, he shifted closer, eyes darkening with reassurance. "You are. It's hard breaking off on your own when you've never done it before. Look, Allagash & Crown isn't that far. Why don't we drive there and see if someone can talk to you about your trust account?"

She nodded but couldn't help saying, "Maybe I was overconfident about all this. I've never paid attention to more than the interest from my trust and don't know how much is in it. There's a difference between paying for shoes and paying for lawyers."

"Believe me, the fact that it's with Allagash & Crown proves you'll be fine."

The first open appointment was at one o'clock, and Cora took it. After they were escorted back out of the black marble building, Sam

checked his watch and then eyed the park across the street. "That gives us about an hour. Feel like lunch?"

Many employees from the surrounding businesses had the same idea, but the lines at the street vendors moved quickly. She chose salted fries, wanting something she could eat without spilling on her outfit. He got a hot dog and had already finished by the time they reached the park. A brass band played in the pavilion, attracting a large audience, but when Sam glanced at her with a silent question, Cora shook her head. She didn't want to listen; she wanted to *talk*, and they settled on a bench over by the pond instead. She watched several ducks drift through the water, already feeling bubbly again, especially when Sam settled an arm behind her and began lightly stroking the back of her neck.

When she turned to him, though, he was staring distractedly at the peaceful pond. It reminded her of how tired he had seemed the night before. Even as she took a fry, she found herself asking, "How are you?"

He looked startled by the question until she added, "Obviously, we've reunited in spectacular fashion, but it *was* over a month that we were apart. My side of things was very clear and boring, but what about you? What did you do?"

"It drove me nuts to think of you back under your father's thumb, so I stayed as busy as possible," he admitted. "Here in the city, that meant figuring out how to free you while Jane worked on the enchantment. I also started and finished a quick case. Being associated with you rubbed off on me. Other high society figures are starting to reach out for my sleuthing skills."

"Oh? Who was your client?"

"Louise Wheeler."

Cora recognized the name. They were much alike, she and Louise. Notorious for being caught in scandal, for being fashionable, and for always being with men. But Louise also preferred hobbies Cora had never been interested in, mostly car and boat racing. The girl constantly drove those two worlds mad with how she could keep up with and sometimes even beat the other established drivers.

To Cora's surprise, Sam's hand moved enough to catch her chin and coax her to look at him. Humor glinted in his eyes. "Your scent changed as soon as I mentioned her name. Jealous of her?"

Cora tried not to huff. "She once called me too short to wear ostrich feathers. That doing so made me look like a molted bird. I've never forgiven her because she was absolutely right."

"That's all it takes, huh?"

"Well, that and the fact that she found her way to you as soon as I was unavailable. What was her case about?"

"Someone replaced a bunch of her jewelry with paste copies."

Cora leaned toward him, trying not to sound so gleeful. "Don't tell me—she did it herself."

He was already smiling. "How did you know?"

"She has a horrible gambling addiction. Her motive for hiring you was probably sheer interest. We're all alike, you see. Dying for any new experience."

"No, Bunny," he replied, his eyes suddenly smoldering. "You are nothing like her. Even during our initial consultation, I could tell you were excited to know more about me, not what you could gain from being seen with me. It's a big difference."

It felt like her heart was about to melt, so she made her response just as teasing. "If we're going to talk about sleuthing, then we

should mention our bet before I was packed off to that stuffy retreat. I was right about Harold Beaumont hiding in Mallow Manor."

"Mm-hm. What do you want as a prize?" Even though they were out in public, their mouths were inches apart, and the tone of his words was anything but proper.

"I can't think of anything I want more than to be with you," she said, voice soft.

His growl sounded more like a purr while he kissed her, his hand still gentle against her chin.

Just as her lips parted against his, the clock tower chimed in the distance, startling her. His movements remained smooth as he pulled away with a sigh. "One o'clock. Time to go."

She groaned but knew he was right.

Miss Carmen Jasso wore rigid, conservative clothing decades out of date, but the yards of black fabric and lace added to her tall, imposing frame. Silver streaked her dark hair, which was styled into a pompadour, and her eyes reflected the office lamplight like pieces of obsidian. Jeweled rings hinted at her skills in old-world magic, with fire opals, tiger iron, and brown tourmaline glimmering from the slightest movement of her hands. A black serpent coiled over her shoulders, flicking its tongue at Cora while she sat in the chair facing Miss Jasso's desk.

Cora, who had never been afraid of snakes, merely gave it the same smile as she had to Miss Jasso. She didn't know much about 'heirloom' magic, as it was quaintly termed now that modern methods of thaumaturgy had taken over, but she figured it was better to acknowledge Miss Jasso's familiar than to ignore it.

"Don't worry about Sylvie," said Miss Jasso, petting the serpent's gleaming scales. "Her work is silent and invisible. Now. You came in to discuss your account with us."

"Yes. I want to live on my own, free of my father's money. That will mean hiring lawyers and other possible expenses, so of course I'll need my own income. Can my trust provide that?"

"Easily. Your mother created it with your independence in mind."

"Good. I want to use the money well."

The other woman nodded and opened the file in front of her. "All decisions, of course, must be your own, but my advice will help you make them wisely. Let's first discuss your portfolio summary."

Cora followed along with the explanations, options, and proposed plans easily enough, asking the occasional question for a clarification.

After about fifteen minutes, Miss Jasso paused. "I freely admit, Miss Marshall, to feeling surprised. You have much more awareness and enthusiasm than when I last called to ask if you wished to make any changes to your trust."

"I suppose I've changed since then," said Cora, not looking up from the sheets of figures and sums.

"You must have, if you now plan to move away from your father."

The sudden change in Miss Jasso's tone drew Cora's focus up to her face. The serpent slid along the woman's shoulders, coiling in beautiful patterns against the stiff fabric. Each scale now seemed to be outlined with flickering, golden light, like the glow that could be seen beneath embers in a fireplace. Its gaze seemed as intelligent as Miss Jasso's while they both studied Cora intently.

Then Miss Jasso leaned forward in her seat, gaining actual emotion in her voice. "If you don't mind my saying so, I believe it to be a good personal decision as well as a financially sound one."

"What do you mean?" said Cora, trying to sound calm despite sensing she was about to hear something important.

"I worked with your mother to set up this trust for you. She was a very respectable woman, a very gentle woman, but wary about your father growing too aggressive with his goals. She thought he would one day bring about his own ruin."

"Do you?"

For a moment, Miss Jasso didn't answer. Her fingers brushed over the serpent's glowing scales. Her hand remained unburned. "There are several magical seals on every account we manage. They protect against attempts to take money from its rightful owner. Blackmail, embezzlement, even murder... we can catch evil intent and trace it back. Over a year ago, we noticed one of the seals for your account cracked—this is a sign of an impending threat, if you didn't know. I called to warn you. You seemed very grateful and scheduled an appointment to see me."

"I... I don't understand."

"You missed it. When I called a week later, you didn't remember our previous conversation at all." Then Miss Jasso gave her a meaningful look. "We are, of course, well-versed in recognizing all types of magic, legal or otherwise."

"Oh." In her excitement of having the sigil removed, she had entirely forgotten that there was no way of knowing what memories she had lost to it. "But if you realized I had a binding sigil put on me, why didn't you notify someone? The police?"

"Our position with clients is to protect their money, not kill them. We didn't think you could survive if the sigil was revealed."

The woman's calmness needled at Cora, and she saw no reason to avoid stating the obvious. "And if I died, my father would inherit the trust and your firm would lose all that money."

To Miss Jasso's credit, she looked slightly uncomfortable but admitted, "That was also a consideration."

The concession made Cora all the more glad that she *did* have one person she could trust, and that feeling only doubled afterward when she found Sam leaning against one of the marble columns by the building's entrance.

"What is it?" he said, catching her lingering indignation.

"Oh, everything's all right with the money. It's just that I realized very abruptly that I'll never know what memories Father took from me. It's a little unnerving. And it makes me feel helpless, which I've always hated." Then she looked up at him, determination burning in her chest. "I want to know everything about this case. I don't care if it's considered solved. I want to know what really happened after Father survived that assassination attempt."

She continued to scowl until Sam stepped in close, his eyes sharp with the excitement of a hunt. "Then I guess it's a good thing you've got a detective on your side. How about a drive to my office?"

CHAPTER TWENTY-NINE

It felt wonderful to be back in Sam's office. Mabel, the secretary, was out for the day. Jane had already holed up in her side and only the faint crackle of electricity indicated she was even in the building. It left Cora feeling very cozy while they sat together at his desk, and her focus kept slipping to him instead of the files he handed over.

He had shrugged off his suit jacket and rolled up his sleeves but still looked businesslike while opening and reading the morning mail. Her heart felt ready to burst from the mere sight of him. Eventually, though, she learned all that had happened while she'd been trapped with her father, and each piece of information sobered her further.

When she realized the last file contained the transcript of Sam's final conversation with Isabelle, she hesitated.

He noticed in between letters and shook his head. "It means nothing to me. And it's accurate. I typed that up myself after leaving the execution."

A few sentences in, indignation replaced her doubt. "Every word out of her mouth was meant to hurt you. I can't believe you kept your temper. I would have slapped her silly."

"I was more concerned with the 'missing links' she mentioned."

"Do you think she was being honest?"

He leaned back in his seat, expression absent. "I do. She seemed genuinely surprised that I didn't have the full picture."

"Hmm." Cora read through the rest of the transcript. "Well, if Freddy wasn't working with the Saxbys for money, then he must have had another source. The last time we went out together, he couldn't even pay the bar tab at his boating club."

"What about your friend Violet? She admitted to having a big hand in his cult."

"She spent money worse than he did. Her nature was more suited to enticing the right people into the cult and growing it into what it became. And since Harold Beaumont is her cousin, she was the only source needed to find an enchanter willing to perform illegal magic. I'll bet she simply bullied him into helping her. That's what she did when we were all children."

Sam stared at the opposite wall, running a thumb over the scar by his eyebrow while he thought. She found the small movement to be distracting in the most delicious way, but his voice drew her attention back to the problem. "Even so, they would have needed money. Jane was paid top price for the materials she sent to Davenport's 'Admiral Antwerth' alias."

"Through a bank account?" said Cora, hopefully.

He grimaced. "Cash. Impossible to track."

"I suppose someone else connected to Freddy or the cult could have funded them. It's just that I've read through the list of acolytes

and others tied to it. I didn't see one name that wasn't connected to outrageous spending. A few were already disinherited from their families over their bad behavior even before they joined the cult. They're all just like Freddy and Violet—constantly bleeding money."

"Not all," said Sam, suddenly straightening in his seat. "There's someone who knew about the cult long before it became anything. You said it yourself while telling the Frosthound alpha-queen about your uncle: he got into plenty of fights with your father over forming the cult and losing money through it."

Then he leaned toward her, eyes sharp with a hunter's intensity. "Bunny, I think we're all turned around. We've been looking at who Freddy Davenport could have begged money from. Maybe we should be thinking about who could have approached Davenport with money as a lure. Do you remember when I asked you what happened the day your father left? And what you said in response?"

"Oh, yes." She didn't even have to find the right file. That entire conversation remained clear in her mind. "He told me he was going to New Obsidian for business reasons and would return the next day. At the time, I didn't think that was strange. It was normal for him to spend the night if he travelled out of the city."

"But was it normal for him to *tell* you this while the sigil controlled you?"

"I... no. No, he never bothered. It's not like I could ask him anything. He would simply recite what I should do while he was away." Cora felt herself stiffen as the implication grew clear. "He wanted me to know, didn't he? And not because he was worried. If he had been suspicious about his well-being, he would have simply ordered me to call the police and report him missing once he didn't return."

"Misdirection," said Sam. "He never planned to go to New Obsidian at all."

"But there'd be no reason to lie about the general location of a secret meeting. Businessmen have them all the time. Unless... it wasn't with another human," breathed Cora.

Sam nodded. "The Saxby Pack. The Frosthounds weren't lying and neither was the informant who tried to get them to pay for details. A human financially backed the Saxbys, but it wasn't Freddy Davenport like we thought."

"That's another thing: the fact that Freddy was killed just as he was about to give a new interview. In previous statements, he freely talked about the cult, the serum, and planning Father's murder. So what was he about to say that triggered the enchantment to kill him? Maybe something *else* about Father. Maybe that he was involved beyond being an innocent victim."

Sam's excitement didn't show in his voice but in the way his teeth flashed when he spoke. "Your father had the money. The Saxbys had the idea about the berserker serum. And then they went to Freddy Davenport for his connections and know-how in hiding illegal magic under the city's nose. True to form, the Saxbys backstabbed Isaac Marshall as soon as they felt it was safe, something Davenport also wanted so that the path to using you for his ritual was as smooth as possible."

Cora beamed. "But they didn't expect us to ruin their plans. The pieces all fit, don't they?"

The glint in Sam's eyes warmed as he focused on her, but his words remained cautious. "They do, but there are still plenty of question marks, like your father's motive for getting involved. He seems like a deliberate man, and one who doesn't like wolves. What

did he want out of this? And how did he convince Harold Beaumont to keep him in hiding at Mallow Manor?"

"That's right, he was with Beaumont for weeks. What did he say about that?" Cora quickly looked for the latest interview transcripts with her father, reading parts out loud. "I don't remember the car wreck or how I escaped it. I don't remember my driver acting out of order. I woke up in the room you found me in. Food or water would occasionally be given to me through a slot in the door. That's all I know."

Then she huffed. "It sounds like utter faff to me. There's no detail at all. But he'll never reveal what really happened. Father's not the type of man to crack."

"It's all right. We can find out if he's the missing link Isabelle mentioned even without a confession from him."

Determination filled her full. "What do we need to do?"

To her surprise, Sam gave her a wry grin. "You really enjoy this, don't you?" he murmured. "Helping with detective work."

"More than anything," she said with complete honesty, caught by how his gaze warmed in response.

He was able to hold onto his focus much better than she was, his voice quickly returning to something more professional. "We need evidence that your father worked with the Saxbys and Freddy Davenport before they turned on him. Our options are narrow since Davenport, Violet Granbury, Harold Beaumont, and the only Saxby willing to talk are all dead."

"There's Father's lawyer, Mr. Forrester. Remember when you got him to admit that he and Father had a terrible fight over a potential 'shadow venture?' Perhaps I can pester him for more. Maybe he knew it was the Saxbys that Father was interested in, and why. If I

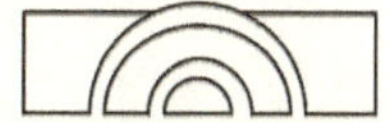

threaten him with the knowledge that I'm free of the sigil and am about to go public with it, he'll know Father won't be a figure worth keeping quiet over."

Sam shook his head. "No, we're not going to put you in danger. Let's stick with your original plan of getting that lawyer and telling the police about the sigil before anything else. I like the idea of talking to Mr. Forrester, but afterward."

"But that means waiting," she protested.

He raised an eyebrow. "I can think of ways to stay busy in the meantime."

His tone was teasing enough to bring a smile back to her face. "Such as?"

The sudden intensity in his eyes was answer enough, but before she could toss the file aside, his phone rang.

It was the lawyer she'd met earlier that day. Mr. Snaith had been busy in the brief time since their meeting, having a representation agreement ready for her to read and sign as well as a proposed team of lawyers, each from a different branch of legal expertise that would be needed for a complicated case like hers. All were willing to meet with her in an hour at Mr. Snaith's office. Cora had to admit, there were benefits to having a renowned father hated by so many. More than a few appointments must have been hastily rescheduled to make room for hers.

When she hung up, she looked over at Sam, who still thumbed through files. "I have a very good feeling that a bunch of lawyers will be helping me before the day is out. Mr. Snaith asked me to bring as much information about the sigil as possible, including the nasty little thing itself if it still exists."

They both looked over in the direction of Jane's office.

The she-wolf rolled her eyes at the sight of them but let them inside. "Don't touch anything."

Her workspace was brightly lit and painfully neat. Each vial and jar that filled the steel shelves looked precisely placed. Some were glass and some were blacked out to prevent light passing through. Reference books waited within easy reach of a workbench. Blueprints of what looked like a submachine gun were tacked to half the walls alongside handwritten notes. There was even an area sectioned off by what looked like hard plastic. Two holes were cut into it at arm-height, and there were thick rubber gloves attached to them so that Jane could work on whatever was inside without contaminating herself or the rest of the room. At the moment, the transparent box looked empty, and the various bottles of powder, wiring, and metal parts on the workbench suggested she was in the middle of something less experimental in nature.

The she-wolf's next words confirmed it. "There goes any hope of working on my own projects today."

Despite her dour tone, Jane looked happier than usual while pulling files from a massive black cabinet. Sam had moved over to the workbench, studying the half-built items there, but Cora was more interested in how Jane seemed to be irritated with her neck, one hand drifting to the skin above her collar before dropping away again. If Cora looked closely, she could just see a smudge of foundation makeup on the leather itself.

Before she could comment, Jane turned in their direction with a handful of files. "Here we are. Copies of Harold Beaumont's records about the sigil and my own notes about the enchantment I made to break it. I hope you're not looking for the memories burned away.

Beaumont didn't list what they were. Most likely, Isaac Marshall was there directing him verbally on what to erase."

When Cora flinched at the words, they both noticed, and Jane actually sounded apologetic as she added, "Sorry, but it's true."

"It's all right. I've just been reminded of it a lot today, and it isn't very pleasant to think about what might have been taken and how I'll never know for sure how much of my mind is left."

Sam's expression turned grim, but in the next moment, the phone in his office rang yet again. "I'll be back in a minute," he murmured to her.

Once he left, Cora sighed, feeling a bit silly. "I'm really all right. I just feel like I hate my father more by the day."

Jane shrugged, glancing over the nearest blueprints. "Understandable. Cruel people are easy to hate, especially when they have power over you."

Cora was again struck by the lack of bitterness in the she-wolf's voice. She didn't know Jane nearly as well as Sam, but the she-wolf had never veered from a caustic attitude toward the world. Cora studied her again, taking in the relaxed way Jane leaned against the workbench. Then she found herself saying, "How are you, Miss Feral?"

Sharp yellow eyes looked her over, but Jane's tone remained mild. "Well and good. I wasn't going nuts like Sam in your absence, though I was equally busy."

"I can't thank you enough," said Cora, sincerely. "You're a miracle worker to free me. If I can ever pay you back..."

"I appreciate the sentiment but don't see how you could. We're not much alike, Miss Marshall. I'll admit, your areas of expertise run

deeper than I thought when we first met, but I doubt I'll ever need help in any of them."

The she-wolf's words sounded so stiff and proper that Cora almost smiled. Sam was so easy-going and confident that she found it easy to forget he and Jane were both strangers to the world they now lived in. She wondered how much of the she-wolf's prickliness was from the discomfort of her situation.

She looked over the she-wolf again and decided to take a gamble. "I don't know about that. For example, I'd advise trying a concealer with a green tint. It will hide the suck marks like a dream, and your skin won't feel irritated from layers of caked-on, sticky makeup."

Jane froze. Then her face flushed scarlet, and she pulled her hair free of its bun to let it tumble around her shoulders. "I didn't have time this morning to craft a cosmetic enchantment."

"We're all very busy these days."

"Hm. Green?"

Now Cora did smile, relieved that the she-wolf sounded tentatively curious instead of offended. "It neutralizes redness on fair skin."

"It does make sense," muttered Jane. "Thank you."

"Of course. I take it Captain Dempsey will be in good spirits if I see him today?"

Jane stared at her in disbelief. "How did you—Sam hasn't even figured it out yet."

"He might be a detective, but he's still a man. They never notice that glow of satisfaction unless they're the one who caused it." Then Cora set her purse on the workbench and perched on the nearby stool. "Don't worry, I won't spill your secret. I'll admit to being very curious, though. When did it start?"

"Soon after he got out of the hospital," admitted Jane.

"Was it at the police station?"

"Of course not." The she-wolf sounded offended by the mere idea. "We're both consummate professionals. He found me in the station's archives one night when I wasn't supposed to be there and escorted me out—all the way back to his place. You can infer the rest. How did you guess it was him?"

"Female intuition. He's always shown much more patience with you than with Sam."

It was Jane's turn to smile wickedly. "Oh, it's 'Sam' now? For the record, I approve. Do you have any other advice for my neck?"

"The concealer should be enough. You could also try convincing the captain to suck on parts that won't be seen in public."

For a moment, she thought she'd shocked the she-wolf again. Then sudden humor glinted in Jane's eyes. "Who says he doesn't?"

They both burst into laughter.

Sam reappeared in time to catch a final giggle from Jane. He stared at her. "Can't remember the last time you really laughed, Jane."

"Call it satisfaction," said Jane, turning enough so she could raise an eyebrow at Cora without him seeing. Before he could respond to that, she brandished the files. "These should satisfy even a lawyer's scrutiny. I'll bring the sigil out in a moment. It's still in the jar."

"You were able to preserve it?" said Sam.

"Of course." Jane didn't bother hiding her smugness. When he gestured at her to hand over the files, she tucked them beneath her arm and added, "Do you really think I'll trust you to explain this level of thaumaturgy? Or to answer any questions they might have

about it? I'm coming with you two. I assume the phone call just now wasn't anything important for us."

"Not as important as this," he said, and then turned to Cora. His smile made her feel like she could take on the world. "Ready to hunt down the truth, Bunny?"

She grinned back. "Absolutely."

CHAPTER THIRTY

As Cora had predicted, Captain Dempsey appeared in high spirits, his sarcasm downright mild at seeing her surrounded by lawyers. "Miss Marshall. I'll take a wild guess and say you're ready to talk about why you left your father."

She offered a shining smile. "That's right."

Mr. Snaith stepped toward the captain, his words as brisk as the movement. "We're sorry to disturb you this late, Captain Dempsey, but we thought this should be brought to your attention as soon as feasible."

Once inside the captain's office, a strange feeling struck Cora while Mr. Snaith and the others laid out the facts about her father and the sigil. There was the sheer anticipation of her father experiencing the hell of a police investigation and media uproar, yes, but also something quieter, something she couldn't name. She sat there in silence, remembering the first time she had been in this office: the day Sam had taken her on as a client to clear her name against murder allegations. She wasn't used to introspection, and it staggered her to think of how her life had changed. She supposed this was the closest she could come to experiencing closure over the sigil and her stolen memories.

Captain Dempsey remained stoic while listening, asking the occasional question for clarification. The smoke from his cigarette added to the moodiness of the dimly lit room. Jane had agreed to give the sigil to Cora's lawyers, and they now offered the jar to the captain. Cora could never understand how men stayed so dispassionate toward a repulsive sight. Only she flinched when the sigil, still in the slug-like form, crawled to the side of the glass nearest to her and grew tendrils to search every inch of the smooth surface.

"As you can see," said one of the lawyers, the expert in thaumaturgic law, "it still senses her."

The captain's gaze flickered over to Cora. She must have looked as sick as she felt, because he pushed the jar out of sight. "So, you want to press charges against your father."

She drew in a deep breath, aware that there was no turning back from this moment. Aware that in the morning, when she felt less overwhelmed by a long day of legal discussions, she would be absolutely gleeful. "Yes. Mr. Snaith and the others have made sure I understand what that will mean."

Dempsey studied her for a moment and then scrawled out a note. As he rolled it up and fed it into the pneumatic tubing system, he said, "All right. I hope you're ready for the grinder."

She raised her chin. "Who am I about to be meat for?"

"Everyone. You'll have to see a police enchanter before you leave the station so he can collect all possible evidence left. Over the next few days, the police commissioner will want to interview you himself. Do you have somewhere to hide when the press finds out

about this? It's going to be big news. Every reporter in town will yap at your heels."

"Miss Marshall is following our advice to remain out of public sight for tonight," came Mr. Snaith's calm reply. "We have someone who will send a press release for tomorrow's morning edition. Since there's no chance of keeping it quiet until you or the city prosecutor makes a move, we decided to control the timing and content of the reveal to reduce the stress on our client."

One of the other lawyers offered yet another sheet of paper to the captain, who read it and shrugged. "Doesn't put any words in my mouth, so I'm fine with it."

As Dempsey stood in a silent signal that he was done with them, he added, "Any other questions or comments, Miss Marshall?"

"Yes. I know you already have men watching Father for his protection. I think that's enough and don't want anyone watching over me."

"Obviously," he said, voice dry. "Once the press is onto this, he won't be able to sneeze without it being reported. Which I'm sure your team here is very aware of. Relax and get some sleep. You've given us plenty to work with."

"All right. Have a good night, Captain." Cora couldn't resist putting a delicate inflection on the words *good night*. The lawyers wouldn't understand it as anything besides an acknowledgment of more work for him and his men, but she thought the captain might hear the slyness in it. His response was a mere shrug, and she nearly laughed at his steady reaction compared to Jane's.

He sensed what she'd implied, though, because as she and her lawyers rose to leave, his next words poked her right back. "Your

retinue is missing a familiar face. I didn't think Sam Hayes knew how to leave your side."

"Oh, he's waiting here in the station with Miss Feral. I believe both expect you to ask for statements on the parts they played in freeing me."

Mr. Snaith cleared his throat while gathering his coat and suitcase. "We've also advised Miss Marshall to keep her acquaintance with him as modest as possible."

The captain lit a fresh cigarette before escorting them out of the office, not even bothering to hide his skeptical expression. "Lost cause, buddy."

The lawyer didn't seem ruffled by the final comment, but as they took the first of the hallways that would lead them to the police enchanters' labs, he told Cora, "Advice is just that—advice, but I really do suggest you avoid spending too much time with Detective Hayes, including finding a separate living situation. We need all the public sympathy we can get for your case, and popular opinion is currently against wolves."

Cora didn't agree but decided she could be diplomatic about it. "I'll certainly consider it."

She certainly didn't, and even after two hours passed with the police enchanters putting her through a ridiculous amount of tests she didn't understand or care to know about, her first thought was wanting to feel Sam's arms around her. By then, it was after midnight, and she wasn't the only one who was exhausted. The lawyers also showed signs of weariness, some taking off spectacles to rub at the marks left behind on their noses and others leaning against the nearest wall.

Yet they were all obviously pleased by how everything had turned out, with Mr. Snaith even smiling at her while they returned to the main entrance room of the police station. "We'll be in touch once I hear anything from the city or your father's legal counsel. Until then, avoid contact with him and try not to worry. There's no reason to."

She nodded, but her sudden eagerness came from spotting Sam near the phone booths. He alone didn't seem tired, his grey suit as crisp as ever and his hat tilted over one of his eyes. When he smiled at seeing her, her heart beat a little faster.

"I'll take over from here," he said, his tone even but also warning the lawyers against arguing.

Cora had to admit, Mr. Snaith and the others took not getting their way with much more grace than her father's retinue, only murmuring a round of polite farewells before leaving the station.

As soon as they were out of sight, she smiled at Sam, who slipped a protective hand to her back.

"Ready to go?" he murmured.

She moved closer to him, her heels loud compared to his silent steps. "Absolutely. What about Jane? Is she still giving her statement?"

"No, we're both done, but she's staying awhile longer. Something to do with her entry for the city's new gun model contract. The deadline is in a few months, and she's getting nervous."

As they drove away from the station, she told him everything that had happened, ending with Mr. Snaith's suggestion. Repeating the words left her more indignant than when she'd first heard them.

To her surprise, Sam said, "Might not be a bad idea to find your own place as soon as possible. Somewhere you can call home."

"But I thought once the news is out about the sigil, I can live with you."

"Bunny, these days I'm hardly at my apartment. And a lot more people know where it is and that I'm there."

"Oh." She tried not to sound crestfallen. Her hope had been that after tonight, they would spend the next several days in bed to make up for lost time. "Is it because you're more involved with the Saxbys now?"

Traffic was sedate enough that he risked a glance at her. Even the glitter of the city's nightlife couldn't compare to his eyes, their gold deep and alluring. "You overheard me and Brom, huh?"

"Yes, a little. You can overhear a lot in that house, especially through its ventilation. Not that I normally try to, but... I was curious. All I heard was that you'll visit the Saxbys tomorrow."

"That's right. At dawn." When he didn't elaborate, she remembered the other wolves' reticence toward discussing their pack in front of her.

Just as she drew in a breath to change the subject, he sighed, expression tightening as if he'd come to a decision and didn't like it. "There's been a lot of upheaval with the Saxby Pack since the city cut it off. The alpha-king has barricaded himself with the remnants of the royal guard in his citadel. The rest of the pack is trying to overthrow him. They're called the breakaway Saxbys since they haven't come up with a new pack name. I've been helping them since I'm the only wolf on their side with firsthand knowledge of the layout and weaknesses of all the royal buildings."

She nodded, taking in the grim set to his mouth. "Is there a good chance they can pull it off?"

He rubbed the side of his jaw, eyes absent. "Yes, there is. Strange as it sounds, the fact that the city has cut off trade with the Saxby Pack created some breathing room. No other pack wants the trouble of mollifying the city if they take over the territory, so even though the Saxby alpha-king's hold on his land has disintegrated, everyone else is content to watch and wait."

"Who will be the new Saxby alpha-king?"

"Whoever the breakaways decide is the best leader for a new pack." He spoke the words with his usual steadiness, but Cora saw more in his expression.

Her voice rose in excitement. "It could be you, couldn't it?"

He hesitated. "Could be. Others have pointed out that I'm already acting like a leader for the breakaways. Right now, I'm solely focused on bringing down the alpha-king to help the others. It's the least I can do to repair the damage his rule has done to the pack."

She didn't understand why he wasn't more enthusiastic about it. "But isn't this all good? You'll be able to return to your pack again and perhaps even lead it. You'll have the respect you deserve from humans and other wolves. It'll be utter freedom to do what you want after having to be so careful toward either side."

He smiled thinly. "I try not to get ahead of myself, especially with complicated situations like this. One step at a time. For tomorrow, that means finding and cracking open some storage rooms. It'll keep the breakaways fed and well-supplied, anyway."

Worry threaded through her next words. "It won't be too dangerous, will it?"

Now his expression warmed. "No. Trust me, I'll be back in time to be with you when the news breaks about your father and the sigil."

"And then onto Mr. Forrester to see what he knows?"

He laughed. "If you're not sick of lawyers."

"Not when it means investigating." Then she also laughed, but a pang went through her heart as she looked out and saw how close they were to Ragbag Way and therefore Minnie's house.

His hand found hers, warm and comforting. "Don't want to go back yet?"

"No. I know I should get some rest, but I'm just not ready. My mind is whirling with how quickly life has changed. All I'm sure about is wanting to spend more time with you before you leave."

When Sam spoke again, his voice brushed her ears like a kiss. "Where do you want to go?"

"Anywhere. I know I mustn't be spotted by people, but that's all right. A quiet place will be just as swell."

His smile in response made her heart jump. "I can think of just the spot."

He drove her to the ocean, finding a rocky part of the shoreline that wasn't popular. There were copses of cypress trees to park a car under, but all the trails down the steep cliff edges were cut right into the stone and sand.

This high above the ocean, the waves sounded lulling instead of thunderous, and the sky was beautifully clear of the typical marine fog that slipped in at night.

An ancient wooden fence waited by the trees, still sturdy enough that they could settle on it to watch the waves glitter under the waning moon.

"This is a lovely spot," said Cora, melting into the warmth of his body. "How did you know about it?"

"When I first left the Saxbys, I used to come here whenever living among humans got to be too much. I'd shift into my fur and run beside the waves, smelling nothing except saltwater and seaweed." He sounded thoughtful, musing, as if remembering those days.

"To escape for a little while," she said, softly, watching how the shadows from the cypresses played off his features. "It must have been terribly hard growing used to us."

"Everything's hard, Bunny. Life in the pack was hard, too."

She nodded, looking out at the ocean. The next words slipped out of her, driven by the allure of moonlight on waves. "Would you like to escape like that tonight?"

There was a brief pause. "You mean, running along the shoreline as a wolf?"

"Yes." Then she wondered if she'd blundered. There was still so little humans understood about wolfkind. "Or is it difficult to change form?"

"Not for me, anyway. It's always been painless and easy. You merely surprised me by asking."

"I don't know why I did. It just seems so dreamlike out here. So peaceful." The wind pulled at the curls of her hair before she added, "I've always thought it must be wonderful to escape being human. I've met quite a few wolves by now, and most look absolutely miserable trapped in clothes and manners. And you know... during the month I was back with my father, only my dreams were truly out of his control. You appeared in them all the time, always as a wolf. It felt so vivid. I can even recall the texture of your fur. It made me feel better whenever I woke back up. People insult wolves by calling them 'animals,' but I don't think being an animal is humiliating at all. I think it means you're free in a way that humans will never know."

He studied her, eyes gold even in the starkness of night. She couldn't tell what he thought. Then he nodded, and his hand brushed her cheek before he pulled away and began removing his clothes. He looked unearthly in the moonlight, and she found herself wondering how humans, herself included, went through their day viewing the wolves as just one more mundane aspect of their lives.

She shivered in awe when he crouched down in his bare skin and began the change. It was smoother than she expected, a hint of true magic taking place. Muscle and bone twisted into new shapes in silent harmony. Fur rippled into life, replacing skin. A soft growl was the only sound he made while shaking himself from muzzle to tail. He looked like smoke and silver while loping to her, and she forgot how to breathe.

At first, she kept still against the fence, unsure of what he was comfortable with. Then a cold nose prodded her hand, encouraging her to touch him. Even through her glove, the thickness of his fur thrilled her. When she took it off and stroked between his shoulders, marveling at how they were as high as her waist, her bare fingers sank in until she couldn't see them. Just like in her dreams. Suddenly, she felt close to tears.

He circled around her, powerful fangs tugging at the thick coat she wore. Despite the ocean's chill, she shrugged it off to free her movements and found herself kneeling to bury her face against his fur. He smelled like clean musk and salt. His heartbeat reverberated, matching her own. He didn't pant like a dog, instead remaining silent while nuzzling at her.

"Thank you," she murmured. "Until this moment, some part of me refused to believe this has all really happened."

Somehow, despite the fact that he was now bone-crushing jaws and bristling fur and deadly instinct, his silent movements held the same reassurance as his kisses while her hands rubbed over his shoulders and through the thick hair over his chest.

She left her hat, stockings, and shoes behind with her coat, too excited to feel the chill of the sea breeze. The trail down to the shore was brightly lit by the moon, but much of it proved steep enough that she kept a hand on his back for balance. The hiss of waves grew into a roar once they reached the bottom, and she could see that rocks as jagged as teeth pushed up through the sand by the cliffside.

Yet there was still a wide strip of smooth shore that ran for a good two miles, and as soon as Sam knew she had her footing, he raced ahead, moving with incredible speed along the damp, hard-packed sand. In that ethereal landscape of black rock, silver waves, and glittering stars, in Cora's eyes he was the most otherworldly sight of all.

She knew she couldn't catch up with him, but it didn't matter. She ran as well, full of an exhilaration that left her laughing each time seafoam washed over her bare feet. The cold air stung her cheeks and calves, but her heart beat strong and fast, gaze always on the wolf speeding over the dusky sand.

He made it to the end of the shore and returned to her before she was even a third of the way along, splashing in and out of the waves until his tongue lolled. Still laughing, she splashed water back at him. She was barely aware of him lunging to erase the distance between them before he had changed form and caught her up in a rough, breathless kiss. With her skin chilled by salt and wind, the heat of his mouth felt shocking. Her fingers buried into his wet hair as his lips

moved down to her throat, his body pressing against hers with the same excitement that had filled his every movement while a wolf.

"Sam," she whispered, just to bring his face back up to hers.

His eyes glowed like the moon as he looked at her, and his grin was almost boyish. Unguarded and in the moment.

I love you, she wanted to say, sure that her heart was about to burst from the truth of those words.

Yet then he kissed her again, as passionately as before, and that butterfly-delicate feeling in her chest brightened into a heat of her own as he began unbuttoning her dress, somehow both unhurried and hungry in his movements. Very soon, she forgot all about those words and anything else that wasn't him.

His skin wasn't chilled like hers but instead hot to the touch, electrifying. His eyes glowed in the dark, brightening when she began gasping against his touch. Then he pulled her to him, and his teeth caught the side of her neck in an unspoken promise that left her senses cresting with the waves. The moon wheeled overhead, bathing them in its gentle, ancient light while they made the most of their night together.

By the time they returned to Minnie's house, they were properly dressed and using their masks of manners once more, but Cora knew she couldn't keep a satisfied smile off her face no matter how hard she tried. Her skin itched from salt left by the seawater, she was so tired that she couldn't tell up from down, and in the morning she would be applying makeup to her neck just like Jane Feral. Frankly, she felt utterly amazing.

Sam escorted her to the door like a perfect gentleman, but before he could unlock it, Minnie Wilkes opened it for them. The old

woman sounded glad enough to see them, but Cora could tell she wasn't about to let them repeat the night before.

Sam didn't bother going in, instead giving Cora that warm, wry smile of his. "I'll be back by breakfast, Bunny," he murmured, eyes gleaming.

She nodded with a tinge of wistfulness. She wanted to say something lighthearted, perhaps even offer a quip back, but all that came out of her was a breathless, "Be careful."

Something flickered in his eyes, but she couldn't tell what it was before he disappeared into the darkness with the ease of someone used to hunting in the shadows of humans.

Inside, the house was quiet and dim, with the main hearth long reduced to embers.

"Everyone else has been in bed for hours," said Minnie, but there was no judgement in her voice. And when Cora only nodded again, the other woman patted her shoulder and added, "Chin up, girl. Sam's gone on much more dangerous visits into pack land and returned no worse for the wear."

Cora managed a smile, believing her, but in her heart, she knew it was more than that. They'd spent the night together, and now her bed would feel empty without him in it.

As she moved for the stairs, Minnie added, "Sleep well, Miss Marshall. Breakfast tomorrow will be at 7:00 like before, but I won't be there. I go to church on Sundays."

"I understand. Goodnight."

The hearth in her room had also burned away to embers, their dim lighting and occasional crackle encouraging her to undress and fall asleep. She had just picked a nightgown when a soft knock at the

door startled her. The silk slipped through her fingers while she turned toward the sound.

"Come in," she said, assuming it would be Minnie.

It wasn't. Instead, Holly stepped inside cautiously, as if expecting Cora to throw her right back out.

"Oh. Hello," said Cora, seeing no reason to hide her surprise. "I didn't realize anyone besides Mrs. Wilkes was up this late."

"I wanted to speak with you." The she-wolf moved with the same silence as Sam but held more grace in her movements while closing the door. She remained there, looking over Cora's suitcases.

Cora didn't know what Holly wanted but thought it was best to get things over with. "Of course. Sit down if you'd like."

Holly didn't, although her gaze briefly flickered to Cora's face. "There's no reason to play coy about why I'm here. Are you aware of Sam's plans?"

Cora decided the best option was to act silly and thoughtless. She had no hard feelings toward the she-wolf but no soft ones, either. "For tonight? He mentioned that he needed to leave and would be back tomorrow."

"I meant his long-term plans. I thought perhaps he shared them with you."

When Cora shook her head, Holly didn't look surprised. "He's never wanted to stay here among humans. In the five years since he had to leave the pack, some of us managed to keep in contact with him. It's always been his goal to return to the Saxbys."

So far, the she-wolf's tone sounded mild, but Cora still felt herself grow restless. Without anything else to do, she began packing her belongings back in her suitcases. When it became obvious Holly

waited for a response, she said, "I understood everything you said, but I don't see what I'm supposed to take away from it."

"His time among humans was for mere survival, including his job as a private detective." Holly studied her again and added with some exasperation, "Including his clients as a detective."

Cora had never been a neat packer, but now she tried, aware that she needed a few extra moments to keep her next words lighthearted. "In other words, we're nothing special to him."

"Yes."

Cora sighed and faced the she-wolf. "If you really believed that, you wouldn't bother having this discussion. So what do you *truly* wish to tell me?"

The insight startled Holly. The she-wolf folded her arms against the oversized, heathered sweater she wore and looked at Cora more carefully. "All right. I'm here to ask you to leave Sam out of your sordid games."

"Games?" repeated Cora, honestly confused.

"You know your reputation. You flaunt it constantly. One of those rich girls of the city that collects men like dresses."

Cora sighed. So it was just the same pinch-faced disapproval after all. "Why should I hide my past? I'd rather be honest about it. But it's all right. I don't expect you to like me. Frankly, most women don't."

Holly eyed her, her posture still stiff. "Can you really be that shameless? The whole city knows about your sordid history and yet you smile like it's a joke. As if you have no heart."

Cora didn't stop packing. "It's just that I've heard this so many times before."

"That's exactly it," said Holly, stepping closer. "You don't understand, so you think it's fine to do to Sam what you've outright admitted to doing to other men."

"Do what? Enjoy each other? I don't see what's so bad about that. You're talking like I've gone out and bewitched him."

"You have! He's distracted by you. Glamored. He trusts you, and that's a terrible thing. Humans aren't like wolves. You don't understand how we view the world. Wolves are loyal."

It was those words that rankled Cora to the point of letting heat slip into her own voice. "Humans understand loyalty, too. Even I do. I was very fond of each man in my past."

"And yet now your attention is so easily focused on Sam." Holly shook her head. "How soon before it shifts again? And even if it doesn't, you've compelled him to care about your problems. To help you far beyond what a client in a case deserves. Can you honestly claim you've brought more good than bad to his life? That he can escape this city while you're clinging to him? What life does he have here, serving humans? He can be a king back on Saxby land, but out of either ignorance or selfishness, you're content to keep him a mere dog among humans."

Cora realized she was breathing so quickly that she felt dizzy. She wanted to tear out handfuls of the she-wolf's long, auburn hair while screaming that none of it was true, but her treacherous brain jumped to how happy he had been on the beach, free of the city and its humanity.

Then she raised her chin, refusing to let Holly's words fill her with doubt. "If Sam wants to end things, then I trust he'll tell me so himself. And I'll believe him. But I won't take anyone else at their

word about it, including you. Is there anything else you wanted to discuss?"

Holly briefly flashed her fangs in frustration, but when she replied, she sounded only formal. "If I can't convince you, then there's nothing else to say. Goodnight."

Cora nodded, still too angry to trust herself to be polite. And once the door shut behind the she-wolf, she paced throughout the room, all exhaustion burned away by confusion and fury. She was so indignant and so sure that Holly would keep talking about her that she even unblocked the vent in the floor that piped air and any conversations happening in the rooms below.

Holly's voice drifted up to where Cora knelt, metallic yet clear. So did the creak of bedsprings, as if she had already settled in for the night. "I'm worried about the human. What do you think of her?"

Her mate, Brom, already sounded half-asleep. "Sweetheart, you're the only girl who exists in my eyes."

"Be serious. What if there's trouble?"

The she-wolf really did sound scared, and once again, doubt itched at Cora. Suddenly, she wasn't angry. Suddenly, she just hoped Holly was completely wrong.

Brom sighed. "For who, Sam? He'll be fine. He survived Isabelle."

"Humans are different. They never want to let things go. And she's an heiress, isn't she? She'll have a lot of sway. If she's soft on him and takes it badly when we all go back home..."

There was a slight rustle, as if one of them shifted to be closer to the other. Then Brom said, "Knowing Sam, he'll let her down gently and have things planned out for her to move on smoothly as possible. It's fine, love. Everything will be fine."

CHAPTER THIRTY-ONE

By the time morning arrived, Cora had pushed all doubt from Holly's words out of her mind. She decided to return to her usual boldness with her outfits as well, choosing a pale pink dress with ruffles at the neck and a white blazer jacket embroidered with gold. The smells of coffee and frying ham reached her while she put on a pair of heels and some earrings, but she resisted breakfast long enough to set aside white kidskin gloves and a hat for later, bubbling with excitement over the idea of spending the day sleuthing with Sam.

She was still smiling while heading downstairs, catching hints of a murmured conversation between Holly and Eve. Butter and jam waited on the kitchen table and so did two half-full cups of coffee, but Holly was already washing the final plate while Eve sat there and nursed the baby with a bottle. The younger she-wolf glanced at Cora and then away again, obviously uncomfortable.

Cora paused in the doorway, assessing the situation. "Did I miss breakfast?"

Holly looked over. The she-wolf had been stiff in her mannerisms before, but now they were absolutely glacial. "Yes. It was at 7:00."

Cora checked her watch. 7:13. Inwardly, she wanted to laugh at the snub but kept her voice serene. "Well, I've always made it a habit to be late, so I suppose I can't complain."

She didn't wait for an answer, instead returning to her room to collect her hat, gloves, and some spare change. In all honesty, breakfast with the others had been dull and strained even when Sam had been by her side. Missing it this morning felt like an opportunity, not a punishment.

Back downstairs, Holly seemed surprised that she was leaving. "You're going out into Ragbag?"

Cora offered a smile while adjusting her hat in the ancient mirror by the front door. "Oh, yes. I noticed a sandwich shop from my window that's open for breakfast. It's barely a block away. Isn't that convenient?"

"But I didn't mean for you to—you'll get into trouble the moment you step outside."

"I don't think so. It's just a sandwich. I'll be back in a bit." Then she was out the door and gone, navigating the grey, dilapidated structures overrun with weeds and trash piles. As she walked, her white shoes skirted broken glass and the occasional bloodstain. Guttural coughing could be heard from one of the leaning shacks built from ripped cloth and broken boards.

Oh, she wasn't a total fool. Ragbag Way had an unpleasant reputation, and she was alone and obviously out of place. For that reason, she had traded her jewelry for her pistol and had left her purse behind. She had also kept every other part of her outfit completely untouched.

The buildings she passed were unlit, but she felt the weight of attention from all directions until she reached the sandwich shop. Matteo's, tiny yet alluring with its mouthwatering smells of peppers, fried eggs, and sausage. A man reeking of whiskey slumped in front of the big display window papered with old advertisements for beer brands and pickles, blinking at her when she smiled at him and continued inside.

The interior was worn yet clean, its air greasy and hot from the griddle in the back. The owner was a boulder of a man, with the thick body and broken nose of an old boxer. He stared at her with the same suspicion and bafflement as those eating at the cramped tables nearby, but said nothing while she ordered a breakfast sandwich and paid. In a few minutes, she left with her food without anyone following.

It was hard not to tear open the brown paper and begin eating, but she resisted until she found an old, crumbling wall to sit on. The fenced junkyard behind it meant no one could catch her by surprise, and the view she faced was rather nice: blackberry bushes overtaking a collapsed house. Red-throated birds swooped over the tangled branches, their chirps bright enough to cut through the drone of heavy machinery echoing from the distant docks. People passed by occasionally, but she didn't expect to be approached, and wasn't.

A few minutes had passed when two familiar figures appeared around the corner: Sam and Jane. Their movements were sharp and careful as if they hunted for something, and even from that distance, visible tension filled Sam while he spoke to Jane. They both caught sight of her at the same time, and she waved before taking another bite out of the sandwich. It really was too good to ignore.

By the time they were within speaking distance, Jane had relaxed back to her usual smirk, but Sam's eyes looked feral. "Cora, why are you out here? What happened?"

"Everything's fine. I just went to that sandwich shop across the way for breakfast," she assured him, shifting to jump down from her makeshift seat.

Yet he had already reached her, ripping off a glove to trace her cheek with bare fingers, as if making sure she was truly there and all right. She smiled at him and watched the concern in his expression melt into relief.

His voice remained a growl. "Wasn't there any at the house?"

He really did seem wound up, but she sensed it wasn't at her. In fact, from the way his body shielded hers from their surroundings, he was ready to rip at any passerby who so much as looked her way. "There was, but you know how I'm chronically late to things."

His hand dropped from her face to check his watch. A muscle jumped in his jaw. "It's not even 7:30."

Jane moved within view, raising an eyebrow. "I told you they'd stop being polite once you left. Eve remains in shock over what happened to her sister, Brom doesn't think if he can help it, and Holly believes you're an innocent lamb being seduced by a fornicatress."

Cora laughed, not seeing any reason to care about what had happened. As far as she was concerned, this was the best sandwich she'd ever had. "And here I thought I'd been called every word known to man. Look, they've really done nothing bad. I'm enjoying a peaceful morning with a delicious sandwich that is much too large for me. Do either of you want the other half? It's bacon, eggs, pepper jam, and cheddar."

Sam still looked too angry to speak without snarling, but Jane turned to her. "Are you fully aware of Ragbag's reputation?"

"Oh, yes. That's why I wasn't worried at all. I mean, look at me. I'm obviously out of place and obviously alone, yet I don't seem scared or confused. There's no sign that I lost my way or got dumped off here. People surely think I'm some sort of police decoy sent out to test how dangerous Ragbag Way would be to a woman walking alone."

"It's *very* dangerous." Sam's teeth flashed with each word. "I was struck stupid when we caught your scent out here on the way to Minnie's. Do the others know you went out?"

Cora hesitated, not wanting to blow things up further.

Her silence proved answer enough, because Sam forced himself calm and told Jane, "Watch over her. I'll be back in a few minutes. Use your protection charms."

"I'll bill you," warned Jane, settling beside Cora on the wall. "The good ones take hours to craft."

"Use them." Then his attention returned to Cora, and for a moment, his fury seemed softened by regret. "I'm sorry this happened, Bunny. I'll be right back."

"But it's really nothing…" Her words trailed off as he left, the set of his shoulders dangerous. Then she looked over at Jane, who pulled a few glass charms from her enchanter's bandolier and rubbed them until they shimmered like opals. "It was a silly little snub, that's all. You should have seen the tricks my old friends played in the name of lighthearted fun."

Jane replaced the charms and then folded her hands, studying Cora. There was no sign of her normal sarcasm. "Keeping breakfast from you wasn't a snub and it wasn't a trick. It was an unspeakably

rude act and an attempt to put you in your place—beneath them. If that sounds like a lot of meaning behind a cup of coffee and some fried eggs, well… consider it an introduction to pack life. And Sam and I are especially sensitive about food. It means even more to us as orphans. Speaking of, are you still offering that sandwich-half? Matteo's is the only thing I miss about living here."

Cora handed it over, hoping she had enough patience to wait to hear more while Jane ate. She needn't have worried. The she-wolf devoured the mound of food with astonishing speed. Despite the sandwich's messiness, not a single scrap escaped her appetite, and when she finished, she neatly wiped her mouth with a thumb and licked it clean.

As the she-wolf replaced her gloves, she said, "Sam's slowed down with practice, but he used to eat like this as well. The Saxbys had a rigid pack structure where food was allotted. Orphans were given the smallest amount because it was an efficient way to see which ones could rise above their situation and be worth something to the pack. So, if someone stole my meal, I either had to fight them to get it back or give it up and go hungry. In that way, the stronger orphans dominated the weaker ones and gained a higher position of power in their group. But the big brutes weren't the only ones who did well. Weaker orphans who were sly learned how to make deals to avoid being attacked for their food. Call it initial education on surviving pack dynamics."

"It just sounds like bullying to me," said Cora, horror itching up her spine. "Was this normal for all the Saxby wolves?"

"Whether you had parents or not, the tactics became abstract once you grew up and were given a position in the pack. Less about brute strength and more about what you could provide to the

stability and growth of the pack. Especially for she-wolves. Not all of us were like Isabelle and had the strength and skill to be a fighter. Many, especially among the royal ranks, can't even change into wolves, so their aggression is literally toothless. A typical Saxby she-wolf will be passive-aggressive with her anger. It's all she knows. And she's often rewarded for being demure, anyway, as if proper behavior is better than her learning how to shift form. The Saxbys are truly an example of the psychoses that happen when you force wolves into a few select roles and tell them that their position means everything for their survival and well-being—and for the pack's as well."

There was a bitter note to Jane's words that Cora wasn't sure how to address. In a soft voice, she finally asked, "What did you do to survive while you were with the Saxbys? It couldn't have been a pleasant life."

Jane smiled thinly. "Sam's always looked after me. For some years, we were too young to fight off the oldest of the orphans, but we could both shift into our fur and catch live prey. I'm a terrible hunter, but Sam was always good at it and always shared with me. Even on the days we went hungry, I felt better about having an empty stomach than giving in. When we were older, enough higher-ranked wolves noticed my intelligence to put me into the researcher division. It was a safety net despite my bad temper and worse tongue."

Cora nodded, not wanting to press the she-wolf further. Yet just as she bit into the remnants of her sandwich, Jane suddenly said, "I'm not explaining all this so you might better understand Holly's actions. I want you to realize how much you've saved Sam. The amount of good you've brought into his life by being in it. By being

as you are. You give him so many things that were missing in his life while he was a Saxby."

Cora blinked, struck by how thoroughly the sentiment crossed what Holly had said last night.

Jane's expression grew shrewd. "So Holly did try to put doubts in your mind. The idiot. Her concern for Sam is genuine and horribly placed. She's unhappy that he clearly cares for you but will never talk to him about it. It's too confrontational. She'll merely sulk and nip at you instead, hoping to drive you away."

"But is she right?" said Cora, hesitantly. "Am I just distracting him as another obligation?"

Jane scoffed and rose to her feet. "Don't listen to her about what he feels. For that matter, don't even listen to me. Talk to him and find out for sure. Here's your chance."

Then the she-wolf looked out at the street. Cora did as well and saw Sam approaching them again. He seemed calmer, eyes back to a normal gold, but his voice sounded rougher than usual when he said, "You won't have to stay there another night. I already collected your suitcases and put them in the car. We'll take them to my office."

"Good," said Jane, looking smug. "I'm sick of dragging her luggage around."

Nothing much was said during the drive. Sam still seemed on edge over what had happened, and Jane showed no interest in another conversation, instead sketching out enchantment ideas on a scrap of paper.

Once at the office, Jane disappeared into her side. Sam took the heaviest of Cora's suitcases, leaving her with just the makeup case to carry while she followed him into the back. Unsure of what to say, she remained quiet while he stacked the luggage beside the small bed.

"You don't have to stay here," he said, still terse. "I'll help you find a hotel if you'd prefer that."

"What I'd really prefer is to talk with you," she said, brushing his arm. Even through the thick fabric of his coat, she felt the tension in his muscles.

At the touch, he studied her as carefully as Jane had back on that brick wall. Then he sighed. "I'm sorry about what happened, Bunny."

"Sam, it means nothing to me. Jane explained why food is important to you and the other wolves, but I—I admit it's what Holly said last night that's got my feathers ruffled."

He growled, looking as wolfish as when he was in his fur. "She admitted to speaking with you last night but didn't want to give details."

"It was about you and your future."

After a short silence, he removed his hat and gloves and then shrugged off his suit jacket and shoulder holsters. She took off her own outerwear, relieved at the sign that he was about to ignore the rest of the world for her. His bare hands felt very warm as they caught hers to guide her over to the bed. Even after they sat there together, he kept their fingers entwined while staring down at them. Stripped down to his waistcoat, it was easy to see the strong, fit lines of his body that had gotten him through years as a pit fighter. All that strength and steadiness, and yet he still looked so *tired*. Her hands tightened against his while she wished she could erase all the worries from his heart.

The movement, small as it was, stirred him out of whatever he'd been thinking, and he looked up at her with dark, serious eyes. "I

don't want there to be any questions between us, big or small. What's worrying you?"

She swallowed hard, not sure she would like this conversation. "Is it true that you've always planned to return to the Saxby Pack?"

He scoffed a little, as if hearing how most of the words were Holly's. "No. I didn't think at all when Jane and I first lived among humans. Once fighting for survival eased into building a life, I had time to realize how deeply corruption ran in the Saxbys and many others. Around the time I got into detective work, I started helping other wolves escape their packs and get a softer starting point among humans than what I had. It helped with but didn't erase my guilt for leaving the Saxbys to their corrupt alpha-king. I feel obligated to help the breakaways with overthrowing him, and I'll enjoy seeing the bastard squirm at facing the consequences for his greed. Those things are what drive me to return to pack land. Nothing else."

He sounded so sure and cold, as if he had thought about it many times before. When Cora searched his face, trying to glean more, he noticed. His tone softened. "I've changed. We're already creatures caught between two natures. Now I'm one caught between two worlds, too. There's a lot about pack life that I don't like. I won't slip back into my old role when it means accepting those things. Holly and the others can't yet understand and maybe don't even want to. It took living among humans to realize how rotten wolves can be. How blind *I* was to the true state of the Saxbys."

"So now you want to help those still stuck in that life," murmured Cora. "What does that mean? Becoming the new alpha-king?"

"Anyone who becomes a king ends up dead inside, paranoid, or gleeful about his power. I just got over being the first type, and the other two sound even more dangerous."

"Oh." Cora blinked, slightly stumped by how unglamorous he made the wealth and power of an alpha-king seem.

As if sensing her thoughts, he smiled a little. "Do I sound bitter? Maybe I am. Maybe that's why I can't forget those I left behind five years ago. They don't deserve the king they have."

She shifted enough to begin stroking his hair, trying to soothe him. Despite the grim nature of their conversation, she had to smile at the way he unconsciously leaned into her touch just like when he was a wolf. "You seem worn down more than anything. Holly made it sound like you've been itching to get away from humans for good."

He had already relaxed enough beneath her touch to wink in response. "A few have grown on me."

She blushed like a schoolgirl, but her hands also dropped to fuss with the quilt covering the bed, smoothing out the nearest wrinkles.

He noticed. "Did Holly put it in your head that you're holding me back?"

When she nodded cautiously, fingers still working away, he sighed and caught her hand, coaxing it close until his mouth brushed her knuckles. The kiss was absolutely chaste compared to some of the things they'd done, but it still soothed the painful doubt that had stubbornly remained.

When he pulled her closer still, her body melted into his, and his next words reverberated against her cheek. "I made up my own mind to help you set up a new life before I join the breakaways to finish off the alpha-king. To hell with anyone who doesn't like that fact."

"I believe you," she breathed against him. "How long will it take to overthrow him?"

"Funny enough, that meeting I had earlier with the breakaways might've improved any answer to that."

Considering the vagueness of his words, she thought he would stop there. Instead, he absently nuzzled the top of her head, still so wolf-like, and added, "Do you remember what I told you about trying to save the Saxby princess?"

Cora nodded. "Princess Liana. The poor girl sent off to be with the mad Sinclair prince."

"She had an older sister who had been mated off to the alpha-king of the Baca Pack. That's what helped make the mating treaty with Liana and the Sinclair Pack seem in earnest. Alpha-king Saxby had done the same thing with his other daughter, Lorelei, and had success with it. As an ally, the Baca Pack joined the Saxbys against the Sinclairs after Liana was killed. By the end of the fighting, they were all dead, including Alpha-queen Lorelei... or so I thought. It turns out she escaped and has been in hiding with a sympathetic pack until now. I met her this morning. It's her all right, and she's hellbent on bringing down her father. The breakaways are willing to rally around her as their new leader."

Cora straightened up to look at him. "But that's wonderful! Then overthrowing the old king should go as smoothly as possible."

In the silence that followed, she added, "Shouldn't it?"

"Yes. Very." Then Sam sighed, grim once more. "Like I said, no questions between us, Bunny. Having Lorelei back on pack land and hungry to take over will push things to a faster pace, but it could still take weeks, even months. And once I'm over for good, we're closing

the territory borders to make sure the alpha-king can't escape. Nobody in... nobody out."

As good as she had felt before, now she felt like a snuffed-out flame. For a moment, all she could do was stare. "What? But... what about letters, or—or news of what's happening?"

"Nothing. We can't risk the alpha-king sending for help, or the other packs pouncing if they hear the wrong news." Then his arms tightened around her. "That's why I'm intent on helping you first. It'll be the last time we can see each other for a while."

"Well..." She struggled to breathe, let alone find some lighthearted words. "Well, that's all right. We never did promise our time to each other, did we? Or anything beyond you taking me on as a client."

"Bunny," he murmured, brushing her cheek. "You're a lot more than that to me. I never knew what love could do to a life until you showed up in mine. But I need to do this. Especially now."

"I understand." And she did, but she wished the idea of months without him didn't hurt so much. "And I won't drag on finding an apartment or anything like that to make you stay here forever. It wouldn't be fair. Which means we have just a few more days together, don't we?"

He nodded.

She drew in a deep breath. "Then let's make it as normal as possible. I want to enjoy our time together without being reminded that it's about to end."

He hesitated. "Are you sure that's a good idea? There are other things I need to tell you, important things that I held back on while the sigil and your father were threats."

"Please," she said, softly. "I'll face reality when it comes. But for now, let me pretend that nothing between us is about to change. I just got you back, Sam."

The gold of his eyes darkened at the sound of his name in her voice. His own voice grew gentle, soothing away her dread. "All right."

"Thank you," she whispered, angling her face towards his for a kiss. A small, painful part of her wondered if he would avoid it.

Instead, he kissed her deeply, as if memorizing her, and broke off only to nip at her lip, a teasing note entering his next words. "Does this mean you want to do some detective work today?"

She smiled in relief that she *could* feel excited at the thought. Ignorance really was bliss, and she was determined to wallow in it. "Yes."

"Good." He kissed her again unhurriedly and then straightened up. "Because I hear Mabel on the stairs outside, and she always brings the morning papers with her. It should help us to see what Mr. Forrester is reading over his coffee."

Cora had read through the press release back when her lawyers had composed it, but she still felt a thrill thumbing through the papers and seeing the results in action. "Oh, Father's face must be absolutely purple by now. I'm sure Mr. Forrester is just the opposite. The man always grows white as a sheet in response to a shock."

"Does he hide, too?" said Sam, skimming through the last of the articles.

"Mr. Forrester? Oh no, he's very proud of never wavering from his schedule. And since it's Sunday, I know just where he'll go after breakfast no matter how disturbed he feels: the golf course."

Sam smiled, almost playful again. "Which one?"

The Cypress Grove Golf Club had a closed membership, but Cora knew more than a few of the members and was recognized by the staff immediately. Despite this, they objected to letting Sam in after one glance at his gold eyes.

"Oh, Herbie, don't be so stuffy," said Cora, looking past him to scan the visible areas of the course for any sign of Mr. Forrester. "You overlook the rules all the time. Or don't you remember?"

The man flushed red against his crisp collar. "Miss Marshall, this place has a reputation to keep."

"We'll be discreet," said Sam, catching one of Cora's elbows to guide her past.

The man gave in with a forlorn, "You're not even dressed to play."

"That's because we're here on business," said Cora, flashing a final smile at him.

"Do you like golfing?" murmured Sam, while they began walking through the course.

"I never tried it. The clothes you're expected to wear are hideous. What about you?"

"Never saw the point in chasing after a ball." His wink drew a laugh from her.

They found Mr. Forrester at the fifth hole playing by himself. He did appear quite pale. He also appeared unhappy to see them.

"Miss Marshall," he said, by way of greeting. "I see the rumor that you had absconded with a scoundrel was true."

"You're a lot less polite than the last time we met," said Sam, his words easy. "Game not going well?"

When the man just scoffed and selected a club, Cora said, "The morning newspapers were quite interesting, weren't they?"

"I have nothing to say about that business."

"That's fine, because I came to you for a different reason. I'd really like to know when Father decided to work with the Saxbys."

Mr. Forrester sputtered. "What?"

Cora smiled brightly, knowing it would irritate him. "You told me Father mentioned a shadow venture to you but you refused to help him."

"That's correct, and that's all I know," he said, stiffly.

Sam glanced at her in a wordless signal before he took over the conversation. "No, you knew more than that. At the very least, you were aware that Isaac Marshall put a binding sigil on her."

The man paled slightly, but Sam gave him no chance to protest. "You admitted to knowing her since she was a child. Are you telling me you weren't suspicious at all when her behavior changed suddenly and radically? You're a smart man and proud of it. You're also a cautious one and would've asked your client how he got his daughter to behave, hoping the answer wouldn't be 'illegal magic.'"

Mr. Forrester was beginning to sweat despite the cool day. Cora decided to press him a little more. "I hope you don't think silence is a swell way to protect yourself. And if you don't wish to talk to us, that's fine. Mr. Forrester, I'm not trying to be a pest. I'm just here to reassure you that the papers aren't exaggerating. Father is about to be in very hot water over what he did to me, and what do you think he'll do when he remembers there are others who know about his willingness to use illegal magic?"

As the man's hand dropped back to his side, the game forgotten, Sam added, "You know how ruthless he was with his daughter. Do you think being his friend will keep you safe?"

The vein in Mr. Forrester's forehead looked like it was about to pop as he snarled, "Friend? No friend would try to convince me to join in on the type of plans he had."

Cora's eyes widened. She hadn't expected the man to give in so easily. He truly must have been rattled by the sigil's reveal. Both she and Sam listened in silence as a torrent of words rushed out.

"I had nothing to do with it. *Any* of it. I only learned of the sigil after it had been placed on you. At my inquiry, he began speaking as if bio-thaumaturgy was the way of the future instead of a death sentence from the city. I couldn't believe it. Not only did he talk about partnering with wolves, but he also claimed he'd finally found a use for his brother's cult."

Then Mr. Forrester seemed to regain some of his composure. "There was no talking him out of it. He was sure the Saxbys would end the violence among the packs that kept spilling into human streets by ruling them all. Stability, he said. That was the goal. The one thing impossible to find in this godforsaken city. All I could do was step aside and wait for disaster to strike. And it did, over and over... whether you believe me or not, that's all I know."

Cora *did* believe him. "Why would Father care about controlling the wolves?"

With his slumped posture, Mr. Forrester's garish golfing outfit made him look like a broken puppet. "Investors outside of the city are increasingly skittish over the wolves' bloodthirst. There are growing rumors that they will overtake the human parts of the city. Isaac decided to strike first. Now. What do you want from me?"

Cora shared a glance with Sam before he said, "A statement to the police about what you know."

"That's it?" Mr. Forrester sounded almost offended.

Cora huffed. "Goodness, I'm not Father. I just want the truth to come out."

"If you ask for protection," added Sam, "they'll hide you away afterwards."

"All right," said Mr. Forrester, heavily. "I'll go as soon as I change."

"We'll give you a lift there," said Sam, his tone implying he wouldn't take no for an answer.

Later, after Mr. Forrester was safely inside the station, Cora watched the traffic thoughtfully while Sam guided the car away. They were nearly back at his office before she said, "It's all solved, isn't it? Our case is finally closed."

Sam nodded, smiling a little. "Good job, Bunny."

She beamed back. "What's left to do now?"

"A lot of waiting. That's the nice thing about being a private detective. The police are the ones who have to collect everything and shape it into charges and a trial."

"Then things will slow down for us?" She couldn't help sounding hopeful, wanting as much time with him as possible.

His voice turned wry while he parked in front of his office. "I wouldn't say that. I can already hear Mabel taking phone calls. It's ringing the moment she hangs back up."

He hadn't exaggerated, and as the following days proved, neither had Captain Dempsey's warning about everyone wanting a piece of her time.

Honestly, it all passed in a blur. She left everything to the lawyers and generally followed their advice, but it still meant hours of discussions with them. The reporters were as terrible as always, but thankfully it had been decided that she should avoid giving

interviews. She made no attempt to contact her father and had no wish to, anyway. Some of her belongings were still at his house, but she was patient enough to let things be hashed out before trying to collect them.

She, Sam, and Jane all had to return to the station at various points to be interviewed by the police commissioner and others; only Jane seemed resentful of her work being interrupted. Although Cora had elected to sleep in the back of the office, wanting to fill up as much of her day with Sam's presence as possible, she rarely saw the she-wolf outside of those instances.

She had never been so busy in her life, and it amazed her how easily time slipped and slid. The only parts of her day that crystallized into clear, shining moments were those with Sam. He was just as busy but somehow found the hours to help her go through apartment listings given to her by a trusted realtor. With him by her side, touring places as a potential new home left her feeling hopeful about the future despite the painful awareness of his need to leave. On his end, he lingered with her as well, always taking her out for coffee or a meal no matter what time of day or night they finally had to themselves. From the look in his eyes, he was memorizing each second as deeply as she was.

Finally, a week after the news broke about the sigil, she signed the lease to a furnished apartment. It was a bright, beautiful morning, and buttery light shone through the windows of the flat, which was on the third floor and of a modest size that would be roomy for one and perfect for two.

She found herself staring at the keys in her hand long after the manager had left. Hayes lingered by the doorway, looking very

striking in his dark grey suit against the bright white geometry of the walls.

She looked over at him in a daze. "It's happened. I have my own life again. No, not again. For the first time, I'm truly in a home of my own."

He smiled, eyes warm with affection. "A little nerve-wracking, isn't it?"

"Exhilarating," she said, still feeling breathless. "It's hard to believe."

"I have something that might make it feel less strange."

"What is it?"

His smile widened as he ushered her into the living room. "I brought it in while you were signing the papers."

It was a radio, *his* radio. The one they had listened to during that blissful day at his apartment.

"Oh..." she breathed, rushing over to turn it on. Lively jazz burst into life, immediately chasing away the stillness and formality of the room.

"So you can listen to Murder Time whenever you want," he murmured.

Cora laughed and held out a hand. "Help me break it in."

Dancing with him felt so right that even her usual chatter faded into nothing as they moved through a lighthearted number. When it slipped into a slower song, she found herself looking up into his eyes, aware of how he had never shifted his focus from her. He was no longer smiling, but there was a fresh intensity in his gaze that left her tilting her mouth toward his.

"Cora," he said, quietly. They were so close that the word brushed her lips like a caress, yet she could hear the deadly seriousness behind it.

"What is it?" Misgiving shuddered through her from how his expression had grown so grim. Surely, he wouldn't leave for pack land already? Not this soon...

"There's one last thing you need to know. Then the case really is over and you're no longer my client." With a sigh, he stepped back from her.

She tried to think up a witty reply, but her throat had gone dry. The air felt very cold compared to the heat of his body, and she shivered despite herself, aware of a rising feeling of foreboding as he moved over to the coffee table and picked up a folder stuffed with papers, something she had assumed was her case file.

"I found your former fiancé," he said, giving no hint of what he thought as he approached with the file. "His name is Roland Archer."

It felt like all the blood drained from her head. She didn't know what to think, much less say. She took the folder from him with numb fingers. Her heart beat very fast, yet she also felt chilled to the bone.

Aware of the need to respond, she managed, "I didn't know. I didn't know you were looking for him."

"You asked me to find your father and no one else, but you looked so sad while talking about how you'd lost him and his love." Then Sam began pacing, as if he was filled with too much tension to stay still. "At first, I had to keep some things secret from the sigil. At first. Then... I went dizzy for you like it was the first time I'd been in love. Once the sigil was off you, it was a relief to have Minnie warn

me not to shock you with any big news. And it was a relief that we both grew busy afterwards with other things. It gave me a little more time. Made me feel like I wasn't holding back on telling you about him. But I was, and it wasn't fair to you."

He looked back at her with a lopsided smile. "You know what they say about wolves. We're greedy. Well, I got greedy for your company."

But not enough to stay, thought Cora. She wasn't angry; she was miserable. It hadn't escaped her attention that his pacing had left them feet apart. The news about him leaving for an unknown amount of time had been bad enough, but this was much worse. She wasn't about to hear *see you soon*. She was about to hear *goodbye*, and she already had plenty of those from other men.

He seemed concerned by her silence, stepping closer to search her face. "I should've told you sooner. You deserve the closure. And the news about the sigil has long reached everywhere. He and the rest of the city know your innocence. It's a good time to look into what I found out about him and decide what to do from there. If you want."

Tears were beginning to prickle in her eyes. The conversation she'd overheard during that night at Minnie's cut into her shock with perfect clarity. *He'll let her down gently and have things planned out for her to move on smoothly as possible.*

"H-how long have you known his identity?"

"Before your father was found."

Weeks, then. And no fella shoved another in his place unless he was done and moving on.

It was obvious he was downright uncomfortable, glancing away again as if struggling with what to say. When he drew in a deep

breath and looked her right in the eyes, she knew what was coming next.

"Thank you," she burst out, clutching the folder to her chest. The edges cut into her fingers from the tightness of her grip. "I never thought I could get anything back from the sigil. Any—any closure over what I lost. It's so overwhelming that I don't know what to say other than... thank you."

Nothing in that flow of words was a lie. She *was* overwhelmed, completely so. The truth was, she knew she couldn't face once more hearing the tired phrases that all fellas used when ending things with her. They all boiled down to the same sentiment: *You mean the world to me, sweetheart, but it's over.*

She couldn't bear it if he used them on her, too.

And if she didn't want to hear him finish things, then she had to do it herself. "It's all over. The case is solved, I'm free of Father and his control, and now..." She stared at the papers crinkling against her grip, unable to believe there was a person in there. "Now I have a chance at the life that I thought I'd lost."

Then she forced herself to look up. Sam still studied her intently, as if uncertain about her words, but finally nodded.

Despite herself, she asked, "Will you be all right? Overthrowing a king *is* dangerous, isn't it? You might get hurt or worse."

His voice grew wry, but she still felt the gulf between them. "Tell you what. The day I come back, I'll call you to let you know I'm fine. In the meantime, don't worry about me, Cora. Enjoy life now that it's finally yours."

She forced herself to smile, wondering how on earth she was supposed to do that without him in it. "I certainly will."

CHAPTER THIRTY-TWO

Captain Albert Dempsey rubbed a crick from his neck and rose from his desk. He'd just finished for the day and was ready to go on a final circuit of the station. It was something he always did, even if it meant running into a problem that cost him a few more hours of sleep. Tonight, everything seemed quiet. All the other detectives and officers who worked in the day had long gone, desks cleared and phones silent.

All except Enchanter Byrd's office.

To Al's surprise, it was not only lit but the main secretary, Grace Hoffman, had fallen asleep against her typewriter. Al scanned the room for any sign of Byrd and then knocked against the open door, jerking Miss Hoffman awake.

The girl quickly adjusted her spectacles and ran hands over her prim sweater to smooth out the wrinkles left by slouching. "Captain, I'm sorry. I didn't realize I'd dozed off."

"Who does? Why's Byrd got you up this late?"

"He's still in the station."

Al checked his watch. "At this hour? You're kidding."

"I would never spread misinformation, Captain," said Miss Hoffman, tone severe. "Even as a joke. He's in the Level 5 zone of the firing range."

Now Al understood. Level 5 was the area for weapons unapproved by the city for official use. Lately, it had become the test zone for all entrants hoping to win the new submachine contract. In a rare show of smarts, the police commissioner had decided it was safest to offer up the station's firing range for all testing, and to have a senior enchanter present each time.

And he could just guess which of those entrants was there this late in the night.

Miss Hoffman's next words confirmed it. "The appointment was booked for Miss Jane Feral. The she-wolf. She's been there for over two hours. Here's the form she filled out."

Al skimmed the sheet of paper, muffling a sigh. "All right. I'll check it out. Go on home, Miss Hoffman."

Relief fought with doubt on the girl's face. She hadn't yet figured out that this type of job would suck her dry if she let it. "But Master Enchanter Byrd might need a message sent or a report filled out."

"The man knows how to write." Then Al jerked his head toward the door. "Go on, get some sleep. Your bed's going to be softer than a typewriter."

After she left, he read the form more thoroughly. In the section reserved for Byrd's notes, he saw that this was Jane's first visit to the firing range. She probably wasn't doing too well.

His suspicions were confirmed when he reached the right level and found her firing one of the standard-issue submachine guns while Enchanter Byrd and Raymond Lodato, the firearms

instructor, looked on. Jane seemed focused but her aim was godawful, hitting the jelly barrier on the walls all around the target, which was easy enough to spot even at that distance: simple silhouettes of a gunman holding a hostage.

Al hid his concern as he took in how her arms shook from holding the gun as properly as she could manage. She clearly wasn't used to the weight as much as the recoil, but kept trying, aiming with care before each shot as if aware of how Lodato watched her like a hawk.

She was so focused that Al was able to join the other men unnoticed, receiving greetings from both. He gave Byrd a nod before turning to Lodato. The noise-dampening spells were in effect, so he pitched his voice low. "Christ, the bags under your eyes. When's the last time you saw a full night's rest?"

"Amelia started teething," the other man admitted, still watching Jane. "And Gertie just learned how to open doors. My brother keeps telling me raising boys is more trouble, but right now I don't believe him."

"You're not the only one who's tired." Then Al glanced over at Jane. From the fresh tension in her shoulders, she'd caught his scent over the gunsmoke. She hated him catching her at "imperfect moments," as she called them. He wished she didn't. He was always tickled to see her fight with a snarl in her hair, or to find writing ink smudged on her hand.

He kept his voice mild as he added, "She's shaking. How long has she been at this?"

"Too long," said Enchanter Byrd, glaring at the firearms instructor. "This is beyond farcical."

When Al looked at Lodato for an explanation, the firearms instructor said, "I want her to hit the target before she tests her prototype weapon. She took instruction well, but she's stubborn. I told her she's unlikely to improve her aim enough with only tonight under her belt. She didn't like hearing that."

"What's the point of letting her try?" hissed Byrd. "She's clearly not able to satisfy your requirements, so let her move on so we can all go home."

"We know what to expect if she misfires with the standard weapon. We don't with her experiment," shot back Lodato. "The protective wards will stop a bullet from going in your face. Can you say the same about the unknown ammunition her prototype uses?"

Byrd turned to Al with an expression that pleaded with him to override the decision.

Al shrugged. "Lodato is our firearms instructor. He's the one who needs to be comfortable with her accuracy."

The enchanter sighed. "What about having her get the other wolf to test the gun in her place? He's a good shot, isn't he?"

It was Jane herself who answered that, still firing in between words. "Sam is not in the city. He's in former Saxby territory and has been for almost two months. I can't contact him. He can't contact me. I don't even know if he's alive."

With that last word, a bullet tore through the target. She stepped back, shaking her hands out before giving them a hopeful look. "There. I did it. Can I use my prototype now?"

Al rubbed his forehead. "You shot the hostage. He'd be bleeding his guts out right now."

"I'm not happy. Why should he be? Besides, he's still part of the target. It should count." Then she noticed Lodato's expression and added, "Can we please move past this useless part of the protocol?"

"It's all useless!" burst out Enchanter Byrd. "The new gun has already been decided on. Next week is just a formality."

Everyone else there stared at him, including Al. He had known Byrd would be on the judging panel, but this was news to him. "Who got the contract without officially testing it?"

Byrd had gone pale over his slip but knew better than to avoid answering. "McCoy, of course. An established company headed by the mayor's godson. Besides, his design isn't inelegant and will drop the city's silver imports by 83%."

Al and Lodato shared a glance. A decision made out of nepotism and by men who would never handle the actual weapons. He wasn't surprised, but he was irritated. The feeling surged into anger when he looked at Jane and found her stiff with shock.

"Shut it down for the night," he said, using a tone that killed any further conversation. "I'll escort Miss Feral out."

By the time he had her out of the station, her silence had become charged. The night air was thick with fog, and he couldn't study her until they stepped within reach of the harsh streetlights. "I haven't seen you shoot anything besides the creature in Davenport's ritual room, and that thing was the size of a whale. Is your aim always bad, or did you hear something about Sam?"

Her response was glacial. "Did you miss what I told Byrd earlier? It's impossible to contact anyone inside the former Saxby territory. No information in and no information out."

"Not even when one of the city's best enchanters wants to know something?"

"You're off-duty, Captain. I don't have to answer any of your questions." When he gestured at her to hand over the heavy case containing her prototype, she ignored him.

"In this kinda mood, huh?" Now he was even more convinced that she'd heard something before coming to the station. Ever since Sam had left the city, she'd been a bundle of nerves, but when she bristled like this, it meant she was flat-out scared and trying to hide it.

"Mood?" she repeated, glaring at him.

"Mm-hm. I don't need to be a detective to know you're upset."

"I'm not upset," she snarled.

He raised his eyebrows.

She noticed and stopped dead, still a few feet from his car. "Al, I enjoy our nights together, but I can't tolerate your scrutiny right now. I want to be alone."

When she began walking off, he remained by his car. "If that's how you feel, I won't chase after you. And if you're just saying that so I'll coax you back and stop asking questions, then I still won't chase after you. I want to help, Jane, but I won't cuddle away your problems when I don't know what they are."

She glanced back, eyes glowing in the fog. "How hard-edged of you."

He shrugged. "It's better than misunderstanding each other."

After she scoffed and disappeared into the fog, he lit a cigarette, deciding to hang around a while longer. He wasn't even a quarter of the way through it when she reappeared, not quite looking in his direction.

Gaze on her feet, she stopped beside him. "Fine. I'm upset. I'm furious. And it is about Sam. He's fine so far, but there's something I

learned this morning, and I don't know what to do about it. There's nothing I *can* do about it. There's also nothing I can legally kill around here, so I'm sulking instead. It feels miserable, and being alone would only increase that, so I... I don't want to be alone tonight. And that's truly how I feel."

Al nodded and kept his next words gentle. "All right. That's all I wanted to know. Any other talk we have is up to you."

She relaxed enough to regain that sharp tongue he enjoyed so much. "I thought men disdained emotional conversations."

"Depends. Look, you're already shivering out here. How about we head back to my place?"

Her response was one of those uncertain side-glances that told him more than she ever suspected. It was the kind of look that revealed volumes about the nastier behaviors from her old pack and how badly she'd been marked by it.

"I know you're not in the mood. I'm just thinking about getting out of this fog. We can go to your office instead."

"No. No, your apartment is much nicer. And warmer."

Nothing much was said during the drive, but once they were inside, she prowled around while he shrugged off his coat and hat. She eyed the cream walls and sparse furniture of the small living room and said, "It always looks like you recently moved in."

"What are you talking about? There's not a cardboard box in sight."

The comment got her to smile a little. "I'll concede to that. There are some at my office that still act as my closet and bookshelf. I don't mind. I never had a life outside of work, so why pretend otherwise? But now I've noticed how empty it feels."

Al nodded, removing his holsters. When he pointed at the nearby whiskey bottle and glasses, she shook her head. He didn't feel like any either, and settled on the couch while loosening his tie.

She paced near him for a few more seconds before sitting beside him. Her body remained tense, as if she was ready to spring back up at any moment. "You're right... as usual. I put secondary instructions on the enchantments I made for the breakaway Saxbys. Whenever one is activated, it collects all conversations and transcribes them back to me as letters."

"Does Sam know about this?"

"No. He would have objected. He trusts the breakaways. I don't." Finally, she looked at him. "Tonight is the final push to reach the alpha-king and kill him. The breakaways will succeed easily, especially with Sam involved. It's expected that the king's surviving daughter will be crowned in the morning and become queen. It's also expected that she will choose Sam as her king."

Al lit a cigarette to hide his sigh. He knew he had to tread lightly; Sam was like a brother to her, and if she wasn't fiercely criticizing him, she was just as ferociously defending him. "Can he refuse?"

"Yes. If he wants." Then she was back up and pacing, and he knew her hidden fears were coming out even before she added, "If his damned sense of duty allows him to. He ruined his chance at happiness two months ago, so who's to say he won't crush the remnants tomorrow?"

Al could guess what she meant but just blew out some smoke while she paused to flip through the newspapers left on the kitchen counter. She needed to talk through all this or it would stay bottled up in her heart and start poisoning her. Her eyes were bright and

furious as she opened one up to the gossip columns and began reading out loud.

"Heiress Cora Marshall continues to be seen out and about with her former fiancé, Mr. Roland Archer, while her father remains hidden in his home from the public eye amid fresh scrutiny. A source close to the police confirms that new charges may be pressed against Isaac Marshall, unrelated to the binding sigil he had allegedly placed on his daughter. Miss Marshall has refused to speak out since her initial statement about her father, but she shows all signs of recovering from the hardship and repairing her relationship with Mr. Archer. Rumors have abounded that their original, secret engagement was the reason behind her father's despicable act, and one can't help but wonder whether Miss Marshall's ordeal will have a fairytale ending complete with wedding bells."

Al listened without comment. The article didn't interest him, but Jane's reaction did. She slapped the newspaper back on the counter with a growl. "The idiot."

"Her or Sam?" said Al, voice wry. After Jane had found out Sam had told Miss Marshall about Archer, he'd had to listen to her rant for hours.

She looked ready to rant some more. "Both. They love each other. I'm sure of it. He didn't want to give her up, and she couldn't possibly hold any feelings for the human. They were all burned away."

"You want my honest opinion? It would've said worse about Sam if he'd hidden the fiancé from her. That kind of move would have helped him, not her, and he knew it."

"That doesn't mean he had to give up on being with her."

Al laughed. "You think it's easy for a fella to hang around romantic competition without immediately punching him in the face? Maybe Sam didn't say enough to Miss Marshall before he left. Maybe he said too much. All I know is he's the type to do what he thinks is right, and this time he didn't realize how miserable the right thing would be for the girl as much as him."

Jane returned to the couch, eyes lighting up. "Then you agree that Miss Marshall being with Archer is a stupid idea."

"I didn't say that."

"Fine, that she isn't happy."

"Sure. I've seen the newspaper pictures. She's lost the shine in her smile. Why are you talking to me about all this instead of her?"

"Believe me, I want to. But then I remember how stupid Sam can be as well, and how much he feels he owes Alpha-queen Lorelei and the rest of the pack for being unable to stop the king and save his daughter."

Then Jane sighed before sitting beside him once more, now hunched over. Hopeless. Her voice fell to a murmur. "Sam and Cora were so happy together. I can't believe this is better for them. I refuse to."

When her shoulders slumped, Al began rubbing her back, keeping his hand slow and gentle. She still wasn't used to being touched by a human, but within a breath, she relaxed into his fingers, and her next words came out softly. "But there's nothing I can do, and I hate it. Tonight feels like hell. It's why I went to the station's firing range, because I wanted to take my mind off waiting for any news about Sam and the alpha-queen."

Al shifted closer, easing her into settling against him. He wished he could do more for her, but right now all he had was an apology.

"I'm sorry about the gun contract. I didn't know the city would pull that move. If I had, I wouldn't have encouraged you to enter."

It had taken her a while to show any affection beyond bites and scratches in bed, so it surprised him to feel her body turning into his, her face pressing into the collar of his shirt to nuzzle at his neck. "I know. You're always honest and much less stupid about it than Sam."

He let some teasing come back into his voice. "Well, thanks."

"And I also know the city would never choose a wolf to make their guns. I still intend to show up next week and embarrass them all with the superiority of my prototype. That is, if I don't first embarrass myself by shooting someone on the judging panel."

Al smiled despite himself, realizing how he could help her through the night. "You won't if you listen to me and put in more practice. Want to start right now? Something tells me you're going to stay up, anyway."

She shifted enough to look at him, surprise brightening her eyes. "Where? The station's range is now closed."

"The boardwalk stays open until dawn. They have plenty of shooting games." He rubbed her back a final time and then tightened his tie again. "Come on. I'll have you winning a prize before the night is over. Maybe not a good prize, but something worth keeping."

"And after that? If it turns out Sam isn't coming back?" She searched his face and added, "I won't rejoin the Saxbys if that happens. He would never ask me to, but even if he did, I'd refuse. I can't live with other wolves again. I can't return to pack life."

There it was again—that deep-rooted fear he'd glimpsed a few times. It would hurt her like hell to lose Sam, and she knew it. Al

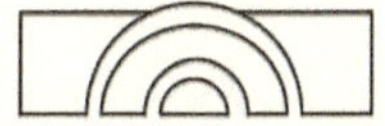

tipped her chin up and kissed her, driving her worry away for now. "I'll help with that, too."

Sam spat out the taste of the alpha-king's blood and stepped away while Lorelei finished ripping her father apart, her fur bristling while she snarled in rage. The rest of the room was just as stained, with dead guards pulled out of the way so the breakaways could watch their new queen take her crown.

All except Sam. He had killed enough times to recognize the look of a body that could no longer fight back, and he left before the alpha-queen changed over and finalized her father's death with a silver dagger to the throat. The howling started behind him before he even made it out of the first hallway. He couldn't remember the last time he'd felt this tired.

He left the citadel completely, returning to an area of the royal quarters that still had working showers. Cold water only, which reminded him of washing off after a pit fight. He didn't feel any different now than he had back then: grim and ready to go home.

When he stepped out of the bathroom, still toweling himself off, his nose alerted him a second before his eyes that he wasn't alone.

The alpha-queen sat in one of the velvet chairs near a dressing table, fully dressed and composed despite the lingering tang of blood. Her face was turned away from him, and she remained silent —polite gestures that gave him the decision to address her or not.

Lorelei had always been the smaller and quieter of the sisters despite being the eldest. Liana had been the rangy, boisterous one, insisting on fencing lessons from the royal duelist and learning how to drive a car in secret to pull a trick on her guards one All Fools' Day. Everyone had been shocked that it was delicate little Lorelei who had been chosen to mate with the Baca alpha-king, a pack known for prizing strength and size above all else.

The bodyguard with her now was a prime example. Aznar was the only other survivor of the Baca Pack, as hulking as Lorelei was small. A nasty slice from a silver blade had left him with a scar on the throat and the inability to speak, but Sam had watched him enough to know he was a mean son of a bitch in a fight and unfriendly even toward the breakaways. A typical Baca wolf.

Sam gave the alpha-queen a nod that was deep but brief, enough to acknowledge her new crown but not enough to acknowledge her as *his* queen. "Your Majesty."

Aznar stared at him while he began dressing, obviously not liking his lack of deference, but the alpha-queen relaxed in her seat and said, "Please, just Lorelei. I'll hardly hear my name from now on, and this isn't a formal conversation."

Sam nodded again, already onto his shirt.

When he remained silent, Lorelei glanced at his opened suitcase. "You brought spare clothing into this room before the final fighting began. It's because you plan to leave right away, isn't it?"

"The old king is dead. I did what I came here to do, and now it's time to go." Already, he was thinking of Cora. Some days, remembering her laugh had been the only thing to keep him steady. Two months was a long-enough chance for the former fiancé. If Sam smelled any excitement in her scent over seeing him again, he wasn't holding back for the human's sake.

The alpha-queen nodded at his answer, her crown gleaming with the movement. To his surprise, she then took it off, setting it on the table. Embedded rubies continued to glimmer beside the fangs of conquered enemies as she said, "Will you stay a few minutes longer? We've never truly talked to each other. Only as part of a larger meeting."

Sam could guess what the topic would be about and bit back a sigh. When he glanced at Aznar, he found the other wolf glaring back, and felt even surer about that guess. He sat at the foot of the bed to face her, now doing up his tie. "Sure, that's fair enough."

Her fingers clasped and unclasped. Without the crown, she looked very young—and was, barely twenty-three. "There has been talk about my future mate. Whether he should secure an alliance with another pack, as my first did, or whether he should be a wolf who will help me rebuild this territory."

"Which do you prefer?"

"I haven't decided, but your name is always mentioned in these conversations."

He said nothing, aware that doing so bordered on rudeness but also too damn tired to pick out a polite way to tell her that he was through with pack life.

"You don't want to be king." It wasn't a question.

He sighed. "Lorelei, this is no longer my home."

"I know," she said, softly. "And I think I understand why you came back at all."

Then she lost enough of her composure to rise from her seat and pace throughout the dusty finery of the room. A ring glittered on her first finger, and Sam recognized it as one that had belonged to her sister.

Lorelei played with it for several moments before speaking again. "As far back as I can remember, I never wanted to be an alpha-queen. I disliked the attention of being a princess, how all my strengths and habits had to be pruned to increase my attractiveness as a mate and my ability to bear heirs. My sister was far louder about her disdain toward being a 'living doll,' as she called it, but I sympathized with her. All I wanted was to be a quiet creature who lived with her books. Unnoticed except as a scholar."

Only to be mated into a vicious pack like the Bacas. Sam felt real pity for her. "I'm sorry."

She looked at him, seeming surprised more than anything. "Don't be. I've also long known how comfortable it is to be a princess. I never had to worry about food, or being challenged, or feeling cold or tired. I *was* a doll, pampered and fussed over, but I also had far more power than anyone else except my parents and never had to earn it or feel the consequences. As a princess, I dreaded the idea of ruling over a pack. As a queen, I'm absolutely *terrified*. There is nothing to stop me from turning into a leader like my father. I have only my own determination to prevent the corruption of wearing a crown."

Then she approached Sam, true pain etched into her face. "I know you came back because of what my father did to you for trying to save my sister. I know you will never trust pack life again. I am so

very sorry that he took your loyalty and used it for something unforgivable."

Sam could smell her earnestness and her grief for her sister, but all he could do was be honest. "You're not the one who needs to apologize. You were caught in his greed like the rest of us. But now we're all free, and I'm not interested in a crown."

"Perhaps that sentiment makes you all the more suited for one," said Lorelei, quietly. "Perhaps it's part of what makes you a true leader who has guided and protected the pack for the past two months. You are my first choice, Sam Hayes, to rule with me, because I think we both understand the price and power of duty."

For him, too well. As he rubbed at his face, she added, "I won't expect love. I won't ask for it."

Even with his hand over his eyes, he sensed Aznar bristle again. It helped along words that could explain the decision living in his heart from the moment Cora's scent had left his clothes. He rose to his feet as well, looking at Lorelei. "I believe you, but I am looking for love, and that's why I'm going back to the city."

The gossip among the pack had included his closeness with Cora, and he knew the alpha-queen had heard about it. As he suspected, she took his answer with complete calm despite just being turned down for a human.

In fact, she looked almost wistful, and as he resumed dressing, he added, "You know, an hour into the fighting, I noticed you shot the royal guard that was close to gutting Aznar even though there was another one threatening Micah, your best tactical advisor. And I also noticed that Aznar has hated me since my name joined the rumor mill of who you'd choose as your king."

There was a sudden movement from Aznar, but the alpha-queen stopped him with a brush of her hand. She looked cautious, the muscles in her slender throat as tight as wire. "I can see why you have a fine reputation as a detective."

He smiled wryly and put on his hat. "It's hard to stop noticing things. Trust me, Your Majesty, if there's one thing I learned, it's that duty will suck you dry as badly as power. You need love and trust like anyone else."

The anger in the bodyguard's scent only increased, but Lorelei briefly searched his face and relaxed. "You truly mean that, so I'll take it to heart. Thank you. Please believe you're always welcome to visit."

He nodded, relaxing himself. "Goodbye."

Aznar gave him a final flash of fangs when he passed by, but Sam couldn't blame the other wolf. He had the same feeling whenever he thought of Roland Archer touching Cora.

It was hard to believe he was back in the city until his taxi turned down the street to his office. The afternoon sun burnished the glimpses of the ocean in between buildings. He could taste the salt in the air. He was even glad to hear the screeching gulls as they wheeled overhead.

The cab stopped in front of the building, and he paid the driver before getting out for his luggage. He had barely grabbed his suitcase before the office door flew open and Jane ran down the stairs for him.

She clung to him in a hug. "Idiot. Moron. Lunk."

He grinned. "I missed you, too."

His relief matched hers as they made it inside. Everything looked like he left it, and he collapsed in the chair behind his desk, feeling boneless. "It's swell to be home."

He would have reached for the phone next, remembering his promise to Cora, but just then Jane sat on the desk, blocking him. She looked excited, eyes bright and wild. "Then you're not going back?"

"No way in hell." Then he studied her. "That look on your face... you knew about the alpha-queen's interest in me."

"Did you think my sanity could survive the past two months without making sure you were alive and well?"

He laughed, leaning back in his seat. "Little spy. Where's Mabel?"

"On vacation."

"You must've been driving her nuts. She never takes a day off. She's up to a whole month of saved vacation hours."

Jane shrugged, smirking slightly. "Not anymore. She's been gone for about three weeks. It's given me all the peace and quiet I need to work on my prototype."

"Three weeks?" repeated Sam, with the first pang of misgiving. He knew how obsessive Jane grew over a project when left completely alone. She would even forget to eat. "Have you kept up with all the things she usually does?"

"What's there to keep up with? You were gone, so there weren't any clients."

"Collecting the mail."

When Jane merely shrugged again, he added, "The mail, which contains the bills we need to pay. Did you pay last month's bills?"

The smile left her face. "Um..."

He reached around her to grab the phone, stomach sinking. The line was dead. "Jane, when's the last time you remember any of our phones ringing?"

"I might have overlooked a few things," she admitted. "But at least we still have electricity."

"Here, anyway. What about at my apartment? Did you miss any bills for it?" When her expression changed again, he groaned. "Did you visit it at all?"

"Once. The day after you left."

"Then my car hasn't been moved for street cleaning for two months."

"It's *possible* that they chose not to impound it."

When he rubbed at his face, her voice grew small. "I'm sorry, Sam."

"It's all right." He looked at her as reassurance that he meant it, but as he got up and moved for her office on the off-chance her phone line hadn't been killed, he couldn't help saying, "Just... what have you been doing this whole time?"

He was already through the doorway when she realized what he was doing. Her voice rose after him. "Wait, let me go in first. I have, um—"

He stopped short, staring at the area of her workspace cleared as a desk. A tiny stuffed teddy bear sat beside the phone. "Jane, what the hell? That's the kind of prize they hand out at the boardwalk."

"So what?" She sounded defensive while picking up the bear, cradling it protectively.

He eyed it and then her. "The boardwalk is fun. You never have fun."

"It wasn't fun. It was educational. I needed to do something while waiting to see if you'd survive last night, so I practiced my aim."

"You... won that?" Still baffled, he glanced toward the alcove where she kept a cot for sleeping near her work.

She tried to block his view, even standing on tiptoe. It didn't work. Another teddy bear, this one as big as Jane, filled the cot. "That can't be yours. They only give those to someone who made every shot."

Then it hit him. He couldn't hide his horror as he looked back at Jane. "You and... no."

She flushed bright red. "I can have personal relationships, too."

"But with Al Dempsey? Why? You hate authority."

"Not when it comes with such impressive attributes," she snapped, glaring at him. "Shall I start with his physical ones?"

Sam cringed. "All right, forget I asked. I need to go out and get everything up and running again."

"I'll come along to help," she said, already mollified. "Since it *is* my fault."

As they gathered up their things to leave, she added in a more serious tone, "You haven't asked about Miss Marshall. Or her former fiancé."

"There's no need. I plan to find out for myself." Despite exhaustion and the list of irritating errands ahead, eagerness filled his movements. "I'll give her a call at the nearest pay phone, and if she's out, I'll find her as soon as I get my damn car back. I'm through with duty."

CHAPTER THIRTY-FOUR

"Evening, Nell. Were there any phone calls?" said Cora, as soon as she squeezed inside the front doorway with all her shopping bags. Any hopeful excitement had seeped from the question weeks ago, and now she asked out of mere stubbornness.

Her maid met her in the living room, already dressed in her hat and coat. "Twelve, miss. How was tea with Mrs. Archer?"

"Very stiff and proper. I'm convinced that woman truly hates me." Cora unwound her hands from the bag handles while glancing over the other girl's neat handwriting on the notepad by the telephone. The first message was from one of her lawyers, but she wasn't surprised. They called constantly these days, anticipating tactics from her father now that he had finally been charged and the trial had been set.

Today's call probably had to do with the discovery that a private detective had been hired by the defense to find every scrap of her past that could be used to question and condemn her character. Even now, all she could manage in response was a sigh over how a detective had come back into her life—but not the right one. She didn't know what was wrong with her. She had always felt so strongly, especially when it came to her father, but now her responses were muted if not outright apathetic. It was really very hard to muster up any indignation that her father would stoop so low.

She glanced through the second message, which was from another lawyer, before noticing Nell was about to leave. It was the other girl's night off, and she seemed more excited than usual. Cora could guess why. "What movie are you seeing?"

Nell's eyes lit up. "Lonny's taking me to the new horror with George DeHart. *Night of the Madman*. Have you gone to it?"

"No. I've just managed to coax Roland to see a mystery tonight, and even that seemed impossible for a time. He thinks using death in entertainment is gauche."

Cora didn't realize how wistful she sounded until pity flickered in Nell's expression. Before the other girl could respond, she quickly added, "Enjoy your night. You'll have to tell me all about the movie tomorrow."

"All right. Goodnight, miss."

Once alone, Cora put away her new clothes. She had to admit, the shopping hadn't been very satisfying even though these were the first things she'd bought for some time. Truthfully, she had only done it because Mrs. Archer had spent the entire tea making pointed comments about the frivolous spending habits modern girls had. Truthfully, every time that shrew of a woman went on about her son's virtues, Cora felt even more irritated with her—and not because she disagreed. In the two months since she had reached out to Roland and began a tentative relationship, she had come to learn that he was a responsible, trustworthy man and devoted son. No

terrible vices or alarming behaviors. Not even a bad habit. No, he was respectable with a capital R. There was nothing wrong with him, and yet he was entirely wrong for *her*. She could feel it.

She wished she could fool herself into wondering what had attracted her to him before the sigil had burned away her memories, but it was clear enough to her even now. Roland never made her breathless with desire, but he was handsome, gentle in manner, and absolutely steady. His interest in her would *never* waver because he treated life as a series of pieces to slot together. She satisfied him as one such piece: a pretty, charming girl who loved him and wished to be his wife. It was all he needed, and while he had her, he would never look at anyone else. And that was what irritated her so much—she had once fallen for him because he was willing to keep her. Because he was the first man who wanted her to be part of his life. It was frankly desperate, even pitiful on her end, and she hated feeling like either.

But that wasn't Roland's fault.

Just then, the clock chimed, reminding her how it was already evening. She'd have to hurry to be dressed before Roland arrived.

She chose a silk gown that flowed like liquid against her body, highlighting its champagne color with a white fur stole and elbow length gloves. A diamond necklace and rose-gold bracelets completed the look, but she still hadn't picked her shoes when a knock came at her door. Roland, she knew, and almost groaned at how she'd be late again.

When she answered the door, he smiled at her. She tried her best to be lost in the sight of him, focusing on his sharp, lean looks, his curly blond hair, and his clear blue eyes as he said, "Hello, darling. How are you? Mother said she had a nice time at tea."

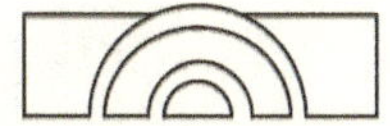

A brief kiss on the cheek was all she got, and she muffled a sigh at how proper he always was, even when they were alone. "I'm swell, thanks. How are you?"

"Fine. I'm still not sure about this play you want us to see. Mysteries always end up being sordid nonsense. I have to score them all the time at the station."

"I think they're exciting once you give them a try. Do you want something to drink while I finish dressing?"

Disappointment seeped into his expression. "You're not ready? You promised to be better about that."

"I know, and I am. I can be ready in five minutes instead of my usual half-hour." She offered him a bright smile.

He didn't smile back while checking his watch. "Darling, why do you always do this? You knew what time we were supposed to leave."

She tried not to let her strain show while picking up the notepad by the telephone. "I know, but I haven't checked all the messages left for me while I was out. I thought I could glance them over before choosing my shoes and purse."

"If you do all that now, we'll be late."

She hesitated and peeked at the last message Nell had written. It was from a downstairs neighbor complaining that she played her radio too loudly in the evenings. With a sigh, she said, "I suppose you're right. Two minutes and I'll be ready. I swear it."

And she was, although the drive to the theater remained relatively quiet. Once, while at a stoplight, she nearly jerked in her seat at the sight of a male silhouette that looked painfully familiar while waiting to cross the street. The tilt of the hat... and the color of the hair...

Then the figure stepped into the pool of light from a nearby street lamp, revealing very human eyes and a face that was nothing

like Sam's. The disappointment felt crushing, but Cora hissed in a breath and turned to Roland, determined not to sulk. "I'm sure the play will be worth all this traffic. It's gotten wonderful reviews. Everyone says the twist ending is worth the ticket price alone."

"If you say so." His tone was pleasant but disinterested.

"You haven't already made up your mind to hate it, have you?"

"No, but I doubt it will play fair with the audience. These types of mysteries are always half-baked clues rendered useless by a twist ending that makes no sense. What's the point of paying attention when it's impossible to guess the culprit?"

Cora fluffed up her stole, refusing to lose her brightness. "You never know. I'm usually quite good at figuring out the mystery."

His mild blue eyes looked genuinely affectionate as he said, "Believe me, darling, I love your enthusiasm, but no one solves these things."

The hope that she could finally coax some playfulness out of him was too much to ignore. "Is that so? How about a friendly bet, then? During the intermission, I'll write out the murderer's name and give you the paper to hold. After the play is over, we'll see how right or wrong I was."

"I don't like to gamble. It's a treacherous habit."

She muffled a sigh. "There aren't any stakes involved. It's just for fun."

"Well... all right."

The fact that he'd agreed left her hopeful that the evening would only improve as it deepened into true night.

The play was as entertaining as she'd heard, and she made careful note of all the characters, mindful of the bet. The actors were all excellent, with the victim proving to be a known blackmailer and all-

around rotten girl. The twisty fun of the mystery faded, however, when the detective entered the story. He was a fat old man who liked to gesture with his pipe to add to his absentminded air, but his presence still sent Cora tumbling into thoughts she had tried very hard to ignore for the past two months.

There in the dark, caught in an audience and sitting beside a man whose biggest virtue was that he wanted her in his life as long as she behaved, there was nothing to muffle her heart. She missed Sam so badly. With every other fella who had left, she had been able to move on after a lot of crying and shopping. Each day had smoothed out a little more until she met a new man who erased the last of the old hurt.

Not this time. Instead, each day felt duller. Nothing bright slipped in, not even with Roland. Oh, she felt sure that her past self *was* excited beyond belief to become his wife. A steady life away from her father would have been heavenly compared to all she had known at the time: uncaring friends who loved drama above all else, brief flings with men that always turned sour, and a home of cold silence.

Yet she was no longer that girl and knew far more about herself. She had met Sam. She had learned how much better it felt to have someone believe in her over merely being an attractive doll on an arm. And she had discovered what she truly wanted out of life: investigating cases with him in the day and going home together at night. Seeing that boyish smile he so rarely gave. Feeling his thick fur between her fingers while their hearts beat in the same rhythm. She should have known a wolf could disappear as easily as a man.

Once or twice, she had tried to prod daydreams from her sluggish mind, concocting a life where she went off on her own as a private detective since she liked the work so much. But the imaginings had

collapsed before fully formed, leading to a realization that she didn't care much about anything anymore, not even the future.

It was a frightening fact, and she found herself staring several moments after the stage curtains had been drawn and the lights turned on for the intermission.

She came back into herself and wrote the character she suspected on a scrap of paper. When she folded it in half and offered it to Roland, he took it with a smile. Since he disapproved of drinking, she had stopped as well—normally. Tonight, she was rattled enough by her thoughts to order a scotch. It drew a side-glance from Roland, but before she could defend her decision, a man called out his name while weaving through the crowd of bodies. Cora vaguely recognized him as one of the other musicians who worked alongside Roland at the radio station, and she wasn't surprised when they both fell into a lighthearted conversation.

It was rude not to join them, but just as the bartender handed over her drink, two figures slipped up by her side.

"Miss Marshall," said the Frosthound alpha-king, gesturing for two shots of whiskey. "You're looking well for someone who's very unhappy."

Cora started, almost spilling her scotch as she twisted to face him and his queen. The pair looked as sleek in their tuxedos as ever, very much at ease despite being the only wolves in the room.

Cimorene *tsked* at her king before turning her attention to Cora. "He's excited. It makes him rude."

"Has something happened? Is Sam—Detective Hayes—all right?" Cora's heart clenched in her chest.

"He's among the living," assured the alpha-queen. "I would know if he had met the Lady and her eternal peace. I meant that

Thane is enjoying the play. Even I am, and I far prefer opera and its pageantry."

"Oh, I see." Cora managed to keep the relief out of her voice, and to resist asking more about him.

As the alpha-king handed one of the whiskeys to Cimorene, she said, "Who do you think murdered our unlikeable victim?"

Cora sipped at her drink, feeling a little bit of life come back into her. She couldn't remember the last time she had spoken without care. "Funnily enough, I have a bet about that. I think it's the detective himself who killed her."

Cimorene laughed without showing her teeth and then glanced at Thane. "He told me the same thing when the intermission began. Yet this detective is the only character with no motive."

"That we know of," replied the alpha-king, idly playing with his empty glass. They were all taking up space at the bar, but no one dared to tell them to move.

Cora nodded. "That's true, and besides, what would be a more perfect way to hide evidence of your guilt than to 'solve' it and pin the blame on another? And if he's been in retirement for years, why come out of it now?"

"The host of the dinner party is an old family friend," pointed out Cimorene.

"Yes, and think of how many similar requests the detective has surely received over the years. Why did he respond to this one?" Cora didn't realize how much her expression had lit up until both wolves studied her intently.

"So you do miss him," said Cimorene, a trace of sympathy in her voice.

It was impossible to play dumb about who the alpha-queen meant. Cora kept her own tone breezy. "I've moved on and built a new life as much as he has, I'm sure."

The alpha-king had already widened his focus to the people around them. "And here you almost made it through the conversation without telling us a lie."

"It wasn't a lie," said Cora, refusing to be cowed. "After all, I haven't said how I feel about that fact."

The response drew a glance of grudging respect from him. His queen looked outright amused, but she quickly grew serious again and said, "We've been in the city since this morning. If news has finally come out about Sam Hayes and the breakaway Saxbys, we're ignorant of it. Yet I do wonder if you know even less than us. The play won't resume for another fifteen minutes. Come sit with us and have a conversation that I believe you need."

The offer made her breathless with anticipation, but she had to admit, "I'm not alone. I'd have to ask my—well, his name is Roland Archer, and he might not be comfortable with that. He's very traditional in his thinking."

The alpha-king now looked over her shoulder. "I can see that, and I can see what his answer will be, too."

Cora turned and saw Roland ducking around people to reach her. She had never seen him so upset, and as he caught her by the arm, the first words out of his mouth were, "My God, Cora, what are you doing?"

"It's all right. I know them," she said, starting to twist toward the two wolves again. "This is—"

Before she could introduce them, she found herself being dragged away in Roland's grip. She resisted, aided by the crush of bodies hoping to get a drink. "Will you stop? They won't hurt us."

"They're wolves," he shot back. "Do you really believe they've never torn out throats?"

The alpha-king watched them with a sardonic smile. "Relax, fella. You'd be too boring of a kill."

The comment drew a glare from Roland before his hand tightened against Cora's arm. This time, he used all his strength to pull her away with him. It hurt enough to draw out her own anger, but before she could do more than hiss his name, the alpha-queen called out to her.

"The path you want isn't closed." Cimorene looked as calm and direct as ever, but her voice rose like a howl of warning. "You lost sight of it, that's all. It can be found again, bloody as before."

Cora tried to glance back a final time, but Roland had a long stride, and within moments they were outside of the building. As the doors swung shut on the lights, smoke, and laughter, she jerked her arm free. "There was no need to be so rude."

"Rude?" he said, incredulously. He was still wound up, smoothing out his hair and checking his tie with shaking fingers. "They looked ready to eat you alive."

"That's just how they are. They're the Frosthound alpha-king and alpha-queen. Even the other packs are scared of their reputation, but they're really very nice. They just wanted to talk, Roland."

"They're murderers," he said, his voice flat. "How can you possibly think of them as nice?"

"I..." Her argument deflated as she realized he would never understand the answer. *Because at least they're honest about their natures, which is more than can be said for all the humans I know.*

"All right," she said, wishing this night was over. "Let's just go back to our seats and wait out the intermission."

He shook his head, catching her arm again. His hand wasn't as tight as before, yet it remained tense against her skin. "Not while there are wolves inside. We're leaving."

"What?" She was shocked enough to walk with him. "You can't be serious. The play isn't over."

His mouth just tightened into a thin line. Even once they were inside the car, his silence simmered.

Cora bit back a huff of breath while looking out the passenger window, arms folded. Soon, she noticed that he followed any stoplight that turned green first, as if trying to put as much distance between them and the theater as possible. She managed to stay quiet for all of a minute. "This isn't the way back to my apartment."

"I know that," he snapped. "I'm so damn shocked that I can't tell east from west right now."

Cora stared at him. Roland, swearing? She couldn't believe it. "Shocked at seeing wolves enjoying a play?"

"At your behavior," he burst out. "When we first met again and spoke about what had happened, you told me that the wolves you knew were all related to the case. That you had never... *associated* with them before."

"Yes, and that's the truth. Including the Frosthounds."

After a few breaths of silence, he pulled the car over and parked it there on the street. They were now far from the theater, in one of the

more rundown areas of housing, but he only seemed interested in studying her face.

At least he looked calmer, and his next words sounded grim and carefully spoken, as if he knew how important they were in deciding their future together. "Cora, I must ask this. That wolf you hired. The private detective."

Cora drew in a shallow breath. "Yes?"

"It was impossible not to hear the rumors about him and you. That your connection with him wasn't professional." He seemed slightly embarrassed to broach such a subject, but his eyes remained fixed on her face. "Is that true?"

Was this what bitterness felt like? A lump in her throat that she almost choked on? "Detective Hayes was a consummate professional when we met, and a consummate professional when we parted ways. Do you really need to know more than that?"

Doubt flickered in his eyes, but he looked away. His hands flexed against the wheel before he said, "It's just that you seemed all too comfortable with those wolves just now. Quite... companionable."

"Is that why you pulled me out of the theater? It really is, isn't it? I thought you were scared of them, but you just felt scandalized by my behavior."

He grimaced. "It's not like that."

"Then what is it like?" When he didn't answer, she slumped back in her seat, dully wondering how the night had turned out like this. "And now we've missed the play."

"Willam told me who the murderer was back at the intermission," he muttered, as they both stared ahead. "It was the detective."

She wished she could feel more satisfied over being right. "Aren't you going to check my guess?"

With a sigh, he pulled out the slip of paper and read it. "Who told you?"

"No one. Like I said, I'm quite good at mysteries." Then she tried to sound lighthearted, although she felt anything but. "Don't you believe I'm smart enough to solve a puzzle?"

When she saw the look on his face, she turned numb. Her voice sounded very thin as she answered for him. "You don't."

"I didn't say that," he said, quickly.

"But you don't. You think I'm a silly, emptyheaded heiress like all the rest. I—you—" Suddenly, she couldn't bear to be with him for another moment, and lunged out of the car. The world had blurred over.

"Cora. Cora!" Then came the sound of a car door opening and shutting.

She ignored him, heels clicking against the crumbling pavement. She didn't know where she was going; her surroundings were dim and empty of any other people or even street lamps. Only the occasional light from a window outlined the road.

When Roland caught up to her, she whirled to face him, all frustration spilling out. "At this point, I wonder if there's anything you *do* like about me. You didn't like that I drank, so I stopped. You didn't like that I carried a gun, so I stopped. Now you apparently don't like that I can think. What am I supposed to do, pull out my brain?"

"It's not like that," he insisted, his voice growing as heated as hers. "I love everything about you, but I did warn you that your life would change if we became a couple again."

When she just huffed and began walking again, he followed. "I know it's been hard adjusting to what your father did to you. I recognize things can't be the same as before, when we were about to elope. But you have to understand that what you got away with as Miss Cora Marshall won't be allowed as Mrs. Roland Archer."

"By you?" she snapped.

"By society." Then he stepped in front of her, forcing her to stop again. He looked both fed up and disappointed as he added, "You know this city as well as I do. Having the right name, connections, and balance in your bank account means nothing can ruin your life. Do you think your father, with all his misdeeds, would still be comfortable in his home if he weren't Isaac Marshall? Any normal man would have been charged, tried, and hanged weeks ago. And that's what I am, Cora: a normal man. A scandal is enough to ruin me and my family. I can't be blithe about my behavior. And now, neither can you."

Her anger pulsed into something white-hot from being lectured. "You've made that clear enough, but what does that have to do with questioning my relationship with Detective Hayes? If it's my present behavior that worries you, why ask about my past? Would you find me repulsive if you found out he had ever touched me? Is my reputation more important to you than who I am as a person?"

He didn't want to answer that, she could tell.

Just then, a rough male voice behind them said, "Hey. Hey!"

They both looked over and saw a short man with a cap pulled low to keep his face in shadow. He stood a few feet away with his hands in his pockets. "You lost or something?"

Roland responded first. "No. Thank you."

"Just having a bad night," muttered Cora, shrugging her stole further around her.

The man had good hearing. "Well, it's about to get worse."

Then he pulled out one hand and flicked it, revealing a small but nasty-looking knife. The blade gleamed in the moonlight as two more shadowy figures slipped up behind him. "No hysterics. Just give me everything you got."

"Oh, my God," said Cora, freezing. "Roland."

His voice turned tight. "Just do what he says."

"*Roland*," she hissed again.

The man sighed and made a feint with his knife. "Do I have to start cutting you up?"

In response, Roland jerked back until he was behind her, leaving her to face the blade.

Even as she gasped in outrage, the mugger chuckled. "What a swell guy. Come on, both of you. Toss all your things to me, including the jewelry."

"Fine. Why not? It's such a perfect resolution to a *wonderful* evening." Cora ripped off her bracelets and necklace, shaking with rage and embarrassment.

Roland remained silent while throwing his wallet on the ground by the man's feet.

"The lady's coat and shoes, too."

"What?" Her voice rose. "But they're my favorite pair. And how am I supposed to walk around barefoot?"

Another twitch of the knife, and she gave in, hands on her hips as the mugger disappeared back into the darkness with his companions. Then she turned around and began walking in the opposite direction.

When Roland called her name, she didn't glance back. "Oh, don't even talk to me. I can't believe you gave me all that guff only to hide behind me like a coward."

"Don't be ridiculous. Let's just report this, go home, and forget that this night happened. The car is right here."

"I'm not getting in there with you," she said, heatedly. "I couldn't stand to sit that close to you for even a minute."

His voice grew just as vehement while he opened the passenger's door. "Cora, get inside. We'll talk about it later."

"No. It's over. We're obviously completely wrong for each other. Whatever I felt for you is long gone, and I'd rather die alone and miserable than become Mrs. Roland Archer. So just leave."

"Fine," he said, his tone growing cold. Then he slammed the door shut and walked over to the driver's side. "Goodnight and goodbye, Miss Marshall."

When the car started up and sped past her, she gasped, running after it for a few steps. "I didn't mean for you to actually do it. I don't even know where I am!"

In the silence of an empty street surrounded by unlit buildings, she groaned. Then she looked up at the sky until she found a constellation that would guide her north until she found something familiar. By the time she did, her feet already felt sore against the rough pavement. Worse, the sight wasn't reassuring at all. It was the huge city clock tower itself, which meant her apartment was at least 30 blocks away.

The police station was only 20. She counted. As she stumbled up to the front entrance, the mud-stained hem of her gown trailing over the steps, she was too exhausted to feel more than a dull relief that it was so late and no one was around to see her sorry state. Inside, she

ignored the empty front area and its cubicles meant to service the public, all shuttered for the night.

She also ignored the one officer on duty there, who gave her a double-take. "Miss... Marshall? Are you all right?"

Her answer would either be a scream or crying, so she simply continued shuffling down the hallway that led to Captain Dempsey's office. As expected, it was the only one still lit, and she opened the door without knocking.

The police captain looked up from behind his desk, papers spread out before him. As she slumped into the chair across from him, his irritation morphed into astonishment. "What the hell happened to you?"

Cora drew herself up, pretending she wasn't a disheveled mess. "I never thought I'd say this, but I'm happy to see you, Captain. It's been a horrible night. I was mugged and left without any money for a phone call or a taxi. I've been walking all night to get here. I'm tired, my feet absolutely *ache*, and it's another 10 blocks home. And... and... and worst of all, you're now the only friend I h-have in this *entire city*."

Then her voice rose into a wail, and she started sobbing into her hands. She couldn't even say if it was out of rage or sheer tiredness.

Dempsey pulled the phone on his desk closer without taking his eyes off her. "No, no, no. Just hang on a minute."

Despite crying so hard that her breath hitched in her chest, she dimly heard him dial a number and mutter, "Pick up. Pick up, damn it."

No one did, and he sighed before hanging up. "All right. Try to shut off those tears and explain what happened."

He passed a handkerchief over before lighting a cigarette for himself. After wiping her face dry and feeling fresh tears run down her cheeks, she began wringing the fabric instead, voice thick and strangled. "What happened? I'll tell you what happened. Responsible, proper, morally upright Roland Archer left me there in the street. He *left*—just like all the other men in my life!"

The police captain rubbed his head, expression resigned, but before he could respond, Cora heard a deep, painfully familiar voice speak from behind her. "Bunny. What—are you all right?"

Her heart bucked in her chest, but her mind refused to believe what she heard until she twisted in her seat and saw Sam Hayes standing there in the doorway. He looked as put-together and composed as the first time they'd ever met, but those brilliant gold eyes darkened with shock as he took in her state.

Under his attention, sweet exhilaration filled her. So did fury. "Don't you 'Bunny' me! You're one of them."

The seething words didn't stop him from stepping inside and crouching before her in one smooth movement. "What happened?"

"You left me for months, that's what. You just disappeared after telling me to make up a new life. As if I could switch off how I felt about you. As if I could stop caring about whether you survived or whether I would never—never see you again." Then she dissolved into fresh tears, too overwhelmed to do more than hide her blotchy face in her handkerchief even as Sam's hand eased against her arm, warm and gentle against her chilled skin.

Dempsey eyed her. "Can't you have this conversation somewhere that isn't my office?"

"No." She managed to glare at the police captain. "I behaved like a proper lady for that prig for two months, Captain, and now I'm going to make a scene whenever I want."

He sighed out a lungful of smoke. "All right." Then he resumed going through the paperwork on his desk, scrawling on some and rolling up others to shove into the pneumatic tubing.

Before she could do more than wipe at her raw cheeks, Sam shifted closer to her. "Bunny—Cora."

"Miss Marshall," she insisted, despite how her heart fluttered at the sound of her name in his voice.

He nodded, slowly taking her hands in his own. When she didn't resist, he said, "I don't blame you for being angry. Do you want me to leave so you can talk to the captain in private?"

The enraged part of her was tempted to say she didn't give a fig about what he did, not anymore. The rest of her remembered what had happened with Roland and the car. After drawing in a deep breath, she said, "No. That's not to say I've forgiven you, but it won't take long to go over what happened. Then we can get back to arguing, because I'm not nearly finished. I'm—I'm smart, and I can do things, and I deserve better than being set aside for some alpha-princess or *anything* else without even having a say in the matter. I have thoughts as much as anyone."

He nodded, studying her with a warm, heavy gaze.

The police captain broke through her indignation by pulling over a notepad. "Let's hear it."

As she explained what happened, she felt Sam's tension increase with each detail. He remained silent aside from the occasional question, thumb running over her knuckles, but by the end, she

could tell he was as furious as she. A large part of her wanted to rest fingers against the muscle jumping in his jaw, but she resisted.

Once she finished, Dempsey pulled over some forms and lit a fresh cigarette. "Usually, you'd fill these out, but I know I'll get you out of here faster if I do it. They'll be shot over to the theft division, but don't hold out hope of getting everything back."

Cora nodded. She hadn't expected anything more. When the police captain fell silent except for the brisk scratching of his pen, her focus returned to Sam. It grew harder by the moment not to lose herself in the deep gold of his eyes, but she kept her voice stiff. "I suppose everything went well with helping the Saxbys."

"We won, if that's what you mean." Then he sighed. "I didn't know I'd be gone that long. Believe me, I didn't enjoy it. I came back as soon as I could."

She huffed. "What about the next time that alpha-princess wants your help?"

"Alpha-queen," said Dempsey, now waiting on the phone. "He got her the crown twelve hours ago. The city passed down word to all its branches to acknowledge the Saxbys again."

Her throat was so raw that her shriek came out as more of a squeak. "You've been back that long? You said you'd call me."

The angrier she grew, the more soothing his voice became. And he still studied her as if she was the most amazing creature he'd ever seen. "I did. The maid said you were out."

"Aren't detectives supposed to look for people?"

He sighed. "I haven't been feeling like a detective today. I've been feeling like an idiot who let the most stunning girl I've ever known slip away. I thought it was better to clear up both our pasts. Get rid of any questions. And maybe I thought a respectable human who

once wanted to marry you would make you happier than a wolf who collects scars and not much else. I'm sorry, Miss Marshall. I can smell your hurt and it kills me that I caused it."

She swallowed hard, voice falling quiet. "C-cora. And you didn't cause all of it. I could have broken off things with Roland much earlier. Even before tonight, I knew he was stuffy, and boring, and... and nothing like you. I should have listened to my heart much earlier, back when you gave me the file on him. I should have admitted right there what I already knew. I'm in love with you, no one else. I just couldn't bear to say it and then hear you explain that we were still through, anyway."

"Through?" His eyes turned feral. "I wanted to burn that damn file, not hand it over. Right now, it's driving me nuts to smell him on you."

"Oh." He did look very intense at the moment, she had to admit. There was nothing reserved in his expression at all, but she found herself saying, "I thought you were passing me off to him. Holly told me that—"

His voice roughened into a growl. "Holly and the rest can go to hell. I know what I want, and it's right in front of me. Whether they like it or not is their problem."

"You're not going to become the alpha-king?"

"No." Then he caught her face with one hand, his grip gentle but tense with an unmistakable hunger. "I swore to myself that I wouldn't be like your father and hide things for my own benefit. Well, now I swear that you've got my heart whether you want it or not. Nothing else can distract it. Not a crown, not the past, and not my own damn stupidity. Cora Marshall, I love you."

Her lungs didn't want to work properly, gasping as if she was close to passing out, but she felt deliriously happy. "You do?"

"Yes." The word came out as a rasp. Despite his fine, tailored suit, at that moment he didn't look human at all.

Her laugh was small and watery but real. "Then why are we fighting?"

He smiled, that boyish one she loved, but the answer to her question didn't come from him.

"Because you both stupidly talk past each other even when trying to have an honest conversation." Jane Feral leaned against the doorway, holding a pink sheet of paper in one hand. She appeared very smug while brandishing it at them. "Unlike you, I wasn't about to leave the line after waiting in it for over five hours. Here's your vehicle release form, so go get your car and take her home. She looks terrible."

"Don't take her to her place," said Dempsey, hanging up the phone to check the fresh messages from the pneumatic mail. "It's been hit."

"What?" said Cora.

Sam swore under his breath. "The mugger used a key tracker?"

"Looks like it." Then the police captain glanced at Cora. "Did you keep your apartment key in your purse? Thought so. A lot of thieves use magic to trace a key in their possession back to its lock. Then they walk right in and clean out the place."

"They took all my things?"

"According to your landlord. Looks like Mr. Archer escaped that problem since they only stole his wallet."

Cora stiffened in her seat. "Wait a minute. Roland already filed a report here at the station?" When the police captain nodded, she added, "Did he mention me?"

"No. He also wasn't any help with describing the mugger. I've got the report right here. 'Short male in dark clothing and cap.' Detective Walton will probably ask if you remember any details when he gets the case tomorrow."

Cora huffed. "I can tell you right now. We were at eye-level before I had to hand over my shoes. The left sleeve of his jacket was torn at the cuff. He tried to keep his face in shadow, but I saw it was triangular in shape and that his left eyebrow was notably higher than his right. Oh, and he was left-handed."

"Spoken like a true detective," murmured Sam while the police captain dutifully wrote it all down.

Despite having a stuffy nose and a headache from crying so much, Cora beamed at him.

Dempsey glanced up again. "Don't distract her with that puppy dog look until I'm done getting information. Miss Marshall, where are you going to be until we're through investigating your apartment? I need a contact number."

She shared another glance with Sam, heart beating faster as he said, "My place."

"All right. Sign here and you can go."

As she did, Sam rose to his feet to take the release form from Jane, who looked extremely satisfied by the turn of events. The she-wolf even smiled while saying, "Don't wait for me. I'm going to practice with my prototype down in the range."

Cora didn't miss the significant glance Jane gave the police captain. Neither did Sam, because after she left, he said, "I know you've been helping her with her aim. Among other things."

Dempsey leaned back in his seat, expression indifferent. "So?"

Sam shrugged. "She's happy, so I'm fine with it."

"Good. Now start acting smart over your own girl." The police captain flicked ash from his cigarette and looked at Cora. "You're all done. Get out of here."

Sam's car was waiting by the impound lot owned by the station, and once they got inside it, he explained what had happened. Cora listened while their hands rubbed together, sinking into his voice like a hot bath. Her head felt both thick with a headache and incredibly light, and she had to close her eyes against another round of tears. She couldn't believe this was real.

After he finished, she said, "Is this what you had to do all day?"

"No. I also had to get the lights and phones switched back on at my office and apartment. I had to call you from a phone booth."

His wry smile made her laugh. "I suppose neither of us had a very good day. But tonight is looking much brighter."

Just then, she saw his apartment building and softly gasped. "Oh..."

Then she turned to him with shining eyes. "You can't imagine how many times I dreamed of being back in your apartment."

"Same here, Bunny," he murmured, giving her a look that made her feel like her gown was about to crisp right off her body.

Inside, she didn't even notice the dust while he flicked on enough lights to lead her into the shower. All her attention narrowed to his hands slipping the dirtied silk down from her skin. His fingers were

rough with calluses, drawing out the sensation in the most delicious way as they skimmed her shoulders, breasts, and hips.

Her breath was already shallow when he finished and raised his eyebrows. "No underwear?"

"I had to revolt against respectability in *some* fashion." She arched into his fingers, feeling like sparks danced on her skin wherever he touched her.

In response, he growled against her neck, one hand already between her legs while he turned on the shower. She managed to take off his tie and shirt, kissing at the new scars she found until his fingers found a rhythm that made her cling to him for dear life. He sucked at her throat while her body shook through sweet, blinding release.

By the time she recovered, they were beneath the water. The spray prickled against her inflamed skin, but it was his mouth that left her gasping, his teeth and tongue tasting every part of her within reach. As she melted against him, it really seemed like her body was as ephemeral as the steam surrounding them, gaining the delightful ache of flesh only wherever he bit her.

The water threatened to turn cold before they finally left the shower. He wouldn't even let go of her to grab a towel, and fresh desire shivered through her while he nipped at the tender skin beneath her ear.

"I still smell him on you," he said, voice as hot as his eyes.

She ran fingers through his wet hair while he pulled her body tight against his. "I don't see how. He barely ever touched—"

His mouth caught hers, cutting off the rest. The kiss was rough in the absolutely best kind of way, coaxing her to forget words.

Offering her a taste of just what kind of wolf he would be now that he had decided to give her his heart, and trust, and loyalty.

Then he lifted her up until their noses brushed. Her legs instinctively wrapped around him as she stared into his eyes, grinning in sheer excitement. His own eyes were wild, intense, taking in every hint of her reaction while he pushed into her. She just moaned, nuzzling against him while he adjusted his grip to take all of her weight.

He held her easily, arms strong around her while she panted against his mouth. Then he shifted his hands until she found herself arching back into them, exposing her throat to his hunger. It all felt so delicious and right. She found herself arching further still, laughing as her flexibility left her looking at the world upside down while his hands kept a firm grip on her waist, their hips working together in time to her racing heartbeat. Never in her wildest dreams could she have imagined feeling like this.

But this wasn't a dream. This was real... and it was just the beginning.

CHAPTER THIRTY-FIVE

Cora had never felt so blissfully happy in her life, a feeling magnified by the sweet simplicity of dozing in bed with Sam. His arm had wrapped around her to keep her close. The back of her head fit against the hollow of his throat, and she could feel his heartbeat against her back. They were in their own little bubble, oblivious to the rest of the world.

Eventually, though, the world came knocking. Quite literally—brisk, impatient raps sounded against the front door. Neither of them moved to answer it, although Sam did shift enough to nuzzle the back of Cora's neck and murmur, "It's Jane. She'll probably use her keys next."

Cora hummed wordlessly, determined to soak in the weight of his body until the very last moment.

Then the front door unlocked, and Jane's voice drifted through to them. "It's been three days since you both holed up in here. Your messages are overflowing, but I thought you'd be interested in the latest one in particular. The police found the man who mugged Miss Marshall. I'll be waiting in the kitchen."

At that, Cora stirred enough to sit up and brush hair out of her eyes. "Maybe they recovered some of my things."

Sam kissed the tender skin beneath her ear before getting out of bed. "Sounds like we're about to find out."

Cora had contacted her tailor after her first night back together with Sam, having remembered that a new outfit would be ready to pick up. She'd had it delivered instead, and the elegant gold boxes waited on the dressing table. Eager to hear the news, she decided to slip into one of Sam's shirts instead, which left her more modest than in many of her outfits.

Sam had already dressed, but at the sight of her in one of his shirts, his eyes glimmered with a hunger she was beginning to recognize. His attention felt as sweet as honey, even when he restrained himself to a lingering kiss and a brief squeeze of her hip beneath the fabric.

Jane only raised an eyebrow at her casual appearance, seeming more interested in drinking a pilfered cup of coffee. The case containing her prototype waited beside her on the kitchen table. She gave Sam a smug look while he greeted her and began skimming through the mail she had brought over, but her attention quickly returned to Cora. "You're not dressed yet? It's late afternoon."

"I haven't been paying much attention to the time." More to the point, there hadn't been any reason to; she and Sam had been constantly at each other. "What's the news about the mugger?"

"He was stupid enough to brag about what he did to friends. He's keeping quiet to the police, however, so they haven't recovered any of your belongings."

"He probably sold them to one of the hundreds of pawnbrokers working in this city," said Sam, voice absent while he looked through the final bundle of letters. His focus sharpened on Cora's disappointed expression, and his tone warmed as he returned to her. "I'll get them back, Bunny. Maybe not everything, but as much as I can."

Cora found it so easy to smile when she was with him. "It's all right. The only thing I really miss is the radio you gifted me. Losing my clothes *does* sting, but I've decided to fill out my wardrobe by taking back the ones still in my father's house."

Jane looked skeptical at the idea. "How? Police officers guard his house, and his bail conditions include a clause that he cannot accept visitors aside from legal counsel."

Cora shrugged. "I don't care. I'm tired of pushy men controlling my life. Those are my clothes and I want them back now, not whenever the lawyers finish fighting with each other."

It was a thought that had crystallized into a firm decision in the past few days whenever she had bothered thinking, but not one she had brought up with Sam. Now she glanced at him, unsure of his response.

He smiled, eyes dark and relaxed. "I've broken in there before. Follow my lead, and we'll never be noticed."

As Cora beamed, leaning backwards into him, Jane finished her coffee and said, "Will you need enchantments? No? Good, because I'm already busy tonight."

"Your prototype?" said Sam.

"Good to know your deduction skills haven't rusted from a few days off." Despite the acerbic words, Jane's expression lit up, and her

hand stroked the case as she added, "I'm showcasing it to the judging panel at eight o'clock."

"Why that late?"

"My decision. They wasted my time under the premise that I had a chance at winning the contract, so now I'm returning the favor. They're going to miss all their cocktail parties, operas, and galas tonight."

"Does that include Captain Dempsey?" said Cora, keeping her voice innocent.

"He isn't one of the judges, but he might be there to see how my aim improved." Then Jane's tone grew more serious. "That's the other reason I'm here, Sam. I didn't have a chance to say this at the station, but I... appreciate your decision to accept Al and me."

"Can't say I expected to come back to that, but you're happy. That's all I wanted for you. Just don't give me the details." Then Sam's smile turned wry, and he nodded at the prototype. "Are we going to get a look at that thing since it's ready?"

Cora moved closer with him while Jane snapped open the case, just as interested. It was a sleek thing for being a submachine gun, black as oil except for the three cartridges that replaced a conventional weapon's magazine—those were a much lighter grey. She kept up with Jane's explanation even though she had never seen a gun that used energy blasts instead of bullets or shells, but did ask, "Why three cartridges instead of one?"

"Different power levels." Then Jane pushed the first, clicking it further into place. It lit up yellow. "Shoot with one cartridge active, and it delivers a disorienting shock."

Pushing the second brightened the glow from both into orange. "Two cause temporary paralysis."

"And three?" said Sam, watching the light flare into red as the third cartridge locked into place.

"Like getting hit by lightning." Then Jane pressed them all again to pop them back into their *off* position. "The public isn't allowed to be there at the testing, or I'd otherwise invite you along to see it in action."

"Oh, I've had enough of the police station," said Cora, watching her put the prototype back in its case. "In fact, the only place I want to visit right now is my father's house."

The sky glimmered with the fiery orange of sunset when they arrived at the gloomy, imposing mansion, parking under a tree just outside the entrance to avoid being seen by the police guard on duty.

As Sam led her around the ivy-covered brick wall that circled the house, she said, "When did you break inside before?"

He glanced at her, briefly losing the hunting gleam in his eyes. "After your father took you back home. I knew I couldn't let you see me, but I had to make sure you were all right. Or as well as you could be with the sigil active."

Cora felt her heart swell but tried to keep a cool head as they reached the servant's gate at the back, aware of how careful they would have to be. "You know just how to make a girl swoon."

He broke his concentration long enough to give her a smile that really did threaten to make her melt. "Well, hold off if you can, because I can smell the cop patrolling the grounds, and we're about to slip past him."

They got in through an open window. Sam stilled her with one hand and listened for a few breaths. "Your father's scent is fresh, but he's not on this floor."

"Good. Do you know how many servants are left?"

"I smell five so far." Then he checked the hallway before motioning her to follow. His movements were sharp and careful. "All of them are terrified."

"I can't imagine Father is ever in a good mood now," said Cora, but she studied their surroundings just as carefully.

Inside her bedroom, she was surprised to discover that everything had been left intact—her makeup compacts and lipsticks still waited on the dressing table, and her closet looked as full as she had left it. She hadn't been sure what to expect, only that her father would have erased her from his life as thoroughly as she had erased him from hers. Seeing her old things covered in a light layer of dust gave her an unexpected shiver, as if she had stepped into a tomb.

Sam prowled around the room while she quickly picked her favorite clothes and packed them in a spare suitcase. It would be agony not to take all her shoes, but she knew it was too much of a risk to do this twice. She was just deciding between a pair of beige and brown sporting boots with beautiful stitching and rose-colored satin pumps when Sam growled softly to catch her attention.

"There's a maid coming," he murmured, just before Cora heard the soft tread herself. "The one you've talked about before. Maisie."

Cora made a split-second decision induced by her curiosity. "Then it'll be all right if she sees me. Besides, I'd like to learn why the staff is so nervous. You can slip out with the suitcase if you want to speed things up."

He shook his head and stepped behind the dressing screen as the door to the room cautiously opened. Maisie peered in and then gave a strangled gasp at seeing Cora.

"It's only me," said Cora, quickly. "I came to get my things and leave again. Maisie, are you all right?"

The girl looked thin and sleepless, her face haggard far beyond her years. Her hands wrung together as she said, "I—I just came in to check whether the windows were locked. Miss Marshall, you can't be here!"

"Why not? Has Father found out?"

"He's..." Maisie swallowed hard, as if her throat had gone dry. "He's not in."

Cora resisted glancing toward Sam's hiding spot. "What? But he's supposed to stay here until his trial."

The girl looked ready to cry. "Please, miss. Just leave before there's real trouble."

Then came the muffled clank of something very heavy and very far below them. The walls creaked, resettling their weight.

"What on earth was that? It sounded like it came from the old wine cellar." Cora looked up from the floor and found that Maisie's expression had shifted into sheer terror.

"I have to go. I can't stay, I can't!" Then the girl fled, her footsteps disappearing down the hall.

Sam slipped out from behind the screen, silent and careful.

Cora looked at him. "What on earth is going on?"

"I don't know, but she's not the only servant leaving. We're about to be alone in this house from what I can hear and smell."

"How fresh is Father's scent?"

"15, 20 minutes."

In his expression, Cora saw the same question that she had, and she said it out loud while staring at the floor again. "Then is that him down there or someone else?"

Since it was an old house, the wine cellar could only be accessed through the large kitchen pantry. The crooked, wooden door looked

the same as she remembered, and chilled air drifted out when Sam carefully opened it, his other hand close to his gun. Fat lamps lit stone stairs that sank down and out of sight.

Cora couldn't hear anything, but her skin still prickled from the cold dampness seeping out through the doorway. "What do you think?" she murmured. "Would going down there be a very bad idea?"

"Yes, because it's your father." Sam's hand was already back on the door, ready to close it again.

Just then, Isaac Marshall's voice boomed up from the darkness. "Whoever is up there, close the door. It's already dusk, you fool."

The sound of that imperious, scathing tone rang through Cora's mind like a ponderous bell, shaking free all the memories of her father condemning her for whatever fault he found in her character. How many times had her cheeks burned while he called her thoughtless, silly, witless? How many times had she smiled at him as if those words couldn't possibly bother her?

Worst of all, how many times had she believed him, just a little?

Her own voice shot through the thick air high and furious, honed from years of pent-up rage. "I'm no more a fool than you are, *Father.*"

Sam tensed beside her, staring down into the darkness with equal intensity, but remained silent as her father's baffled response drifted back. "Cora?"

"Yes, it's me." Dimly, she was aware of Sam murmuring her name, but she was just too angry to keep herself from lunging down the stairs. She'd had enough. She'd had just enough of dueling with her father through lawyers and news articles. Here was a chance to give him a piece of her mind, and she would take it.

In the flickering light, the dirt tunnel morphed into concrete walls so fresh that she still smelled the lime. The air grew even colder as she reached the floor and began weaving past racks of wine.

Her father called out again, perhaps alerted by the rap of her heels. "Cora, don't come down. Get back upstairs."

Still ordering her around. Still acting like he always knew better. She was shaking, but not from the underground chill. Then Sam caught her arm, stilling her just as she reached a large steel door that was slightly ajar. Lamplight glowed inside.

When she turned to him, still furious, he met her gaze, his eyes dark and serious. "Cora, it's all right. What he says doesn't matter. He can't control you anymore."

"But he's still trying to. I can't hold back, Sam. I can't!"

He sighed. "And it has to be right now?"

"Yes." Her voice cracked. "Because after this, I never want to see him again."

Another moment of study and then he traced the curve of her cheek. "All right. Let me go first."

She nodded, heart pounding and fists balled at her sides while she followed him inside. Then she blinked, stopping dead. "Father? Why are you in a... a cell?"

Cell was putting it mildly. The steel bars dividing the room in two were obscenely thick and bolted into the floor. Her father sat in a plain wooden chair. It was the only thing present on his side. Even all the lamps were carefully placed beyond reach of the bars. It really seemed like a dungeon more than anything.

Despite his rigid posture, her father didn't look well, sweating and shaking in his evening dressing gown. His eyes were bloodshot, and his words sounded strained as he said, "For God's sake, Cora,

leave before Siebert locks the door. He's ordered to do so at dusk no matter what."

The sharp click of metal sliding into metal at their backs suggested it was already too late.

Sam growled while trying the door's handle. When he shook his head at Cora and then shrugged off his coat, obviously preparing to break them out, she turned back to her father. Her pulse pounded in her ears.

Her father groaned and slumped over. The act left his face in shadow as the lamplight flickered erratically. "You're the same as always, dear daughter. Unable to understand anything."

"I don't believe in that claptrap anymore," she shot back. "I'm smart. I know lots of things. And I deserve to know a lot more, especially when it comes to all that you did to me. You want me to leave, Father? Then tell me why you're in here."

When her father's shoulders bunched, she thought he was drawing in a breath to shout at her. Then she heard Sam growl again. Suddenly, he pushed between her and her father, staring at the man in horror. His expression cleared some of her fury, and she didn't resist when the press of his body urged her back toward the door. "We need to get out of here. Now."

Just then, her father shuddered and raised his head again. His eyes were a bright, feral yellow, and oversized fangs flashed in his mouth as he forced out, "I'm in here, you little fool, because it's a full moon."

With those final words, he began seizuring, falling out of the chair to writhe on the stone floor. His voice dwindled into a gut-wrenching groan.

"Sam?" managed Cora. "Is... is he..."

His response remained calm, but she could read the tension in the lines of his body as he motioned her closer to him while his other hand pulled out his knife. "He's changing form, but not into a regular wolf. His smell is different. I think he's turning into the same goddamn creature as Dominic Tierney. Do you have your pistol? Good. Keep it on him in case he finishes before me."

She did, amazed at how steady her hands were. A scream rose in her throat when sharp, cracking noises filled the room and she realized they were her father's bones breaking and reforming. After swallowing her horror back down, she said, "What are you going to do? The lock is on the outside."

"The hinges are in here with us. Once I knock the pins out, we can swing the door open and get the hell out of here." Then Sam began using the hard metal of his knife's pommel to do just that.

The noise quickly grew muffled by the snapping and gurgles coming from her father. His transformation was nothing like Sam's smooth, painless shift, and she was too shocked to look away. The features of his face bubbled, tongue lolling like a man choking in a noose. His eyes bugged out until she thought they would pop. His spine contorted in quick, shuddering movements, vertebrae bursting through the silk fabric of his dressing gown.

It wasn't until a tail sprouted out that he finally began screaming. His voice thickened into something guttural and utterly wretched while the muscles of his body convulsed and swelled, sloughing over the exposed bone of his back. Hands scratched at the ground until fingernails broke past the quick. The movement pushed his sleeve up past his left arm, and that was when Cora saw it—old scar tissue bubbling and swelling until it ripped into a fresh wound again. She had known enough roughshod men to recognize what a bite from an

attack dog looked like, and this was a much larger, uglier version of that. Even as she fought not to feel sick, the wound sprouted greyish fur.

The next time her father twisted to where she could glimpse his face, his stately sideburns had thickened into the same fur and spread, covering his skin. His teeth were even larger, pushing out of a distorted muzzle without rhyme or reason. Another spasm left those terrible fangs clamping down on a still-human tongue. The froth on her father's jowls grew bloody.

After that, Cora had to look down and concentrate on breathing steadily. The pistol remained cocked and ready in her hands, leaving her unable to cover her ears against the wet, tearing noises of flesh reassembling itself, or the agonized howls that still sounded like her father's voice. Only the steady pounding from Sam driving out the pins in the hinges kept her focused.

The beautiful chime of one falling to the floor jerked her gaze toward him. He was sweating but intent, fingers incredibly steady as he straightened up to the second and final hinge near the top of the door. His voice sounded just as calm despite rising above another thick scream from her father. "Cora, brace a hand against this area of the door to keep it straight. If it starts twisting, there'll be too much pressure on the pin to pop it out."

She tried not to pant while following his directions. Despite the awful noise shaking the room, he glanced at her, eyes clear and reassuring. "It's all right. We're almost out of here."

Just as she nodded, a bubbling groan from her father shifted into a rumbling growl. Then came the scrape of claws against stone, and panting breaths that vibrated the walls. Cora instinctively aimed her

pistol again, eyes widening as the form behind the bars shuffled closer to the lamplight.

Glowing eyes stared back at her in a mountain of muscle. Rivulets of drool streamed from a blunted version of a wolf's muzzle. The creature that was somehow her father had grizzled fur tipped with silver, as if even in this form he felt the ravages of age. He moved awkwardly, on limbs unfit for either walking upright or bounding on all fours. A patchwork creature designed by a madman, a grotesque mimicry of wolfkind sharpened by size and power. The entire room felt tiny with him in it.

A large, wet nose snuffled at the air, pointing in her direction. Then came an earth-shaking growl, and all that weight slammed against the bars holding it back. Steel groaned in response. Bent. Her father snarled, dripping saliva from a mouth that could fit around her entire head and crack it like an egg.

Then came the clang of the second pin falling free, and Sam snarled back at her father while ramming the door open with one shoulder. "Come on. Hurry!"

As they raced through the cellar together, Cora said, "Do you think this room will hold him?"

The sound of cracking cement answered her question. Sam's voice was nearly a growl. "I wouldn't count on it."

They burst out into the kitchen, leaving behind the echo of crumpling metal. By the time they reached the front entrance, Cora heard splintering wood and cooking pots clattering to the ground. He was already out of the cellar. She wasn't even sure how she was still running; she felt numb from head to toe.

Light spilled out into the night as they fled out the door and down the steps, alerting the police officer who was on duty.

"Run!" she screamed at the startled man.

Then Sam jerked her aside. An incredible noise filled the air, as if the entire house crumbled beneath a great weight. Then came a guttural roar, and she felt more than saw long claws rake the space where she had just been. They caught the officer instead, ripping him in half.

Cora shrieked as blood splattered her from head to toe, convinced they would die next. Only Sam's hand at her back kept her moving as he said, "The police car is right there. You drive it while I shoot at the bastard."

For some reason, climbing into the driver's seat was more terrifying than running. Even with her father distracted from attacking the limp pieces of the body, her hands shook as she started up the car and slammed on the gas pedal as hard as possible. Even with the reinforced metal of a police vehicle, they would be crushed like a tin can if he got to them before they reached a fast speed.

Somehow, they were out of the driveway and onto the private road before the hulking form appeared in the rearview mirror, shaking blood off fur. Cora tried to stay as calm as Sam, who had found the standard-issue shotgun and was checking to see if it was loaded.

"I'm so sorry," she said, trying to hold back tears as her father began chasing them. Despite his awkward run, he moved fast and was already closing the distance. "I've probably just killed us."

At that, Sam looked over at her. "You think I'm angry with you?"

"I'm certainly kicking myself right now."

To her surprise, he actually laughed. Despite both of them being covered in blood—despite how she could already hear panting growls and a heavy lope behind them—his next words brushed her

ears like velvet. "Let me tell you something, Bunny. I've been itching to kill your father from the moment the sigil left you crying and bleeding in my arms while trying to force you back to him. Now I have the chance to fill him up with silver buckshot. Do you really think I'm angry about that?"

She managed a watery smile. "No. For that matter, neither am I." Then she drew in a deep breath, determination filling her full. "We need to lead him somewhere. We're about to barrel off the property and onto a public street."

"The police reports said silver didn't do much to Tierney, so we need something else to stop him."

"What about Jane's prototype?"

Sam opened his window, ready to lean out with the shotgun. "Even if that doesn't work, something else at the station should. Ready?"

She nodded, focusing on the road. With the city's thriving nightlife, this was about to get hairy.

She began honking the horn as well as blaring the police siren when the first cars appeared in front of them. A glance in the rearview mirror proved that she couldn't slow down. Her father bounded with awkward but distance-swallowing lunges. The moment they stopped, he'd be on them. Sam's aim never missed, and each shot drew an answering roar of pain, but her father never faltered for more than a breath, his thick hide smoking from the silver.

With her hand on the horn, she wrenched the car onto the sidewalk. Pedestrians scattered with shouts and screams. The shrieking changed pitch when people saw what chased after the car.

"He's staying focused on us," yelled Sam, while reloading. "That's the good news."

"And the bad?" She prayed that no cross traffic was about to pull in their way as she crossed a street, scraping a massive cement flower pot. The sharp crack behind them suggested that her father had just barreled through it.

"He's getting closer."

Just then, she saw the Telladay Conservatory, its many glass facets glittering with reflected light. "I think I can slow him down. Get back inside!"

With the siren still blaring, she veered past the opera house and turned as tightly as she dared to point the car at the lowest part of the conservatory across the street. When the car lurched from its wheels bumping off the sidewalk and onto the front lawn, she sensed Sam twisting to see where they were headed. Then he saw the looming conservatory and quickly shut his window, realizing what she was about to do.

Glass shattered against the car, bright and deafening. Cora felt her hands sweat against the wheel, but nothing punctured through to them. From the change in her father's roaring, he wasn't so lucky. Cracking and scrabbling continued behind them as she drove as fast as she dared through the plants.

"It's working," said Sam. "The pieces that aren't sticking into him are slicing him into ribbons. It's a lot of damage to heal from."

The police car destroyed the man-made stream and sideswiped the spiral staircase before she glimpsed the other side. Just then, she heard Sam swear. "Veer left. Left!"

She did but still felt the car jolt as her father lunged, catching them with a glancing blow. She wrenched the wheel, trying to keep

control even as her father's grotesque face crashed through the passenger window, foam dripping from open jaws.

Sam fired point blank, sending the creature back with a spray of blood. Her father's massive form twisted and writhed, crashing through the glass ahead of them to paw at his face. By the time Cora got the car through the broken shards and back outside, two eyes glowed at them while mountains of fur shook off blood and debris.

Screams sounded all around while people realized what was happening. Cora just kept driving, hoping that her father would remember enough of himself to continue chasing after her.

"How many shells are left?" she shouted above the earth-shaking roars and the wailing of their siren.

"Not enough to keep him focused on us throughout the city until we reach the police station. What about tearing through the Cypress Grove golf course? It curves around most of the high risers. We'll pop back out a few blocks from the station."

"And no one else will be in the way, either." Then came the screech of metal as claws raked the back of the car. Cora stomped against the gas pedal and veered the car in the right direction.

The golf club's entrance was flanked by cypress trees. She rammed through the large *members only* sign and the decorative wooden gate instead to get inside. The windshield cracked but held as broken boards and posts flew into the air. The siren was knocked off, dying with a final wail.

The headlights were just enough to keep her away from the sand pits, but the grass wasn't used to the weight of a police car, slowing their speed. Her father was also having trouble, ripping up great clods of earth with each step. Out here, it was eerily silent aside from her father's panting and the car's engine. With the endless swathes of

green grass turned silver beneath the moonlight, it almost felt like they were all trapped in an eternal hunt.

Then the glimmer of water warned her to steer left. Her father lunged straight ahead, some dim instinct encouraging him to take the shorter distance to cut them off. Instead, he landed with a great splash, and all that weight immediately sank further.

"Oh, no," she muttered, hoping they were clear enough of the pond's edges to avoid any mud. The front tires dipped slightly into the softer ground but kept rolling. The back tires sank in with a sickening lurch, stopping them dead.

"No!" she screamed, stomping on the gas. The wheels spun uselessly. They were stuck, and from the looks of it, so was her father, who writhed and roared while trying to contort his limbs free.

Sam stopped her with a hand. "Wait, wait. Use the brakes instead. I think I can give the wheels enough traction to get back onto solid grass. Here, take over with the gun in case he escapes this mud before us."

Her skin prickled as she slid out of the car with the shotgun, unsure of what was about to happen. As water frothed and splashed around her father, Sam grabbed a few fence boards that were still wedged against the windshield. Within moments, he placed them in front of the back tires, ignoring the mud flicking onto his clothes and hands.

Cora made sure she was out of the way while he got into the driver's side and carefully pressed on the gas, coaxing the wheels to lurch forward enough to catch the rough grain of the wood. Her father was also working himself free, the line of mud on his chest and back showing how much of his body had escaped the pond's grasp.

When he snarled at her, she shot without hesitation, unable to tell what was blood and what was mud in the stark moonlight.

Then the car rolled back onto firm ground, guided by Sam's steady steering. She shot her father again just as his hind legs emerged from the water and ran for the passenger's side.

"I can't believe he's still chasing us," she said, as they raced through the rest of the course with him close behind. His breathing sounded more labored, but he showed no other sign of pain or tiredness.

Sam's voice grew grim. "It's just what the Saxbys wanted with their berserker serum. Fighters that would never stop."

"But how? Did they infect Father as well as Tierney? That can't be right, though. Isabelle Saxby admitted that they wanted to kill him."

"With a serum invented by a madman. Something must have gone wrong. Tierney didn't kill your father, but he passed it on somehow. The traits are all the same: his appearance, his immunity to silver, and the fact that he changed on the full moon."

Cora remembered the ugly bite on her father's arm revealed during his transformation. "He bit him. There was a scar I saw on him while you worked on the door. It was a terrible wound. My God, has this happened to Father on every full moon since then?"

"Would explain why he went to Beaumont after escaping Tierney. And why Beaumont had him in a reinforced room." Then Sam's voice tightened. "Hang on. We're about to hit city streets again."

Cora nodded, bracing herself for a fresh round of chaos.

They smashed through some bushes and a decrepit wire fence to reach a road. Branches and barbed wire slowed her father to a limp,

his growls bubbling wetly in his chest as he fought to free himself, eyes always glowing right into the rearview mirror. The massive police station rose high into the night, illuminated by so many lights that it appeared gold. Their car barreled down the sidewalk on the wrong side of the road, as battered as her father.

Despite the time of night, there were a few cars parked in front of the long stone stairway up to the entrance, and a group of people made their way down the steps. Through the broken windows, Cora could hear their voices and recognized some of the figures.

The police commissioner barked orders to a young, neatly dressed man who nodded and took notes. Other equally distinguished-looking gentlemen murmured to the commissioner while angling their hats and tugging their gloves into place against the night chill, making their way to the cars. Further behind on the stairs was Jane with her prototype in its case, a handful of police officers and enchanters, and Captain Dempsey.

They all stopped and stared as Sam screeched to a halt, nearly hitting the commissioner's car.

As they both lunged out, Cora raised her voice. "Jane! Get ready to use that prototype. He's coming!"

"What is the meaning of this?" said Commissioner Keene, his mustache bristling as he glared at them.

Sam guided Cora to circle around until the cars would block them from her father whenever he emerged from the dark end of the street. When he spoke, it was to Captain Dempsey. "Get reinforcements. Her father changed just like Tierney. He's been chasing us for the past goddamn hour."

Cora glanced down the street long enough to search for glowing eyes. There weren't any, which somehow made her even more terrified. "We have to get inside. All of us."

"Don't be ridiculous," said the commissioner, and then turned to the younger man beside him. "Jackson, the door. What kind of assistant are you?"

Jackson bobbed his head and hurried toward the car. Just as he opened it, a massive shape lunged out from the darkness, trailing barbed wire behind it. Glass chips pelted the ground. Mud obscured all but the fangs and eyes as a giant mouth snapped down on the commissioner's head.

This time, it was someone else who ended up covered in blood, not Cora. Sam had already pulled her further back, hiding them both from her father's view behind one of the iron statues that circled the station.

Jackson froze despite the blood dripping down his face, managing only a whimper as the massive creature in front of him dropped the commissioner's body to study him instead. As the creature's shadow fell over the man, he shrank back against the car, squeezing his eyes shut.

Then orange light shot into the creature, splitting into lightning that crackled all over its heaving form. It convulsed, roaring with true pain.

Cora watched her father, openly impressed that Jane's weapon affected him so much, but beside her, Sam swore and said, "She's out in the goddamn open."

Captain Dempsey's voice roared out a moment later. "Jane, take cover!"

Just as Cora realized that Jane was standing at the top of the stairway in clear view, her father saw the she-wolf and lunged, fur still smoking. Jane tried to dart back but he was already there, backhanding her with enough force to send her and the prototype flying in different directions. Her body hit a pillar with an audible snap, and she fell to the ground in a motionless heap. Cora's heart jumped into her throat.

Before her father could grab the limp she-wolf, officers began firing from behind the other pillars. Their bullets peppered her father without any effect beyond bewildering him in who to go after next. Dempsey had already pulled Jane out of sight. Cora still held the shotgun, but her attention had shifted to the prototype, which had landed several yards from her and Sam. Two out of three cartridges glimmered orange at her.

She lunged for the weapon, every muscle feeling electrified. The third cartridge clicked into place beneath her touch, flickering red to show the gun was now at the highest power level. Then a wave of hot breath blasted her side, and she looked over her shoulder to find her father towering over her. Shock burst through her chest just as a bullet caught him clean in the eye, sending him reeling back.

As he roared and clawed at his face, Sam shot him again, expression feral. His snarl was just as ferocious. "You're not going to hurt her, you son of a bitch."

Cora steadied her stance and then let out a scream that shredded her throat to get the creature's attention. "Father!"

His head swung back in her direction, fangs bloodied.

"You won't take my life away *ever* again." Then she fired.

The night brightened into a white heat as overwhelming and vicious as a lightning strike. Even after Cora closed her eyes, her vision remained red. The sizzle of burning flesh filled the air.

When she opened them again, she found her father twitching on the ground, his body reduced to a crater of charcoal from neck to hip. Shockingly, within a moment, he drew in a breath. Then another. By the time her eyesight had completely recovered, he panted sluggishly, surrounded by a ring of officers ready with their weapons. She had never seen the police captain look so mad.

Sam joined her side and shook his head. "Just like Tierney. He's still breathing despite everything."

"Isn't there anything that can kill him?" she said, staring.

It was Jane who answered, slightly unsteady on her feet as she approached them and the smoking body. "Not until he transforms back. Remember how Tierney only died once he was human again?"

"Sunrise, then," said Sam. "Because it was the full moon that triggered the change."

"What do we do until then?" said Cora. "Shoot him whenever he recovers?"

"Sounds good to me," growled Captain Dempsey. He waved over Enchanter Byrd, who seemed both in shock and fascinated by the sight of the creature. "Byrd, let's put him in one of your containment rooms. We'll watch over him until dawn."

Cora sighed, all tension draining away as she handed the prototype back to Jane. Sam pulled her close, nuzzling the top of her head, and even with hours of night ahead, she knew the danger was over.

As it turned out, that single shot was enough to keep her father down. His body had healed by the time lavender tinged the sky, but

he seemed unconscious, breathing shallowly. Cora shared a cup of coffee with Sam while waiting in another room, knowing they'd be called by the enchanters once her father had changed back into human form and had been revived. Several times, she had to hide a smile over how Captain Dempsey kept checking on Jane, his professional mask slipping whenever the four of them were alone. Jane herself simply looked smug, stroking her prototype in its case.

It was nearly an hour after sunrise when Enchanter Byrd escorted them back to the containment chamber. Captain Dempsey was also there. Her father looked much as he had in his wine cellar, only now his dressing gown was plain cotton and his sickly pallor was brightly lit. He faced them all without expression, as composed as if he was in the middle of a board meeting.

"Well, then," he said, finally. "I expect you all want something out of me."

Dempsey answered first, his cigarette in his mouth. "Do you remember what happened?"

"Oh, yes."

When he said nothing else, Cora decided to speak up. All her anger had melted away, crystallized by the finality of the situation. After all, nothing better suggested an end to any chance at a relationship with her father than shooting him. "I'm sorry you were infected by the serum, Father. I really am."

He barely reacted to her, instead sipping at his coffee with shaking hands.

Sam sounded less sympathetic. "Are you willing to tell your side of the story now?"

At that, Isaac Marshall glanced up. "Is it necessary? You have the air of someone who knows and simply wishes me to confess."

"I think your daughter deserves to hear it. It's the least you can do for her."

Her father scoffed, but after another heartbeat of silence, he gave in. "This godforsaken city is going to the animals. Humans are the dominant force only because the packs are too busy fighting each other to truly come after us. The Saxbys looked poised to win with their berserker idea. I agreed to give them capital in hopes of securing future deals with them."

"And soon regretted it," murmured Sam. The cold glint hadn't left his eyes.

Isaac Marshall took a final sip from his coffee and then set it down. "I didn't like the others who were picked for this plan. Too unreliable. Too impulsive. All too soon, my fears proved true. The berserker serum created by that hack of an enchanter had so many flaws. For God's sake, its best iteration turned the berserker into something infectious, transferring its shifting ability to whatever it bit—the very opposite of what the Saxbys wanted as an elite, special force. Once I realized the enchanter was an utter madman, I wanted to back out before my losses ran too deep. That's all I know, although I can surmise the Saxbys were behind my misfortune with my driver in Corpsewood."

Cora said nothing, realizing that any comment she made might annoy her father enough to shut him up. Instead, she watched Sam pace and share a glance with Dempsey in an unspoken signal.

When Sam spoke, his voice remained flat. "I can tell you what happened. The Saxbys used human connections to infect your driver, Dominic Tierney, with the serum while he got a new tattoo. Another pawn of theirs set up a meeting for you to ensure you'd be driving with him at night during the next full moon. Nothing too

tricky to time, and they knew you were too arrogant to think they'd try anything, anyway."

Isaac Marshall nodded. "I remember being attacked by him. Something distracted him before he could finish me off. Other people, I think. I was able to stagger off and disappear into the forest. I knew that miserable Beaumont was hiding in a manor within walking distance. I thought he might cure me. We worked on it for weeks before he grew too drunk one night and accidentally killed himself. I was locked in that room for three days without food or water."

Now Sam stopped in front of him. His teeth flashed as he said, "Why did the Saxbys want Cora so badly?"

For the first time, her father deigned to look him directly in the eyes. "My God, so there is a sordid attachment between the two of you. I shouldn't be surprised at this point."

Cora swallowed hard, moving up beside Sam. When she brushed his arm, he understood her silent request and moved away so she could face the man she was ready to cut out of her life. "Father, it's no use trying to bait me. I'm thoroughly over all that. And I just wanted to say that I'm going to move past what you did to me with the sigil. I found Roland again, and... well, it's all over with now."

"Yes, preventing your elopement has been my greatest regret."

Cora felt tears fill her eyes, realizing it was the closest to an apology she would ever receive from him.

Then her father added, "Yet there wasn't a better excuse than the boy."

Out of the corner of her eye, she saw Sam turn toward them again. She knew his body language well enough to understand he was just as startled by the words.

Dempsey blew out some smoke while studying the other man. "Mind elaborating on that?"

Her father faced her as if she had asked the question instead. There was still no hint of emotion in his eyes. "I didn't care about your plans to elope, Cora. I cared that you'd found out about *my* plans with the Saxbys. Probably from sneaking in one night after a rendezvous with the boy. Beaumont told me you would still have awareness of losing memories, and that it was best to hide the true reason by taking other memories as well."

"You... you mean..." was all she could manage.

Her father continued as if she hadn't even spoken. "I decided to use your plans with the boy as an excuse. I didn't want to. I would have rather let you disappear once and for all. It would have greatly simplified my life. But I still found a way to make the situation useful. Since Beaumont was already working on you, I told him to use your blood for the serum as a fail-safe against the Saxbys trying to cut me out of the deal. I knew wolves couldn't be trusted, and thought making my daughter an essential component of the serum would prevent them from replacing me with another rich human. I now admit I assumed too much."

"You rotten bastard," said Sam, quietly. "I'd hoped it was something the Saxbys insisted on to keep you roped into the plan."

"You... *you*..." Then Cora felt something deep inside her snap. Hands grabbed at her as soon as she lunged, and she was left scratching at the air until Sam pulled her into his arms, his voice low and soothing while she screamed at her father's impassive face, tears streaming down her cheeks. "You miserable old man! How could you? Did you ever love me? Did you ever even try?"

When his expression only darkened in disgust, she finally broke, slumping against Sam while he guided her out of the room. Tears reduced the world into blurred light and his warm touch.

When they were to themselves, she cried against him until his shirt was wet. It felt like everything was spilling out of her, every bad memory, every moment of pain, every neglected piece of her childhood. He just held her close, steadying her with his warmth. Once her sobs became sniffles, he offered her his handkerchief. She took it, wringing it as if it were her father's neck. "I could kill him. I could really do it."

He traced the curve of her cheek, his tone teasing yet gentle. "Once isn't enough?"

Minutes ago, she'd thought she would never smile again. Now she found her lips twitching toward one even as fresh tears ran down her cheeks. "Maybe not."

Then she sighed. "I always knew he was cold. I didn't realize he was *hateful*."

At that, Sam caught her chin. His gold eyes were intent and hot, thawing the chill behind her ribs that had appeared with her father's final words to her. "It's all over, Bunny. He's not part of your life anymore. And believe me, now that he's killed the police commissioner, the city will have him tried, convicted, and hanged within a month. He can't take anything else from you."

She nodded, resting her head against his chest again. Her breath already felt steadier. "Will you take me home?"

"To your apartment?"

Despite her stuffed-up nose, she shifted until she could kiss him. She still hurt but already felt the parts of her heart that would heal

with enough time. "No. Yours. It's the only place that has ever felt like home, and that's where I want to start my new life. With you."

"Isaac Marshall was hanged by the neck and pronounced dead at 6:05 this morning, putting an end to a dastardly conspiracy that instigated a city-wide plague of strange, complex, and grotesque crimes that were at times too strange to believe. Twelve members of the public and his daughter, Miss Cora Marshall, were the official witnesses to Marshall's death. Miss Marshall, herself a victim of her father's deeds, was said to remain composed throughout the execution but refused to speak to the press afterward. And now for the weather. It's a bright, sunshiny—"

Cora changed to another station, and then another, searching for music. She had just found a jaunty little jazz number when Sam stepped in from the kitchen with coffee and the morning mail. She ran a hand over the radio before taking a cup from him. "I can't believe you got it back. I thought it would be stolen forever."

He grinned, settling beside her on the couch. "I had to shake down a few pawnshop owners, that's all. The jewelry is probably gone for good, though."

"I don't care." She had already taken off her black dress and shoes, and was now only in her underclothes, cuddling against him. "Everything important to me is right here in this room."

He nuzzled her neck before turning his attention to the mail, squeezing her nearest thigh whenever he had a free hand. She looked out the big window across from them, watching a raft of white ducks in the pond.

It would have been a lie to say she felt normal. After all, she had watched her father die less than an hour ago. But she did feel good and happy, and she most certainly felt loved.

"What do you want to do today?" she said, once the sunlight had brightened into true day. "I assume it'll be only us again. Jane has been busier than ever since the city gave her that special gun contract."

The fact left her smiling. The she-wolf always looked happy these days, although whether that was from the money and recognition or Captain Dempsey's continued attention, it was difficult to tell. Then Cora's focus flickered over to Sam. He was also much happier than when they had first met, more willing to drop his reserve and bring out his smile or laugh.

As if sensing her attention, he glanced at her, the gold of his eyes deepening. Her heart skipped a beat even before his hand left her leg to catch her chin, drawing her into a tender, lingering kiss that filled her full. When he broke off to let her breathe, he murmured, "Are you happy with your new life?"

"Of course. You're in it." She had never known she could feel so good even after such a grim morning. "Are you?"

"Every day with you feels like heaven. Never thought it could be like this." Their noses brushed before a hint of teasing appeared in his voice. "Maybe this letter will answer your first question."

Then he handed it over for her to read. "It's from Miranda Dewhurst, the famous actress. She says there was a murder during a play she was in, and that the police consider her a suspect. She's asking for my help."

"Hmm." Cora quickly went through it. "I know her a little. Dramatic like all actresses, but she doesn't have a malicious bone in her body."

"Feel up to visiting her today?"

She pretended to think about it. "As what, your assistant?"

Sam smiled, the look in his eyes all but melting her heart. "No, Bunny. As my partner."

Then he kissed her again, and the last of her somber thoughts from the morning vanished. Maybe she would always sense the ragged edges of her mind where her father had taken her memories, but that was all right. She was making new ones.

Her answer bubbled out, bright and ready for the day. "Absolutely, Detective."

ABOUT THE AUTHOR

I've always loved writing about monsters and the girls who love them, which means I write a lot of werewolf romance. In my spare time I like to do things where I don't have to take myself seriously, like bike riding with my husband, baking anything that sounds good, and painting monsters and horses.

I like scotch, wine, and cats.

Enough about me; if you want to know more about my work, my personal website is juliemidnight.com, and my Instagram handle is @juliemidnighter